COME TO DUST

COME TO DUST

Greg Matthews

WALKER AND COMPANY

New York

First published in the United States of America in 1998 by
Walker Publishing Company, Inc.

Published simultaneously in Canada by Thomas Allen & Son
Canada, Limited, Markham, Ontario

Library of Congress Cataloging-in-Publication Data
Matthews, Greg.
Come to dust/Greg Matthews.
p. cm.
ISBN 0-8027-3317-4 (hc)
I. Title.
PR9619.3.M317C66   1998
823—dc21   98–12212
CIP

Series design by Mauna Eichner

Printed in the United States of America
2 4 6 8 10 9 7 5 3 1

for

Joel and Deborah

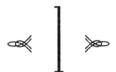

1

ost writers share a common fantasy: the Unexpected
Encounter with a Reader of One's Work. The writer
imagines that the reader he notices in some public place
will be engrossed in the writer's latest effort, lips slightly parted,
eyes wide, rapidly scanning the masterpiece. A casual inquiry
launched at the reader results in an outpouring of praise for the
book in hand, a declaration that the author of such a work must
surely be a genius. At this point the writer reveals his identity,
if the smitten reader is an attractive member of the opposite sex,
or else accepts the praise in quiet satisfaction; another fan
confirmed; further word-of-mouth sales anticipated; life is good.

It happened to Moody at Redondo Beach, Los Angeles, on
a Thursday late in May 1944. His latest manuscript had been
safely dispatched just an hour before to his agent in New York,
Morris Dubrov. His wife was away from home and would continue to be absent for the next few days, and Moody was unable
to come up with any better plan for the afternoon than trailing
his toes through sand while watching the waves. He drove to the
beach, parked, and walked down to the shoreline, trying to re-

member when it was that he had last removed his shoes in public and allowed wavelets to lap around his bony ankles. Sunlight revealed, beneath his rolled-up pants, a surprising amount of hair on his big toes; why had he never noticed that before? He squirmed his feet an inch or so into wet sand to hide them, wondering if shaving his toes would solve the problem, or simply make it worse over time.

He looked around. There were fewer people than he had expected to find sharing the beach with him, women for the most part, accompanied by small shrieking children. He supposed that most of the men, unless classified 4-F like himself, were in uniform, fighting the war, or else occupied in the usual fashion inside office buildings and factories. Moody felt a little guilty over the intense pleasure he was experiencing as his feet continued to squirm beneath the sand, clenching and unclenching the slippery wetness; he felt about six years old.

A wave more insistent than the rest splashed his pants. Moody extricated himself from the sand before stepping back to shallower waters, his shoes in one hand, socks in the other. A small boy clutching a beach ball was watching him. Moody came back up the beach toward him, smiling in what he hoped was a friendly fashion; children always made him nervous. "Swell day for it!" he enthused, his smile widening. The boy threw the beach ball directly at him, knocking Moody's glasses from his nose. He stooped to retrieve them from the sand and replaced them to see the boy hurrying toward the safety of his mother, a large woman basting beneath a layer of glistening suntan lotion. The boy looked back at Moody. The mother appeared to be asleep, so Moody kicked the ball as far in the opposite direction as he could, then stuck his tongue out. The boy began to cry. Moody marched away down the beach, annoyed that his simple pleasures had been compromised by the brat.

A hundred yards away from the incident he slowed his pace, determined to recapture his former happiness, and no sooner had he decided to do so than he caught sight of a familiar object. It was a book, in the hands of a heavyset young man just a short distance away. The book was Moody's first published novel. The reader sat cross-legged, his feet beneath him like a Buddhist's. He wore bottle-end glasses and a handkerchief knotted into a square in lieu of a hat; his feet, despite their location beneath his plump buttocks, were encased in heavy boots. His upper lip, with a single lizardlike movement of the tongue, was cleared of sweat while he gazed fixedly at the book in his lap. Moody was entranced; here was one of that mysterious, seldom-seen tribe, the Appreciator of Finer Things. This was no cheap thriller with detective and moll and gat on the cover; this was *Below the Salt* that the reader consumed, its jacket tastefully decorated with a picture of the main character, an actor, removing a theatrical mask to reveal another mask beneath. Clearly, the reader was absorbed completely with the tale. Moody watched his eyes dart back and forth. He was about halfway through the book, near the important chapter where the actor Jason is revealed to be schizophrenic, much to the disgust of his overbearing father.

The reader, unaware of Moody's scrutiny, paused occasionally to look up and scan the long horizon before him, as if to find brief release from the dramatic intensity lying opened in his hands. It gave Moody a definite thrill to see his words, his characters, his plot, drive a reader to this kind of involvement in the story. Abruptly, he decided to ask his opinion of the book. Such an opportunity might never arise again. Creator would consult consumer for an honest appraisal.

He squatted beside the young man, smiling. "Excuse me."

The reader read on, and Moody couldn't blame him; a riveting story was hard to tear oneself away from.

He tried again. "Excuse me, I was wondering if that book you're reading is good enough to recommend."

Moody had his attention now. The eyes behind their amazingly thick and distorting lenses were raised from the page and directed across several feet of blistering sand into Moody's own.

"Huh?"

"That book, is it any good? I've been thinking about reading it myself. Would you recommend it? I'm sorry to interrupt. I just wondered if it was a good book, in your opinion."

The reader stared at Moody, then glanced along the beach in both directions. There was no one closer than seventy yards from them.

"What?"

Moody was beginning to suspect that his reader was less intelligent than his glasses and choice of reading matter had led him to assume.

"I just wondered if it was a book you'd recommend."

The reader reached inside his jacket, a battered hunter's thing that had probably never been among trees other than the palms of Los Angeles. Though yet to reveal his identity as the book's author, Moody fully expected the hand to be withdrawn from the reader's left armpit clutching a pen with which to obtain an autograph. Maybe the picture of Moody on the back of the dustcover had tipped him off. The reader would most likely want him to scribble some kind of dedication on the flyleaf. The gun that was brought out into the open didn't resemble a pen at all. Had the reader misinterpreted Moody's approach, thought him a solicitor of perverse acts? Moody quickly readied an explanation and an apology, but neither was required.

"Wallet," said the reader.

"Pardon me?"

"Wallet, you deaf? Shake a leg."

"I'm the author of that book, as a matter of fact."

"All the money, now, okay?"

"Of course."

Moody reached for his cheap and depressingly slender wallet.

"You might be disappointed with this," he said, knowing it contained just three dollars. "I'm a starving writer. You've heard about us, haven't you?" He opened out the wallet. "That's my book you've got there. How about that for a coincidence."

"It's *my* book. I paid for it."

The wallet was snatched from Moody and rummaged through with one well-practiced hand; the other kept the gun barrel pointed at Moody.

"Three bucks?"

"I know. Most people assume that if you're an author you're rich, just because you had a book published, but actually most writers don't make a lot. That's what kind I am. It can be tough."

"Three bucks?"

"You're welcome to all of it."

"Gimme the rest. Where's it, in your shoe?"

"No, you see, there's no more. . . . Maybe I didn't explain as clearly as I should have. I'm a writer, and I don't earn a lot of money—"

"You don't gimme the rest, I'm gonna put one right in your guts, I mean it."

"There are women and children around—"

"I don't care about them, just you. Gimme it."

His lip was gleaming with new moisture. The wallet, minus its three dollars, was dumped onto the sand. "I'm not gonna wait, stupid." He sounded calm despite the sweat. Moody saw that his only chance lay in talking his way out of the situation. Words, his stock-in-trade, would be his best defense.

"I'll gladly autograph your book. It's a first edition. They're always worth a lot more."

"What? What are you saying?"

"You have a first edition of my book in your lap. It's worth money if it has the author's signature inside, believe me."

Moody didn't tell him that a first edition was the only kind of edition *Below the Salt* was available in, because there were no subsequent editions; in fact, most of that first edition had ended up on the remaindered shelves within six months of publication.

Understanding began to dawn behind the bottle-end lenses. "You wrote this?"

"Indeed I did. Notice the picture on the back?"

The thief did so, one-handed, then looked back at Moody, faint surprise easing the tight line of his mouth.

"Keith Moody. . . . It's you! You wrote this book?"

"Yes, I did. Are you enjoying it? I'd really like to know."

"Well, yeah, on and off. There should be more stuff happening with the brother though, you know, whatsisname, the one that steals."

"Michael."

"Right, Michael. More stuff about him, not this other boring actor with the disturbed mind and all, but it's okay, basically, I mean I got this far, right? So yeah, I like it okay."

"There's more about Michael later on, so keep reading. I think you'll like the way it turns out for Michael in the end."

"You write any other books?"

"As a matter of fact, my next one has just this morning been sent off to my agent. *A Desert Island of the Mind.* That's the title."

"I don't like it. That's not a good name for it."

"It's a reference to everyone's need to have a private place, where no one else can go, or even know about, a kind of desert island with nobody there but yourself, only it's inside your head, not out in the ocean somewhere."

"I don't like it. It's dumb. Change it."

Moody smiled. The young man with the gun and book was not just a criminal but very possibly insane. "Okay, I'll do that. I always had doubts about it myself. Too pretentious maybe."

"Make it shorter. Book names should be short, like the movies are."

"Good point. Something short and snappy."

"So whaddaya gonna call it?"

"Uh . . . how about *Too Much Heat*?"

"Good. What's it mean?"

"Too much pressure. Psychological pressure, you see, too much emotion and mental turmoil . . . and so forth."

"Okay, I like that better than the other name with the island in it, only don't put in too much of the mental and psychology. Make it with plenty of action. Guns, cars chasing around, Jimmy Cagney stuff."

Moody's critic was ignoring the fact that the book had already been written. Not just criminally insane, but stupid as well. Moody maintained what he hoped was a friendly smile.

"Would you like that signature now? Remember what I said about signed first editions?"

"Why wouldn't I remember? You just now said it. Are you saying I'm too dumb to remember what you said just now?"

"Certainly not. It's clear from your choice of reading matter that you're a fellow with an alert and discerning mind."

"Okay, then. Jeez, it's hot. I'm from Wisconsin, but don't go thinking I'm a Swede. There's other people in Wisconsin. It don't get this hot there, well, maybe sometimes. I came out here to find my aunt. She lives here, somewhere here. I didn't find her yet."

"Really. What's her name?"

"Flowerdew, Amanda Flowerdew."

"Charming name, if you don't mind my saying so."

"Why would I mind? Anyway, you already said so. It's too late if I minded, right?"

"Right."

Moody caught brief flashes of dialogue from the Mad Hatter's tea party and kept on smiling.

"What're you grinning about?"

"Oh, I'm not. I'm squinting. It's the sunlight reflecting off the sand. I should've brought my sunglasses. When I squint my eyes, it sort of pulls my cheeks up and people think I'm smiling, but actually I'm not."

"You got a pen?"

"Pen? Uh . . . no. What for?"

"For the signing in the book!"

"Oh, yes—"

Moody produced a fountain pen from inside his jacket and reached for *Below the Salt*. He had to exert slight pressure to pull it from the chubby fingers.

"Would you like a personal dedication as well as the signature?"

"Is it worth more money that way?"

"Definitely," lied Moody, wanting only to know the name he would need to gasp out with his dying breath if his reader decided to shoot him.

"Okay, put 'To Kurt Flowerdew with . . . uh . . . respect. From his friend'—that's where you put your name. And the date too, I guess."

"To . . . Kurt . . . Flowerdew . . ." Moody wrote it all down as requested. "Interesting name, Kurt."

"You said it was charming before."

"That was with Amanda in front of it. With Kurt in front of it, that's an interesting name."

"I hate it, but what can you do, right? I got in more trouble on accounta that name—I could write a book about what happened to me in my life."

"I'm sure you could," said Moody, who had heard a similar claim from dozens of people over the years. He handed back the book.

"You wanna help me write it?" asked Flowerdew.

"Help you?"

"Yeah, you know, to make it more of a professional job. You talk better than me."

Moody looked quickly up and down the beach. Not a single cop in sight.

"That might be possible, of course, if your story's really interesting."

"It is," stated Kurt Flowerdew. Moody didn't ask for proof.

"It's a long story, even if I'm only twenty-two."

"Well, then, this is obviously not the place to be telling me, not in all this heat, and I don't have a notebook with me either."

"Okay, where do we do it?"

Flowerdew's expression was infused with sudden enthusiasm; it made him look even more peculiar, almost demented, in Moody's opinion.

"Do you know a bar called Ferguson's, on the corner of Eighth and San Pedro, downtown?"

"No," said Flowerdew, an answer Moody expected, since no such bar existed.

"It's easy to find, just ask around. It has a big sign outside with neon cocktail glasses that blink on and off. You can't miss it, really. Why don't we meet there tonight at, say, seven-thirty?"

"Eighth and San Pedro. Ferguson's. Is there good-looking women there regular?"

"It's a real hot spot. Maybe we should meet somewhere else, so there are no female distractions from our work."

"No. We're gonna do it there."

"All right, Kurt, it's your story, after all." Moody got awkwardly to his feet and felt pins and needles begin attacking his legs; the entire conversation had been conducted while squatting on his haunches. "Well, I have an appointment with my dentist this afternoon, unfortunately. Until tonight, then, Kurt. Oh, may I have my wallet back, please? You're very welcome to keep the three dollars. I know how it is when you're new in town."

Kurt flipped open the wallet and studied Moody's driver's license. "Thirty-three oh four El Segundo, apartment six. They got all these wop names in this town."

"Spanish, actually." Moody hoped Kurt wouldn't be offended at having been corrected, but the comment seemed to have passed completely over his head.

"This is where you live, this place here?"

"Naturally, if it says so on my license."

"Because if you don't show up at this Ferguson's joint, that's it, I mean I'm coming after you. Nobody tells a lie to Kurt Flowerdew, ask anyone. I get lied to, I get mad, then I get moving, know what I'm talking about?"

"You have nothing to worry about, Kurt, I'll be there."

The wallet was tossed over to Moody. "You better be."

"Until then." Moody dipped his head and turned away. He began walking along the beach, half expecting to receive a bullet in the back. There was no shot, nothing but the sounds of children and waves and seagulls. He reached his car and collapsed behind the wheel. His hands were trembling a little; had they been doing that while he talked with the maniac Kurt Flowerdew? No, Kurt would have noticed and commented: Whaddaya shaking for? Nervous, huh? I do that to people.

Moody started the engine and backed out of his parking space. He'd gone to Redondo in anticipation of a quiet moment of inner reflection and the mundane pleasure of squeezing wet sand between his toes. What he had encountered was unexpected and ugly, completely at variance with the surroundings; a turd in a salad bowl. He drove away, pushing at the pedals of his Ford with his feet still shoeless.

Making a report on the incident at the nearest police station was a frustrating experience. Moody was questioned by two different officers, who each obliged him to repeat the story in its entirety. When he had finished telling the second officer, the first one entered the room and they both left together. Moody suspected they were comparing notes. After fifteen minutes they returned.

"Okay, Mr. Moody, let's go down to the beach and see if he's still there."

"He probably won't be by now," Moody said, trying not to sound irritated.

"Oh? Why would that be?"

"The time factor."

"Time factor?"

"The delay incurred by my having to repeat myself to you gentlemen. It's been more than ninety minutes now since I walked away from him. Why would he stay there?"

"He got three bucks off you, Mr. Moody. Could be he'll try it with someone else."

But there was no Kurt Flowerdew to be seen when they

arrived at the same spot in a squad car, then drove a half mile in each direction along the beach road. "See?" said Moody. "He's a dangerously unstable individual, and now he's gone who knows where."

"He'll turn up someplace else, sometime. Anyone like you described, he's bound to make himself known."

"When he finds out there's no Ferguson's bar, that's when he'll make himself known. He'll be furious, and he has the address from my driver's license."

"You're asking for police protection, is that it, Mr. Moody?"

"I don't require that at all. The address is out of date. My wife and I live somewhere else now."

"So okay, no problem," said the larger of the two cops.

Moody said, "It might be a problem for whoever lives at the old address now."

"Maybe we'll give them a little warning," said the smaller man.

"How long since you moved, Moody?"

"We moved when we were married, about eighteen months ago."

"And you haven't got yourself an up-to-date address on your driver's license in all that time?"

"I've been rather busy."

It sounded lame. Moody saw the cops exchange a look.

"That's an offense, Moody, what you did. You move, you get the new address on your license pronto."

The other cop said, "You're eighteen months into an offense because of what you didn't do about that license. That's a long time not to go reregister."

"Police work, Moody, it's not what you think, all squealing tires and blazing guns like in the movies, is it?" he asked his partner.

"Nothing like it. Police work, mainly it's reading stuff."

"Files," added the other. "Information about who lived where, so we know where to go and maybe ask some important questions for an investigation."

"Very unglamorous, but it pays off."

"But only if the information's up-to-date. The information isn't up-to-date, there goes our investigation."

"We have to start all over again when that happens, chase down a new lead that's got up-to-date information in it."

"You see what we mean, don't you, Moody? Getting your license up-to-date, that's your civic duty."

"Otherwise you just make life hard for guys like us. We waste time that we wouldn't have wasted if the information hadda been up-to-date, that's what we're saying."

"I understand," said Moody. "I'll change my license this afternoon."

"You do that, and stay off the beach meantime so this guy doesn't catch sight of you again."

"I'll certainly do that."

The squad car was turned and driven back to the station. Moody felt like a schoolboy who had been lectured for not bringing the correct textbook to class.

The big cop lit a cigarette. "So, Moody, what books did you write?"

"The first was called *Below the Salt*. The second is currently in the hands of my agent. It's called *A Desert Island of the Mind*."

"I never heard of 'em," said the smaller cop. "Did you?"

"Neither one," said the big cop. "I would've remembered a name like that desert island one."

"That's the one as yet unpublished," Moody reminded him.

"I know that, Moody." The cop's voice was less friendly now. "All I'm saying, if a book like that ever got in the stores, with that name on the front, I'd remember it."

"Because of the strangeness," said his partner.

"The strangeness," the big cop agreed, "and the fact that I don't like it. I'd be more likely to forget a name if I liked it, but if I really don't like something, it kinda stays in my mind, you know?"

"It's like that with life, not just book names," said the smaller cop. "Like how you remember all the bad stuff that happened to you, but the good things, if you get any, you just let it slide right outta your head, don't you?"

"You do," his partner said.

A window was cranked down; warm air rushed through the car, replacing the warmer air inside. "You oughta write for the movies, Moody. That's where the money is. *Gone with the Wind.* You shoulda wrote that one."

"Yes, I should have. I should have written it while I had the idea, but like a fool I sold the idea to Margaret Mitchell for fifty dollars."

"Who's she?"

"The author of the book the movie was based on. You're aware it was a book before it was a movie?"

"We know that, Moody. You really sold the idea for fifty bucks?"

"You sold out cheap. Five hundred. Hey, five thousand, yeah, that's more like what I woulda got for it, a good idea like that one."

"You must kinda like squirm when you see how much money that movie made," said the big cop. "You must kick yourself plenty about that."

Moody nodded. "Margaret has been big about it, though. She sends me a case of champagne every year on my birthday."

"Yeah? That's good, champagne, a case. That's so's you won't be a sore loser, am I right?"

"You're perfectly correct. You may not know this, but Margaret hasn't published anything since then. No ideas from me, you see."

"That right? Revenge, huh? If you got another good idea, you wouldn't sell it so cheap this time, I bet."

"Indeed I wouldn't."

"If you ever get another good idea like the last one, and they make a movie out of it, you'd tell us, wouldn't you, Moody, so's we could tell all the guys in the station we knew you when you were nobody."

"Naturally."

"You're some bullshitter, Moody. Is that what writers are like, all bullshitters like you are?"

"We're cops, Moody. We don't fool so easy. We heard it all, every kinda bullshit story there is."

"That Flowerdew thing, for instance. That's a bullshit story, right, Moody? Nobody's called Kurt Flowerdew."

"Nobody from Wisconsin, anyway. 'My name is Yon Yonson, I come from Wisconsin.' "

The cops laughed.

"You made it all up, am I right?"

"No."

The squad car pulled up outside the station. Both cops faced Moody.

"Don't you do this again, hear me? We got plenty of real crime to deal with. You're lucky we don't charge you with making a false statement, you know that? Only reason we won't is, you made us laugh. *Gone with the Wind.* Jesus H. Christ."

"The wind from my butt," said the other cop, and they both laughed.

"You get that license address changed today, Moody, so we know where to come get you when someone tells us they were bothered by some drunk that says he's a writer that shoulda been famous because he's the one that wrote that big movie. That'll be you, Moody, that drunk."

"May I go now?"

All three exited the squad car.

"You bear in mind what I said, Moody."

"Bear it in your desert island mind, Moody."

The cops mounted the station house steps, laughing again.

Moody went home.

e missed his wife. If Myra had been there to share the experience with over a drink, Moody would have been better off. But Myra would be gone until the weekend, visiting the small town in Idaho where she had been born, to attend the reading of a will; her uncle had died in April. On his own, Moody sat and fretted and listened to the radio and read the newspaper, but nothing could distract him from the probability that Kurt Flowerdew, armed and angry, was at that moment wandering in the region of Eighth and San Pedro, looking for a bar called Ferguson's. He wouldn't be happy in his search: Whaddaya mean, there's no such place, feller? My friend the famous writer Keith Moody said he'd meet me here, and he's a guy that don't lie to a pal. Nobody tells lies to Kurt Flowerdew.

Moody considered ringing the police station to ask if the officers he'd spoken with had done as they said they would, and contacted the current resident of 3304 El Segundo. Had they actually said they would, or did they say they *might*? He tried to recall the conversation; the word had been *maybe*. Maybe we should warn them, the little cop had said. But then they as much as accused Moody of making the whole story up. He should never have cracked wise about Margaret Mitchell; he'd undermined his own credibility, and now someone not connected with any part of the sorry incident might be hurt as a result. He had to be sure.

His car was parked on the street. Moody and Myra had shared a small detached house in Alhambra since their marriage, and its only drawback, so far as Moody was concerned, was the lack of a garage. Myra still drove the convertible she had owned when he met her at the Empire studios in '42, and it had been stolen twice since then by joyriders because Myra never bothered putting up the top unless rain was threatening. Moody made it his task to go out to the curb every evening and put the top up, and Myra let him do it. "It wasn't hurt when they took it, so I don't know why you make such a fuss. That's a lucky car. It doesn't need fussing over." Moody fussed anyway, because that was the way he was; the car hadn't been stolen since he began his fussing. His own car was an older coupe. He'd always wanted something bigger, newer, but being fired from his position as screenwriter at Empire had obliged him to hold on to the Ford. It was Moody's hope that the end of the war, said to be no more than a year or two away at worst, and the resumption of civilian car production in Detroit would coincide with a bestseller from his typewriter, maybe a second best-seller, or even a third by that time, and a movie deal to boot, something that would earn him a Cadillac.

He drove without urgency in the direction of El Segundo. The evening was warm enough to roll his window down, and he enjoyed the sound of eucalyptus and palm rattling dryly in the breeze whenever he stopped at an intersection. He wanted to be rich, he wanted to be famous, a Great Writer, but *Below the Salt* had passed across the literary landscape like a tiny cloud, unnoticed by all, and Moody was beginning to wonder if *A Desert Island of the Mind* was similarly destined to win him no prizes. Maybe he should be aiming at the larger readership of detective fiction or historical romance, something Hollywood might consider buying for the screen.

Moody had made good money at Empire turning out B-feature rubbish for several years before being fired. His literary output since then was more refined, from an intellectual standpoint, but far less profitable. He was proud of his two books, but it hurt Moody's pride that his wife had to work in a small insurance office downtown to keep the rent paid, the cars gassed. He once had apologized to Myra for his fiscal shortcomings, and been told, "Pish and piffle, who cares about that. Say, those are terrific names for our yet unborn twins. Pish would be the girl, I guess. Piffle is more boyish, don't you think?" The newlyweds had taken care not to impregnate Myra, and their bedroom practices had continued, both acknowledging that children were not yet a viable option, the family checkbook lying flat and unprosperous as it did. Maybe the recently deceased uncle in Idaho had left Myra something worthwhile, a million acres of prime timberland perhaps. Myra had said he was a storekeeper, so such riches were unlikely. "He sells hardware in a one-horse town and collects stamps for a hobby," she had told Moody when news of the demise had come, "so don't go expecting to hit the big time. He probably left me a nice big bucket of nails."

As he neared the apartment house where he used to live, Moody's thoughts returned to the matter at hand. He parked and approached his old doorway on the second story, knocked, and waited. The door was opened by a middle-aged man with a napkin tucked into his shirt collar. His head was balding, his manner polite despite the obvious interruption of his dinner. "Yes?"

"I'm sorry to disturb you, but have the police been in touch with you today at all?"

"Police?"

"Yes, concerning a certain individual called Flowerdew, Kurt Flowerdew. He thinks I still live here, and he's . . . he's not going to be very happy with me tonight."

"I beg your pardon?"

"I used to live in this apartment eighteen months ago, and . . . it's rather complicated, I'm afraid. The thing is, sir, you might be in danger. He has a gun, I saw it myself."

"A gun? Who has a gun? Who are you?"

"Moody, Keith Moody. I do apologize for the intrusion. I went to the police, but they didn't take me seriously, I'm afraid, so I thought the very least I could do, after putting you in harm's way, so to speak, was come here and let you know what kind of trouble there might be as a result."

"Trouble?"

The less than tantalizing odor of a poorly cooked meal was wafting through the doorway past the confused diner, whose manner was becoming less friendly.

"I think you'd better leave. I don't understand a single thing you're telling me. I'm busy eating. Come back later."

"Sir, it'd take less than five minutes to explain the matter fully and completely—"

"Go away!"

The door was abruptly slammed shut. Moody rapped it with his knuckles, trying to convey a sense of urgency. "Sir, please open up! This is terribly important! He's a dangerous man, and he'll come here, I'm sure of it. . . . Sir?"

From inside came a muffled voice. "I'm calling the police!"

"Good idea! Tell them to come right away! I'll wait right here!"

The next door along the landing opened, and a woman's head appeared. "What's the rumpus?"

"Nothing, ma'am, nothing to be concerned about yet. The police are on their way."

The head was withdrawn, the door shut, and at that moment the door in front of Moody was opened again. He readied a friendly smile to reassure the man he had so clearly upset, and the smile was confronted with the end of a shotgun barrel, long and unwieldy. "Get away from here," Moody was told, in a voice pitched higher than it had been the first time. "Get away right now and don't come here ever again!"

Moody was already taking steps backward, propelled by instinct.

"Uh . . . sir, that isn't necessary. It isn't me who might be intending you harm, it's Flowerdew. If you'd just let me explain the situation—"

The gun was lifted to its owner's shoulder and aimed squarely at Moody's chest.

"Actually, sir, I'm reassured to know that you're armed, just as he is. When he comes knocking, which he might or might not do, be sure and have your weapon handy. In fact it might be wise to open the door with it already in your hands, just to let him know you can't be intimidated. . . . Thank you, sir, and a pleasant evening to you."

He was walking backward down the concrete steps by now, and the shotgun was aimed at him until the upper landing rose past his chest, his eyes, his hat. Moody turned then and continued on down to the courtyard. Looking back, he saw that the door was now closed. He had attempted to do the fellow a good turn, possibly save him from physical harm, and this had been the result. The wages of the Samaritan were meager indeed. He continued on to his car, unlocked it, and drove home.

. . .

BY TEN O'CLOCK Moody was worried again. Kurt Flowerdew had had plenty of time to locate the apartments on El Segundo Boulevard and do whatever it was his intention to do. Was the man with the shotgun all right? Had anything at all happened? Maybe he should drive back there and assess the situation, without knocking this time. If he stayed where he was, fretting over the possibilities, he wouldn't sleep anyway. He was just about to reach for his hat when the phone rang. He knew, somehow, as he picked up the receiver, that it would be Flowerdew. Moody's name and new address were in the telephone directory, after all, a fact that had escaped his attention until that moment. Sudden sweat made the phone slippery.

"Hello . . . ?"

"My my, is that what writers refer to as a voice filled with trepidation?"

"Myra . . ."

"The same. Is anything wrong? You sounded as if you thought I might be an income tax auditor."

"No, I . . . thought something else. How are you?"

"Wealthier. They read the will this afternoon. Guess who got the hardware store."

"You?"

"Guess again. No, don't bother, it was my cousin Norman."

"What did you get, if I might be so mercenary as to ask?"

"I got the bird, that's what I got."

"The bird? You mean you inherited a parrot or something?"

"Nothing so amusing. The bird in this case is a figure of speech. I might just as well have said I got the elbow, or I got the shaft. Am I making myself clear, darling?"

"Perfectly. Your uncle left you his sincere good wishes and a fond fare-thee-well, I take it."

"Almost. I triumphed over all other members of the family from far and wide. They all wanted the not so antique nut bowl with the nickel-plated squirrel on top, I could tell by their smiles, and I definitely heard the grinding of teeth as I was given Uncle Barney's stamp album. It's just as well I wasn't awarded further treasures, or I might not have made it out of the lawyer's office alive."

"A nut bowl and a stamp album. I see. And what exactly was it that you did to alienate your uncle Barney? Were you a peevish child who irritated him while visiting, or did you smash his window at some time or other with your slingshot?"

"I have never in all my life owned a slingshot. I was a bow-and-arrow girl, as a matter of fact, and no, I didn't put out his eye or skewer the family cat. I only met Barney a few times. We lived over in Spokane from the time I was three. Actually, the stamp album is rather nice. Do you know anything about stamps?"

"I know where to purchase them, how to lick them, and the appropriate corner of an envelope in which to place them."

"Have you never appreciated the fine old stamps of yesteryear? Some of them are quite fascinating. They make stamps today look boring and unimaginative."

"I'm glad you've chosen to look on the bright side. You'll probably find the chromed squirrel is quite charming in its own squirrelish fashion if you just look at it long enough."

"The squirrel is for you. He rather resembles you, with that earnest expression of his as he quietly nibbles his nuts."

"I'm flattered."

"I'll start driving home tomorrow. Bess misses you."

Myra had taken Moody's dog, a large black poodle, with her

on the trip to Idaho, at Moody's insistence. "Bess will protect you if uncouth types attempt to inflict themselves upon you," he had said, and Myra did admit that most ruffians will cower instantly at the sight of a poodle.

"Give her a pat for me."

"Is everything okay down there in civilization?"

"Perfectly fine."

"I'd kill for a martini. In this town they have beer and whisky, generally taken together to cancel out the taste of each."

"You're too sophisticated by far for such a frontier outpost. Hurry home. No, don't hurry, you might have an accident."

"I think that's why I married you, darling, to have someone who'll worry needlessly over me."

"It's a dirty job, but someone has to do it."

" 'Bye for now, lover. Friendly wags of the tail from Bess."

"See you soon."

He hung up the phone and stood for several minutes, experiencing a pleasant sensation of warmth that had crept over his entire body during the phone call. Moody assumed this was an essential clue to the way he felt about his wife; if he didn't love her to distraction, he wouldn't have become so warm at the sound of her voice. He was a lucky man.

The clock in the hall chimed the quarter hour, and Moody recalled his anguish of several minutes before. He had almost made up his mind to go back to the apartments on El Segundo and sniff the air, just drive past the place and make sure everything was all right, when Myra called. Did he still want to do that? And there was the possibility now that Flowerdew was on his way to Alhambra, courtesy of the phone directory. Moody wished his number was unlisted. Was all of his worrying for nothing? Flowerdew might very well have forgotten the meeting at Ferguson's completely. He was obviously demented in some way; maybe he'd been distracted by some other encounter later on in the afternoon, and was not interested in either location. That was probably the case. Myra sometimes told him he tended to worry about nothing because it was his nature, as a writer, to extrapolate from dreary reality a more exciting narrative thread than everyday life tended to provide. "You can't walk inside a grocery store without wondering what might happen if a robbery occurred while you were there and were taken hostage. You invent plots all over the place, darling, because you can't help it. You're too clever for the mundane world, that's your problem, too intent on ferreting out something dramatic from absolutely nothing."

He sat down in his favorite chair, then got up and made himself a drink, then sat down again and reached for a cigarette. Watching smoke curl toward the ceiling, Moody told himself he would do the right thing by doing nothing; he had done all he possibly could by warning the occupant of apartment six that Kurt Flowerdew was about to enter his life—maybe. He was extracting the possibility of mayhem from thin air. Today's events would not coalesce into some thrilling agenda for terror, as it would in a movie; instead, the peculiar incident on the beach would fade from memory, having resulted in nothing more than a few hours of nervous concern. That was life. He raised his glass.

MOODY EXPECTED MYRA would be home by late Sunday; that allowed her three full days of driving to cover the twelve hundred miles separating Yellowtail, Idaho, from Los Angeles. She called on Friday from a hotel in Tacoma, Washington, and again on Saturday from a motor court cabin near the Oregon-California state line, and was confident that Sunday night would see them together again. Moody told her nothing of Kurt Flowerdew; that episode was already in the past, its protagonist obviously nowhere near as dangerous as his threatening manner had led Moody to believe; the entire piece of foolishness was best forgotten. He spoke with Bess over the phone and sent her into paroxysms of yipping at the sound of his voice. "Oh, God," said Myra, "now she's searching under the bed for you. I don't think talking to her was a good idea; in fact I don't think bringing her along for the drive was such a good idea. I had to argue and argue with the hotel manager last night to let her sleep in my room. No problem where I am tonight, though."

"Next time you go on a long trip, I'll come too."

"I wanted you to come with me this trip, but you wouldn't, you rat."

"Darling, I had to finish the book. You know I hate to stop work on something when I'm near to finishing."

"The artistic-temperament excuse."

"Precisely. I worked like blazes and sent it off to New York Thursday morning."

"You did? Why didn't you tell me when I called Thursday night?"

"I was distracted."

"Blond or brunette?"

"Neither. He was chubby and obnoxious and wore a handkerchief hat."

"Keith, you haven't turned all swishy on me, have you?"

"I'm referring to a fellow I bumped into on the beach Thursday afternoon. I wasn't going to tell you because I didn't want you worrying."

"You bumped into him—and then what? Did he sue you for knocking him down? You aren't giving me the full story."

"Actually, he robbed me, at gunpoint, right there on the beach in broad daylight. I couldn't believe it was happening."

"So it was him who bumped into you, not the other way around."

"Well, no . . . you see, he was reading a copy of *Below the Salt*, so naturally I stopped to have a few words with him, find out if he liked it and so on, and the next thing I knew, he was aiming a gun at me. He took everything I had—three dollars."

"Poverty has its bright side. Imagine how upset you'd be if he stole hundreds. I suppose the real blow lies in the fact that you found one of your readers, and he was a pig. I'm terribly sorry, darling. I'm sure there are absolutely wonderful people out there who appreciate your book, it's just that you'll never know who they are."

"It was an eye-opener, definitely."

"Give me all the details tomorrow night, after we've made frantic love together on the sofa and the floor, and possibly the table."

"I'll begin taking my vitamin supplements immediately."

"Goody. Until then, darling."

Myra hung up. Moody was pleased to notice the beginnings of an erection behind his fly buttons. "I certainly do like my wife," he said aloud.

ON SUNDAY AFTERNOON Moody cleaned the house and set to rights all signs of the domestic slovenliness he had allowed himself during Myra's absence, then went out to purchase a few expensive items for dinner, including some of Myra's favorite wine. He arranged everything to his own satisfaction, then began waiting for the arrival of his wife.

He had picked up a copy of *Variety* at the store. Usually he avoided any news of Hollywood, since reading of movie deals and the amounts of money being flung around by the studios depressed him. Ever since his firing from Empire Productions by Marvin Margolis, for reasons that Moody could not logically have been held accountable for, he had felt a sense of bitterness tinge all thoughts of movieland and its maddening ways. It was better to be poor and happy, in complete control of his work as a novelist, Moody reminded himself, than to be at the beck and call of arrogant and foolish men like Margolis, who had never appreciated his talent in any case and had thrown him out to cover Margolis's own rear end when the studio was involved in scandal following the murder of its up-and-coming star Baxter Nolan, Myra's brother. Moody could never forgive Empire and Marvin Margolis for that, and yet his dismissal from the studio had allowed him to find his feet as a novelist, so perhaps it had been a fortuitous moment after all, rather than one of anger and regret.

It was a picture of Marvin Margolis on the front page of *Variety* that had caught Moody's eye. The headline was EMPIRE SIGNS ENGLISH STAR. Beside Margolis was the picture of a far more handsome man, Nigel Lawson. The article compared the signing of Lawson to the signing by MGM of Laurence Olivier to star in *Wuthering Heights* some years before. Lawson had contracted to star in ten movies for Empire, the first of which would be a wartime espionage story called *Traitor's Dawn*, in which the Englishman would portray a Nazi double agent working secretly for British Intelligence.

Moody read the article twice, then threw it down in disgust, knowing that whichever screenwriter Empire assigned the task of scripting *Traitor's Dawn* would earn fifty times what *Below the Salt* had earned for Moody. It was better not to dwell on such incongruities of fortune; he was now engaged in writing of a superior type altogether, dealing as it did with reality, human psychology, and the vicissitudes of fate, not with daring heroes who bounded from one scene of impossible odds to the next with the ease of a superman. Empire's new star, reputed to be an actor of actual talent and accomplishment on the London stage, would doubtless have to accept roles of far less substance than he was used to. Let him blot his tears with dollar bills, thought Moody.

Myra was late. Expected by sundown, she still had not arrived by nine o'clock, and Moody began to worry. Myra had always been a reckless driver (his nickname for her was Leadfoot) and insisted on motoring with the top down in anything but a rainstorm, a rare circumstance in California. Had she taken a curve at excessive speed and left the road? Rolled the car? With no metal roof above her, she would be killed instantly. Moody hated convertibles for their dangerous impracticality, but he had never been able to persuade Myra she should trade hers in for something safer. He pictured her, a broken doll flung many yards from the overturned car, and began pacing back and forth anxiously. Fifteen minutes later he called the Highway Patrol to ask if any accidents involving a blue 1940 Pontiac convertible had occurred. None had, but Moody continued to worry until the phone rang. He snatched it up and let out a literal sigh of relief as Myra's voice filled his ear.

"God, what a rotten day it's been. First I had a flat tire this morning, which wasn't so bad because a very nice truck driver helped me fix it, and then, wouldn't you know it, this afternoon something went wrong with the engine, the fan belt or something, and I've been stuck in Fresno for ages while the garage man hunted around in stores all over town for the kind of belt I need. He had every kind except that one, can you believe it? Anyway, darling, I'm all set now, and I'm going to press on until I get home. I couldn't stand to spend the night here. Were you worried at all?"

"Me? No, of course not. You have a lucky car, as you're always reminding me."

"Don't stay up late waiting for me to get in. It'll be the wee small hours before I get there. I'll pounce on you in the bedroom and wake you up with my lascivious touch."

"You'll do no such thing. You'll drag yourself into the house utterly exhausted, and I'll have to undress you myself."

"Sounds like a good beginning."

"I guarantee you'll be fast asleep by the time I reach your underwear."

"Fifty cents says you're wrong."

"I accept your bet. Drive carefully."

"Actually, I'm going to drive ninety miles an hour through the dark, just to reach you sooner."

"No, you won't. You'll drive at a safe speed and present yourself before me in an unbroken, unscarred state. That's a friendly order."

"Which I'll obey, of course, because your stern, compelling voice obliges me to."

"I should hope so."

"See you later."

"Much later, because you'll be driving slowly."

"I might. 'Bye."

He set the phone down and inspected the dining room table. He'd done a good job setting out Myra's fancy table-cloth, and he knew she'd like the red candles. The welcome-home meal would simply have to be postponed until tomorrow night. He turned on the radio. The Ink Spots were singing "A Lovely Way to Spend an Evening." Moody pulled a wry face and poured himself a whisky. He drank it down and poured another, deciding he may as well get slightly drunk while waiting, rather than go out to a movie. He was in no mood for serious reading, so booze and the radio would be his companions.

He fell asleep on the divan after midnight, and was awakened by a knock at the door. Moody rolled onto the floor in surprise, picked himself up, and went to answer the door, then stopped. It was Flowerdew outside, he knew it! The knocking came again, louder this time, more insistent. Moody had no gun in the house, not even a baseball bat or golf club with which to defend himself. The best thing would be to pretend he wasn't home. He tiptoed to the wall switch and turned out the lights. There was muffled conversation outside his door when he did this. Flowerdew had an accomplice, and they had seen the sliver of light beneath his door go out—and there were the windows too, with shades that couldn't conceal light or the absence of it from the street. He had made his move too late, and by doing so confirmed he was behind the door. Now Flowerdew knew he was afraid. Moody's actions so far had been unforgivably stupid.

"For chrissakes, Moody, open the door," said someone outside.

"We know you're in there. We're waiting, Moody," said a second man.

Neither of them sounded like Kurt Flowerdew, yet Moody was convinced he had heard those voices before.

"Who is it?" he asked, staying away from the door in case bullets should come tearing through it.

"LAPD, Moody."

"Don't go making us wait no more."

"We hafta wait, we get mad. Don't make us mad, Moody."

He opened the door. They hadn't changed at all. Even their coats, drab and unpressed, were the same.

"Finally," said the tall one with the mustache. "Remember us, Moody?"

"We remember you for sure."

"Uh . . . it's . . . Huttig, isn't it? And Labiosa?"

"Lieutenant Huttig," said the tall one.

"Sergeant Labiosa to my friends, which you're one of, Moody," said the short one.

"How you been, Moody? Been okay since we last had a little chat with you?"

"We were wondering," said Labiosa, "always wondering about our good friend Moody since the last time. All those murders, Moody, remember?"

"None of which had anything to do with me, if you'll recall," said Moody.

"That's what you told us then, and because you're a pal of ours, we're gonna keep on believing it, only we wouldn't want you to think we swallow that kinda story from just anyone, Moody."

Vinnie Labiosa added, "Most guys tell us a buncha crap, we make our displeasure known, that's a fact."

"But bygones are bygones," said Huttig, smiling.

"We still iike to listen to you talk, Moody. You tell the swellest stories."

Moody opened the door wider. "Naturally you fellows want to come in."

"Sure we do. We make a call on a pal, we don't wanna just stand around on the doorstep. That'd be unpolite."

"Impolite," Moody corrected.

"Same difference on my street."

The detectives swept past him and looked around without bothering to remove their hats.

"Nice little place. You still got that black dog?"

"Yes, I do. She's not here at the moment. My wife has her."

"You got married, Moody?"

"Yes, about eighteen months ago."

"To that nice-looking dame we saw that one time when her brother got killed?"

"That's her."

"That was some murder, that was. Movie star, right?"

"Baxter Nolan, yes. May I ask you what it is you need to talk to me about?"

"No need to ask. We're ready to do plenty of that ourselves."

Huttig sat on the divan. Labiosa stayed standing, moving around the room, lifting things up and putting them down again as his partner spoke.

"Moody, you used to live in El Segundo, on the boulevard there, right?"

"Until I moved here, yes."

"Only, there's been some trouble down that way tonight. Someone got hurt."

"Kurt Flowerdew," said Moody. "I knew it."

"Say who? The injured party's called Morton Dulkis. He's the one that lives in your old apartment. Who's this Kurt—what was it?"

"Flowerdew. He's a maniac. He has a gun. Was Dulkis shot?"

"Strangled. His neighbor lady next door told us he called the local station Thursday night to complain about a feller by the name of Keith Moody that came around and said he was sending a pal of his to do some damage, and tonight it happened. Soon as we heard that name, our ears pricked up, right, Vinnie?"

"Pricked up so hard I thought they were gonna have sex with my head."

"Keith Moody, the lady said, so naturally we had that old-time feeling about our Hollywood writer friend that always gets tied up with falling bodies, and we got your forwarding address from the manager of the apartments there, so here we are, all curious to hear what you're gonna tell us about this, Moody."

"To begin with, Mr. Dulkis was confused. That wasn't what I told him."

"What wasn't what you told him?"

"That I was sending a pal around to do him harm. Flowerdew's no pal of mine. I tried to let Mr. Dulkis know that Flowerdew might show up there looking for me, and that if he did, Dulkis should be prepared for trouble. He ran me off with a shotgun."

"We saw that there," said Labiosa. "It was never fired."

Huttig said, "So you were definitely there Thursday night, correct?"

"Certainly. I went there to warn him."

"No kidding. About what?"

"Flowerdew, for God's sake. Am I not making myself clear?"

"Who's this Flowerdew guy, some kinda fruit? That his real name?"

"I couldn't say. I believed him when he told me."

"Told you when, where?"

Moody sat down and related the Thursday's events in their entirety. When he was finished, Huttig and Labiosa looked at each other. Labiosa removed his hat and scratched at his bald scalp.

"So this guy's after you because you stood him up on a date?"

"It wasn't a date, it was a meeting."

"In a bar that don't exist."

"You can understand why I did it, though, can't you? The man's a lunatic."

"And you're telling us it's just a coincidence, you bumping into him on the beach and he's got a favorite book of yours in his hand."

"Not a favorite book, a book I wrote. I explained that."

"We thought you were a movie writer, Moody."

"I was, but now I'm a novelist."

Labiosa said, "Is that better?"

"From the intellectual point of view, yes. Financially, no. Not yet, anyway."

"This desert island book you were talking about, does that have swell dames in bathing suits in it? I've seen books like that. There was this one book I remember, *Torrid Zone*, I think it was called, and it had this guy shipwrecked on an island with these seven women, and they were all hot for him, except these two that were hot for each other. There was all kindsa stuff happening on that island. That was a good book."

"Quite different from mine, I assure you."

"I figured you're too refined for that kinda stuff, Moody, so don't get all offended."

"What we need now is for you to come see the crime scene, maybe tell us if you notice anything strange, different, you know, since you lived there."

"But of course the place will be different. It wasn't a furnished apartment, so the current tenant—I'm sorry, what was his name?"

"Dulkis."

"Mr. Dulkis's possessions will make the place different from what it looked like when I lived there. I don't see the point."

"Just to humor your buddies on the force, huh, Moody? Just to please Vinnie and me so we can make a full report, and the captain don't say to us how come we never took you down there, which we need to do, even if you don't know why, see?"

"No, I don't see, but if you insist, I'm ready."

Huttig and Labiosa escorted Moody to their unmarked car. Labiosa drove.

"Oh, wait," said Moody. "I should've left a note for my wife. She'll be home soon. Can we go back?"

Ignoring the request, Huttig asked, "Where'd she go this time of night? You got marriage problems, Moody?"

"She's been in Idaho. Her uncle died and left her something."

"Yeah, like what?"

"A nut bowl with a squirrel on it, and a stamp album."

"You're kidding me. That's all?"

"I'm afraid so. She wouldn't have driven all that way if she'd known her uncle Barney was a practical joker. There was a thriving hardware store up for grabs, but Myra's cousin got that."

"Tough," said Labiosa. "My uncle did that to me, I'd go piss on his grave, I mean it. A squirrel and a stamp album. Some people got no decency."

Moody said, "I suppose you've put out an all points bulletin, or whatever you call it, for Flowerdew."

"Not yet. You just told us that name a minute ago."

"Yes, but it's obviously his work. You should put out a description of the man. He doesn't have a home. You should alert all the cheap motels. Uh . . . I just remembered something important—"

"You want us to go back so you can put the cat out?"

"Please, I'm serious. I just this moment remembered that he told me he was looking for his aunt, Amanda Flowerdew. It could be that he located her, and he's staying at her house. There can't be that many Amanda Flowerdews in Los Angeles."

"We'll look into it," Huttig said, without displaying interest.

"You fellows seem very casual about all this."

"One more dead guy," said Labiosa. "We seen plenty of 'em over the years."

"Too many," Huttig agreed.

"You get so you don't get all in a panic about one more dead guy, Moody. That's how it is in police work. Your kinda work, sure, you see a dead guy and you panic."

"Maybe not our good pal Moody," Huttig reminded his partner. "He's seen plenty. This one we're taking him to, he won't panic when he sees it, I bet."

"Could be," Labiosa conceded. "You gonna panic when you see a dead guy that you already saw before, Moody?"

"Is this a trap, gentlemen, or an innocent question poorly expressed? For the record, yes, I've seen Mr. Dulkis before, on Thursday night, but no, I haven't seen him dead, or alive for that matter, at any time since then."

Huttig wheeled the car around a corner onto El Segundo Boulevard. "You can't fool a guy that writes words for a living, Vinnie."

"Guess not."

They parked outside the apartments and went up to number six. A patrolman was stationed by the open door. Inside, a forensics team was taking samples and photographs. There was no corpse in sight, but a large pool of blood occupied the center of the living room. Huttig became angry. "They took him away already? I said hold on till we got back! We got a man here needs to see the stiff!"

The patrolman shrugged. "They put him in the coroner's wagon twenty minutes ago, Lieutenant. Nobody told me he had to stay put."

"This goes in the report, dammit! Go get that dame next door."

The patrolman left. Moody said, "If it'll help, I'll go to the morgue with you to identify him."

"We already got identification from the lady next door," Labiosa said. "It wasn't that, it was something else."

"You mean you wanted to see my reaction to the dead man, I take it."

"Anyways, he's gone, so just take a look around, okay, Moody? Take your time."

"I still don't quite understand what I'm looking for."

"Maybe you'll know it when you see it, so go look. Don't mind these other guys. You guys just about done yet already?"

A forensics man said they were. Moody watched them pack up their equipment and leave. As they passed through the door, the patrolman returned with a woman wearing a flowered dressing gown.

"This the guy?" Huttig asked her.

She nodded. "That's him. He was shouting at poor Mr. Dulkis."

"I most certainly was not," Moody protested.

"Thank you, ma'am. The officer will take a statement from you."

The patrolman escorted her out. Huttig jammed a cigarette into his mouth but didn't light it. Moody watched the two detectives. Labiosa said, "Never mind us, go look around like we said."

Moody went from room to room, breathing the odors of another man, his clothing, his food, his life. The apartment didn't look like the one he had lived in for years. A few simple changes of furnishing and decoration had transformed it into a place he could barely recognize despite the familiar placement of floors, walls, and ceilings.

"Any luck, Moody?" Huttig called from the living room. Moody was in the bedroom by then.

"No, nothing."

He passed through the bathroom, noting that Dulkis used an old-fashioned cutthroat razor strop that dangled like a long leather tongue beside the mirror. He hadn't looked like a straight-razor man, more the safety blade type. Moody returned to the living room.

"So, anything strike you?" asked Labiosa?

"No, not really. Well, his razor's gone, if that means anything."

"Razor?"

"He uses a cutthroat, at least there's a razor strop in there. I didn't see the razor itself. Maybe it's in the cupboard. I didn't want to open it. Fingerprints, you know."

"The fingerprint team just left. You can touch anything you want, Moody."

Huttig sat down on the dun sofa. "We noticed that about the razor too, didn't we, Vinnie?"

"Yeah, but it wasn't no puzzle to us like it is to Moody."

"Know why that is, Moody?"

"No."

"Because the razor's what the killer used on Dulkis."

"I thought you said he was strangled."

"Yeah, he was, and then the killer used the razor. It's on its way downtown in an evidence bag right now."

"Lieutenant, I wasn't here tonight, and if I had been, and committed this murder, I certainly wouldn't be so stupid as to draw attention to the razor's absence, now would I?"

"Maybe, maybe not. You mighta said it just because you knew we wouldn't be expecting you to say a word about the razor."

"Reverse psychology," said Labiosa. "We know about that."

"Got nothing to say, Moody?"

Moody was staring into a corner of the room. He pointed. "Umm . . . I think I see something there—"

"Yeah? What is it, Moody? You find a clue for us or something?"

Moody went to the corner and stooped to reach beneath a small table. He stood up with a piece of paper in his hand, his expression triumphant.

"There! You see? It *was* Flowerdew!"

"What's that you got there, Moody, Declaration of Independence maybe?"

"Must be awful important, Vinnie. See his face?"

"I see it."

"This," said Moody, "is the dust jacket, or the back part of it, of my book, my first book published last October, the one I told you about. Flowerdew had it with him on the beach! It proves he was here, don't you see?"

"Give it over," Huttig said without enthusiasm, and Moody realized the detectives had known the mutilated dust jacket was where he found it.

"This that desert island book, Moody? All I see is a picture of you."

"No, that book hasn't even been sold to a publisher yet. That's the jacket from my first book, *Below the Salt*. Flowerdew was reading it. That's what started this whole insane business. I wish to God I'd simply kept on walking and left him to his reading."

"I bet Dulkis wishes it too," said Labiosa.

"Look, I went to the trouble of going to the police immediately after I got away from Flowerdew, and I also took the time to warn Mr. Dulkis of what might happen if Flowerdew came here looking for me. I didn't have to do that, but I did. Shall I tell you why I did it? Because I suspected that the police officers

I reported the incident to didn't take me seriously enough to warn Dulkis themselves. And now he's dead."

"That sounds like a serious criticism of the department, Moody, what you said about those cops."

"You can take it as such if you wish. I have nothing further to add. Did you really think I'd come here, clutching the dust jacket from my own book, murder someone I have no grudge against, and then leave the book cover as a convenient clue for you to find? Do I really look that stupid?"

Labiosa shrugged. Huttig flipped the unlit cigarette from one side of his mouth to the other.

"I want to go home now," Moody said. "You couldn't possibly have any charges prepared against me, it's just too ridiculous." He glared at the detectives. "Well?"

"I thought you had nothing further to add."

"Please take me home now, or else take me to the station and prefer charges—that is, if you want the department to look completely incompetent. It's up to you."

"Whaddaya say, Vinnie?"

"I say take him home. We can always talk to him some other time if we want."

"Okay, Moody, let's go."

Moody was dropped off outside his house.

"Don't leave town," Huttig advised him.

"I have no intention of going anywhere."

"Good. We like cooperative people. Cooperative people don't get hurt."

Moody got out of the car and slammed the door.

"Don't do that, Moody. That's department property you're banging there."

"Terribly sorry. I'll be more careful next time. I have such respect for the department, after all."

"Sarcastism, Moody, it don't become you."

" 'Sarcasm' is the correct pronunciation, and I can't help it."

He turned away from the car and approached his front door. The car behind him pulled away from the curb while he fumbled for his keys. Entering the hallway, he felt relief at finally being home again. That feeling lasted only for the few seconds it required him to flip the light switch.

Everything within sight of the front door had been disturbed: every rug pulled back and tossed aside into corners; every chair overturned; every picture on the walls turned face inward and left lopsided; every drawer in the living room china bureau yanked open, the contents dumped and smashed, the drawers flung across the room, the bureau itself splintered across the back, ruined.

Moody went through the house, his mouth hanging open. It was the same in every room; no place was undisturbed. Every single piece of furniture was destroyed, as if with an ax. The mattress had been ripped open, the springs and stuffing exposed. What had the burglars been searching for with such frenzied abandon? Such mayhem couldn't possibly have been the work of just one man—unless the man was Flowerdew. But why would Flowerdew, whose target was Moody, look for him inside chests of drawers and crockery cabinets where no human could hide? Even the old-fashioned cabinet radio had been broken open, the insides lying in a jumble of tubes and wires.

He stood, baffled, attempting to assign a reason for the destruction surrounding him, and still had not found a plausible answer when the front door opened. Moody was in the kitchen when he heard the sound, and he quickly snatched up the largest of the knives strewn about the floor and tiptoed out to confront what he assumed was the perpetrator, returned to complete unfinished business. He would have run from the house if he could, but there was no way outside from the kitchen that did not oblige him to pass whoever had just entered the front door.

"Oh, my God—"

It was Myra. Bess began barking, aware that her mistress was upset.

Moody came around the corner, and Myra screamed. Moody dropped the knife.

"Sorry—" he said, then had to ward off the friendly attack of his adoring dog.

"Bess! Down! Get down, Bess—!"

"What happened?" Myra wailed. "Oh, God, who *did* this?"

It was almost dawn before the police departed, following Moody's telephone call to report the break-in. He had half expected Huttig and Labiosa to walk in and accuse him of faking a crime scene in order to establish the viability of his nemesis, Flowerdew. The smashed back window, point of access for the intruder, was taped over with a square of cardboard, and husband and wife sat down to drink coffee together. Moody added a dash of whisky to his.

Myra said, "I just can't turn my back on you for five minutes, can I?"

Moody's expression caused her to add, "Just a little joke, darling."

"I can't handle jokes right now, if you don't mind. You know we can't stay here."

"Surely you don't think he's going to come back again?"

"He's insane. He's capable of anything. Look at this place—"

"The insurance will take care of most of it."

"I don't want you to have to collect a nice fat sum from my life insurance as well."

"Just think, if I hadn't had trouble with the car and been late home, I might have been here when he came around, or walked in on him while he was smashing things up. I always said my car was lucky. Even when it breaks down, it's lucky. Is this Flowerdew person demented or something?"

"Myra, he murdered a man who had nothing to do with me at all, just because I sent him on a wild-goose chase to find a bar that doesn't exist. Obviously he looked me up in the phone book afterward and came here. We have to leave. He won't stop at killing me. He'll kill you too, just for being here. I want us packed and out of this place before noon. You and I are targets now. Until he's caught, I won't be able to rest easy."

"He's really got under your skin, hasn't he?"

"Under my skin and practically to the marrow."

"Would breakfast help? A little humdrum wifely activity to settle the nerves?"

"I couldn't eat."

"I'm going to make something anyway. If you don't want it, Bess can have it."

The dog, drowsing on the floor between them, lifted her head at the sound of her name.

"He'd kill Bess too, if he could," Moody said. "I'm glad we don't have children."

"Actually—"

"Yes?"

"Nothing."

Moody set down his coffee cup. When Myra said "nothing," it generally meant plenty. "You're not pregnant, I hope."

"Why would you hope that?"

"Because—because obviously we're in no fit state to be parents!"

"Ahh, yes, the entrenched alcoholism on your side, the dementia and nymphomania on mine. . . . You're right, we wouldn't make a good mom and dad."

"Don't joke! Are you in fact pregnant?"

"I am in fact pregnant. You, in fact, did it to me, you mindless lecher, you."

"But . . . we've always been so careful."

"Nature accepts accidents as a good enough reason to begin a new life."

"When did you find out?"

"Just before I went up to Yellowtail. I didn't want to tell you until I found out if I'd inherited a gold mine from Uncle Barney. That way you wouldn't have been able to plead the poverty excuse for not letting the little blobby inside me turn into a big Moody."

"Unfortunately, Uncle Barney has given you cause to think again."

"We could christen him using the squirrel nut bowl. Or her."

"And the stamp album will be his college fund, yes?"

"It might be. I have to have it looked at by a stamp person."

"Philatelist."

"Thank you, yes, one of those, to see what it's worth. There are hundreds of stamps in it. I haven't unpacked the album yet. Do you want to see?"

"You're avoiding the issue. Hunted husband, pregnant wife. Do they flee, or do they sit around the house looking at stamps until the killer returns?"

"Definitely the former, since it's obvious you don't want to do the normal thing and ask for police protection."

"I wouldn't trust the police to protect Bess when she's in heat, frankly."

"God, yes, one pregnancy at a time, please. All right, dar-

ling, I'll start packing the minute I see you eat something. I won't
have you keeling over from hunger, even if Jack the Ripper's
after your blood."

AT NINE MYRA called the office where she worked and
declared herself absent for the day, despite the reluctance of her
boss to accept the excuse of a burglary, on top of her absence of
almost a week; he insisted she come in or face the consequences.
Myra asked what these might be, and her boss told her she would
be fired. "Consider me fired, then, Pruneface," Myra said, and
slammed the phone down. "I've just put us a little closer to the
fiscal cliff," she told Moody. "I no longer have a job to pay for
the groceries."

"We could always sell the house. We have quite a bit of
equity in it now."

"Certainly not. I like our little love nest. I'll get another job,
working for nicer people, and you'll write a best-seller."

"I just wrote one, well, a potential best-seller, remember?
A Desert Island of the Mind?"

Myra had read the novel in manuscript. She said, "It's far
too good a book to be a best-seller, Keith. Please don't take that
the wrong way. When you write the next one, make sure it's
about rich people, doctors or lawyers or something, and make
them all handsome, with interesting sex lives. That should do
the trick."

"You're joking, of course."

"Of course I am, darling."

But Moody could tell she wasn't.

The insurance agent arrived a little after ten. By then
Moody and Myra had filled both cars with as much as they might
need for the next few days and were pondering where to set up

house temporarily. Moody favored any cheap hotel, miles away, and stipulated that it would be a different cheap hotel each day until Flowerdew was caught. Myra shook her head. "Nix to that. I won't be knocked from pillar to post on account of this disgusting creature. And there's Bess to consider. How many hotels will accept a dog? No, we'll pick a suitable place and stay there. The police will want to know where you are in any case, so they can keep an eye on you. Even if you think they can't."

"Naturally your mind is made up."

"Naturally."

The insurance agent went from the living room to the bedroom, giving them a professional smile in passing; he hadn't stopped scribbling in his pad since he came through the door. "Nasty business, this," he said.

"Nasty indeed," Myra agreed. "Can we leave all the details of mending the window and such to you? We're leaving soon."

"All taken care of, Mrs. Moody. Golden State Insurance knows how to look after a valued customer in an emergency."

"Thank you." She turned back to Moody. "Well?"

"Well what?"

"Where are we going?"

"I don't know. I can't seem to think—"

The telephone rang. They turned to stare at it.

"It's him," said Moody. "I just know it's him, calling to gloat and threaten—"

Myra stood and went briskly to the phone, snatched it up, and snapped, "Yes?"

She listened for several seconds, then offered the receiver to Moody.

"It's for you. It isn't him."

Moody stood and went to her. "Who is it?"

"Empire Productions."

"Empire? This is a joke."

"I don't think so. She says she's Marvin Margolis's secretary."

"It's a woman?"

"Or a castrato. Shall I ask?"

Moody took the phone from her. "Hello?"

"Mr. Moody?"

"Yes."

"Mr. Keith Moody?"

"Yes."

"Good morning, Mr. Moody. This is Katherine Harrison, Mr. Margolis's secretary. Perhaps you remember me?"

Moody recalled a middle-aged lady of regal bearing and severely tailored outfits who inhabited the outer room leading to Margolis's inner sanctum, the intimidatingly large office behind massive bronze doors. Someone at Empire had once quipped that Katherine Harrison was a dog, meaning Cerberus, who guarded the gates to Hades.

"Yes, Miss Harrison."

"Are you free to meet with Mr. Margolis today at one?"

"I . . . uh . . . possibly. Why does he want to see me?"

"I believe some kind of contract for your services as a screenwriter is the point of the meeting, Mr. Moody."

"Really? I find that most unlikely, Miss Harrison, given that Mr. Margolis threw me out on my ear two years ago, for no good reason at all, I might add."

"I have no knowledge of that alleged incident, Mr. Moody. I know only that Mr. Margolis has graciously offered to provide you with a limousine to bring you here. What address shall I give the driver? You're at home, of course. Shall that be the address given?"

"Wait one moment, please—"

He covered the mouthpiece and looked at Myra. "The bastard wants me back!"

"Good God, whatever for?"

"My talent, obviously," said Moody, slightly annoyed.

"Of course, but . . . I'm sorry, it just doesn't make sense."

"Miss Harrison? I'll make my own way to the studio, if that's all right."

"Mr. Margolis was most insistent regarding the limousine. It really would be the best thing, Mr. Moody, don't you think?"

"Um . . . all right, but don't send it here. We just . . . had a nasty fire, and the house won't be inhabitable for some time, which means I don't have the slightest notion where I'll be for the rest of the week."

"Where shall I direct the driver, Mr. Moody?"

"Oh . . . the corner of Venice and Western. I'll be carrying a copy of the *L.A. Times* and wearing a purple ostrich feather over my left ear."

"Twelve-thirty sharp, Mr. Moody," said Miss Harrison, distinctly unamused.

The phone clicked. Moody set it down.

"I don't believe this."

"Why would he change his mind after all this time?"

"A special project," concluded Moody. "Something no one else is capable of doing. It can't be anything else."

"Darling, don't take offense, but the only thing you ever wrote for Empire were those awful Westerns for Smokey Hayes."

"I wrote a war movie, *China Skies*, remember?"

"Which was never produced. You didn't even have a chance to finish the script before Margolis bundled you out the door, so whatever the reason he wants you back, it has nothing to do with your ability as a writer."

"Thank you for that vote of confidence. I prefer my theory."

The insurance agent appeared again, snapping his notebook shut. "All done, Mr. and Mrs. Moody. I'll see myself out. Please get in touch with us before the end of the week so we can arrange delivery of the compensation check."

"We will," said Myra, "and thank you for such prompt service."

"Not at all. Good-bye."

As the door closed, Moody said, "Maybe Margolis has turned into a decent human being, and just wants to make amends."

Myra smiled and patted him on the arm. "No, darling."

THE LIMOUSINE ARRIVED exactly on time. Myra had dropped Moody off at Venice and Western five minutes earlier and driven back to the Homeaway Hotel in Ladera Heights, their new home for the immediate future. Stepping inside the enormous Lincoln, Moody felt like an utter fraud, a mountebank masquerading as a potentate. He sank into the deep upholstery and watched the sunlit world outside glide silently past.

"Mr. Moody, remember me?"

Moody looked at the back of the chauffeur's capped head and could not recognize the closely shaved bull neck.

"I'm sorry, no."

"Lester Montgomery. I was on location for some of your Smokey Hayes pictures."

"Oh, Lester, yes, I remember now. I couldn't quite place you in that uniform."

"My own mother wouldn't. I had this job six, eight months. A horse fell on me and busted both my legs, so I wasn't much good for location work anymore."

"I'm sorry to hear that."

"I'm not complaining. This job's easier, even pays more. Do less, earn more, can you figure that out?"

"If you ever do yourself a serious injury and wind up in the executive building, you'll ask yourself that same question, only you'll ask it very quietly."

Lester laughed. "That's a good one, Mr. Moody."

"Keith is fine. I'm only a mister to small children. How's your family, by the way? I seem to recall you had a couple of kids?"

"They're all okay. I got my brother Marty living with us now, in the back room. Doris and me, that's my wife, we got this nice little place over in Maywood. Marty pays us a little rent, so that works out fine. He works for this funeral company. It's real interesting, and the pay ain't so bad either. We all get along. You got any brothers, Mr. . . . Keith?"

"No, no sisters either."

"That's too bad. A man needs his family. Marty, you know what he did? He took the hearse he drives, this big old Cadillac hearse, he takes it out at night without the boss knowing, he's got these spare keys to it, see, and he takes the Cadillac out on a date, what I mean is, he takes his date out in the Caddy, and she won't even get inside the darn thing at first, I mean, you can see why, but in the end he talked her into it and they went to this fancy restaurant or something, where she drank enough so she sees the funny side finally, and Marty, he even says to me he got her to go all the way in the back there with him, in a darn old hearse, can you believe that? Marty, he's got a way with women. I guess that's why his wife went and left him. All the way in a hearse. You couldn't put that in a movie."

"No, you couldn't. Dating in the hearse might be okay, though. That'd be funny."

"Yeah, Marty, he wants to take the hearse out every time now because of this one date that worked out so great for him. He's gonna get caught someday."

"So how are things at good old Empire?"

"You mean since you got fired? Word is, the profits are way down, and nobody knows what to do. That's strictly out of the back room by way of the ventilator, if you know what I mean."

"But Empire just got hold of Nigel Lawson. I wouldn't think he came cheap."

"He cost plenty, they say. Mr. Margolis is hoping he'll be a big box office draw and pull the place outta the red before too long. That's the scoop, anyway."

"I don't suppose you've heard any whispers about why Margolis needs to see me?"

"Nope. It sure is good to see you coming back on the lot, though. You know, I always liked those Smokey Hayes pictures. What I mean is, there's plenty worse out there."

"Thank you, Lester."

"Maybe they want to let you finish that war movie."

"Maybe."

"I see every war movie they make, whatever studio makes it, I don't care. My cousin, he's in the Pacific, island-hopping. I just hate them Japs. If it's a war movie about killing Japs, I prefer it better than the ones about the Nazis. But I'll watch any war movie, like I say."

The limousine swept through the familiar gates of Empire Productions, and Moody was driven directly to the broad steps leading up to the front office.

"This is it," said Lester. "Hope it means good news for you."

"Thanks, Lester. I could certainly use some."

Minutes later Moody approached Miss Harrison, who

smiled frostily and told him to go on through. Moody pushed open one of the bronze doors and stepped inside the office of Marvin Margolis. Nothing had changed: The carpet was the same, impossibly lush; the dimensions of the office offered no comfort to the intimidated; and the polished surface of the aircraft-carrier-size desk at the room's far end was still magnificently empty of papers and clutter. Empire's head of production beckoned Moody forward.

"So good to see you again. Sit with me, Keith."

Moody advanced and seated himself on one of the ornate armchairs facing the desk. Marvin Margolis alarmed him by creasing his smooth face with a smile. The man was dressed as usual in a sober suit of distinctly expensive cut, his only concession to Hollywood a faint green pattern lurking inside his salmon-colored tie. He had lost a lot more hair since Moody had last seen him, but somehow this didn't make him appear older; Marvin Margolis had always looked old. What had not changed one iota was the message passing like an invisible wave across the desk between them, the message that has always flowed from the powerful to the powerless: You are here because I summoned you; I am strong and you are weak, but because I want something from you that torture and humiliation would never successfully accomplish, I shall smile at you and pretend I respect your lower caste. Welcome to my parlor.

"Back in the old corral, eh, Keith."

"Yes, and wondering why, to be perfectly frank."

"Let's both be perfectly frank with each other, Keith. Honesty is always the best policy, in this or any other business. A frank and honest exchange of views. Let me have your best guess, however wild the thoughts inside your head. Why are you here once again as before? That is the question."

"Miss Harrison hinted at a screenwriting assignment."

"Miss Harrison is correct. Can you imagine, Keith, what assignment lies waiting for you? Miss Harrison informs me you have been the victim of a fire. I trust you suffered no serious injury? Your home was not incinerated completely, beyond the possibility of savior? That should happen to no one. A man's home is his castle."

"My wife and I are perfectly safe, thank you."

"Keith, you married? Why was I not informed? Tell me the name of your wife, Keith."

"Myra."

"A splendid name for someone I know is a splendid woman. A man such as yourself, Keith, would be satisfied with nothing less."

"She used to work here, doing research. She was Bax Nolan's sister."

"Ahh, yes, it returns to me now. The young lady left our family of employees at around the same time you yourself did, Keith."

Both of us fired by you, you asshole, thought Moody.

"A tremendous loss to the studio, young Baxter. My own health suffered considerably as a result of our misfortune. You'll appreciate what I have to tell you, Keith, with regard to your present return. There's a connection, you see."

"A connection?"

"Between the unfortunate loss of your deceased brother-in-law and the reason I have summoned you here today. Can you grasp the connection, Keith?"

"I'm afraid not."

"We have a replacement at last. A young and vigorous man of unbounded talent and charm. An actor without peer from across the water, Keith. Someone with even greater potential for long-term success than the late lamented Bax."

"You're referring to Nigel Lawson."

"The same. What a presence! We had to leap beyond the offers made by other studios, *far* beyond, to capture the prize. Nigel Lawson represents an investment of unparalleled importance to Empire Productions, Keith. This is our golden opportunity to raise ourselves to the forefront of magnificence. A man of such importance, Keith, deserves the very best we have to offer. The very best production values. The very best director. The very best story we currently have available and suitable for this actor's very special talents. The very best screenwriter to bring out that story's strengths, Keith, and erase its possible weaknesses. What we must have at the end of the day is a script so exactly perfect for Nigel Lawson, the man will weep genuine tears when he reads it. That is why you're here, Keith, to write that script. No one else will do. Only the very best talent is appropriate for a venture of this size and potential for success."

"I'm a novelist nowadays, Mr. Margolis, not a screenwriter."

"A novelist, yes, so I have been informed, and that is why you're the perfect choice for this project, Keith."

With a conjurer's flourish Margolis produced from behind his desk a book. He pushed this across the polished teak toward Moody, who was obliged to stand and reach across a considerable expanse of wood to pick it up. He looked at the cover: *Traitor's Dawn* by Jeffrey Hubbell.

Margolis continued. "As a novelist and screenwriter, Keith, your perspective will give you the tremendous advantage of being able to appreciate the prose before you, while at the same time enabling you to render the story—and a superb example of the storyteller's art it is, Keith—in terms suitable for a motion picture audience."

"You want me to adapt the novel for the screen."

"Precisely. Empire Productions seldom extends a chance for fortune and fame as generous as this that I'm offering you. One thousand dollars a week, Keith, and the use once again of the Writers' Building."

Moody looked down at the book before him. A handsome black-uniformed Nazi with a Luger in his hand was glancing over his shoulder down an alleyway ending in darkness. This was presumably the character Nigel Lawson would play, the British double agent Moody had read about in *Variety*. One thousand a week. He needed the money. His second book was not yet sold, and the first had been an awful flop. Myra was pregnant. Moody was being hunted by a lunatic, and might possibly be killed by him before too long. A single mother would struggle on, all alone in the world, her bank account depleted by the untimely death of her foolish husband, who died poor when he might just as well have accepted an offer of work and at the very least left her a nest egg to carry on with.

Moody took a breath.

"Fifteen hundred a week," he said.

"Accepted," said Margolis, beaming again. "Welcome aboard, Keith."

"A pleasure to be back." Moody's smile was every bit as sincere as that of Margolis. Why is this happening? Moody thought, his cheeks beginning to ache with the unaccustomed stretching. What's Margolis not telling me?

"Nigel himself is anxious to meet you, Keith."

"He is?"

"Just this morning he expressed that very wish. The man awaits without."

"Pardon?"

"Nigel is, at this very moment, waiting in the outer office to meet you."

"How . . . nice."

Margolis stood. Assuming they would go together to the outer office, Moody stood also, but was waved back onto his seat by Margolis.

"Remain as you are, Keith. Nigel will join you presently. A meeting between two artists mustn't take place in the hearing of a secretary, so I've surrendered my own office for as long as you both require it. Even the Head of Production sometimes is superfluous to such a meeting of minds. Wait one small moment."

Margolis began walking toward the bronze doors. Turning in his chair, Moody was rewarded with the rare sight of Marvin Margolis in motion, seen from behind. Most encounters with the most important man at Empire took place while the man was seated; in fact, a popular rumor at the studio for years had credited Margolis with being a cripple who hid his wheelchair behind the formidable teak desk. Moody knew this wasn't so, having been inside Margolis's house at the end of the Baxter Nolan affair. The man did have an unusual way of walking, however: a stiff-legged, almost robotic swinging of the legs, as if they might not bend at the knee. Perhaps he was indeed crippled, the owner of wooden pins. No, Moody decided; if Margolis had wooden legs, he'd lurch and roll like a drunken sailor instead of moving smoothly and unnaturally across the carpet. A bronze door opened, then closed with a muted clang.

Moody looked about himself, as lost in the spaciousness of Margolis's office as a model airplane inside a hangar designed to house a flying fortress. It was all very strange, and he was only being told a small part of whatever it truly was that had brought him back to Empire. He would keep his mind sharp and discover the real reason for his reinstatement as screenwriter at fifteen hundred dollars per week. Myra would be pleased; more than that, she would be relieved. He would write a fine script (but not too quickly) and defy Kurt Flowerdew's plan that he be dead. Life would be good.

The door behind him opened. Moody turned again to watch the entrance of the actor. Nigel Lawson was exactly as his publicity pictures depicted him: tall, lithe, his blond hair with a slight wave where length permitted. He covered the distance to Moody, who stood to greet him, in a few energetic strides, his right hand extended, a slow smile making his face, already handsome in the classic sense, even more appealing at the personal level. Moody realized it was the smile that came across more than anything else on film; without it Lawson would have no more than the physical perfection of a menswear window dummy; the expensive slacks and sports jacket completed that impression. His eyes were as bright as his brilliantined locks and gleaming teeth, and Moody, ever the cynic, was won over regardless, deciding that the smile couldn't possibly have been anything but genuine; nobody could be that good an actor. He accepted Nigel Lawson the instant their hands clasped.

"May I call you Keith? I'm definitely to be called Nigel, although I'll probably respond to Nige or Nigers when we get drunk together. I've read your book, old man."

"My book?"

"*Below the Salt.* Amazingly perceptive study. I don't think anyone's ever captured the mind of an actor so precisely. The fact that Jason the schizophrenic actor and his brother Michael the thief are one and the same man was handled so well I didn't suspect a thing until the last chapter, when the asylum doc makes Jason break down and reveal the other side of himself. Fantastic plot development! Sorry, didn't mean to rant and rave so soon after meeting you."

"Oh, rant and rave by all means. The writer's ego requires petting just like anyone else's."

"That's right. Writers and actors, two sides of the same coin, really. One side's all deep thoughts and looking inward, and the other's all fireworks and preening. Philosophers and show-offs, that's us creative buggers. Better let you have your hand back."

Moody realized Lawson had been pumping his hand all along. Each released the other's fingers. Moody was smiling as broadly as Lawson by then.

"Look at us," said the actor, "both standing about, burning energy, when we might just as easily be relaxing in these marvelous chairs. That Margolis chap, what a tremendous fellow, really, the heart and soul of tact and diplomacy, a superb mind hidden inside a body of common clay like the rest of us. Pretty much of a titan in the industry if you ask me, don't you agree, Keith?"

Moody was flabbergasted by the outrageously overflattering content of Lawson's praise, and for a moment he considered ditching all his good feeling toward the actor; then he saw that Lawson was nodding his head vigorously, still smiling, and pointing at the ceiling, then cupping his hands over his ears to mime a listening spy. Margolis's office had a hidden microphone! Moody swayed between surprise and outrage, but he was able to recover and do some acting himself.

"I've always thought so. MM and I have had our little differences in the past, as you may or may not know, but there's always been mutual respect between us, especially from my side."

"I'm glad we both agree. You know, this is going to be a damned important picture for me, Keith, first one made in America. Got to make it count at the old box office, many bums on many seats and all that. Still, what need to worry when MM's behind the scenes, making it all happen the way it ought to, eh?"

"Exactly. With him at the wheel, we're already steering the right course."

Lawson mimed copious vomiting. Moody had to keep himself from laughing aloud as the actor stood and puked with exaggerated abandon across Margolis's desk, then mimed hosing it off with a stream from his penis. Moody sagged against the side of his chair and held his lips together.

"You know, Keith, it was me who insisted that you be the man to write the screenplay, and MM, being the genius that he is, didn't attempt to impose his own opinion on me, the way most studio heads would have. No, he's so clever himself, he saw immediately that I had the right idea and was gracious enough to let me have my way. You know what, Keith? I'll bet MM doesn't even claim to others that the idea was his own, which is what a lesser man in his position would do. He's going to acknowledge openly that it was me who brought you into the fold for *Traitor's Dawn*. What a man!"

"Indeed he is, Nigel. I couldn't agree with you more."

Nigel looked at his wristwatch. "Bloody hell. Here I am, gasbagging away, and you probably haven't even had lunch yet. How about getting our heads into the trough over at the commissary? Have you sampled their wares? Of course you have, silly me, you used to work here before. Shall we partake of the viands together, old man? My tummy's tugging urgently at my throat."

"Excellent idea."

Moody stood up and had his arm taken by Nigel. They passed along the length of the office arm in arm, Nigel doing a rubbery-kneed imitation of a drunk that brought Moody to a state of silent laughter again.

Nigel flung open both bronze doors together, like a hero entering the enemy's stronghold, and turned his charm like a searchlight beam upon Miss Harrison, whose hands hovered over the papers on her desk. She was as captivated by the presence of Nigel as a rabbit in the shadow of a splendid python.

"Miss Harrison," said Nigel, his precise British diction commanding the air between them, "please inform the big chief my new friend and associate, the renowned writer Keith Moody, and my humble self are retiring to avail ourselves of the groaning board, where we shall stuff ourselves to repletion on fine American cuisine. Good afternoon to you, Miss Harrison."

Nigel swept past with Moody still in his grip.

The frost that Miss Harrison had presented to Moody was thawed instantly.

"Yes, I . . . I'll tell him, Mr. Lawson."

Nigel whispered to Moody, "Look back over your shoulder."

Moody did so, and saw Miss Harrison reaching down to perform some task beneath her desktop.

"She's turning off the wire recorder in monstrous Margolis's office. It's a laugh, isn't it? They say the whole rotten setup was installed by the FBI. MM's a great fan of J. Edgar Hoover. They both see themselves as the moral custodians of America. Both on the lookout for moral degeneracy and contrary opinions, you see. Bastards."

"How on earth do you know all this?"

They were strolling down the corridor now. Moody observed passing secretaries undergo a sudden change of expression as they caught sight of the English matinee idol, yet he was not jealous; mere minutes had passed, but he felt, against all logic, that Nigel was truly his friend, and as a friend, Moody could only admire the ease with which Nigel melted the hearts of women simply by passing them by.

"You mean, how can a new chum in town like myself possibly be privy to secrets?" He tapped the side of his aquiline nose. "Ask not who whispers to whom in the dark, for 'tis better not to know. Everything's an open secret in Hollywood, Keith, old sport. The sensible thing to do is accept it and have a jolly good time anyway, within reason, of course. Can't kill the fatted calf and the golden goose at the same time, not without getting awfully bloody, anyway. God, I'm starved!"

The commissary was crowded with extras in exotic costume, echoing with the din of cutlery and conversation. Moody and Nigel lined up for their trays and moved along the counter displays of meals and desserts. Twice, Nigel was welcomed to Empire by women dispensing the food, and to both he gave back thanks that seemed to Moody the very essence of charm and sincerity. Extending his bowl to receive asparagus soup, Moody felt a momentary pang of doubt concerning his new friend; the man seemed absolutely perfect, and Moody had always harbored a healthy sense of doubt concerning the rich and famous. Yet he put this aside, chiding himself for a sour misanthrope. Nigel Lawson was a talented and engaging man, and Moody was lucky enough to have been chosen, sight unseen, to be his friend. It was an unusual situation to find himself in, and he had better rise to the occasion.

Their trays filled, they sought out a quiet corner table and began eating.

"Damn good nosh they serve here," commented Nigel. "Actually I feel a bit guilty. There's bugger-all available to John and Jane Public back in dear old Blighty. Ration cards for everything, and 'everything' doesn't cover much at all, yet here I am scoffing down a meal fit for the king, and being paid handsomely to do it. Funny old world, eh, Keith?"

"I often find myself laughing in my sleep over it."

"You know, I've got the feeling you and I are going to get along like the proverbial burning house. Stop me if I get too gushy, old man, but the moment we met, I knew I'd made the right choice for screenwriter. Just between you and me, I almost fell over when Margolis said he'd hire you for the job. It happened very early this morning, as a matter of fact. I think MM crawls out of his crypt at first light, sort of a reverse vampire or something. Anyway, he had me over at his house for a special meeting at some ungodly hour to thrash things out with my agent and myself, fine-tuning the deal and whatnot, and I took a chance and mentioned you. You should have seen his face. There was a tiny little thundercloud brewing between his eyes, and he started chewing his lips and drooling—all right, I'm going over the top a bit, but he obviously wasn't pleased, so I thought I'd press on anyway, just to see what happened. The old agent was having kittens, I could tell, but I wasn't going to give up without a fight on your behalf, and blow me down if Margolis didn't come over all smiles a few minutes later. All I had to do was point out the obvious to him, really."

"Which is?"

"Well, just look at your book, old fruit. Here's this actor chap in *Below the Salt* with two sides to him, each separated from the other by the nonreflecting mirror of madness—gosh, that sounded poetic, didn't it! Anyway, that's the key to the character in *Traitor's Dawn*, you see, he's able to be two people at once, working for British Intelligence and at the same time being a perfectly convincing Nazi. That's the problem with Jeffrey Hubbell's book, though, Keith. It's a darned good read and very exciting, with all those hair's-breadth escapes and so forth, but Traven, the double agent, is a bit thin, just a Bulldog Drummond type who happens to find himself mixed up with the Nazis."

"You feel the character lacks depth."

"Motivation, that's what's not there. I hate that word, personally, 'motivation.' Every silly tart of an actress is always wanting to know what her bloody motivation is for every single piddling little scene. 'What's my motivation for opening the door, Mr. Director?' Bloody annoying. But in this case it's the right word. I want you to round him out, make him more like the mad actor chappie Jason in *Below the Salt*, you know what I mean, with all kinds of interesting internal conflict going on."

"Why would an Englishman experience internal conflict over spying against the Germans? It's his patriotic and moral duty to do so, I'd have thought."

"Well, yes . . . and no. You see, he's so very damn good at it, there has to be some kind of switch inside his head, something normal people don't have, that enables him to assume the persona of the Nazi on demand, rather as an actor has to slip into character."

"I think I see what you mean. Of course, I haven't read the book yet—damn, I left it on Margolis's desk."

"Not to worry, I've got several copies. The thing is to slip this extra stuff into the script with a subtle enough hand so that MM and the other philistines don't get wind of it and throw it all out in favor of more leaping out of planes and romancing the Jerry countess and all the rest of it. It'll be there, the psychological underpinnings of the fellow, if you like, for anyone of intelligence to see and appreciate, but it won't interfere with the demands of the plot for lots of good old-fashioned action and derring-do."

"I understand. It shouldn't be too difficult. There'll have to be some kind of key scene that explains the spy's inner workings, the thing that makes him better than good at his job. It'll be something that lets us know he's not just doing it for king and country, he's doing it because he's compelled to do so, by something or other in his past."

"Exactly! I knew you'd get it."

A young woman, one of Margolis's secretaries by the look of her tailoring and deportment, approached the table. She began blushing the moment Nigel turned to look at her.

"Mr. Lawson? You have a fitting appointment in Wardrobe at two o'clock."

"By golly and by gosh, so I do! Clean forgot about it." He turned back to Moody. "Have to run along, Keith old man. Do have a think about what we were discussing. Just between you and me and the lamppost, all right?"

"Of course."

"See you later, then." To the girl who had reminded him he said, "Thanks so much for roping me in. I'm a forgetful sod at times."

She simpered wordlessly under his gaze. Nigel winked at Keith and turned away to lose himself among the commissary crowd. The girl watched his departing shoulders and wavy fair hair until he was gone, at which point she looked at Moody with considerably less admiration.

"Miss Harrison says you left a book in Mr. Margolis's office, and you have to go back anyway to sign a contract."

"Thank you. Please tell Miss Harrison I'll be there directly, following my peach cobbler and cream."

The girl turned away. Moody had seldom been successful with women, especially attractive women like the one walking away from him. It often surprised him to recall that he was married to an attractive woman. With a start, Moody realized he had, from the instant of meeting Nigel Lawson, not given a moment's thought to his pregnant wife, nor had he worried over the looming presence in his life of Kurt Flowerdew. Nigel certainly possessed some kind of magic about himself, to be capable of erasing such things by his smile, and Moody was reminded again of the mysterious process by which such ability is captured on celluloid and blasted on streamers of light across darkened theaters to kindle on the screen an exact, or possibly enhanced, replication of itself. Nigel needed little enhancement, which meant, perforce, he was destined for stardom. And he was Moody's friend. It was more than flattering; in an odd sense that Moody could not properly define, it was comforting.

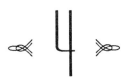

The temporary home of the Moodys was a gargantuan edifice erected in Hollywood's silent heyday to accommodate the influx of young men and women streaming to southern California in ardent search of fame. The Homeaway's clientele from that time until the present had been uniformly attractive, naive, and—almost to a boy and girl—disappointed. The Homeaway Hotel remained a beacon for those small-towners desperate for the stuff of fantasy, and so cunningly named it provided at least a little reassurance for anxious parents that the destination their beloved but foolish sons and daughters were heading toward would not be so very different from the familiar comforts of home.

No such ambience existed at the Homeaway, of course, or the zealous young things flocking to its reception desk from Union Station and the Greyhound depot would never have stayed. Stay they did, savoring what, for most of them, comprised absolute freedom within the law. Many love affairs were begun in the labyrinthine corridors and rooms of the Homeaway, and an equal number ended there, sometimes tragically. The utility doorway to the roof had been padlocked shut in 1927 when three young women plunged to their deaths within the same month, victims all of professional disappointment and personal betrayal. Their ghosts, it was rumored, still haunted the byways of the Homeaway; they were called the Flying Starlet Sisters, and the flippant remarks and unkind wisecracks made at their expense were the only lasting fame they achieved in Hollywood. Even fame such as this outlasted those among the living who passed through the narrow halls, waiting and hoping for a phone call, until they wearied of it and settled for the kinds of job ordinary people content themselves with, or else went home again to Indiana and Iowa and Kansas, relinquishing their rooms and their dreams to a fresh influx of lambs.

Myra was still unpacking their cases and arranging clothes in drawers and closets when Moody arrived back at the hotel, transported by another chauffeured limousine from the studio. Bess leaped at Moody and whirled in circles to express her delight. Moody looked around at their rooms, smelling the ancient carpet and the lingering odor of transient lives in the air, a kind of invisible perfume, musty and sensual and sad, that even the opened window could not expunge. If only they had waited until after his meeting with Margolis, they could have moved into something far more grand; still, the Homeaway did accommodate the quirks and eccentricities of its guests, and this included the keeping of pets, provided the creatures were not unusual enough to disturb the staff. A fifteen-foot python had escaped from one of the rooms in 1938 and finally been located in the basement, slowly consuming, uniform and all, a young bellboy who had been missing for several days.

"Well?" said Myra. "Has he declared you his long-lost son, or what?"

"Not quite. He declared the next-best thing—I'm hired, at fifteen hundred a week."

"Are you joking? Marvin Margolis took you *back*?"

"He almost went down on bended knee. Told me only *I* can give Empire what Empire needs."

"And what does Empire need, to the tune of fifteen hundred a week?"

Moody tossed *Traitor's Dawn* onto the bed. "That, in screenplay form."

Myra picked it up. "Oh, I've heard of this. Isn't it the hot new thriller?"

"It is, and it'll be even hotter now that Nigel Lawson's been signed to play the hero. He'll be Edward Traven, double agent."

"Lawson? Isn't he just a bit too scrumptious to play that kind of role?"

Moody knelt to pet the dog and rub behind her ears. "Being handsome doesn't necessarily exclude a man from espionage. What better way to find the enemy's weaknesses than to charm your way into the heart of darkness in Berlin. I think he'll be excellent."

"But why did Margolis pick you, and not one of the dozens of other writers he has on tap?"

"Lawson insisted. It's him we have to thank, not Margolis."

"Lawson picked you? Keith, that's extraordinary."

Moody explained the connection with *Below the Salt*. Myra became animated.

"Darling, you'd resigned yourself to the book being a flop, and instead it's going to earn you tons of cash!"

"Well, indirectly."

"We can replace our smashed-up things with something much nicer!"

"Only after Flowerdew's behind bars. I need to make a phone call."

Moody called the Homicide Division and asked for Lieutenant Huttig.

"Yeah? Huttig."

"Lieutenant, this is Keith Moody."

"You call to confess, Moody?"

"No, nor to make jokes. You've probably been informed by now that Flowerdew was at my house last night, while I was over at El Segundo with you."

"Say again?"

"They didn't tell you? That's completely unprofessional."

"Wait a minute, Moody. Who didn't tell me what?"

"The police who were at my home last night, after you and Sergeant Labiosa dropped me off. I made a point of telling the officer, I forget his name, to tell you what happened because of the Flowerdew connection."

"What Flowerdew connection?"

Moody heard a click and assumed Labiosa had picked up an extension to listen in.

"It was Flowerdew," he continued. "When he didn't find me at the El Segundo apartment, he did the obvious thing and looked up my new address in the telephone book. I wasn't there, so he went through the entire house, smashing every stick of furniture, ripping out drawers and emptying them. He even slashed open the mattress. Sheer wanton vandalism."

"Sounds more like he was looking for something."

"He was looking for *me*, Lieutenant. Would he expect to find me inside a mattress? The man's insane."

"He leave any kind of a message?"

"I'd say destroying furniture sends a fairly eloquent message, wouldn't you?"

"Maybe, maybe not. Did anyone see any of this happening, the neighbors or anyone?"

"No."

"So there's no definite proof it was Flowerdew that did it."

"Who else could it possibly be?"

There was silence at the other end of the line.

Moody said, "Oh, I see. You're insinuating it was me who did it, presumably to establish Flowerdew as a real person instead of the character I made up to cover my tracks at El Segundo, is that it? What a brilliant hypothesis. What reason would I have for killing Morton Dulkis?"

"Beats me, Moody."

"But I'm a suspect anyway, correct?"

"If we figured you for the killer, Moody, you'd be down at the station right now under them hot lights you movie writers say we use to get confessions outta people."

"So I'm not a suspect."

"Not necessarily. Maybe there's a whole lot more to this case than you know, or we know. Maybe there's another guy doing this. Your pal Flowerdew hasn't exactly left his autograph anywhere, not at Dulkis's place, and not at yours either, so for right now, we're gonna leave it open till we get some more facts."

"What about the aunt, Amanda Flowerdew? Did you locate her?"

"There's exactly three Flowerdews in the L.A. phone book, and none of them's an Amanda. You got anything to add, Moody?"

"I . . . no."

The phone clicked.

"Idiot," Moody said, setting the receiver down.

"They can't seriously suspect you of murder, surely."

"Nothing is beyond the bounds of absurdity where Huttig and Labiosa are concerned. Actually, I don't think I'm on their shortlist, but I'm not so sure they don't think I invented Flowerdew, that's the annoying thing."

"Don't they realize a professional writer wouldn't create an alibi for himself with such a ridiculous name?"

"The habits of professional writers probably don't come up in police training."

The phone rang. Moody picked it up.

"Hello?"

"Front desk, sir. A gentleman here says he wants to meet with you."

"What name?"

"Uh . . . Flowerdew, I believe."

"Kurt Flowerdew—!"

"The gentleman didn't give his first name, sir. Do you want me to ask?"

"No. Does he appear . . . Does he seem . . . all right?"

"All right, sir?"

"Yes, I mean, does he appear to be demented in any way?"

"The gentleman appears quite normal, sir. Do you want me to ask how he's feeling?"

"No! Is he able to hear this conversation at all?"

"The gentleman is reading a newspaper by the lobby door, sir."

"How the hell did he know where to find me?"

"Sir?"

"Nothing. Call the police, Homicide Division, and ask for Lieutenant Huttig. Tell him a murder suspect is right there in the lobby. Tell him it's Flowerdew, he'll know what to do. And tell Flowerdew I'll be down in a couple of minutes, stall for time, you know."

"Like in the movies, sir?"

"Exactly."

"Your wife was telling me you're a movie writer yourself, sir."

"I used to be. Well, as a matter of fact, I am again, just today. . . . Are you calling the police?"

"Certainly, sir."

"Good, and stall Flowerdew. This is terribly important."

"I'm sure it is, sir."

The desk phone was disconnected. Myra's face had whitened a shade or two.

"Is it really him?"

"Who else?"

"You're not going down there."

"How else am I going to hold him until the police arrive?"

"Wait up here. Let them handle it."

"He's not going to gun me down in the middle of a hotel lobby."

"How do you know he won't! He's insane, you said so yourself!"

"Listen—"

The sound of a police siren came through the window. Moody rushed across the room and threw it open farther, then stuck his head and shoulders outside. The room was located on the side of the hotel, however, so he was unable to see if the police car was approaching the lobby entrance. It was definitely getting louder.

"That can't be them," said Myra. "It's too soon."

"There must have been a prowl car right down the block. Damn, I should've said not to turn on their siren. He might be scared away—" The siren suddenly quit, winding down in a discordant snarl. "Damn! I can't see a thing except the alleyway. I'm going down there."

"No! Wait here until they call up. Let them grab him first."

"They'll have done that by the time I get down there."

He sprinted for the door.

"Keith!"

"There's nothing to worry about. Back in a minute."

He flung himself out into the corridor and hurried toward the elevators, decided they were too slow, and went sprinting down the echoing concrete tower of the service stairs, so intent on reaching the ground floor he barely paused to brush past a couple engaged in upright sexual intercourse between floors four and five. Reaching the door marked LOBBY, he eased it open and peered out into the capacious and pillared room before him. The desk clerk, presumably the one he had been speaking with, could be seen across the way, past the potted ferns, his attention directed elsewhere. There were no sounds of scuffling and shouting. The air smelled of old cigars and wasted time.

Moody stepped out into the open and went across to the front desk. The clerk, a casting director's dream of wizened servitude, broke open his face with a welcoming smile. "How can I help you today, sir?"

Moody cast a quick look behind himself. No cops, no struggling Flowerdew. A half dozen people sat in the overstuffed armchairs positioned about the lobby, apparently undisturbed by recent events.

"Did they take him away already?" Moody asked.

"Who, sir?"

"The police. They certainly know their stuff."

"Your party is over there, sir."

"Party?"

"Yes, sir, over there, with the large-brimmed hat and newspaper."

Moody turned and saw a man of this description beneath a large poster extolling the virtues of transcontinental travel by train. He turned back to the desk clerk, who continued to smile; Moody imagined he might smile even in his coffin.

"I'm . . . confused. Didn't the police come? And that isn't the man, by the way. Flowerdew's younger and chubbier."

"There have been no police here today, sir, although I did hear a siren just a few minutes ago. The gentleman over there wants to talk with you, sir."

"You didn't call the police, did you."

"Oh, no, sir, I wouldn't do that. I've worked here far too long, sir."

"Too long?" Moody prompted, wondering if it was the desk clerk or himself who was missing the point.

"Yes, sir, too long to let a little joke be taken seriously. You writers and actors, sir, what a bunch of pranksters, always without malice, of course, but a fellow gets to know when his leg's being pulled, sir, after all this time."

Moody took several breaths. "That gentleman over there?"

"Yes, sir."

Moody approached the man in the broad-brimmed hat. He was middle-aged, thin to the point of desiccation, his short-sleeved shirt revealing elbows so gnarled they resembled woody knotholes.

"Mr. Flowerdew?"

Moody fully expected the man to answer no; instead he looked up and said, "Kind of."

"Kind of?" Moody felt he was being kidded. Was the visitor in collusion with the desk clerk, practicing some kind of practical jokery based on misdirection and misidentification?

"In a way," said the man, showing his perfect dentures. "Young Kurt, he's my nephew. My name's Gallagher."

"Mr. Gallagher, I'm a little confused about all this."

"Don't blame you one little bit, son. I'm a mite confused about it myself."

"The desk clerk said you were called Flowerdew."

"Him? That old fossil's half senile, most likely. What I told him was, I'm here to see you with regard to Kurt. He must've got it mixed up in his head."

"Oh, I see. Mr. Gallagher, how did you know where I lived?"

"Followed you from your place over Alhambra way. There was you and a nice-looking young lady driving two cars, looked like they were loaded up with bags and such. Didn't notice a '31 Dodge trailing along behind, did you."

"Uh . . . no, I didn't."

"I would've talked with you sooner, but you got here to this place, and ten minutes later you went someplace else, with the lady driving. I lost you in traffic, got stuck behind a bus, with an army truck alongside of me, and when I got free of them, you were gone, turned off somewhere I guess, so I came back here to wait."

Moody sat beside him. The armchairs they occupied were so huge they were separated by at least five feet. "What can you tell me about Kurt, Mr. Gallagher?"

"I was kind of hoping you'd be the one to tell me. Kurt, he's not one to communicate his thinking too well. I got your name off of him and looked you up in the book. He was pretty darn scared, that boy."

"Scared of what?"

"Wouldn't say, only he wanted to talk with you real bad."

"You're aware that the police are after him."

"Hell no, he didn't mention that fact at all. What'd he do?"

"Well, he seems to have . . . murdered someone."

Gallagher looked at Moody for a long moment. "Murdered, you say?"

"Yes, a man called Morton Dulkis. It happened last night."

Gallagher shook his head, bemused rather than shocked.

"Mr. Moody, that boy couldn't hurt a fly."

"I don't suppose you're aware that he carries a gun."

"He wouldn't do no such thing, not Kurt. I offered him an air rifle when he's just a boy and he said no, he wanted a big book about lizards, with color pictures."

"Mr. Gallagher, where does Amanda Flowerdew live?"

"Amanda? Out Pasadena way, why?"

"Because Kurt told me he was in Los Angeles looking for his aunt Amanda."

"He'd have trouble doing that, even if he used the phone book."

"Why is that?"

"This place she's at, it's real quiet, just a home for old folks out that way. Amanda's got to be getting on for eighty years old. Her sister-in-law, Kurt's mama, she was a lot younger than her. She's been dead a long time now, up in Wisconsin. Her name was Mary Gallagher before she got married. My sister, she was. Kurt's old man, that's Amanda's brother, he never knew how to take care of him after Mary died."

"When did you speak with Kurt, Mr. Gallagher?"

"This morning. He was shook up pretty bad about something."

Moody explained what that something might be. Gallagher shook his head.

"Nope, don't believe he had a darn thing to do with it. Could be he was there when it happened, that'd explain him being all upset, but it wasn't him that did it, killed this feller Dulkis. You can take that to the bank, Mr. Moody, and would you mind explaining to me what exactly is your connection with Kurt? He was kind of closemouthed about that."

Moody gave a brief account of the meeting on the beach,

emphasizing the fact that Flowerdew had made a note of the address on Moody's driver's license, the out-of-date address that was occupied by Morton Dulkis.

"So you're telling me that Kurt got mad at you and went around there to kill you, only he ended up killing this other feller instead."

"Unfortunately, yes."

"No, sir, not that boy."

"How was Kurt able to locate you but not his aunt, Mr. Gallagher?"

"He had my address wrote down on a piece of paper. Told me he had that piece of paper folded up six ways from Sunday inside of his coat pocket all the way from Wisconsin. I expect he wanted to see Amanda first on account of he was kind of a favorite of hers, being that Amanda never did have kids of her own. Course, I'm just supposing that's why, he never did say."

"And what is your address, Mr. Gallagher?"

"I'm just not prepared to say, right this minute. You might go telling the cops, and then there'd be no peace on earth for yours truly, now would there? They'd be forever hanging around the place waiting for Kurt to show up, when what they oughta be doing with the taxpayers' money is go find the real criminal that did it. So no deal."

"I can't make you, of course."

"Damn right. I need to stick by my nephew. He's sixty cents short on the dollar, but he's family, and he's no killer."

Moody saw it was pointless to argue.

"Mr. Gallagher, I have a favor to ask. Please don't give Kurt the address of this hotel. I'm not convinced he isn't after my blood. I appreciate your sentiments concerning family obligation, but I also have a family. My wife is pregnant, and this business with Kurt is upsetting her."

"Fair enough. I'll keep him steered away from here, and you quit telling the cops you figure it was him that did this murder."

"My opinion is already on record with the police department, Mr. Gallagher, there's nothing I can do about that now."

"But in your mind, do you still think he's the one?"

Gallagher's expression, until that moment hard and uncompromising, became vulnerable. Moody felt terrible. Could he be wrong about Flowerdew?

"I'm . . . uncertain. It's in the hands of the police, in any case. My thoughts on the matter are pretty much irrelevant at this stage."

Gallagher levered himself up and out of the armchair. "I won't take up any more of your time, then, Mr. Moody. You tell your wife she doesn't have a thing to worry about from Kurt. I'll be taking care of that boy myself, get him out of town maybe, before he gets in any more trouble. No need for you to go telling the police none of that."

Moody said nothing. Gallagher nodded at him, then walked across to the revolving door and was gone, absorbed by the sunlight outside. Moody stayed where he was for a short while, then noticed the desk clerk signaling him. He struggled out of the armchair and approached the desk. The clerk was holding up a telephone. "Your wife, sir. She wants to know if you're injured. I took the liberty of assuring her you weren't."

"Thank you." He took the phone. "Hello, I'm all right. It wasn't him, it was his uncle on his mother's side. I'm coming straight up."

He handed the phone back. The desk clerk said, "Just for a moment there, sir, I was tempted to play along and tell her you were taken away in the blood wagon. A fellow gets to where he knows which side of the line he belongs, though, professionally speaking. We get all sorts here, sir, with all kinds of funny notions about behavior. The Homeaway accommodates everyone, regardless."

"That's most reassuring."

"Was your friend in on the gag, sir? Just curious."

"Oh, yes, absolutely. Did you notice the way we both pretended to be engaged in earnest conversation? Fooled you, didn't we. Actually, we were discussing the role of the amiable dunce in contemporary film and fiction. Your name came up, as a matter of fact."

"Did it, sir? Thank you, sir."

"Don't mention it."

Moody rode the creaking elevator up to his floor. Opening his door, he was greeted by a stinging slap across the cheek from his wife. "That's for being an idiot!"

"Myra—"

"I could just kick you for what you did, running out into danger like some stupid movie hero!"

"There wasn't any danger, dammit—it wasn't him!"

"But you didn't know that when you went down! Do you want your child to grow up fatherless?"

"Don't be ridiculous."

"I'm not being ridiculous. If I wanted to be ridiculous, I could take lessons from you. Five minutes' observation should be enough."

"I'd prefer to end this conversation now, if you don't mind."

"There's a not-so-subtle difference between writing about courageous heroes and being one, you know."

Moody took the Los Angeles County telephone book from the phone stand beside the sofa and began leafing through it. Myra watched him, then said, "You're not listening to me."

"Sorry, darling, things to do. Care to make me a sandwich while you rage?"

"Idiot. We don't have any food here."

"Takeout will be fine. There's a wonderful little sandwich shop just down the street. Take your time, I'll work up an appetite."

"Are you deliberately being obtuse? If you want a sandwich, phone down to room service."

"Can't do, darling." He picked up the phone and began dialing. "I am, as you can clearly see, otherwise engaged with the telephonic device."

While Myra fumed, Moody called three different old people's homes in Pasadena, each time asking to speak with Amanda Flowerdew. On the third attempt he was told Miss Flowerdew was unable to come to the phone.

"May I ask why? She isn't ill, I hope."

"Miss Flowerdew is taking her late-afternoon nap." The voice at the end of the line was female, crisp, authoritative.

"And your visiting hours are?"

"Seven through eight, Sundays excluded. Are you a relative?"

"A friend of the family."

"May I have your name, sir? Just for our files?"

Moody hesitated. "For your files? I don't quite understand."

"At the Morning Glory Retirement Home we're most careful with regard to the emotional well-being of our guests. It doesn't do to allow visitation from the wrong people. Such visitations may result in undue stress, which we absolutely must avoid."

"I think Miss Flowerdew would be very pleased to see me, really. I'm a close friend of her nephew Kurt. That's her nephew on the father's side. Has Kurt been to visit lately, by the way? He told me he was most anxious to see Amanda again."

"Your name, sir?"

"Keith Moody."

"And your visit is intended on which evening?"

Moody looked at his watch.

"It's a little late to be driving out there tonight, so shall we say tomorrow?"

"Thank you, Mr. Moody. Your phone number, please?"

"My phone number?"

"So that we may call you back in time if Miss Flowerdew declines to meet with you. We wouldn't want you to make a wasted trip."

Moody gave the number and his room extension at the Homeaway, then hung up.

Myra asked, "Are you stepping where angels fear to tread?"

"I may be. I'm seeking out danger, you see, so that my wife can slap me again. I think she secretly enjoyed it, and my primary mission in life is to keep her happy."

"You can slap me back if you like."

"Wouldn't dream of it."

"I was upset. It wasn't the usual me who did that."

"Apology accepted. There'll be a price to pay come bedtime, though. My every command will be obeyed enthusiastically, without hesitation."

"Oh, really?"

"I'm afraid that's the price of forgiveness nowadays. You can refuse the offer if you want to."

"What exactly would I be refusing?"

Moody told her. Myra responded by accusing him of having been reading naughty literature, at which Moody bridled. "Literature has nothing to do with my demands."

Myra met his demands just a few minutes later, without bothering to wait for bedtime. Then, lighting a cigarette to share with her panting husband, she asked, "What are you doing, Keith?"

"Recovering nicely, thank you."

"I'm referring to your plans for visiting Miss Flowerdew. Are the police going to be invited along?"

"I doubt that a woman of Amanda's advancing years will whip out a switchblade when I start asking questions. Why don't you come along? She might respond better to a woman. Interested?"

"I might be. There's a stiff price tag attached to my cooperation, though."

"What price tag?"

Myra informed him. Moody accepted, and proceeded to deliver every last cent of it. After which they both slept, then went out to eat.

Returning to the Homeaway, Moody picked up *Traitor's Dawn*. "I'd better get started on this so I can see what I'm in for."

"Read on. I'll entertain myself with my knitting."

"What are you knitting, darling?"

"A cockwarmer for Hitler. It shouldn't take a minute."

AT TWO THIRTY-THREE in the morning, the bedside phone rang. Moody fumbled for it in the darkness and spilled an ashtray onto the floor. He managed to separate the receiver from its cradle and croak, "Yes?"

There was silence on the line for several heartbeats.

"Hello?" Moody said.

Beside him, Myra wakened and rolled over. "Who is it?"

A soft voice, muffled to prevent identification, said, "Moody?"

"Yes—"

The caller hung up.

Myra asked again, "Who is it, Keith?"

Moody replaced the phone. "No one. Wrong number."

"But I heard you say yes, as if you were asked if you're you."

"Darling, I've always known that I am me. There's never been any doubt in my mind about it. The caller was some obnoxious drunk. He asked me if I liked champagne. I responded in the affirmative, and he told me to call him Charlie, then hung up. Probably the wrong extension. This place has the most interesting clientele."

"If you're saying I chose wisely, thank you."

Moody lay awake for a long time after that, while Myra drifted back to sleep. He had read all of *Traitor's Dawn*, finishing a little before one in the morning. The book was very enjoyable, filled with exciting action scenes and more than a little gripping tension, but he could see that what Nigel Lawson wanted was missing. Inserting a few psychological keys into the plot would present no difficulty, and Moody was looking forward to starting work. Easing aside the mask of the master spy Edward Traven would be a pleasure, and a richly rewarded pleasure at that. He hoped he would be able to concentrate on the work he was being paid to perform. Simply to ignore the Flowerdew problem was impossible, however, so Moody would have to do what the fictional Traven did; Traven lived in two worlds, that of the Allied powers and that of the Nazis, simultaneously. Moody by day would be the consummate Hollywood screenwriter, wringing every scene for its essence, pleasing his powerful yet capricious master at Empire and his secret ally, the actor's actor Nigel Lawson. Moody by night would ferret out the truth behind his chance encounter on the beach with Flowerdew, and the murder that followed. He suspected he had barely begun to draw aside the curtain of mystery hiding things from him.

The phone call had come from the other side of that curtain.

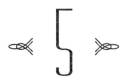

One of the best offices in the Writers' Building was made available to Moody, and he began work on the standard twenty-page scenario, adhering closely to Jeffrey Hubbell's plot but hinting with a line or two at material that would be his own—scenes concerning the inner workings of Traven's mind, the reasons for his ability to slip from one role into another in a heartbeat. Moody left the actual reason vague, since he hadn't yet worked out what it might be, but the subject had to be included in the scenario, or Marvin Margolis might object at some later date. MM liked everything planned out well in advance of shooting and habitually referred back to synopses and scenarios to point out what was missing in the original concept, if a director went over budget by including scenes that were not planned for from the beginning. Even the most casual jottings from the creative team at Empire ended up in the so-called script vault for future use as ammunition against erring directors. The writers wished Margolis could be a more accommodating studio head, more along the lines of Darryl F. Zanuck over at Fox, who allowed his people more leeway, but it was clear MM distrusted anyone with artistic leanings.

No one interrupted him, and the bulk of the work was accomplished by early afternoon. Moody took a late lunch break, then went back to his office and continued working, a Chesterfield dangling from his lips. When he was three-quarters done with the scenario, there was a knock at the door. Moody yelled, "Come in!" He expected to see Nigel Lawson when the door was opened; instead it was Terry Blackwell, the director slated to helm *China Skies*, the project Moody was involved in until the murder of Bax Nolan caused Margolis to fire him. Blackwell wore his customary fedora and a smile that Moody detected was genuine.

"Well, for gosh sakes, Keith Moody, alive and well and back at Empire! I thought that was about as likely as seeing Johnny Weismuller in a tutu."

"Hello, Terry."

"How on earth did you do it? I couldn't believe it when someone told me you were seen in the commissary yesterday with our new golden boy."

"Lawson's the reason, actually. He handpicked me to write the script for *Traitor's Dawn*, and Margolis let it happen, claiming it was his own idea, of course."

"Of course. Ready for some déjà vu? Yours truly will direct."

"Really? Congratulations. It's going to be a terrific picture."

"You're speaking as the modest author of the screenplay."

"Naturally. We're going to stand the usual transformation of a good book into a not-quite-so-good script on its head. This time the movie will be better."

" 'We?' "

"Nigel and myself. It was his idea, and I agree with him."

"Better let your director in on the secret, Keith."

Moody explained Nigel's wishes, and Blackwell agreed it made sense to include an extra dimension to the character that was not present in the novel. "Lawson's not just another pretty face, seems like."

"Far from it. Have you met him yet?"

"Briefly. He doesn't come on as strong as I thought he would, not such a prima donna as I expected. I think you're right, this is going to work out fine for us all."

"Quick, touch wood. Remember how we expected great things from *China Skies*?"

"Oh, hell, that was different. MM set that thing up too fast. Bax getting killed was just the last straw in a whole bale that came down on our heads, especially yours."

"Best forgotten, then."

"Never look back, my friend. Listen, I won't disturb you any more, I just wanted to reassure myself your being back wasn't a rumor."

"I'm here in the flesh, doing what I do again."

"See you later."

Alone, Moody wondered if the pairing of himself with Terry Blackwell a second time amounted to stacking the deck in favor of a jinx. He shook his head, throwing off such superstitious thinking. This time everything would proceed smoothly and according to plan, the very antithesis of the *China Skies* debacle. He was also aware, now that he thought back to the knock at his door, that he was disappointed it had not been Nigel who came in with a cheery word or two. The actor was probably busy elsewhere, maybe still getting fitted for his costumes. Moody resumed typing.

· · ·

"HOW DID IT go, darling?"

"It went well." Moody flung his hat onto the stand by the door and began removing his jacket. Bess attacked him with fierce devotion and brought him down while his arms were still entangled in cloth. "For God's sake, Bess!" Having reached the floor, still helpless, he twisted his face away from the dog's adoring tongue and called for help. Myra yanked Bess away, enabling Moody to sit up. "Did you take her for a walk today?"

"Yes, I did, a nice long one. She can't help it if she loves you."

"I wouldn't be offended if she loved me a little less."

He stood and took off his jacket, coping as best he could with the paws scratching at his shirt. He knelt and made a fuss of the dog, then stood up again. "Guess who's directing *Traitor's Dawn*."

"Cecil B. DeMille?"

"Not enough chariots and swords in it to suit C. B. Guess again."

"Alfred Hitchcock."

"He'd be perfect, but no. Exhausted your options? Terry Blackwell."

"The one who was going to make *China Skies*?"

"The same. I'm amazed Margolis is putting us together again, after what happened last time."

"That wasn't Blackwell's fault, or yours. Now it's my turn to ask irritating questions. Guess what I did today."

"Had your hair done?"

"Guess again."

"Is this an exercise in mental telepathy?" Moody closed his eyes and massaged his brow. "I see . . . I see a young woman.

She appears normal to the eye, but deep within there are strange stirrings. . . . She's a siren, calling to men with her irresistible song . . . luring them to their doom while asking them to guess what she's doing. . . . She's an enchantress . . . a temptress . . ."

"Idiot. I went to have Uncle Barney's stamp collection appraised. There's a place just eight blocks from here—Stamp of Approval, it's called. Isn't that clever?"

"About on a par with calling a laundry the Sudsy Dudsy."

"More guessing. Guess what the man there told me."

"That you have beautiful eyes and a figure to drive men mad."

"No, he said we own a fortune."

"He said what?"

"Well, he didn't actually say so with words. It was more his actions that told me what he was thinking."

"Are you sure it wasn't mental telepathy?"

"Just listen. At first he was very dismissive and snooty, barely even looking at the pages, not paying any attention to the individual stamps at all, really, and then he stopped, and I swear, Keith, his face went white. He stared and stared at one stamp, and then he turned the page, trying to convince me nothing had happened. He pulled himself together finally and said it was a very ordinary collection, but he'd give me fifty dollars for it. I took the album out of his hands, and guess what. He actually resisted letting me have it. What a giveaway! When I got it off him, he said he'd give me a hundred, then two hundred. Well, I wasn't going to let him have it at all, not after the way he tried to trick me. I knew there was something he'd seen on that particular page that wasn't ordinary at all."

"Clever you. What page? Show me."

Myra picked up the album from the coffee table and brought it back to Moody.

"I remembered where it was because the page had a little dog-ear in the corner. This is it."

She opened the album and presented it to him. Moody let his eyes roam across the small colored squares tucked neatly into clear cellulose pockets. Every stamp before him was unusual, to his unpracticed eye; none more than another, though. "They all look interesting to me. I like this one with the ibis, and this one with the hot air balloon. Which one was he so taken with?"

"I couldn't tell. There are twenty-three stamps on that page, and one of them's worth something. Tomorrow I'm going to another stamp-collecting place and see if the same thing happens. We might have something worth thousands of dollars, Keith!"

Moody began loosening his tie. Bess sat and gazed at him, tail wagging.

"Where would your late uncle Barney have found such a stamp? He never even left Idaho in his lifetime, did he?"

"You don't need to go sailing away to foreign countries to collect stamps. You get them from places like Stamp of Approval, dealers and so forth. Uncle Barney sent away for his stamps, ordered them from catalogs, I suppose. The point is, he must have got one that's rare by mistake. His hardware store was a good business, but it didn't make him rich. There's a stamp here he never should have received. I'd love to know which one. I bet it's this one from Peru."

Moody looked at the stamp, which depicted the helmeted head of a Spanish conquistador with bristling beard and greedy eye.

"It might be. Who's to say?"

"Someone tomorrow might be able to, if he's honest and doesn't want to trick me out of it. Wouldn't it be wonderful if I went all the way to Idaho for something that turned out to be valuable after all?"

"It's about as likely as the squirrel nut bowl turning out to be solid silver instead of nickel plate."

"Pessimist. You think you know everything."

"I know that hardware store owners in Yellowtail, Idaho, don't own rare stamps."

"If you're wrong, I intend kicking you hard, just to let you know how much you don't know."

"I yawn with terror."

THE DRIVE OUT to Pasadena was pleasant. Bess stuck her nose through the open window, breathing in the evening air. The *Los Angeles Times* had reported Allied forces ousting the Germans from Cassino, and finally moving north from Anzio toward Rome. Moody felt the end for Hitler was now more of a certainty than ever before. It was so very far away, the blood and suffering. He had no right to be motoring along a southern California road with his wife and dog, gainfully employed once more, with expectations of considerable success in the offing. Being labeled 4-F didn't spare a man feelings of guilt. Moody had to remind himself he still faced his own peculiar brand of threat in the elusive shape of Kurt Flowerdew, but his initial fear was fading.

Somehow Flowerdew's uncle, Gallagher, had conveyed to Moody his own doubts concerning the young man's tendency to such violence as had been committed against the unsuspecting Morton Dulkis. It might possibly have been sheer coincidence after all. But then he remembered the torn dust jacket from his book found at the murder scene. That was stretching coincidence too far. There was an unsatisfying lack of understanding, of motive and opportunity, that Moody kept rolling around in the back of his head. He hoped that Amanda Flowerdew would be able to shed light onto the darkling landscape through which flitted Moody's indistinct memory of the reader on the beach.

The Morning Glory Retirement Home was a rambling Victorian pile, its silhouette against the evening sky a jumble of crowded spires and cupolas, turrets and balustrades. It stood among extensive lawns shaded by trees planted in the previous century. Moody followed the curved gravel driveway and stopped in a marked parking space a short distance from the glazed front doors.

"This seems rather pleasant," Myra said, watching several old people talking among themselves on a bench beneath the trees nearby.

"I'll remember to send you out here once you're ancient," Moody said. "That'll be in ten or twelve years. Should we book you in while we're here?"

"Don't be a pig, darling, or I'll have to discipline you. Is it seven o'clock yet?"

"Just on, thanks to my flawless navigation and driving expertise."

"Aren't you ashamed to be perfect? It makes the rest of us feel so inadequate."

"Suffer in silence, that's my recommendation to you all."

They left the car window cracked for Bess and approached the front steps. A wheelchair ramp had been constructed along one side. Moody was near this as they climbed. An elderly man in a wheelchair was already rolling down the ramp at what Moody calculated was an unsafe speed, a cane raised in his hands, leaving the wheels of his chair undirected. Moody couldn't understand what the old gentleman was lifting his cane for, and was concerned for his safety as the wheelchair began gaining speed halfway down the ramp. The cane was swung in a tight arc as the wheelchair and Moody passed each other, and

Moody's arm was whacked with considerable force. Having delivered the blow, the cane wielder broke into harsh, barking laughter.

Clutching his arm, Moody turned to watch as the wheelchair and its occupant rolled off the end of the ramp and across the driveway, losing speed quickly as the narrow rubber tires sank into gravel. The wheelchair reached the driveway's far side and hit a dividing border of concrete, at which time it tipped over, dumping the laughing man with the cane onto the ground. Already attendants in white were hurrying down the steps. Moody heard one young woman call out, "Mr. Hardiman! You know you're restricted, Mr. Hardiman!"

Myra said, "I thought this place was for old people, not crazy people."

"He looked pretty old to me," said Moody, rubbing his arm. "Old but certainly not feeble."

Two orderlies picked up Hardiman, warding off his flailing hands. One of them picked up the walking cane, and the other righted the wheelchair. The young woman walked back to Moody with an apologetic expression on her face. "I'm so sorry. He escaped. That is . . . he wasn't where he was supposed to be at visiting hour. Are you hurt?"

"Not at all."

Hardiman was escorted back across the driveway, his legs moving stiffly, bent at the knees; arthritis, Moody guessed. As he passed by, Moody said, "You should channel that move into a golf swing, sir."

Hardiman stopped and stared at Moody, then said, "I won't eat custard!"

"I've never liked it myself," admitted Moody.

"They try to make me eat it, and I won't!"

"I don't blame you at all."

"Mr. Hardiman, *please*—" admonished the young woman. Moody felt a little sorry for her embarrassment. Her hair was drawn tightly to a bun at the nape of her neck, and her eyes were hidden behind lenses the size of Moody's own. He said to her, "We're here to see Miss Flowerdew."

"Oh, yes. One moment, please."

She watched as one of the orderlies assisted Hardiman up the steps, while the second wheeled the empty chair, the cane hooked across its back. When Hardiman reached the top step and was being led with the docility of a sleepy child to the front doors, she turned back to Moody and said, "I'm Nora Worth, special assistant to Mrs. Yaddigan."

"Keith Moody. This is my wife, Myra."

"I'm so sorry you were given a bad first impression of Morning Glory."

"Not at all. You seem to have everything under control here. May I ask who Mrs. Yaddigan is?"

"The administrator. All appointments for visitation are made through her."

"Ahh, then I've spoken with her already."

"Please come in."

Nora Worth led them through the finely etched glass doors and into a foyer of impressive size. All the original woodwork had been preserved, the finely crafted surfaces gleaming brightly, exuding a faint smell of lemon oil. Staff members, mainly women, uniformly white and starched, came and went in attitudes of silent concentration.

Miss Worth invited them to sign the visitors' book, and Moody complied, then asked, "Where would we find Miss Flowerdew?"

"Upstairs. I'll take you there myself. Is your arm quite all right, Mr. Moody?"

"No pain at all, Miss Worth." Moody had noted the ringless fingers.

At the foyer's far end was a staircase worthy of a Hollywood soundstage, a soaring, sweeping curve of polished mahogany leading steadily upward to a higher realm; Moody imagined a stairway to heaven might look something like this at its base; an infinite number of corkscrewings would wind their way up to an impossibly distant paradise, with lucky souls ascending in the wafted scent of lemons to their life's reward.

Myra asked, "How many patients do you have here?"

Miss Worth answered, "We have no patients here, Mrs. Moody, but we do have fifty-three long-term guests."

"Excuse me, it must be the white uniforms."

"Those are Mrs. Yaddigan's innovation. She feels the uniform is reassuring to the guests. They might not respond so positively to a staff member dressed casually. The uniform represents a caring, protective surrounding. The guests are happier seeing us this way."

"What about the disobedient ones?" Moody asked.

"I'm not sure what you mean, Mr. Moody."

"Mr. Hardiman, for example. He didn't seem to have too much respect for the staff."

"Mr. Hardiman is a trial to us all, sometimes. He used to be a rodeo rider, I believe, and he seems to think he can gallop around and do as he pleases, despite severe arthritis. Mrs. Yaddigan has had to reprimand him herself several times."

"Who pays the bills here, Miss Worth?"

"The bills?"

"Accommodation in this wonderful place you have here can't come cheap. Does Mr. Hardiman have some kind of Rodeo Riders Hall of Fame pension fund to ensure he doesn't get thrown out?"

"Morning Glory would never do any such thing. We exist to serve the needs of the elderly. They have made their contribution to society, and now we must contribute to their well-being. Mrs. Yaddigan refers to our philosophy as the Circle of Reward."

"The Circle of Reward," Moody repeated. "It certainly has a poetic ring to it."

"Mrs. Yaddigan might not want me to tell you this," said Miss Worth, lowering her voice, "but she does in fact pen occasional verse."

"That's so reassuring," said Myra. "One hates to think of the elderly being managed by uncaring philistines."

"Indeed not, Mrs. Moody." Miss Worth seemed to inflate her meager chest just a little. "Mrs. Yaddigan has a distinct style of her own. In her capacity as administrator, I mean."

Moody was beginning to appreciate Mrs. Yaddigan's other style. Having reached the top of the circular staircase, they proceeded along a broad corridor, richly carpeted. There were many doors leading from the corridor, and between each door, where a picture might usually reside, were embroidered homilies: *The Heart at Rest Knows It's Been Blessed; The Soul At Peace Awaits Release; A Life Well Lived Has All Forgiv'd; In Twilight Years We Waive All Tears.*

"These are splendid sentiments, Miss Worth." Moody indicated the framed embroideries. Nora Worth actually blushed.

"Those are my own handiwork," she admitted. "The words, of course, are Mrs. Yaddigan's."

"I suspected they might be."

The message on the walls, by Moody's interpretation, encouraged the guests to be glad they were old and enfeebled, and to anticipate with smiles their own imminent demise. It was as self-serving a collection of sanctimonious nonsense as he'd ever come across. He composed several antidotes as they walked on: *Get Out of Bed Before You're Dead; Don't Wait for Death, Grab Every Breath; Be Very Suspicious of Staff So Judicious; The Sky's a Big Hole to Swallow Your Soul.*

"Here we are," declared Miss Worth. "Lavender, that's Miss Flowerdew."

The door was labeled in ornate script: *Lavender.*

Miss Worth explained, "Every single one of our guest accommodation rooms has a name, either a pleasant herb or flower. Once we had a gentleman by the name of Basil who actually occupied the Basil room. Everyone was very amused because the gentleman was convinced it was his name on the door. He thought so until the end—"

As if she somehow had betrayed the Morning Glory ethos of cheeriness and smiles by mentioning senility and death, Miss Worth suddenly yanked open the door, her face less composed than it had been a moment before.

"Miss Flowerdew? Your guests have arrived." To Moody and Myra she said, face downcast, as if still embarrassed by her own words, "The gong will sound at eight."

As they entered, the door was closed behind them. The room was large, high-ceilinged, elegantly appointed in a style of decor that Moody knew Myra termed Nineteenth-Century Clutter. Every square foot of wall space was occupied by framed pictures, large and small, and much of the floor was set with tables jammed with similar stuff. Glancing at them, Moody received an impression of unusual persons in costumed variety. Then his attention was arrested by the occupant of Lavender.

Amanda Flowerdew sat by the window in an ornate armchair, watching them. She was a small woman, wearing an old-fashioned neck-to-ankles dress of somber hue, from beneath which peeked the toes of button-up boots that scarcely touched the carpet. It was impossible to determine her age, because the face of Amanda Flowerdew was entirely covered in hair; every part of her head, with the exception of eyes and nostril apertures and lips, was blanketed in a thick pelt of auburn hair tinged with gray. The effect was of a tall, highly intelligent simian of unknown species dressed up as a Halloween prank. Moody heard Myra suppress a gasp.

Amanda Flowerdew's lips parted in a smile beyond interpretation; without the usual amount of exposed skin surrounding the parted lips, the movement of her lower face might denote anything from friendly welcome to soundless snarl. Her teeth were small and slightly yellow, the teeth of an old woman.

"Nobody told you ahead of time?" she asked.

"Uh . . . no, ma'am," said Moody, recovering himself.

"These people here, they act like I'm something that ought to be locked in the cellar. Come closer and take a good look. I won't stand up and bite you. I can barely stand up anyway. Sit yourselves here and tell me why you came."

She indicated a love seat a few feet from her. Moody and Myra sat, at a loss for words. Amanda Flowerdew smiled again. "No need for you folks to be self-conscious about the way I am. God made me this way, so it's all right by me. The doctors have a funny long word for it, but that doesn't explain a thing, does it now. It's made me a bundle of money in my time. When I was a little girl I just wanted to run away and hide. You can't imagine the miserable condition I was in. Even my own family couldn't bear to look at me. My own mama said it was a curse of God on them for my daddy's drinking and whoring around. You understand, her God isn't the same feller my God is. Different as different can be. I made my cash on the carnival route, starting in 1880 when I turned sixteen. I started with a little outfit in Wisconsin, then I was discovered by Colonel Lupton, of Lupton's Human Oddities Travelling Menagerie, and got paid a lot more. I was the star draw, bigger than the six-hundred-pound woman, Colossal Cora. Bigger in the sense that more people wanted to see me than her, you understand. Cora and I were friends, but she was the unhappiest female on the face of the earth, always fretting about men, as if it ever would've worked out between her and a man, for goodness' sake. I told her the story about the passionate mouse and the elephant, and after I did that we weren't such good friends anymore. What were your names again?"

"I'm Keith Moody, and this is my wife, Myra."

"I knew I didn't recognize the name when they told me you wanted to stop by, but I didn't let on. I said you were well known to me. They wouldn't have let you come here otherwise. They don't like people coming around, isn't that sad? Of course, most of us are here because our folks can't be bothered stopping by in any case, so it doesn't make that much difference, I suppose."

"Are you visited often, Miss Flowerdew?" Moody asked.

"As often as I care to be. Human company isn't all that interesting to me. I like canaries. They make such a pleasant fuss and racket, don't you think? A distraction from human woes is the canary bird."

Moody saw Myra looking around for a birdcage, but there was none. Amanda Flowerdew's room held no birdsong. Moody was unsure how to proceed; was the hair-faced woman before him eccentric, or was she daffy? She appeared incurious about her visitors, watching them watching her, an air of equanimity surrounding her small frame. She was so still, so very much in repose, that Moody thought she resembled a display of some kind, a museum offering dedicated to the unusual.

"Has Kurt been here recently, Miss Flowerdew?"

"Yesterday evening. His uncle brought him around."

"Mr. Gallagher?"

"That's him. My brother Daniel married his sister Mary. Daniel, he didn't have more hair on his face than the general run of man, just the beard as usual. My condition is more startling on a woman in my opinion. That's why Colonel Lupton took me across to Europe and I got to see the crowned heads over there. I shook the hand of the czar and czarina of Russia, so how about that? There's a picture of it over there on the bureau. The czarina, she wanted to see for herself if I had fingernails or claws, but I wasn't offended. I got presented to Queen Victoria too, the year she died, and a bunch of other littler crowned heads. How many folks have done that?"

"Precious few, I'd imagine," Myra said.

"You imagine right. My, but you're a pretty thing."

"Thank you."

Moody asked, "Did Kurt mention my name, Miss Flowerdew?"

"No, and Henry Gallagher didn't either. Henry, he hardly ever stops by, even if he lives not so very far away. I believe he's ashamed to have someone like me in the family, even if by marriage. People are a big mystery to me sometimes. I don't care anymore, though. I made my pile off people's curiosity about me. I'm just fine for the rest of my days here. The czar and czarina of Russia, imagine that."

"Was there a purpose behind Kurt and Henry's visit?"

"Purpose? People want to look at me all the time. Kurt, he hadn't seen me since he was little, back in Wisconsin. He said he remembered me even though he was so small because he had nightmares about me for a long time afterward. He's the kind of young man that says what's on his mind, but not because he's honest. He says it because he can't help it, like a little child. I wondered after they left if Kurt was any older than the last time

I saw him. Brain feeblement, there's no telling where and when a family's going to be afflicted."

"Did Kurt or Henry say anything to you about Kurt being in trouble, Miss Flowerdew? I don't mean to intrude upon your family's business, but it's rather important."

"What kind of trouble would that be? Did he lift someone's skirts to see what's under there?"

"Kurt is a suspect in a murder case, I'm afraid."

"Murder? That boy wouldn't do any such thing. Murdered who?"

"Morton Dulkis."

"Never heard the name. Kurt didn't do it."

"I didn't mean to upset you."

"I'm not upset. I haven't been upset since I was a little girl. He just didn't do it. I would've been able to tell if he killed someone. I can tell about people. It's a gift. He was upset, I won't say he wasn't, I could see it in his eyes, but he never did kill anyone."

"I'll accept your judgment, Miss Flowerdew, but he's still suspected by the police. Mr. Gallagher shares your opinion, by the way."

"Henry, he's a farmer, so he's got sound judgment. He's a no-nonsense man, Henry. We don't see eye to eye like maybe we should, but he's not one to get fooled."

The door to Amanda Flowerdew's room was suddenly opened from outside. Filling the doorway was a woman of formidable size and aspect. *Battleship* was the word that sprang to Moody's mind, and not only because the woman's dress was battleship gray. She moved swiftly forward into the room, and Moody, caught up in his initial impression, could almost detect a surging bow wave in the atmosphere preceding her impressive bulk. There could be no doubt this was Mrs. Yaddigan. Perched on her pug nose were tiny rimless glasses; below these were the chin and jowls of a bulldog; parting the waters were the bosom and waist of a giantess. She steered a tight course around the tables filled with mementos and dropped anchor before the love seat, eyes glowering with suppressed rage, nostrils flaring (Moody couldn't help himself) with steam from her boilers.

"You must leave," she announced.

"Pardon me," said Myra, "we made an appointment. It isn't eight o'clock yet."

"You'll leave immediately!" boomed Mrs. Yaddigan.

Moody caught a glimpse of Nora Worth lurking in the doorway, wringing her hands.

"May we ask why?"

"You are not family members. Please leave."

Moody said, "I made it clear when I spoke with you on the telephone I was a friend of Kurt Flowerdew—"

"And that was a lie. I've just this minute received a call from Mr. Gallagher, warning me to beware just such an imposture as you have made. Leave immediately, or I'll send for assistance."

Moody stood. "No need for that, Mrs. Yaddigan. We'll leave peaceably."

Myra stood also. "Miss Flowerdew," she said, "thank you for having talked with us. It was a pleasure to have met you."

Amanda Flowerdew's expression, hidden behind hair, was indecipherable. She simply nodded her head. Moody reached out and shook her hand. "A privilege, ma'am."

"Leave now," Mrs. Yaddigan ordered. Moody and Myra headed for the door, escorted closely by the bulk of the administrator. Nora Worth backed away from the door to let them pass, her eyes downcast, willing to accept responsibility for having allowed the visitors access.

"Miss Worth, show these people out."

The small woman bobbed her head and shoulders in submission. "Yes, Mrs. Yaddigan." Moody felt sorry for her.

"Mrs. Yaddigan?" Myra said.

"Yes?"

"You have a small blob of dried snot dangling in your left nostril."

Mrs. Yaddigan's florid features seemed to expand, the color across her bulldog cheeks deepening to an alarming shade of crimson. "Get out!"

"But it suits you," protested Myra. Moody took her elbow and steered her along the corridor. Mrs. Yaddigan remained behind. Myra said over her shoulder, "If you could just manage a similar effect in the other nostril, for balance—"

Nora Worth hurried ahead of the Moodys, afraid to look back at them. She scuttled down the winding staircase as if the building were ablaze and crossed the foyer to hold open one of the glass entrance doors. Eyes still fixed upon her shoes, she whispered, "I'm so terribly sorry," as they walked past her and out onto the front steps.

"You did nothing wrong, Miss Worth," Moody assured her.

The door was closed behind them. The sky was darkening as they walked a short distance along the gravel driveway to the parking spaces, their shoes crunching loudly in the evening stillness. "What a revolting specimen of womanhood," Myra said.

"Unpleasant personality," Moody agreed.

"Did you find out anything worthwhile from Miss Flowerdew? What a charming lady, despite appearances."

"Nothing concrete. Gallagher's first name, that's about all."

"How do you feel about Kurt now?"

"Less and less convinced it was him at the murder scene. But part of the jacket for *Below the Salt* was there, and I know he had a copy of the book just a few days before."

"There must be dozens of copies of *Below the Salt* floating around."

"Hundreds, actually, if you don't mind. The first print run was exactly one thousand copies. I like to think that the bulk of them went to the remaindered tables rather than the pulpers."

"Sorry, darling, didn't mean to disparage your wonderful book."

"I'm an author. That means I'm sensitive on certain subjects, especially my lack of success."

"You can't be that much of a failure. Nigel Lawson read the book and was impressed by it."

"One reader, one copy. I need several thousand more Nigels."

"And several thousand more Flowerdews. Without homicidal intent, of course."

"Naturally."

"Is that man waving at us?"

"What man?"

Myra pointed. In one of the ground-floor windows the figure of a man could be seen, waving frantically with both arms. It was Mr. Hardiman.

"He probably wants to apologize for hitting you," Myra said. "I'll get the car while you talk to him. Let me have the keys."

Moody handed them over, then looked to make sure he was not under observation from the entrance to the building. He walked across to the window, which, he now saw, was barred on the inside. Hardiman was able to reach through the bars, unlatch the window, and slide it up.

"Been up to see her, huh?"

"If you mean Miss Flowerdew, yes, we have."

"She don't know," said Hardiman, shaking his head. "She's close to the jumpin'-off place, and she don't know."

"Doesn't know what? What's a jumping-off place, Mr. Hardiman? I'm not sure I follow you."

"Foller *me?* Hell, I'll be follerin' *her.* She's a damn sight closer'n me to the jumpin'-off place. You don't know what that is?"

"I'm afraid not."

"That's the last place you're at when you ride the black bull. You ride the bull, then you jump off. Then you're gone, see."

"No, I don't see. What do bulls have to do with Miss Flowerdew?"

"Son, are you an idjit? She's close to death as a woman can be, everybody knows it, even if she don't like to make a fuss. She don't hardly eat at all, starvin' herself to help it along, I guess. She went and decided it's time to jump off, told me so her own self just a couple days back. Only she don't know, see, and that's sad."

"Doesn't know what?" said Moody, beginning to feel he was following a conversational circle.

"About the plan they got laid by for her."

"What plan is that?"

"To put her in that place."

"What place?"

"The museum place down Miami way."

"I'm still not sure I understand, Mr. Hardiman."

The old rodeo rider was becoming agitated. "The goddamn place where they send all the freaks, that's where!"

"Freaks?"

"Like old Amanda there. Sideshow people, carnival freaks, you know?"

"How can they send her there when her professional career is over? She's retired, if I understood her correctly."

"You bet she is, and just about dead to boot. Son, here's the situation. They're gonna stuff her like a Christmas goose and send her on down there for folks to gawp at. They done it already to a bunch of others like her, two-headed people and them that're joined at the hip and the tallest man in the world and such. They're all down there in that place, Lupton's Human Oddities Museum right there outside of Miami for folks to put down fifty cents and come see the stuffed freaks."

"Miss Flowerdew is to be . . . stuffed?"

"You bet. I heard 'em talkin', Yaddigan and this feller she knows that runs the mortician place. Anyone dies in this place, that's where they go for buryin'."

"You overheard Mrs. Yaddigan discussing a plan to . . . preserve Miss Flowerdew's body with the aid of this mortician fellow?"

"Ain't that what I just said? One thousand dollars, that's what some other feller down in Florida's gonna pay her for Miss Flowerdew, just because that lady's got hair on her face. Is that a dignified thing to happen? A body that can't rest in dignification, that's a cryin' shame. Greed, that's all it is. You got to stop it, son. Tell her kin, tell the police, so someone—"

Behind Hardiman the door to the room he was in opened, and Mrs. Yaddigan hove into view. Hardiman turned from the window and picked up his cane. As Mrs. Yaddigan bore down on him, flanked by two male orderlies, Hardiman waved his cane back and forth in his own pathetic defense. "You get the hell away from me, you goddamn bulldyke! Can't a man go where he damn well pleases and talk to whoever he wants? You tell them two they better not come no closer—!"

Mr. Hardiman was seized by both orderlies with a practiced maneuver that had him pinioned in less than three seconds. His cane fell to the floor with a clatter. He was lifted between the two men and carried away while Moody stood, transfixed with helplessness. Mrs. Yaddigan reached through the bars and brought the window sash down with a bang, then stood there, staring directly into Moody's eyes, as if daring him to do something about the scene he had witnessed. Abruptly she turned away; seconds later Moody was looking into an empty room.

He turned around as Myra drove up and stopped beside him.

"Keith, what's the matter?"

"Nothing." He got into the car, resisting Bess's willingness to lick his ear. "Drive us away from here, please, before I get sick. My God, that woman—"

"Miss Flowerdew?"

"Yaddigan. I'd pay money to see her harpooned and rendered down to oil."

"Jeepers, darling, it's not like you to say such things."

"Drive, Myra, please."

Myra drove.

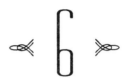

On Wednesday afternoon, while Moody was finishing the scenario for *Traitor's Dawn*, he was visited by Terry Blackwell and a striking blond. Moody recognized her instantly; Gloria Gresham had been Empire's leading lady for the past year, and had made *Lessons in Love* and *The Emperor's Lady* into box-office successes. Both these costume epics had been set in Europe, both aimed squarely at the female audience. Gresham was able to convey a certain Europeanness to her roles because of her lifelong ability to mimic the accent of her maternal grandmother, who had been born in Kraków. Gresham was from Scranton; her father was a hosiery salesman.

"Keith, we have your German countess," announced Blackwell, shepherding the actress into Moody's office. "Gloria, meet Keith Moody, who'll give you all the best lines."

"Hello there, fellow slave. Are they paying you enough? I could bribe you for those lines if they aren't."

Moody liked her style. "Bribery is unnecessary, Miss Gresham, and in the unlikely event I write some less than scintillating dialogue, it won't matter. Dud lines would still fall from your lips like pearls."

Gresham did a double take and held on to Blackwell for support. She stage-whispered to him, "Does this guy always come across so gallant and sophisticated, or did you tell him I was coming over?"

"Keith doesn't do rehearsals, Gloria. He's a writer, not an actor. Of course, he might have polished that smooth line for just any old actress who happened to limp through the door and tell him she's got the role, right, Keith?"

"Untrue, Terry. Miss Gresham has always had my respect. I can't think of better casting than this."

Gresham squinted at Moody with mock suspicion. "Mean to say you don't think Garbo would be better at playing a Kraut countess?"

"Well—"

"Don't answer that," she told him. "Empire hasn't got Garbo, it's got me, and damn lucky they are to have me."

Moody silently agreed. Gloria Gresham had been compared by the critics to the late Carole Lombard, and was credited with the same quick-witted responses in real life as her characters tended to mouth on-screen. It was said that she had talent enough to play comedy and drama with equal panache, and was reckoned to be a star-in-waiting, the kind who would, given the right string of successes, become a mainstay of the studio lucky enough to have her under contract. Casting her as Countess Maria von Eschen, the wife of a top Nazi, would allow her to break free of the lightweight roles she had carried off brilliantly to date.

"Forget Garbo," Terry Blackwell said. "Comparisons are for also-rans. Here at Empire we break the mold every time. New names, new talent."

Gresham said, "You two should be a team—The Fabulous

Smoothie Brothers. I don't know that my tiny ego can support this kind of praise for too long."

"Honestly, Keith, won't she be perfect for von Eschen?"

"Yes, and nobody's paying me a bonus to say so, Miss Gresham—"

"Gloria, always."

"Gloria, it's the role that'll lead you to better things. Wait—that didn't come out right. The role that'll persuade the brilliant men who run Empire Productions that costume dramas, although well served by your presence, are not where your destiny lies."

Gresham let out a breath. "Better and better! You guys are great. Pretty soon I'll not only think I'm better than Garbo, I'm better than Barrymore—Ethel, not John or Lionel—and then you'll have a raging egomaniac on your hands. But keep it up, fellers, I like it."

Blackwell and Moody laughed. Knowing she had their attention, she continued, "But listen, Keith, this Countess von Eschen broad is a bit lily-white in the book, don't you think? There she is, the only one in all of Germany who finds out that Traven's a spy, and she doesn't turn him in because she's fallen in love with him. Okay, Traven's a dish, just like Nigel Lawson, but she fell in love with him while she still believed he's a Nazi. How's that going to come across on the screen?"

"I've thought about that. A lot of the German aristocracy, the 'vons,' aren't exactly crazy about Hitler, but they went along for the ride. I can stress that Maria's marriage to Bruno von Eschen was pretty much arranged by her father, and von Eschen himself isn't that fond of the party. He's not such a monster, for example, as Traven's nemesis, the altogether evil and odious *Obergruppenführer* Kaltenbrunner. That guy's a real Nazi, so he's the one everyone will hiss at, not Maria's husband, who's a lot older than her, let's not forget, and who gets the sympathy vote when he realizes his wife's fallen for a younger fellow and yet doesn't slap her around. Then, when he finds out Traven's real identity, he doesn't report him to the Nazi high command, because to do so would mean that his wife, who's planning to escape to England with Traven, would be captured and tortured, which he can't allow, being a basically decent sort."

"That's great for the husband. I'm playing the wife."

"Oh, okay, I was getting beside the point, wasn't I. Here's the angle on Maria—she doesn't like Nazis, and doesn't have to, because her Nazi husband's one of the aristocrats who went along with Hitler for the sake of political convenience, and when she meets Traven she *senses* that he's another of the same ilk, not a real spitting, screaming Nazi, and that's why she can fall for him. It'll be a lot more subtle in the screenplay."

"Not too subtle, Keith," warned Blackwell. "This has to get past MM."

They laughed together. Keith suddenly felt that *Traitor's Dawn* must somehow be blessed by circumstance; he approved of the casting, he approved of the director, and the script was in his own hands; could anything possibly go wrong? The project, handled correctly, would catapult all concerned into positions of greater influence in the Hollywood community, from which exalted position they could pick and choose among the best of the million and one projects floating in the atmosphere over Beverly Hills and Bel Air. It would be the making of them all, and barring catastrophe, it would happen. It was Ordained; it was Destined to Be; as a writer Moody would have to say, it was Written. *Traitor's Dawn* was already riding a greased rail toward success; all everybody had to do was play their part, and the rest would follow naturally, as a well-aimed arrow follows its path to the target.

"Okay, I'm reassured," said Gresham, unaware she spoke also for Moody. She plucked Blackwell's fedora from his head and placed it on her own. With exaggerated huskiness, she intoned, "I am a spy. I am incognito, darlinks."

More laughter. Moody knew that Lawson and Gresham were going to fall for each other offscreen as well as on, and because he liked them both—had liked them literally from the moment he met them—he wished them well. It would be interesting to watch them together for the first time, to see the current flow between them. Word would get out to the gossip columnists and movie magazine writers that, for once, reports of romance between stars Handsome X and Lovely Y were in fact true. Interest in *Traitor's Dawn* would escalate accordingly, and box-office success was virtually guaranteed before the final cut was even ready for distribution. Nigel and Gloria would attend the premiere together, arm in arm, and take the opportunity, there in front of the nation's newsreel cameras, to declare their love and announce their impending marriage. It was a Hollywood dream, beautiful, glowing, nascent with the possibility of perfection.

Contemplating it, Moody felt a tiny crack developing at its polished marble base, the intrusion of uncontrollable reality with its myriad invitations to disaster. He hastily mended those cracks, erased them with sheer willpower; he was only human, only a man eager as any other to believe that happiness is not only possible but certified, bonded, and secured for those possessing the magical qualities of heightened appearance and presence. Movie stars deserved everything they got, was the message running through Moody's mind, and as he became aware of it he paused in his smiling beatitude of optimism and professional good fellowship, and realized that he was thinking like anyone else, anyone else at all out there beyond tinseltown—Keith Moody was thinking like a Ticket Buyer.

. . .

"MR. MOODY?"

"Yes?"

It was almost seven-thirty in the evening. Moody had been reading the newspaper when the phone rang. Myra was not at the Homeaway but had left a note: "Gone to San Diego—back this evening. M." Moody had no clue why she might have gone down to San Diego, and was mildly annoyed that Myra had not gone into a little more detail in the note. When the phone rang he assumed it would be she.

"Desk clerk, sir. I have a Mr. Flowerdew here to see you."

"Send him right up, please."

Moody set the phone down, shaking his head. The desk clerk was a consistent fool, once again garbling the message given to him by Henry Gallagher. What could the farmer want with Moody this time? Hadn't he said he wanted no further contact? Maybe he'd changed his mind about his nephew and now wanted advice on how best to hand Kurt over to the police. Nothing would surprise Moody, given developments so far.

He was, however, very much surprised when he answered the knock on his door. Kurt Flowerdew stood outside, wearing the same clothing he'd worn at the beach, minus the knotted handkerchief on top of his head. Moody stared, unsure what action to take; did Kurt have his gun with him this time?

"Hey, how you doing?" said Kurt.

"I'm . . . doing very well, thanks for asking. How about you . . . uh . . . Kurt?"

"I'll tell you when you say to come in outta the hallway here."

Moody considered slamming the door, then took a chance and stepped aside.

"Come in, Kurt. Can I take your jacket?"

"Why? I'm wearing it."

"Just thought you might be more comfortable." Moody had wanted to see if a shoulder holster was still snuggled in Kurt's armpit. "Please sit down."

Kurt sat in the most comfortable chair, Moody sat in another.

"I'm very surprised to see you here, Kurt."

"I bet you are. You figured you weren't gonna see me again ever. That's why you gimme that dummy address. Jeez, I was mad about that. You got me in trouble, Moody."

"Trouble?"

"Yeah, at that place you lied about living at. I waited a couple or three days, then went there to chew you out about the first lie, that Ferguson's joint, only you weren't at the place you said you lived either. That's two big lies. I hate it when people lie to me!"

"I apologize, Kurt, but let's face it, you weren't exactly the kind of guy a person puts his trust in."

"How come?"

"Kurt, you pulled a gun on me and stole my money."

"Only three bucks."

"That's hardly the point. Why would I give you a rendezvous, let alone tell you the address was out of date? That'd be inviting further theft, wouldn't it?"

Moody felt he was lecturing the school bully, a hulking simpleton who habitually stole lunch money and could see no reason why he shouldn't.

"Rondy . . . what?"

"Rendezvous. A meeting place. You can see my point of view, can't you, Kurt?"

"But we hadda deal! You were gonna help me write about my life story."

"Yes, I did say that, but I said it only to appease you."

"What's that mean?"

"To leave you in a happy frame of mind. You still had your gun and my three bucks, remember."

"Yeah, but a deal's a deal, I figure. You're not honest."

Moody had no response to this. Kurt fidgeted, looking around.

"So you live in a hotel, huh?"

"Yes, for the time being. We didn't feel safe living in the house anymore."

"Yeah? Why not? What house?"

"The one you went through like a hurricane, ripping everything apart, looking for me."

"Huh? I never did that to noplace!"

"What about what happened at my old address, Kurt? Why did you do that to Morton Dulkis? Were you mad at him for not being me?"

"Whaddaya talking about? Which one was Merton Dookis? The dead one or the other guy?"

"Other guy?"

"That was there. I knocked on the door, see. It took me a long time to find the place, because I hadda ask a lot of people where to find it, so when I knocked I didn't want trouble outta you after what you made me go through to get there, so it made me mad when I heard someone inside but he don't wanna open the door for me, which is rude. So I walked right in there. It wasn't locked even, and he's standing there, this big guy, just looking at me very surprised that I walked right in there without getting invited, but he made me mad not answering or nothing after I heard him moving around in there, so who's he to act like I'm the one not being polite, huh?"

"Morton Dulkis was small. Did you happen to notice him lying around the place?"

"Just the big guy, who I asked him if he knows where the owner is, that's you, Moody, and he kinda looks sideways with this funny look on his face and that's when I see the other guy, the dead guy on the floor there. I saw right off it isn't you, so I ask him, the big guy, if he knows where you are, and I take out the book and show him the picture on the back, and he says no."

"Then what happened?"

"Then I ask him about the guy on the floor, what's wrong with him, he looks dead, and then the big guy starts beating up on me, so I got away. I ran out the door fast as I could. He was a lot bigger than me. You woulda run away too, he's that big."

"I'm sure I would have, Kurt. Can you describe this fellow a little more?"

"Yeah. He's big."

"I understood that. Mustache? Clothing?"

"Uh . . . no mustache. But he had clothing."

"What kind of clothing, Kurt, can you recall?"

"It was . . . pants and a shirt with a jacket on top of the shirt."

"I see. Was the man fair or dark?"

"He had a hat. I forgot about the hat. The hat was dark."

"The man on the floor, was he surrounded by a pool of blood?"

"No, I woulda remembered. I don't like blood."

"Then he was probably just unconscious, not dead. He was killed with a razor after you left."

"Jeez, what for?"

"I have no idea. After you ran away, you didn't report what you'd seen to the police, did you?"

"Hell no! Think I wanna get mixed up with dead guys in your place?"

"It wasn't my place anymore, Kurt, it was the dead guy's place, Morton Dulkis."

"Well, how was I to know that with you lying to me like you did!"

"And you didn't use the phone book to find my current address, that is, the house I lived in until I moved here?"

"No. I shoulda done that."

"Then it wasn't you who went through that house, destroying every stick of furniture?"

"Not me. Why'd that happen?"

"I don't know. It scared my wife and myself enough to make us move here. By the way, how did you get the address of the Homeaway?"

"My uncle, he had it wrote down in a book. It's a recipe book, but he keeps addresses and phone numbers in it. There's a duck on the cover, flying."

"What made you go to the book, Kurt? Was there a particular address you wanted?"

"Yeah, my aunt Amanda. I told Uncle Henry I wanted to see her and he says okay and we went there, but I already saw your name there, wrote down. Moody, Homeaway Hotel, Ladera Heights. I hadda ask a lot of people how to find this place here. When do we start?"

"Start?"

"On the book."

"What book?"

"The goddamn book of my life! I want you to do it. I finished that other book. Boy, you had me fooled. Those brothers, that Jason and Michael, right up until the end I thought they were two people, and then it turns out it's one guy that's crazy! I hadda go back a couple pages and read it again, just to be sure I got it right, which I did. That's what you wrote, that the two brother guys are just one guy. That was very surprising."

"I'm glad you enjoyed it. Unfortunately, Kurt, I won't be able to assist in the writing of your autobiography just now—"

"Why not?"

"Because I'm busy writing something else. I can't set aside a professional commitment to produce something just because you want me to."

"Why not? Who's this other guy you're writing for? I asked you first!"

"Kurt, listen closely. You're in serious trouble. The police believe you murdered Morton Dulkis. They're looking for you."

"Me? I didn't do that. It was the big guy!"

"And I believe you, but you'll have to tell the police what happened."

"No! I don't wanna! I don't like cops. One time they hit me on the head and put me in jail because I didn't have no money. That's why I take people's money sometimes, so they won't hit me on the head and put me in jail again because I got no money—"

"Listen to me, Kurt. It's highly likely that the man who murdered Dulkis is the same man who tore my house apart. For some reason he had my old address, just as you did, and when he found out I didn't live there anymore, he found out the new address by way of the phone book and went there, not knowing that the police had come to take me back to the first address to accuse me of murdering Dulkis."

"You murdered him?"

Moody took a breath. "No, Kurt, the big guy murdered him. I was a suspect in the case, briefly, because the police found a picture of me at the crime scene, the picture torn off the back of your book when you struggled with the killer."

"Yeah, the cover fell off. It had the back half gone. I didn't see that till later on."

"So there you have it. A classic case of double mistaken identity. The police thought it was me, then I told them it was you, and the assumption was wrong both times."

"You said it was me? Why'd you do that?"

Moody had to resist rolling his eyes. "Because you threatened me with a gun and stole my money. Because I knew you had my old address and would very likely be annoyed with me for deceiving you. Motive, you see, Kurt. That's what made me tell them it was you. If you come with me now to the police, we can clear this mess up and set them on the path of the big guy."

Kurt Flowerdew looked at the floor, shaking his head. "No, I don't like the police. One time they hit me in the head and put me in jail just because I didn't have no money."

"Yes, I recall you telling me that. Well, what do you intend to do?"

Kurt considered his options for a long time, gazing at the carpet between his boots.

"Go home," he concluded.

"To Wisconsin?"

"To Uncle Henry's. He said I can stay there with him if I work hard. He's got a little farm with some cows and chickens and a dog. I like dogs. Do you?"

"Yes, I have a dog. She's with my wife at the moment, down in San Diego."

"What kind?"

"A black poodle. Big, not one of those silly little yappy things."

"I guess I'll stay there."

"That might be the best idea. Would you mind giving me the address, Kurt? I might need to get in touch."

"About the book?"

"Uh . . . possibly."

"It's this farm, on this road. The road hasn't got a name, just a number, I forget what, but there's trees along it. It's real pretty out there."

"I need more specific directions than that, Kurt. Think hard."

"It's . . . uh . . . it's near Santa Clara, someplace like that."

"Santa Clarita?"

"Yeah! How'd you know that?"

"Just a wild guess. How did you get into town from there, Kurt?"

"Oh, a bunch of folks gave me rides along the way. That's how I come out here from Wisconsin mostly, rides that folks gave me. I never took no money from them."

"That was wise, Kurt. What are your plans now? Does Uncle Henry know where you are?"

"No. Go back there, I guess."

"Would you like a lift?"

"Yeah! In your car?"

"Certainly."

"What kind is it?"

"A Ford."

"I like Fords!"

"I'll just leave a note for my wife."

While Moody scribbled hastily, Kurt informed him he also liked Chevys and Dodges too; Kurt liked all automobiles, also trucks of all kinds, whatever their make, plus tractors and combine harvesters; in fact, Kurt had to admit he was fascinated by vehicles of every description. He began talking about planes as they left, and ships as well.

On the drive north to Santa Clarita, Kurt fell into an unnatural silence that Moody was disinclined to disturb. Kurt finally announced, "My aunt Amanda, she's got a beard on her face."

"More than just a beard, Kurt. Her entire face is covered in hair. Her entire head, I suppose. But she's a very nice woman, wouldn't you say?"

"How come you know about the hair?"

"I paid her a visit yesterday."

"Oh."

"Do we go through town to get to your uncle's place, or do we turn off somewhere along the road before we get to town?"

"Go through."

Moody motored through Santa Clarita, and on the north side Kurt began picking out landmarks despite the darkness. "I seen that water tower before! And that bridge! I come over that bridge, so it won't be long now—"

He recognized the turnoff to Gallagher's farm several minutes later by the tall eucalyptus trees flanking the road, and Moody slowed down to make the turn. Less than ten minutes after that Kurt pointed to a lighted window off to the left. "That's Uncle Henry's! There!"

Moody turned into the ungated driveway and pulled up outside the main house. He could see several equipment sheds and a barn, and some old-fashioned split log fencing that seemed more decorative than practical. The light beside the front door came on as they stepped out of Moody's car. Henry Gallagher stood waiting until Kurt hurried up to him, gabbling excitedly about his hitchhiking trip down to Los Angeles; then Gallagher slapped him hard across the cheek. Kurt stopped talking instantly, a stunned expression on his face. "What'd I do? What'd you do that for?" He sounded like a sulky child.

"That's for running off and not telling me. Get inside and

sit yourself and don't say nothing till I say you can. Go on now and do it."

Kurt sidled past his uncle, shoulders slumped in defeat, and disappeared inside the house. Gallagher said to Moody, "He give you any trouble?"

"None at all. I thought it best to bring him straight home, though."

"That's the correct thing, all right. You better come in and talk."

They passed through an empty hallway to a living room redolent of old dog and old man, an inescapable mustiness enhanced by the lingering odor of pan-fried food and seldom-changed clothing. Moody became aware that Gallagher had cleaned himself up and put on his Sunday best for his own trip to the big town two days earlier. The Henry Gallagher before him now was pure farmer: bib overalls and checked shirt, facial stubble and heavy brogans. A dog of obvious antiquity lay on its dusty flanks between a mismatched sofa and armchair, unnaturally blasé about the presence of a stranger. The walls were decorated with calendars, most of them out of date, depicting scenes of mountain and prairie and whooping Indians. Kurt selected the armchair for himself, and Gallagher waited until Moody had placed himself at one end of the sofa before sitting down at the other. An awkward silence followed.

"Well now," said Gallagher. "I got coffee if you want it."

"No need to trouble yourself, Mr. Gallagher, I won't stay long."

"Thank you for bringing him home." To Kurt he said, "Did you thank Mr. Moody for bringing you home like someone with good manners ought to?"

"Thank you," mumbled Kurt.

"No problem at all," Moody assured them.

"He don't always think before he does what he does," explained Gallagher.

"I understand."

"And you were right about him having that gun. I made him give it to me. It was a real gun all right, only the firing pin was took out so it can't be used. He says he got it in a pawnshop and never even knew it didn't work on account of he never did buy any bullets for it. I made him throw it away. He's no genius, but he's not harmful neither, like I told you."

Moody said, "Miss Flowerdew said much the same thing."

Kurt blurted out, "He knows about Aunt Amanda and the hair on her face! He went and saw it himself! Ask him!"

"That right?" asked Henry.

"I visited Miss Flowerdew yesterday evening, out of curiosity. She mentioned you and Kurt had dropped by the day before."

"It's a shame about that woman. A good woman, I bet, and the Lord did that to her."

"She seems remarkably well adapted to her circumstances, even a little proud, it seemed to me."

"A body's got to feel that way when you get near the end, otherwise how could you face what's to come? It's all behind her now. She's got the cancer inside her bones, don't hardly eat at all anymore, they tell me, just waiting for the end. All over and done with, so it don't hardly matter anymore if she never had a man and her face is the way it is. Amanda's all set to go with her dignity still there at the end."

"She's that close to death, Mr. Gallagher?"

"That's what they told me. That big woman, Yaddigan, said so."

"Did you actually speak with a doctor?"

"I expect they have a doctor there someplace. Couldn't run

a home for old folks without one. People that old, they'd get sick and die every other week, I expect."

"But you didn't speak with a doctor, just Mrs. Yaddigan?"

"Are you saying she'd tell me something that isn't true? Amanda, she's skin and bone. She wasn't always like that till these last few months. You can't see her face to tell if she's on her way out, but her skinniness says to me she's on death's doorstep."

"This is probably none of my business, sir, but did Mrs. Yaddigan have you sign any kind of papers after she gave you the bad news concerning Miss Flowerdew?"

"Papers? I recollect something she had me sign, some legal thing for the burying."

"May I ask what was on the paper?"

"Couldn't rightly say. I never did think to bring along my reading glasses to visit with someone. I saw it clear enough to sign my name along the bottom, so it's all done, been taken care of legal."

Moody debated the wisdom of pursuing the topic further; it was really nothing to do with him. He pictured Amanda Flowerdew proudly willing herself asleep forever, and found her admirable. Then he pictured Mrs. Yaddigan, and was less favorably inclined.

"The reason I ask is because of what happened while I was there, at Morning Glory."

"Happened?"

"Have you met a gentleman called Hardiman?"

"The wheelchair cowboy? We bumped into each other a time or two. Used to be a rodeo champ in his day. What about him?"

"Mr. Hardiman told me that Mrs. Yaddigan is making plans to dispose of Miss Flowerdew's body in a way that I'm sure you won't approve of."

"What way's that? I told them go ahead and bury her. I was thinking about burning, you know, at the cremation place, but then I thought that'd be wrong, like I was ashamed of the way she was with her face and all? So I said bury her in a nice coffin. Mrs. Yaddigan, she said that was what Amanda wanted too, so that's okay, and the money side's all taken care of in advance. Amanda, she made a good living with her face, never really had to work, just sit there and let folks stare at her. I guess that was her compensation, not having to do real work like the rest of us."

"Did Mrs. Yaddigan happen to specify a closed or open coffin?"

"I believe she said it'd be open for any of the old folks there to go pay their respects when the time comes, then it'll be closed up for burying."

"According to Mr. Hardiman, between the open coffin display and the burial, Miss Flowerdew's body is likely to be taken from the casket."

"Why'd he say something like that? What good's burying an empty coffin?"

"Mrs. Yaddigan has apparently made arrangements to have Miss Flowerdew . . . stuffed."

"Stuffed?"

"Embalmed, I should say, for public display in a . . . freak museum down in Florida."

"Say what?"

"I can't vouch for the truth of what Mr. Hardiman told me. He said he overheard the arrangements being made. Quite frankly, Mr. Gallagher, I believe him. Mrs. Yaddigan, in the short time I was confronted by her, struck me as a person inclined to do things very much her own way. I'd look into the situation if I were you, before it's too late."

Kurt said, "They're gonna stuff her like a turkey?"

"Not if I can help it," Gallagher said. "Damn, but that bitch has got some nerve. That's an insult to the family, stealing her away like that after she's gone. That's not dignified."

"It's probably something you should mention to the police. You might need the services of a lawyer to guarantee the body's handed into your care for burial. I wouldn't let Yaddigan know where the body's buried, either. She may dig it up in spite of you."

"She might at that, but I don't like police and lawyers. I can handle my own business anytime I want, always have done. I never did like that woman. She bullies that little helper lady of hers something terrible."

"I noticed," said Moody.

"Uncle Henry?"

"What? We're talking serious business here, Kurt."

"I just wanted to say . . . I think—"

"Think what? Speak up and say your piece."

"I think . . . Ben's gone, Uncle Henry."

"He's right there at your feet, so how can he be gone?"

Moody deduced Ben was the prone dog with the graying muzzle and unwagging tail. He hadn't seen it lift its head since walking into the room.

"But he's not breathing—"

"Ben!" Gallagher commanded. "Ben, get up and stir yourself!"

Ben lay as before, perfectly still. Moody sensed the worst had happened while they had talked of another death in the offing, perhaps before. The dog was utterly immobile despite Gallagher's entreaties. The farmer eventually got down on the floor and lifted Ben's head.

"Oh, God, and he never even let out a breath that says he's

gone. . . . Oh, damn, but he was a good old dog, was Ben. . . . Snuck out from right under my feet, gave up the ghost silent as you please. . . . Damn!"

Moody was embarrassed to witness the genuine grief Gallagher was attempting to hide behind bluster. Tears were already rolling from his eyes, and he could no longer speak, just cradle in his hands the dog's heavy head. Moody suspected Gallagher's social world was narrow—a dying hair-faced woman; a nephew of limited mental ability; his dog—and becoming narrower. Ben alone could have accounted for the tears and stifled sobbing, but probably he did not. Moody decided he should do whatever he could to assist Henry Gallagher. He had no idea what practical assistance to render, but was ready to do whatever was asked of him, if anything should be.

Ben was buried by lamplight behind the barn. Kurt and Moody shared the task of digging a hole. Gallagher sat nearby on an upturned bucket, drinking occasionally from a whisky bottle. The diggers declined to share it with him until they were done and Ben was consigned to the earth. Kurt coughed and spluttered as the liquor hit his throat. Warned by this, Moody sipped just a little of whatever cheap brand it was that Henry preferred and was able to avoid a similar reaction.

"Damn, but he was a good old dog," Gallagher repeated by way of a eulogy, and all three men went back inside. Moody picked up his jacket, aware of the tingling of incipient blisters on his palms. "I'll be going now, Mr. Gallagher."

Henry nodded glumly, already partway drunk, his thoughts elsewhere. Kurt waved good-bye to Moody, although they were separated by only a few feet. Nobody saw him to the door or accompanied him across the yard to his car. Moody was slightly offended by that but dismissed any real disappointment over the behavior of his hosts; neither was a sophisticated man, and both had peculiar burdens to shoulder. Moody had already decided that contacting the police about Kurt Flowerdew was pointless; it would only involve the young man in procedures he could never understand and from which, without the wherewithal to pay for a competent attorney, he would probably never be able to extricate himself. Moody was himself satisfied by then that Kurt was not associated with the murder of Morton Dulkis or the destruction visited upon Moody's home, except by accidental association. He was prepared simply to forget about the shrinking Flowerdew/Gallagher clan, and hoped the police investigation into the death of Dulkis steered them in another direction entirely. Kurt's description of a "big guy" would help no one. It was all none of Moody's business anymore. The break-in at his home in Alhambra had been something unrelated to Dulkis, probably the work of a deranged individual or dope addict searching for something in the wrong house.

He entertained these and similar thoughts on the leisurely drive back to Los Angeles. It was getting late; Myra would presumably be waiting for him with an explanation for her trip down to San Diego. He would broach the subject of returning home; there was little point in remaining at the Homeaway Hotel now that Kurt was no longer lurking in the shadows. There would be a return to normalcy, a concentration on the business at hand of writing a screenplay for *Traitor's Dawn* and securing his renewed position at Empire. The entire Flowerdew sideshow had been a distraction Moody no longer had time for.

It was almost ten-thirty by the time he reached the Homeaway and parked. Entering the lobby, he was signaled by the desk clerk and handed an envelope with his name printed in block letters on the outside.

"Did someone leave this for me?"

"Yes, sir."

The desk clerk's face was smiling, helpful, eager to assist.

"He didn't leave a name?"

"No, sir, no name."

Moody began opening the envelope. "Good news, I hope, sir," said the desk clerk, stretching his ancient smile a little wider.

"Actually, it is," said Moody. "This is notification of my Academy Award. I was told to expect it this evening, hand delivered, you know. They do it that way nowadays."

"That's splendid, sir. Congratulations."

Moody couldn't be sure if the desk clerk enjoyed playing along with the hotel's eccentric guests or was unable to distinguish humor from reality. He opened the envelope.

The single sheet of paper was clearly printed in the same hand as the envelope. WE HAVE GOT YOUR WIFE. SHE IS OK. WILL CALL MIDNIGHT. DO NOT CALL COPS.

"What category, sir? Best actor? Or are you a writer, sir? I believe you told me you were."

Moody began walking toward the elevators, blood pounding in his ears.

"Best screenplay is it, sir? Best picture?" As the elevator doors closed behind him, he heard the desk clerk calling, "Best musical score?"

The elevator operator, a young man with an actor's good looks, said, "You'll have to excuse old Knobby. He's nuts." Moody said nothing, the capitalized message repeating itself inside his head like an endless ticker tape. The young man continued, "There's been complaints, but the management don't listen. Knobby, he's someone's uncle or grandpa or something, so they keep him on. Maybe he saved the manager's baby from getting run over by a runaway wagon, something like that. They say he's been a little crazy ever since those little gals jumped off the roof here way back when, those Flying Starlet Sisters, you know? I heard one of 'em was his daughter, how about that. Maybe it's true. Anyway, just ignore him. You feeling okay tonight, sir?"

"Yes . . ."

"Good. We like to know our guests are happy at the Homeaway. The Homeaway is a home away from home, sir. Nine, isn't it?"

"Nine . . ."

Moody got out at his floor and walked unsteadily along the corridor. The sconce lamps mounted along the wall seemed to shed light as old and cold as the moon. Myra, kidnapped. . . . It had to be the same man who had murdered Dulkis and smashed up the interior of the house at Alhambra. . . . Or else it had nothing to do with any of that, was a completely different mystery. At least he knew Kurt Flowerdew had nothing to do with it.

He placed his key in the lock and went inside.

Myra . . . Kidnapped . . .

For what?

He smoked eleven cigarettes while waiting for the call. It came promptly at midnight.

"Moody?"

He didn't recognize the voice, since it was not deliberately muffled like the call that had awakened him early on Tuesday.

"What have you done with my wife!"

"Nothing, Moody. We aren't criminals. She's fine."

"Let me speak with her!"

"Maybe, if you're a good boy and do as you're told."

"I won't do anything until I know she's all right."

"First things first, Moody. We need to know where it is."

"Where what is?"

"The book."

"What book?"

"With the stamps."

"I don't know what you mean. Are you sure you've kidnapped the right person?"

"Don't be cute. We haven't kidnapped anybody yet,

just . . . looking after your wife for you, Moody, until we get what we want. It's a trade, not kidnapping."

"I still have no idea what you're talking about."

"The stamps, Moody. The big book with all the stamps in it is what I'm talking about. Go get it. The book's there, isn't it?"

"I . . . suppose so. Wait just a minute."

Moody went to the bureau where he'd seen Myra place the stamp album. The squirrel nut bowl stood on the same bureau; for some reason Myra had insisted on bringing it with them to the Homeaway. The squirrel was there, the album was not. Moody felt panic rising from his chest into his throat. Where the hell was the album?

He went back to the phone, anxious to gain more time. "Hello . . . ? Look, I can't seem to lay my hands on it at this exact minute. . . . Hello?"

"Moody, you lay your hands on that stamp book or we start laying hands on your nice little wife, and I don't mean healing hands, Moody. Go get the book."

Moody set the phone down, and as he did so, he caught sight of a newspaper folded into sections, with one large advertisement circled in pencil. It lay right beside the phone stand, on the floor; why hadn't he seen it before? He picked it up and scanned the advertisement. American Philatelic Society, he read, and stopped breathing for a moment or two, then went on. The society was assembled for three days in San Diego for its annual get-together. Tomorrow was to be the last day. All stamp aficionados were invited to attend. . . . He flung the newspaper down and began panicking all over again. The stamp album was with Myra, obviously taken to San Diego for some expert opinion on the contents of the page with the dog-eared corner. But if the man on the phone had Myra in his clutches, then he must surely have the album as well. . . .

Moody tried to concentrate. He had to know if Myra was in the custody of others.

"Hello? Yes, I have it here. It wasn't where I thought it was."

"That's good, Moody. Now, here's what you do—"

"I want to speak with Myra!"

"Look, you don't want to make her suffer, do you? See, she's got tape across her mouth to make sure she minds her manners, and if she has to speak to you we're gonna have to tear the tape off, Moody, and after you're done, it gets put back on again, which it then has to get taken off again later on after you give us the book and we give you your wife back. You want her to get the tape pulled off twice in one day, Moody? What kinda husband are you, anyway?"

"What do I do with the album?"

"You take it to the corner of Hollywood and Vine, you know, where everyone you ever met in your life is gonna come by sooner or later? You stand there with the book in your hands at one A.M. Can you make it by then, Moody?"

"Certainly."

"Someone'll drive up and you give him the book, then you get your wife back."

"I refuse to hand over anything until Myra's safe, where I can see her clearly."

"You don't trust me, Moody?"

"Why should I?"

"All I want is the book, not blood on my hands."

"Why? Is there something valuable about it?"

"Is your wife valuable to you, Moody? That's how valuable the book is, to the penny. You get yourself down to Hollywood and Vine and wait for the car."

The phone clicked. Moody set it down and considered his options. There was a chance the caller was bluffing, just as Moody was. One party didn't have Myra, the other party didn't have the album. Myra and the album presumably were together in San Diego, or else on the road between there and Los Angeles. But it was past midnight now, and she still hadn't returned, which tended to suggest she'd been detained by a person or persons unknown. Unless, as on her return journey from Yellowtail, she'd run into car trouble.

Moody dialed the front desk.

"Hello?"

"This is Keith Moody up on nine. Did my wife call at any time this evening to leave a message?"

"Your wife, sir? Let me check."

Moody waited, fingers drumming nervously on the phone stand.

"Mr. Moody?"

"Yes."

"A message came through at nine thirty-seven. 'Staying overnight Oceanside Hotel maybe exciting news tomorrow.' "

"Thank you. Is there some reason why that message wasn't given to me earlier, along with the other message in the envelope?"

"Indeed there is, sir. The telephone message was in the telephone message rack, and the envelope was in the mail slots, sir. Someone else must have taken the phone message. I would have delivered them both to you at the same time, sir, I assure you."

"Wouldn't it be a good idea to leave both kinds of message in one place, the mail slot, for example, then it wouldn't matter who took what message, all messages would be waiting in the same damn place?"

"A brilliant suggestion, sir! May I appropriate it? The management may reward me in some small way for streamlining the system."

"You're very welcome—" Moody almost said, "Knobby."

"Thank you, sir."

"Get me the Oceanside Hotel in San Diego."

"Certainly, sir. I'll ring when I have the connection."

Moody hung up, then crossed his fingers. The phone rang a moment later.

"Yes?"

"Your number, sir."

"Thank you."

He heard the quiet burring of a phone a hundred miles south of Los Angeles.

"Oceanside Hotel, how may I help you?"

"Do you have a Myra Moody registered there?"

"One moment, please. . . . Yes, sir, we do."

"Put me through, please."

More burring. Moody found himself holding his breath.

"Hello?"

"Myra . . . ? Thank God—!"

"Darling, it's so good to be appreciated this way—"

"Are you all right?"

"Of course I'm all right. You took your time returning my call."

"It's that idiot Knobby."

"Who?"

"Never mind. Someone tried to tell me you'd been kidnapped."

"Pardon?"

Moody explained. Myra was dumbfounded. "They took a chance, trying to fool you that way. They must know I'm not there, or they wouldn't have tried bluffing you."

"I agree. You're sure you weren't followed today?"

"Not that I was aware of. I have Bess with me. She would've bitten anyone who tried to nab me. Keith, we may be rich!"

"One of the stamps?"

"Yes! Do you recall the one from Finland with the two rings on it?"

"I'm afraid I don't. What about it?"

"It's the drabbest one on the page, but it's worth a lot, apparently. It has two rings, one inside the other, with little bumps inside the inner ring. It's very rare, from 1901. There are only five in the whole world, or so Mr. Moxham told me."

"Who might Mr. Moxham be?"

"Only one of the country's greatest stamp experts. He's doing some investigating on my behalf. We should know tomorrow what kind of figure to expect from the Finland stamp. Isn't it exciting?"

"No, it's terrifying. Someone else obviously wants the stamp. He's already killed once, and you're the target now. Where's the album? You didn't let this Moxham fellow take it away with him, did you?"

"It's in the National Bank of San Diego on Harbor Drive, in the vault. I rented a strongbox overnight."

"Clever girl. . . . Wait, something doesn't ring true here. . . . If they know you're in San Diego, presumably with the stamp album at the philatelic convention, then why are they attempting to arrange an exchange of you, whom they don't have, for the album, which they must surely know I don't have?"

"I don't know, darling. Maybe they don't know I'm down here, they just know I'm not there. For all they know, the album's with you at the Homeaway. Lock the door, Keith. They'll be angry when you don't show up at Hollywood and Vine."

"But I *am* going to be at Hollywood and Vine."

"Keith! Don't you dare!"

"It's all right. I'll stay in my car and watch for them as they cruise by in theirs, then I'll tail them to wherever they live. Then I'll call Lieutenant Huttig, and the police will do the rest."

"I don't like that plan."

"Piece of cake, darling. Absolutely risk-free. I'll call you in the morning."

"Please be careful. Don't do anything foolish."

"I'm a coward at heart, didn't you know?"

"Idiot."

"Thank you and good night."

He hung up, then hurried to the door. He had less than forty minutes to make the rendezvous.

WAITING IN HIS Ford, fifteen or so yards from the corner of Hollywood and Vine, Moody was excited by his own brilliance in having called the bluff of the killer. Morton Dulkis, innocent bystander, would be avenged. It was three minutes before 1:00 A.M, and the intersection was still busy with traffic. Observing this, Moody felt a moment of doubt; how would he know which of the cars passing by was the one with the killer inside? Even if the same car passed back and forth several times, he wouldn't really be able to tell, unless it was some kind of exotic roadster that called attention to itself, and no one involved in this kind of shady business was likely to drive such a vehicle. The best thing to do, under the circumstances, was stand where he'd been told to stand, and when the killer's car pulled over to take delivery of the stamp album, Moody would make a mental note of the license plate number. After that, the police could take over as planned.

He got out of his car, locked it, and strolled to the corner.

He had nothing resembling a stamp album to carry, so he removed his jacket and draped it over his arm, as if concealing
something, then stood on the curb and waited. And waited.
Traffic came and went in four directions at a steady rate, but no
vehicle stopped. Moody became impatient. Had the bluffer
somehow realized his own bluff was called, a trap set in its place?
It was now 1:17, and not one car had so much as slowed to
inspect him in passing.

A young woman wearing too much makeup and a tight dress
approached Moody and asked him for a match. He offered his
lighter, and she inhaled on her cigarette. Moody was alert; could
this be the pickup agent, someone roped into the scheme to
make sure he had the album before the killer approached? If so,
he was in trouble. The young woman was scrutinizing his face,
blowing streams of smoke around his head.

"It's in the car," Moody told her. "I've got it, but it's in the
car. I'm not going to hand it over to you, only to him."

"What's that, sugar? Hand over what?"

"The album. I'm sure you understand."

"Oh, I'm the understanding type, all right. Why don't you
come with me, and I'll listen real hard to whatever you want to
tell me, honey."

"Uh . . . are you here representing someone else?"

"Just me. Are you here representing a guy that needs some
company, sugar?"

"You're not here for the album, then."

"Honey, I don't get you. I've got a little place right near
here. You come with me, and we'll figure out all this about the
album, okay, sweetie? You'll like my place."

"No, thank you. I'm waiting for someone."

"No waiting with me, sugarman. Let's go."

"Please go away. I'm waiting for someone. It's important."

"You don't have to pretend with me, lover."

"I'm a policeman. Leave the area or face arrest."

She blew smoke directly into his eyes, making Moody blink. "Policeman? Shit, feller, I don't think you're even a man."

The prostitute walked away, switching her hips. Moody took a deep breath. Had the right car passed by while he spoke with her? There was every chance the killer was being cautious, stringing out the meeting to convince himself no trap had been laid. This might take some time.

A police car pulled up in front of him. Moody groaned.

"Hey, you."

"Yes, Officer?"

"You've been standing there fifteen minutes now. What's the deal?"

"No deal, Officer."

"Then why are you waiting? That young lady not to your liking, huh?"

"As a matter of fact, no, she isn't."

"Waiting for something else, hey? Some good-looking young guy, maybe?"

"Not at all. Nothing like that."

"Then what? Tell me something I can believe, mister."

"I . . . I'm waiting to see my uncle."

"Your uncle?"

"Someone told me if you stand on the corner of Hollywood and Vine, everyone you ever knew will pass you by, so I'm waiting for my uncle Clarence. I haven't seen him since 1938."

"Mister, get lost. Don't stand around on no street corners, is my advice to you, or you might get in trouble. Your uncle Clarence isn't coming, not tonight or any other night or day. He called me up on the two-way radio and said to tell his nephew to go home and quit waiting. So go on home, okay? I see you still here when I come around again in five minutes, I'll run you in for being a public nuisance, you got that, nephew?"

"Yes, Officer."

"So beat it."

Moody walked back to his car and started the engine. Maybe the killer had driven by, maybe he hadn't. It had been a waste of time. He was suddenly tired, desperately in need of sleep. His bed at the Homeaway beckoned, and he drove toward it at a little above the legal speed limit.

"GOOD EVENING, SIR. Out for a spin? Or should I say good morning?"

Moody leaned against the front desk and looked at Knobby's smiling parchment face. The man remained an irritating enigma.

"I'm going to bed. If any calls come through for me, just take a message and tell me in the morning, unless it's my wife."

"Certainly, sir. She already had a caller herself, and I took the liberty of supplying the number of the hotel in San Diego."

Moody became a little more alert. "Did the caller leave a name?"

"No, sir, he just asked if Mrs. Moody was available, and of course I was in a position to tell him no, unless he cared to call long distance, which he said he was quite prepared to do, so I gave him the number, sir."

Moody felt a sensation akin to icy fingers walking up his spine.

"Get me the Oceanside Hotel, quickly—"

"Certainly, sir. Rather late to be calling, isn't it, sir?"

"Hurry up!"

"As you wish, sir."

The connection seemed to take an eternity. Knobby smiled on as Keith waited.

"Oceanside Hotel, how may I help you?"

"Myra Moody, please."

"One moment."

The phone in Myra's room rang, and rang. The Oceanside desk clerk came back on the line. "I'm sorry, sir, there's no answer. The party may be very soundly asleep at this hour."

"This is an emergency. Please send someone to wake her up."

"Very well, sir. Hold the line, please."

Moody passed the next several minutes in agony. Knobby stared into space with the equanimity of a statue.

"Sir?"

"Yes—!"

"The party is no longer there, sir."

"No longer there? She wouldn't have left at this hour of the morning!"

"Sir, there's a dog—"

"Yes, that's my dog. The dog's there, but my wife isn't, is that what you're saying?"

"Sir . . . the dog is dead. We were not informed the party had a dog accompanying her. The Oceanside Hotel management wishes to inform you they can take no responsibility for the dog, sir."

"She's . . . dead? How?"

"I've been told the dog has been shot, sir. Sir, can you tell me why your wife had a dog in her room and made no attempt to communicate this fact to us? Pets are not allowed at the Oceanside, sir. The management takes no responsibility for accidents occurring to nonregistered guests. Do you understand, sir?"

"Get the manager."

"The manager is not here at this hour, sir."

"Then get the fucking night manager! My wife has been kidnapped!"

"There's no need to shout, sir. Nobody here is responsible for what happened to the dog. The dog should not have been on the premises—"

"Get whoever's in charge, and get him now!"

"One moment, if you please."

Moody sagged against the desk. Myra gone . . . Bess, sweet Bess with the liquid eyes and moist nose and eager paws . . . dead. He felt himself being sucked into a whirlpool of his own devising. While he had waited in vain at Hollywood and Vine, the killer had found out where Myra was staying. He had to have followed her down to San Diego, then lost her trail somehow, and used the ever-helpful Knobby to ascertain her whereabouts while sending Moody on a fool's mission. Moody had cooperated in the kidnapping of his own wife, assisted in the killing of his wonderful dog. . . .

"Sir, are you all right?"

"No, I'm not. Call the police. Homicide. Lieutenant Huttig—tell them to call him at home. Say it's Keith Moody with important information—"

"Homicide, sir? I thought you said your wife was kidnapped."

"Just call them!"

HUTTIG AND LABIOSA arrived at 2:58 A.M. Neither wore a tie; both wore expressions of skepticism and annoyance. They took Moody to a corner of the lobby and sat him in one of the overstuffed chairs.

"Let's get this straight, Moody. You say your wife's been kidnapped down in San Diego because of a stamp album?"

"Containing one very valuable stamp, yes. Have the police down there found out anything yet? They shot my dog. They must've used a silencer. They're obviously prepared to use violence—"

"Calm down, Moody," advised Labiosa. "They find out anything down there, they're gonna tell us pronto. Where'd this stamp album come from? Your wife a collector?"

"No, she inherited it from her uncle Barney up in Idaho. I told you that before."

"I remember it was a squirrel," said Huttig.

"A squirrel nut bowl and a stamp album. We had no idea there was anything valuable about it. It's in the vault of the National Bank of San Diego, on Harbor Drive. Myra had the good sense to put it there overnight, while Mr. Moxham ascertains the worth of the Finland stamp."

"You don't figure this Moxham guy's got anything to do with it?"

"She only met him yesterday. He's an expert on philately, not a kidnapper. This is clearly the work of whoever it was that killed Morton Dulkis and broke into our house. It was all about the stamp. None of it has anything to do with Kurt Flowerdew. There's no connection, barring the coincidence factor."

Huttig said to Labiosa, "Coincidence—we know that word, don't we, Vinnie?"

"We sure do know that word."

"We know that word on account of you, Moody, and that Bax Nolan business."

"Every time we turned around there's another stiff, and all of them connected to you, Moody, and all you could keep telling us was it's nothing but a big coincidence."

"Which it turned out not to be so coincidental in the end, Moody."

"So when you say to us today, 'coincidence,' we don't believe it right away."

"Not after the last time, we don't," agreed Labiosa.

Moody put his head in his hands.

"My wife has been kidnapped. It wasn't Kurt Flowerdew who did it. It was someone who followed her down to San Diego yesterday."

"Why wouldn't that be Flowerdew?"

"Because—" Moody couldn't tell them he had been visiting with Kurt Flowerdew on his uncle's farm earlier that evening, not without inviting an intense police grilling of Kurt to settle the issue, an unnecessary distraction, in Moody's opinion; and there would be repercussions, if only because Kurt had stolen three dollars from him at gunpoint, a crime for which Moody had already forgiven him.

"Yeah, Moody? Because?"

"Because . . . it wasn't. That avenue of inquiry is a waste of time, believe me."

"Avenue of inquiry," repeated Labiosa. "I like that. Vinnie, did you know that's what we did for a living, went down avenues of inquiry?"

"I thought we just pounded shoe leather."

"We have to remember that Moody's a writer, Vinnie. Writers say stuff like that about the avenues of inquiry. Why do you suppose they do that instead of just saying what something really is?"

"They like to hear their gums beat up and down," was Labiosa's opinion.

"Gentlemen," Moody protested, "isn't time being wasted here?"

"What else are we gonna do? If your wife was kidnapped, there's gonna be a ransom demand pretty soon, or maybe not pretty soon but sometime. The one they're gonna wanna talk to is you, Moody, and this is where they're gonna call you up, see? So what we do is sit tight and wait for the call."

"Meantime," added Huttig, "the San Diego cops are doing their part. That's a shame about that dog of yours. One of them black poodle types, wasn't it?"

"Yes." Moody didn't want to talk about Bess. It was only the fact that Myra had been kidnapped that prevented him from bursting into tears over the dog, he realized.

Across the lobby the phone rang. Knobby picked it up, listened, then beckoned to Moody, his face animated, happy for Moody that a call had come through.

"For you, sir!"

Moody hurried over, followed by the detectives.

"Hey, you," Huttig addressed Knobby. "Got an extension handy?"

Knobby indicated a second phone on the desk, and Huttig picked it up, then nodded at Moody, who took the first phone from the clerk.

"This is Keith Moody. Who am I talking to, please?"

"Never mind that. Nothing personal, Moody, but this time we really do have her. You can even talk to her if you like."

There was muffled conversation, then Myra's voice came on the line.

"Keith?"

"Myra! Are you all right?"

"They haven't hurt me. Oh, Keith—they shot Bess. She jumped at them and . . . they shot her."

"I know. What do they want, the stamps?"

"I've already told them where they are. . . . Keith, they say you have to come down here and be their hostage while I get the stamps out of the bank vault first thing in the morning."

"I'll do it—"

The male voice was back. "Did you say you'd do it, Moody?"

"Yes, I did."

"You better not get the cops involved in this. Did you tell them yet?"

Moody looked at Huttig, who shook his head.

"No . . . I didn't want to jeopardize anything."

"Good. The cops down here, they won't know about it till the maid cleans the room tomorrow and finds the dog. By the time that happens, you're gonna be down here, and your wife, she's gonna be walking outta the bank with the stamps. Then you both walk away healthy and happy. Sound good to you, Moody?"

"Of course. The police shouldn't be involved at any stage. This is between you and me now."

"Exactly right. So you get in your car and come on down to San Diego, Moody, and wait for us to get in touch. You park your car next to the Navy Pier entrance. What kinda car you got?"

"A Ford coupe, green."

"You wait outside the Navy Pier, and we'll get in touch. Go get in your green Ford coupe right now, and Moody?"

"Yes?"

"Don't go calling no cops. We don't get that stamp book, she's dead. Understand?"

The caller hung up.

Huttig set down the second phone. "Vinnie'll drive with you, Moody, and I'll follow in the prowler. We'll get something set up with the boys down there."

"But you'll stay under cover until Myra hands over the stamps."

"Sure we will. We're professionals. You leave the stakeout to us. These crumbs that took your wife, they won't even know we're in the neighborhood. Let's go."

DURING THE TWO-HOUR drive south, Vinnie Labiosa amazed Moody by falling asleep beside him. Huttig's cruiser maintained a constant distance behind as they followed the coast highway. Effectively alone, Moody pondered the sequence of events that had led him to this predawn drive. He thought about Myra, and he thought about Bess. He wanted the police to honor their word and stay away until Myra was safe, and then they could do whatever they wanted, so far as Moody was concerned. He hoped for confrontation, a gun battle in which the killer/kidnappers couldn't hit the side of a barn but the bullets of righteousness spitting from police revolvers would find their mark. Moody wanted them dead, stone dead, for what they had done. His body exhausted by anxiety and lack of sleep, he drove on, the highway unwinding like an endless dream before his twitching eyes.

By the time both cars were nearing the northern suburbs of San Diego, the sky was beginning to turn a pale pinkish blue over the Vallecito Mountains to the east. Moody's eyelids were like metal shutters, fighting gravity in their need to remain open. He was beginning to swerve across the highway's dividing line when he heard Huttig's horn behind him. He straightened up, but the horn sounded again. Moody pulled over to the shoulder and rolled down his window. Huttig parked behind him. Labiosa was awake as Huttig approached on foot. "Moody, you falling asleep at the wheel there?"

"No, I'm just a little tired."

"You follow me from here on in. Vinnie, you're with me."

Labiosa transferred, and the cars went on. With the dawning of a new day Moody felt himself gain his second wind. He would sleep when Myra was able to sleep beside him, and not before. His outrage over what had happened made him feel helpless. Unlike any movie scenario, in which he could have concocted a heroic role for himself as Myra's liberator and avenger, Moody knew he was restricted to following police orders. The righting of wrong, in this case at least, was going to follow standard procedure, with Moody playing a secondary role. He wouldn't have the chance to plug a bad man and walk away, knowing he'd made the world a better place.

He followed Huttig to a main road near the ocean, then both cars stopped in a parking lot alongside several other parked cars bearing the whip antennas of unmarked police vehicles. Moody got out. He could smell the Pacific. Huttig and Labiosa conferred briefly with several plainclothes detectives and uniformed officers standing by their cars, then beckoned Moody forward. A large man appeared to be in charge.

"Moody," said Huttig, "this is Captain McAllister, SDPD. Do what he says."

"Mr. Moody, are you ready to play a part in this, or would you prefer to step aside? We can have one of my men play decoy using your car and hat."

McAllister's voice was rough with tobacco and whisky, his breath accompanied by their odors. Moody wondered for a moment if the man had cancer of the throat, and suspected he was a man of few words to spare himself any additional aggravation to his vocal cords. "I'll do my bit, Captain."

McAllister indicated two men in snap-brim hats. "These gentlemen are from the FBI. They were called in when the kidnapping angle made this into a federal crime. Agent Buller and Agent Denton. They'll make the arrest."

They nodded at Moody, who returned the greeting.

"What exactly do I have to do?"

"Get in your car, Mr. Moody, and drive around the corner here to the left, that's Broadway, then follow Broadway till you get to the docks. The pier you'll come out next to is Broadway Pier, which isn't the one they want you outside of, so you turn left again and follow the road south just a little way till you get to Navy Pier. Park on the right side of the road, as near to the pier entrance as you can, under a streetlight, preferably, so they can see you clearly. Then you wait. If and when they approach you, just play along till we make our move."

"What move will that be?"

"Just do what I said, Mr. Moody, and leave the rest to us. My men are already in position. You won't see them, but they're there. You don't have anything to worry about. I suggest you start now."

"Should I . . . uh . . . have a gun?"

"That won't be necessary."

Moody went back to his car, feeling less certain of the plan's success than McAllister appeared to be. He would simply have to trust the professionalism of the SDPD and FBI.

Ten minutes later he parked where he had been told to. There were no moving vehicles anywhere in sight. He could hear the sound of waves, the crying of gulls. The entrance to Navy Pier stood like a false-fronted building on a movie set. There was not a soul in sight. He lit a cigarette and blew smoke out the widow; the smell of salt water came back to him, reminding Moody of the first time he had encountered the Pacific, when he came to Los Angeles before the war to work for Empire Productions. The beach had not impressed him as he thought it would, and the ocean itself was no more inspiring, with its limitless horizon, than the open spaces of Moody's home state, Kansas. But the smell of the place had left a definite impression, with its tangy, slightly unclean bouquet. The line marking the boundary between land and water was, for Moody, made plain not so much by the strip of sand as by the coastal smell of the place; it was his nose rather than his eyes that told him he was standing at the edge of everything. He breathed in that same odor now, its familiarity made more pungent by the addition of marine fuel and floating garbage, and waited.

It was almost six o'clock, the sky a clear blue above, when he noticed a white Chevrolet sedan drive past. The driver looked at Moody, and it was the look that made Moody watch the car in his rearview mirror as it went by. He felt a tug of excitement and apprehension in his chest as the white car turned around and returned. It drew up alongside Moody's Ford, and the driver leaned over to wind down the passenger-side window. Moody could barely breathe. The driver was a tough-looking man in his thirties; Moody had never seen him before. The Chevrolet's engine was kept running.

"Say, is this the way to the coast highway? I've got myself all turned around."

Moody felt a pang, two parts disappointment to one part relief.

"Uh . . . I think it joins the highway farther south, but I couldn't say for sure. I'm not a San Diegan myself."

"No? Where, San Francisco?"

"Los Angeles."

"Moody?"

The excitement and fear and anger returned. He recognized the voice now.

"Yes."

"What's your wife's name, Moody?"

"Myra."

"Just need to be sure you're not a cop. What's your dog's name?"

"Bess. Why did you kill her?"

"Had to, feller, sorry. Okay, you're gonna follow me. It isn't far. You in a cooperative mood, Moody?" The driver laughed at his own joke.

"No," Moody said.

The driver stopped laughing. "So what if you're not? You'll do it anyway."

"Not necessarily," said Moody, his eyes flickering to his side mirror, where a sudden movement was reflected. Two police officers were out from wherever they had been hiding, approaching the Chevrolet from behind, guns drawn.

The driver was concentrating on Moody, annoyed by his attitude. "You better get your head screwed on straight, friend. We mean business."

"You're a coward, that's all. A cheap crook who pushes around dogs and women."

"Brother, you're asking for it now."

The two cops were closer. Moody made himself take his eyes off the mirror before the man in the white car noticed his interest and turned around.

"I want you to know," Moody said, "that I despise you, completely and utterly. People like you are a disgrace to humanity."

"Go fuck yourself. I got a good mind to make you pay for every word you just said to me that I don't like. You get cooperating right now, friend, or your little woman, she won't get outta this deal in as good a shape as she's still in, and neither will you—"

A gun was thrust through the driver's open window, the barrel jammed against his neck just below the ear. The driver's mouth fell open in surprise.

"Don't you move, bud," said the cop behind the gun. "Turn that engine off."

"Sure . . . sure . . ."

The driver reached slowly for the ignition, then abruptly threw the car into first gear. Before his foot was off the clutch, the cop fired. Moody saw a hole open in the side of the driver's jaw on the side opposite the cop; the hole instantly sprayed blood and scraps of bone across the passenger seat, the roof lining, and the front window. Moody felt a small stinging sensation as a bone chip buried itself in his cheek. The driver slumped across the wheel, his weight pressing against the horn. The car, gears engaged but without a foot on the accelerator, horn blaring, began creeping away from Moody's Ford. The cop reached through the open window and switched off the engine. The white Chevrolet rolled to a stop.

More police officers came out of hiding and surrounded the car. Moody sat still for a moment, aware that his left ear hurt from the sound of the gunshot, then got out of his car. McAllister was beckoning him forward to view the dead man. "Recognize him?"

"No."

"You did a good job, Mr. Moody, keeping him talking that way. Gave us exactly the right opportunity to make our move."

"Captain, excuse me, but with this man dead, how am I going to get in touch with the rest of the gang to get my wife back?"

"The thing is, you don't have to. She's already down at headquarters. Been there about ten minutes now."

"I don't understand—"

"There was only one other guy, and he had a heart attack, something like that, according to your wife, and she just walked out of the place they were keeping her. That's it. Show's over."

"Myra's . . . all right?"

"No harm done, just a little put out by events maybe. You're a lucky man, Moody. This could've happened a whole lot different than it did."

"The officer who shot the man, he already knew my wife was safe?"

"Him? No, how could he? He was nowhere near a squad car radio."

Moody let the implications of that wash over him without comment. The FBI agents were approaching in lockstep. Moody wanted simply to drive away and collect Myra, but it was obvious no such escape could be made before official reports had been typed up and filed in triplicate.

BY NOON THE following had been accomplished: Moody and Myra were reunited at police headquarters. Both made statements for the benefit of the SDPD and the FBI. Moody learned, as Myra spoke, that the man who had been guarding her was one Lemuel Spaulding, the Los Angeles philatelist and owner of Stamp of Approval, to whom Myra had first taken the album for appraisal. It was assumed that he had spotted her at the Philatelic Convention in San Diego and mounted an impromptu plan to relieve her of the Finland stamp with the aid of one Paul Geery, a small-time hood with an extensive record in Los Angeles. The prior relationship between these two was undetermined, and now would probably never be known. Spaulding had a weak heart, according to his wife when she was informed of his demise. Several newspaper reporters insisted on interviewing the Moodys before they could depart from head-quarters. When finally they were able to leave, their first stop was at the Oceanside Hotel to pick up Myra's car and the body of Bess. The management informed them that Bess had been taken away by the county dogcatcher for disposal by cremation; a bill for that service was being prepared, and could be paid immediately or by mail. Moody handed over ten dollars, holding back an irrational urge to jam the money into the manager's disapproving face. Their next stop was the National Bank, where Myra collected the stamp album. She then made a call to the hotel room of Elliot Moxham the stamp expert, who informed her that the Finland stamp was worth approximately $80,000.

The drive back to Los Angeles in both cars began. The stamp album was hidden under the front seat of the Ford. They arrived home by midafternoon, and the album was placed in the vault of their bank. They ate lunch together, then tried to get some sleep to make up for their lost night, but so much had happened, the experience had been so harrowing, that neither could sleep, and so they made love instead. Then Moody cried for his dog, and Myra cried for Moody. Finally, worn out, they slept.

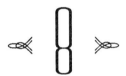

On arriving at his office the following day, Moody found a note requiring his immediate presence before Marvin Margolis. Ten minutes later Moody was under the basilisk gaze of the studio's head of production. Margolis produced a copy of the *Los Angeles Times* and placed it carefully on the desk. Moody sensed trouble.

"You seem to have had an adventure, Keith."

"I'd call it a misadventure, Mr. Margolis."

"Perhaps so. Your wife is unharmed?"

"She's fine, thank you."

"The incident has had extensive coverage, not just in the *Times*, but nowhere do I find mention of Empire Productions, Keith. Publicity such as this is worth its weight in gold. Were you perhaps too exhausted by your ordeal to inform the reporters of your profession, your employment here at Empire, and your connection to none other than Nigel Lawson, not to mention Gloria Gresham? Did these facts slip from your mind as you gave interviews, Keith? I call that a missed opportunity. Your wife was not subjected to torture of any description, I hope."

"None. The man guarding her while his accomplice met with me was so ill he suffered a heart attack right before Myra's eyes. First he pulled off his mask, which is when my wife recognized him as someone she'd shown her stamp collection to, and then he simply fell off his chair, stone dead, apparently. She slipped out of the ropes around her wrists and walked out into the street, hailed a cab, and went directly to police headquarters."

"A woman with a cool head, to be sure. She also turned her back on this golden opportunity to make the public aware of your circumstances?"

"I think she was too relieved to find herself, and me, out of danger, Mr. Margolis. Circumstances such as those don't allow much room for publicity of a commercial nature."

Margolis wagged his head from side to side, just once. "Wrong, Keith. There are no such circumstances. Every moment made available by the Almighty is there to be seized, whatever the situation may be. Seized with both hands and delivered to the members of the press upon whom we depend so very much. Do you have any idea of the sums Empire spends in newspaper advertising for our product nationwide, not to mention magazines of every description and radio to boot? Have you, Keith?"

"I imagine it's a pretty large sum."

"You imagine. The figure is *unimaginable*. The figure is vast beyond the realm of understanding by the man in the street. Such figures are for handling by those accustomed to sheer size, to wealth that would fill a treasure ship every week and sink it to the bottom of the sea. Huge figures, Keith, and you couldn't think fast enough to take back just a small portion of those enormous sums by mentioning the name of your employer, the title of your latest screen venture of which we're all so proud? This didn't even occur to you, Keith?"

"I'm afraid not."

"Then you'll be relieved to hear that I have arranged for a further interview, with an eye to the evening editions. Several representatives of the Los Angeles press will be at your office at noon precisely. Nigel and Gloria will also be there to lend spice to the occasion. Kindly telephone your wife, mmmm—"

"Myra."

"—and have her here at the appointed hour exactly. Between the four of you I expect to reap a considerable story. It has all the correct ingredients, Keith. Murder, criminal activity, a valuable asset . . . The stamp is worth how much?"

"Approximately eighty thousand."

"Amazing. Such a tiny piece of paper. And the final ingredient, Keith—glamour. Yes, I believe it isn't too late to extract the full publicity potential from such a meeting. Your wife is an attractive woman? It doesn't do to let someone suffer by comparison with Miss Gresham's outstanding loveliness. Comparisons such as that tend to make the woman in the street feel inadequate, and that may breed resentment against our movie stars. We need the female half of our audience, Keith."

"Surely they'd be more interested in Nigel, Mr. Margolis."

"A fallacy, Keith. A conclusion reached erroneously and hastily. Research has shown that women not only wish to fantasize about handsome men such as Nigel, they also fantasize that they, the women, are in fact the actress on the screen, the one in Nigel's arms. To accomplish this secondary fantasy they must never feel that the actress is so far above them as to make their fantasy absurd. That would make them resentful, would it not, Keith? And a resentful fan will watch some other movie starring an actress less spectacular in her beauteous appeal." Margolis picked up the *Times* again. "You said your wife was attractive?"

"I find her so, and others have concurred. You have her picture in front of you."

"Newspaper photographs are seldom flattering. All those tiny dots, they blur the features. She does appear presentable despite that. You yourself should have removed your glasses before allowing the photographers to take your picture. Those heavy frames, they dominate the features to an unnecessary degree. If the public can be persuaded that not only are our actors and actresses glamorous, but also our creative staff, think how that enhances the overall perception of the industry in general and Empire Productions in particular. You do see my point."

"Yes, I do."

Moody wondered if he should get Myra to sell the stamp so they could invest the money and live off the proceeds; then he could resign from Empire, leaving behind in the office of Marvin Margolis a scornful bon mot that would convey his true feelings for the man and everything he represented. Then again, Moody wanted to earn his own money; the stamp belonged to Myra. And he wanted to work with talented people whom he liked—Terry Blackwell, Nigel Lawson, and Gloria Gresham; it would be fun, and rewarding in more than the financial sense. He knew he shouldn't arbitrarily throw away the opportunity to write a movie that would almost certainly be successful. Moody wanted his name up on the silver screen for all the world to see. Pride could wait until the ego was satisfied.

"And a wonderful point it is, Mr. Margolis. So astutely made, and so very apropos."

"Thank you, Keith. The studio will accept your absence

from your office all day yesterday without loss of pay. You may go. Don't forget to call your wife."

"Thank you for reminding me."

Moody was unsure, as he closed the bronze doors behind him, that he had bested Marvin Margolis. Maybe his sense of having won some nameless contest was an illusion. Katherine Harrison was at her desk, attending to paperwork. She barely glanced at him as Moody walked by, saying, "You look most professional today, Miss Harrison."

MYRA WAS AT Moody's office by eleven forty-five, just as the first of the newspaper reporters were arriving. She and Moody told their tale once again, without embellishment, in effect repeating what they had told the San Diego press. There was no new angle on the incident to parlay into something fresh for page one; it was a waste of time, from Moody's perspective, but he understood that he and Myra were not the ones the newshounds had really come to interview. The true objects of interest arrived at 12:05, arms around each other's waist, smiles of happiness aimed at all concerned.

"Sorry we're late, chaps," Nigel said. "Had to attend to other matters, and time slipped away."

"Care to tell us what those other matters were, Mr. Lawson?" asked a leering reporter.

Nigel assumed a solemn expression. "A gentleman never tells."

The reporters laughed. Moody was not surprised that Nigel and Gloria appeared to have become lovers, although that impression was not necessarily correct; it might be, he warned himself, that the stars' apparent affection for each other was nothing more than a studio concoction, something prepared by the cynical strategists of the publicity department. But Gloria did seem to be in a carefree mood. She said, "And a lady never admits, fellers." The reporters laughed again.

The kidnapping of Myra Moody and the deaths of two men anxious to possess her Finland stamp were instantly forgotten. The subject of the moment became the smiling, well-dressed couple who ensconced themselves on Moody's office sofa (the "horizontal creative thinking enhancer") and proceeded to do what they did best—entertain. Moody and Myra watched with bemusement as the reporters made fools of themselves over nothing more substantial than charm and a pleasing appearance. Marvin Margolis had been right; this was the real news, a movie based on a best-seller, starring two of Hollywood's newest favorites. Moody winked at his wife, who rolled her eyes in return.

After the reporters had gone, Nigel bounded from the sofa and made retching sounds over Moody's wastepaper basket. "There, now I feel much better. Keith, old man, you haven't introduced me to your lovely wife."

"Myra, in case you hadn't worked it out for yourself, this fellow is Nigel Lawson, and this is Gloria Gresham."

Myra smiled. "Hello to you both. I'm not going to ask for your autograph, so don't worry. And now I'd like to eat lunch so I can get the taste of newsprint out of my mouth."

"God, me too," said Gloria. "Those guys with the note-pads are the limit. Did you hear that one with the big Adam's apple ask me if I was taking a weight-reduction course in the studio gym? The nerve! And I'd like to know who ratted on me. Say, why don't we all go over to the commissary and take a bite together. Myra, I want to hear from your lips exactly what it felt like to be tied up in a little room with a gun held to your head."

"Actually, nobody held a gun to my head, they just pointed

guns in my general direction. I didn't really think they'd kill me, even after they killed our dog."

"You've got balls, honey. Oops, didn't mean to say that. Nigel, you look weak from hunger. Let's eat, gang."

The lunch went well. Nigel and Gloria were both excellent raconteurs, with plenty of movieland stories to tell; Nigel's tended to stress the absurd and idiotic, while Gloria's were of a more earthy nature, consisting of gossip that would have made a scandal magazine editor salivate. Myra and Moody held up their own end of the conversation, and Myra recognized some old friends of hers at another table. After she explained to Gloria that she had once worked in Empire's research department, both women went across to the other table. Moody was impressed that Gloria Gresham didn't consider herself too good to talk with the studio rank and file.

"There's a woman who doesn't put on airs," he said, lighting cigarettes for himself and Nigel.

"Your wife, old man?"

"The same description would apply, but I meant Gloria."

"She's definitely one of the boys, no snobbery about her whatsoever. Damned good looking too, wouldn't you say, Keith?"

"I would, yes."

"Don't worry, I shan't breathe a word of your indiscretion to Myra."

"What indiscretion?" Moody remembered a word often used by one of the studio's older character actors, a Londoner who had specialized in blithering military types throughout the thirties. "Bollocks to you, Nigel."

"Bollocks indeed. Listen, old sport, have you had a chance to come up with that special bit of nonsense we were discussing the other day? I don't mean to rush you, and I do realize you've had quite a bit on your plate in the last forty-eight hours, what with kidnappings and coppers to the rescue and so forth, but I was wondering about it, you see. Had a chance to come up with anything?"

"You mean about Edward Traven and the reason he became a spy?"

"Exactly. Has inspiration struck at all? Muses pounding on the old noggin?"

"As a matter of fact, I did get an inkling of an idea before this thing about Myra's stamp swamped me. You'll appreciate that it's barely formed, not much thought out at all."

"Understood, fire away."

"Well, in the book, the reason Traven's able to pass himself off as a Kraut with such conviction is because he was raised in Germany, the English mother and German father, if you'll recall, but the parents were never discussed much, I mean they both died in a boating accident when Edward was just seventeen, after which he went back to England to live with his godfather, the very fellow who worked for the Secret Service and was able to get Edward into the spying game. At first I thought, well, obviously he's going to be a spy, with a godfather like that, but then, how did he overcome a natural tendency to still love the country that he grew up in, Germany, a place where he was happy until the accident took away his parents?"

"That struck me as well. It wasn't explained properly in the book. I suppose Jeffrey Hubbell, being a solid Brit, thought it was enough to say that young Eddie was born a Brit, so nothing further need be added. In the blood, so to speak. A Brit does what a Brit ought to do, and that's step forward to serve the crown, no doubts allowed, no second thoughts about king and country."

"Yes, and it obviously isn't enough, so what I thought of

was this: The reason Edward is fully prepared to spy against Germany, quite beside the fact that war's declared between the two nations, is because—he hated his father, the German."

"Not bad. Why does he hate him?"

"Because he treated the mother like dirt."

"Aha, classic Oedipus complex, made worse by actual justified loathing for the chap. Yes, that might work. . . . In the book the father's a businessman, but it might be a good idea to make him a military man, the kind who ended up swearing allegiance to revolting Adolf once the Nazis came to power."

"Yes, why not, but don't go talking about Oedipus complexes to Margolis, or he'll veto the entire subplot."

"Naturally. Boys who want to mount their mums aren't good hero material, not here at Empire Productions. MM wants his sex conventional, above the age of consent, and within the bonds of marriage, that's the word around here."

"Exactly. Are you happy with the idea?"

"I think it's a stroke of genius, old fruit. Little Eddie loves his mum and hates his Teutonic pater because of his harsh ways with mater. Gosh, here's a thought—let's suppose it was Edward who arranged the boating accident somehow, not knowing that the father would be accompanied at the last minute by the mother. A thing like that would scramble the kid's mind no end."

"It's a nice touch. He is motivated to spy against the Germans not only by national need and a very personalized hatred, but because he feels guilty about having been responsible for killing his mother. Could guilt be a motivating factor, do you think?"

Nigel stubbed out his half-smoked cigarette. "Don't see why not. It's all a bit involved, the why and the wherefore, psychologically speaking. Think you could put it all in a nutshell?"

"That isn't the problem. The trouble is, Margolis would

never allow anything so ambiguous. The nasty German father's one thing, but a murderous boy who accidentally kills his own mother is something else again. He wouldn't allow it. Margolis does read the final draft of every screenplay the studio produces. It's impossible to slip anything past him."

"Hmmm. Might be just as well to forget that bit, then, and stick with the original thought. Nasty dad and lovely mum meet untimely death together while punting on the Rhine or something, how about that?"

"I think it's best, from Empire's point of view, anyway."

"Jolly good. Just goes to show what can be accomplished by two intelligent fellows getting together without interference from the buggers who think they run things. You know, Keith, if *Traitor's Dawn* is a success, which I'm sure it will be, you and I should get together to make *Below the Salt*. Now, that's a project worth doing, for the psychological twists alone. Interested?"

"Certainly. The book didn't do at all well."

"Too subtle for the average reader, that's why, but the story gains instant commercial viability if yours truly says he wants to play the part, pardon the big head talking."

"No, you're right, that's the way things work in Hollywood. Of course, there's a problem with putting the story on the screen. In the book the brothers have two different names, so it's easy to keep the fact that they're actually one person from the reader because they can't see that Jason and Michael are the same man. That little trick won't work on the screen. Michael will be played by Nigel Lawson, and so will Jason."

"They're identical twins, not just ordinary brothers. That'll take care of that problem."

"That's clever, Nigel. Yes, that'd work."

"Don't suppose MM'd consent to give me double the salary to play both roles."

"Out of the question."

"Ahh, well. . . . By the way, have you got that stamp all safely squared away? What a fantastic thing to happen, inheriting something like that, even being kidnapped for the bloody thing."

"It's in a bank vault. It'll stay there until we decide what to do. Frankly, I'd like to get rid of it before anything else happens."

"Reputable bank? Burglar-proof, I hope."

"Syndicated Bank of Los Angeles. It's supposed to be the best."

"Just down the street from my hotel, I think, the Syndicated Bank. Big square place with pink brick?"

"That's it. Where are you staying?"

"The Wilshire. Not a bad place. MM tells me I need to buy a house in Beverly Hills like the other movie stars. I might, but I'm in no hurry. I'd have to go to all the bother of hiring gardeners and maids and cooks and whatnot, whereas all that's laid on at the hotel without my having to worry about a blessed thing. I'm a lazy bugger, truth be told. Pampering's all very fine if you don't have to worry about paying for it out of your own pocket. The studio's picking up the bill at the Wilshire."

"That's why Margolis wants you out of there and into a house."

"For which I pay the mortgage. No thanks, not till I get kicked out of my room. Ahh, here come the ladies."

Myra and Gloria returned, and the conversation was renewed over dessert.

All too soon, the party was broken up when Nigel and Gloria were obliged to meet their schedules elsewhere in the studio maze. Moody walked Myra back to the visitors' parking lot, passing between the towering walls of the soundstages, concrete chasms populated by every imaginable human type, vividly costumed.

"Keith, is that man supposed to be an ancient Roman? His wig's too long."

"He's an angel, I think. Stage nine is set up for *Heaven Calls*."

"Sounds a bit dismal. Does anyone pick up the phone and drop dead?"

"Actually it's a comedy. The hero has to fulfill several duties before being allowed into heaven, making a rich man give up his wealth, finding a happy home for an orphaned blind girl, that kind of thing."

"A laughing weepie?"

"It's a cross-genre concept."

"Keith, you sound like a studio executive."

"Please, I've just had lunch. Were you bowled over by the manly profile and roguish charm of Nigel Lawson?"

"No more so than you were smitten by the raffish sexiness of Gloria Gresham."

"Actually, they're both very nice people, and I suspect they're head over heels for each other."

"Actually, Keith, are you aware that just lately you've been saying 'actually' a lot? Is it the English influence of dreamy Nigel?"

"Actually, it might be."

They reached Myra's convertible. "You left the top down again," Moody scolded.

"It's a lovely day. I can't be bothered putting it up just to park."

"But it makes stealing the car so much easier this way."

"Keith, are you suggesting there are car thieves lurking on the Empire lot?"

"No, but . . . it's a habit you should get into."

Myra pecked his cheek. "Poor Keith, always worrying about something or other. Rich people shouldn't worry about a thing."

"We're not rich."

"Eighty grand isn't rich? Darling, what high standards you have."

"It should be invested wisely. I'm going to make plenty on this project, and the others that'll follow."

"I love to hear my hubby speak with confidence. It makes my nipples go all tweaky. Care to make love to me on that office sofa of yours?"

"Actually, I have a lot of work to do."

"Actually, I don't think I want to engage in lustful pursuits on the same square mile occupied by Marvin Margolis."

"You didn't always feel that way." Moody remembered the intense encounter between himself and Myra in his old office two years before.

"That was before he fired us both. He hasn't hired *me* back."

"Rich folk don't need jobs."

Myra opened her car door and stepped inside. "You're right. I'll just tootle on home and talk dirty with my stockbroker. And speaking of home, isn't it time we went back to our little love nest and left the Homeaway to those best suited there? If you're convinced this Kurt Flowerdew isn't going to harm you, I mean."

Moody had told Myra the night before of Kurt's visit to the hotel, and Moody's subsequent visit to the Gallagher farm to talk with Uncle Henry and assist in the burial of his dog. "I suppose we might as well. Today's Friday. Let's move back home tomorrow."

"Done." She started the engine.

"Myra . . . you left the key in the ignition?"

"I wouldn't want anyone to damage my lovely car trying to hot-wire it."

"For God's sake, Myra—"

"Toodle-oo."

She backed out, leaving Moody to fume helplessly.

When he arrived back at his office, Moody found a small business card on the floor near his desk. He picked it up.

THE KUMQUAT CLUB
The Right Place for the Right People

He'd never heard of it. The place was probably some downtown dive frequented by reporters, where they could get drunk, escape their wives and families, and talk about the scoops that got away. He dropped the card into his wastepaper basket and got back to work. Oddly enough, he was at the point, in the script's first few pages, of defining Edward Traven's English/German past; he'd discussed the matter with Nigel at exactly the right moment. Serendipity, thought Moody; this project is going to be a lucky one from start to finish.

Official approval of the scenario, which Moody had handed in on Wednesday afternoon, had not yet come back to him, but Moody knew it would and didn't want to waste time waiting for the front office to catch up with him. Marvin Margolis's approval would be virtually automatic. Traven's childhood had been skipped over, merely mentioned in passing, because Moody at the time of its composition had no clear idea what to place there, had only his own and Nigel's wish to insert something of significance, a clue to the boy who would become a man who would become a spy. Now Moody had that key to the character, and rather than inject it into the narrative as a flashback, he decided to begin the story with young Traven witnessing his father beating his mother, or rather, since such graphic stuff would never pass the censors, Traven would see the father push the mother into their bedroom and close the door, after which would come thumpings and stifled screams from the far side, while Edward clenched his fists in impotent rage.

Reviewing the scene, Moody liked what he had written. He wrote some more. By day's end he felt he knew and understood Edward Traven, and had conveyed that understanding to the page. Terry Blackwell and Nigel Lawson would project it onto the screen and into the minds of moviegoers everywhere. It made Moody feel just a little bit omnipotent. He liked that feeling, and smiled. Then he remembered his dog was dead, and the smile vanished. He found tears leaking from his eyes. Only a dog, he told himself. Bess was only a dog, and it was she who had been shot, not Myra. Moody knew he ought to feel grateful for that, and in fact he did, but the loss of Bess was still a terrible thing. "I'm a marshmallow," he said aloud. Here he was, writing about a man who risked his life by spying against the Nazis, a truly heroic character, probably not so very far removed from actual spies engaged at that very moment in bringing down the Third Reich, and what was Moody doing while the world waged war, country against country? He wept for his dog. Definitely unheroic, he concluded, then comforted himself somewhat with the additional thought that, after all, he was only a writer.

AFTER A MEAL in the hotel restaurant, Moody and Myra went up to their room, entering in time for Moody to snatch up the ringing telephone.

"Yes?"

"Mr. Moody?"

"Speaking."

"Front desk here, Mr. Moody."

He recognized the blasé joviality of Knobby the gnome.

"Yes, I thought it might be."

"How are you this fine evening, Mr. Moody?"

"I'm feeling fine. In the pink. Dapper and dandy. And yourself?"

"Thank you so much for asking, sir. I have a headache. Soon I'll take an aspirin, but not yet. I have a message to pass on before attending to my own needs."

"Really? I thought this was a personal call, just a cozy chat between the two of us."

"It could hardly be that, sir. You're a celebrity, a man whose picture has appeared in both the morning and evening editions. Congratulations, sir."

"Thank you. You did mention a message?"

"Ahh, yes, the message. I have it in my hand."

"Please read it to me while I digest my food."

"Have you been to the restaurant, sir? I thought I saw you and your charming wife strolling in that direction. I recommend the omelette to anyone who asks."

"We had lamb. The message?"

" 'Amanda dead. They won't let me have her. They said I signed a paper. Help me get her out.' The message is signed, 'Henry G.' Shall I repeat it, sir?"

"No. When did this message come in? Was it phoned, or is it a telegram?"

"It arrived by telephone at one o'clock this afternoon, sir."

"And is there some reason I wasn't handed the message when I walked into the hotel at five-thirty? And my wife came back earlier than that."

"I couldn't say, sir. Someone seems to have placed it under the registry book. That really shouldn't happen, but I point my finger at no one."

"That's very decent of you. Could you connect me with the operator for directory inquiries?"

"Immediately, sir, and it's certainly been a pleasure talking with you today."

"Likewise, I'm sure."

Moody's head was beginning to swim. If he wrote dialogue like this, it wouldn't be accepted in anything but a screwball comedy.

Myra asked, "Are you talking to that fool of a desk clerk?"

"Not so much talking as drawing blood from a stone. . . . Hello, Operator? I need the number of Henry Gallagher. He's probably listed in the Santa Clarita book. He lives on a farm just outside town, if that's any help. . . . Thank you, I'll wait."

"Flowerdew's uncle? What does he want?"

"Tell you in a minute. It's about Amanda. . . . Yes, please connect me."

"Amanda?"

"She's dead."

"Oh, no—"

"It's no surprise, let's face it. Eighty-odd years old. . . . Hello, Henry? I got your message at last."

Gallagher's voice was high-pitched, almost frantic by comparison with his usual laconic style.

"They won't let me have her, said I signed her body away with that burial paper. You warned me, but I never did lift a finger to find out what it was I went and signed, so now they're saying to me I can't have her and it's all legal what they want to do, which they won't say what it is, so I guess you're right about her being stuffed for the Florida freak show place. Mr. Moody, I just plain don't know what to do."

"Do you have a family lawyer?"

"Nope, don't like lawyers, doctors neither. It won't be a dignified way to go."

"No, it won't. Have you been to Morning Glory to see the body in the coffin?"

"Nope. I won't go there unless it's with a shotgun to make them give her to me."

"I really don't advise that, Henry."

"Kurt, he'd help me. He's mad as blazes about this."

"Keep him away from Morning Glory, Henry, and stay away yourself if you're that angry. Violence won't get her back. We have to think about this, find a way of getting around the document you signed."

"Don't know how. Damn that Yaddigan woman! She's got a heart cold and hard as a cash register."

"I'll think of something, Henry. Leave it to me."

"Think you can figure out a way?"

"I'm sure I can. Try not to worry."

"You figure out a way, and you got me for a friend forever."

"Thank you, Henry. I'll be in touch. Good-bye."

He hung up the phone and informed Myra of whatever aspect of Mrs. Yaddigan's perfidy she hadn't already guessed at from Moody's end of the conversation.

"That bitch! It's too awful to think about. That nice old lady, behind glass, filled with sawdust—"

"I think they have more sophisticated methods of preservation nowadays."

"We can't allow it to happen. Who do we know who knows a big lawyer?"

"I doubt that a lawyer, even a big one, could do anything. Yaddigan's a businesswoman. She didn't get to run a place like Morning Glory without knowing how to cover herself legally.

The paper Henry signed is probably as watertight as Yaddigan could make it. There has to be another way—"

He suddenly snapped his fingers.

Myra said, "Keith, a lightbulb has begun to glow above your head—"

"Very funny. I need to talk to Lester Montgomery."

"Who on earth is Lester Montgomery?"

"One of the studio drivers. He's the one that picked me up in a limousine on Monday. God, that was just four days ago. . . . Do you get the impression we're living a rather hectic life?"

"It's hardly been a dawdle, lately. Why do you need a driver?"

"Tell you in a minute. First I need to talk to Nigel." Moody picked up the phone. "Front desk? Get me the Wilshire Hotel."

"Mr. Moody, sir. How good to hear your voice again. Are you leaving us for the more refined air of the Wilshire?"

"No, I'm not, I just want to talk to someone who's staying there."

"I'm so glad to hear that, sir. We here at the Homeaway so seldom have a celebrity as our guest. We certainly wouldn't want to see you depart, sir, especially to the Wilshire, which already has any number of celebrities staying there."

"I'm not moving to the Wilshire. I'm moving out, that is, my wife and I are moving out tomorrow, but not to the Wilshire."

"Moving out, sir? Sir!"

"I'm sorry, but that's just how it is. The Wilshire Hotel, please."

"Is it the confusion over the messages, sir? I'll accept full responsibility, if that will change your mind, sir, even though it really wasn't me who kept putting them in the wrong place. Would an apology from the manager help, sir?"

"No, just get me the number, please."

"Sir—" Knobby's voice was near to breaking. "Sir—it'll mean my job if you go."

"Don't be absurd. Guests come and go all the time here. My wife and I are going home, that's all."

"You won't lodge any complaint with the management? Nothing about the messages, sir? They won't go astray again, I promise."

"I have no intention of informing the management about anything. Now will you kindly connect me with the Wilshire?"

"Yes, sir. Thank you, sir. Sir?"

"What is it?"

"Who are you calling at the Wilshire, sir? I'm just curious."

"That's for the Wilshire's front desk, Knobby, not for you."

There was a brief silence on the line.

"Who told you to call me that? Who said to call me that name? That isn't my name. My name is Alfred. It was the elevator boy, wasn't it? He calls me that. Well, I don't like it. Nobody has the right to call me by anything but Alfred. I think I'm within my rights in wanting that."

"Excuse me, it just slipped out—"

"A name I don't like, a nickname—no one has the right to call me that. It's offensive and rude. I won't put up with it, not even from a guest."

"I apologize . . . Alfred."

"One moment."

The next voice Moody heard was female. "Wilshire Hotel. How may I help you?"

"Nigel Lawson, please."

"Whom shall I say is calling, sir?"

"Who."

"Please wait."

"No, just a minute—I didn't mean my name is Who. I was commenting on your grammar. . . . Hello?"

Moody tapped his knuckles against the phone stand with impatience.

"I'm sorry, sir, but Mr. Lawson has no knowledge of a Mr. Who."

"You misunderstood me. My name is not Who, What, or Why. My name is Moody, and Mr. Lawson definitely knows me."

"Please wait."

Myra lit a cigarette for Moody and passed it to him. "Darling, you've gone all red in the face. Are you listening to an obscene call?"

"I'm listening to nothing at the moment—"

"Your party is connected, sir."

"Keith, are you playing silly buggers? Who's Whom?"

"It's a mixup, my fault, pedantic nature and all that—" Moody stopped, aware that he was talking like Lawson. "Umm . . . listen, Nigel, I have a favor to ask."

"Ask away, old bean."

"Actually, it's more of a favor for a friend of mine."

Myra whispered, "You're saying 'actually' again."

Moody waved her away. "It's a fairly complicated story, Nigel. Would it be too much of a bother if I came around and had a bit of a chat about it?"

"Not at all. What's the nature of the favor?"

"It's . . . a challenge. That's all I can say."

"Intriguing. Shall we say half an hour?"

"Thanks, Nigel."

As he hung up, the phone rang. Moody lifted the receiver again.

"Alfred Oglethorpe Maynes Junior," said Knobby, still aggrieved.

The phone clicked, and Moody set it down.

"We're definitely leaving tomorrow, after we take care of this other business."

"Hooray! What other business?"

"Medical matters," said Moody, picking up the phone yet again. "Hello. Alfred? I need a number in Maywood for Lester Montgomery."

"I believe you have a telephone book in your room, sir."

"Yes, I do, but I still have to go through you for an outside line, Alfred. I think pleasing the guests is part of a desk clerk's duties."

"If you insist."

"I'm afraid I do, Alfred. I just hate thumbing through the phone book, don't you?"

"Not as much as I dislike impertinence."

"Oh, I agree."

"What was the name again? Montgomery?"

"Lester Montgomery, in Maywood."

"I have the number. I'm dialing now."

"Thank you, Alfred."

The line burred several times, then the phone was picked up at the other end.

ester and Marty Montgomery drove into the Wilshire
Hotel's parking lot at 8:44. Moody and Nigel Lawson were
waiting. They squeezed into the front seat, and the Cadillac
hearse with *Blakiston's Fine Funerals* painted on the doors re-
joined the evening traffic on Wilshire Boulevard.

"Mr. Moody, is that you there?"

Moody was wearing a false beard artfully applied by Nigel.

"It's me, Lester. I'm wearing it for twenty-four hours to
repay a bet I lost. It comes off tomorrow."

"Yeah? Hey, that's better than losing real money. I should
make bets like that."

"Don't be too sure. It itches. I even have to shower in it.
Lester, allow me to introduce you to my good friend Nigel
Lawson. I call him my good friend even though it's him I lost
the bet to."

"Hi there, Mr. Lawson. I'm Lester, and this is my brother
Marty. I guess Mr. Moody, I mean Keith, he already told you
the names."

"Yes, he did. It's a pleasure to meet you both."

Marty Montgomery turned around to stare at the actor.

"You're really him," he said. Marty had the same solid build as his brother, and an identical bristling haircut. "I saw you in that movie that time, what was that called?"

"I'm not sure," said Nigel. "Can you be more specific?"

"Yeah, it was that one where you had this dame crawling all over you, some English picture I saw a couple years back now."

"You're probably referring to *An Affair of the Heart.* Ring any bells?"

"Yeah, that's the one, I think. I had this date with me, she cried and cried. It was amazing how she cried. Me, I didn't cry. That was a dame's movie, yeah?"

"I'd say so. Lots of emotion, not a great deal of action."

"You can say that again. I fell asleep a couple times, then she wakes me up with the crying again, y'know?"

"That must have been very annoying."

"You said it. That's very annoying when that happens."

Lester broke in. "So where are we headed, Keith?"

"Pasadena. I'll give you directions when we get there."

"Okey-dokey."

Nigel looked at Moody and went startlingly cross-eyed for a few seconds. Moody raised his eyebrows and maintained a straight face.

Lester went on, "So it's your aunt or someone there, huh?"

"Aunt Amanda. Yes, she's on display at the moment, but we need to remove her from the old folks' home tonight. They won't allow her to stay there another day, something to do with the rules and regulations. That's when I thought of Marty and his hearse."

"It ain't mine," Marty said. "It's the boss's, but I got the use of it at night, even if he don't know about it."

"So I've heard."

Lester and Marty exchanged knowing chuckles.

Marty asked Nigel, "How come you're here, then?"

"Oh, I'm a friend of the family. Keith was good enough to invite me along for the ride, so to speak."

"I never heard of an old folks' home that throws the body out at night. These people must be real assholes."

"Oh, they are. Morning Glory Retirement Home, ever heard of it?"

"Sure. Dickensen Brothers, they got the business at that joint, I think. They're our competition. I'd like to see their faces when they get told Blakiston's got the stiff insteada them—Say, Keith, I didn't mean to be disrespectable or nothing."

"No harm done, Marty, but I wouldn't let Dickensen's know about this, otherwise your boss might be informed of your unauthorized nocturnal perambulations and be very annoyed."

"He what?"

"He'll find out you took the hearse at night. No more Caddy dates with hanky-panky in the back there."

"Oh, yeah, you're right. So I won't tell Dickensen's. Too bad. I woulda liked to seen their faces."

The hearse arrived at the Morning Glory Retirement Home a little before nine o'clock and drew up in a shower of gravel outside the front entrance. Nigel and Moody got out and stretched for a moment before going inside the building and approaching the reception desk. Moody had hoped to find Nora Worth in the foyer, but her petite form was nowhere to be seen. He would have to deal with Mrs. Yaddigan, and hope the beard and his spare pair of glasses would fool her. There was no one behind the desk, and Moody recalled that visiting hour was long past. He banged his palm against the bell before him and listened while its echo traveled around the foyer and disappeared up the grand staircase.

"Posh-looking place," Nigel commented.

Footsteps could be heard approaching along the upper corridor, beyond the balustrade, then descending the stairs. As she came into view, Moody was relieved to see that it was Nora Worth. She appeared considerably agitated.

"Excuse me," she said, drawing near, "but visiting hours are over."

"This is an affair of business," Moody said, trying not to chew his whiskers.

"Business?" Miss Worth pushed the heavy glasses farther up onto the bridge of her nose. "I don't understand."

"Concerning the late Miss Flowerdew."

"Miss Flowerdew?"

"Was our telegram not delivered this afternoon? I represent Empire Productions."

"There was no telegram that I'm aware of," said Miss Worth. "Empire Productions? I really don't quite know what it is you're saying, Mr.—"

"Wolfgang Hufnagel, ma'am, motion picture director. Maybe you've heard of me?"

"No, I—I'm afraid I haven't."

"But no doubt you've heard of my associate, Nigel Lawson. Nigel, don't just stand there pretending to be shy, say hello to Miss Worth."

"Good evening," said Nigel, in his most honeyed tones. "A pleasure to meet you."

"Nigel Lawson? Oh—"

Clearly Miss Worth was a moviegoer. She dragged her eyes from the Englishman and asked Moody, "But how did you know my name, Mr. Hufnagel?"

Moody squirmed behind his beard; how could he have been so careless?

"Your name pin, Miss Worth."

"But I'm . . . I'm not wearing a name pin, Mr. Hufnagel."

"Never mind. Our scout described you perfectly."

"Scout? This is really most confusing . . ."

"Talent scout, Miss Worth. He was here yesterday evening, visiting with an elderly family member, and heard about the death of Miss Flowerdew and the . . . shall we say, unusual circumstances of her . . . how shall I put it . . . of her appearance? Empire Productions has a pressing need of such an unusual . . . mmm . . . person."

"But Miss Flowerdew only died this morning."

"Precisely. Our scout heard of her imminent demise, and informed us. May we see the body of the deceased? It's still here, I hope."

"Yes, in the Chapel of Eternal Repose . . . but this is all so irregular."

Nigel stepped closer to Nora Worth, smiling like a crocodile. "Dear Miss Worth, the fact is, Empire has need of a woman such as the late Miss Flowerdew for a role in my next film, which happens to be a horror picture titled *They Came in Darkness*. Miss Flowerdew would play a nonspeaking role, naturally."

"You'd actually place her . . . in the picture?"

"Yes, as the matriarch of a peculiar clan of extremely backward types, cretins and morons for the most part, a family that lives deep in the woods, called the Margolises. Miss Flowerdew would simply be placed at the head of the family table and not be required to say a word. The Margolises are vicious brutes of the lowest order, quite grotesque, really, and their utter repulsiveness is manifested by the family curse of facial hair, simply oodles of the stuff, as exemplified by Miss Flowerdew. I do hope I've made myself clear, Miss Worth."

"I . . . yes, I think so. You want to . . . borrow Miss Flowerdew?"

"For just a day or two, my dear Miss Worth."

"I don't know . . . I should really talk with Mrs. Yaddigan about this. It's a most unusual request."

"Is Mrs. Yaddigan on the premises?" asked Moody, his sphincter tightening.

"Not at present. She left this evening to meet with a gentleman from Florida, a business meeting."

"She's gone to Florida?" Moody asked, feeling a weight lift from his shoulders.

"No, just to the gentleman's hotel—" She blushed a deep and instantaneous shade of beetroot. "I mean to say, from where they'll proceed to a restaurant to discuss their business."

"And at what time will she return?"

"Oh, not until late, I was told. Could you possibly wait?"

Moody twitched his whiskers. "Miss Worth, Empire Productions simply cannot wait another hour. The fact is, we're shooting this picture at night, using an old mansion set used by another crew for an entirely different production through the day, and the set is to be dismantled next Tuesday to make room for yet another production. You can see that time is of the essence."

"Yes, but—"

"Miss Worth," Nigel murmured, "if you were to find it in your capacious heart to assist us in our hour of need, I would offer to escort you to the premiere of *They Came in Darkness*. A Hollywood premiere, Miss Worth, of unprecedented proportions, where you and I will mingle with the stars and dine among them too, followed by dancing till dawn at one of Hollywood's most famous nightspots, several of them in fact. Just you and I, Miss Worth, dancing the night away like . . . lovers."

"Mr. Lawson . . . I . . ."

Moody said, "Empire Productions will pay to Morning

Glory Retirement Home the sum of five thousand dollars, for the use of Miss Flowerdew until Tuesday, or the check can be made out to Mrs. Yaddigan personally."

"Tuesday? I'm afraid Miss Flowerdew hasn't yet been . . . prepared. She's on display for the benefit of mourners, but only for a short time, you see, until she can be—"

"Embalmed?" Moody prompted.

"Yes, so you wouldn't actually be allowed to keep her until Tuesday because of . . . because it wouldn't be . . . very nice for all concerned."

"We appreciate what you're saying, Miss Worth, and that makes it imperative that we take Miss Flowerdew with us tonight, so that we have sufficient time for setting up the shots she'll appear in as soon as possible."

"I just don't know—"

"Is it possible to communicate with Mrs. Yaddigan?"

"No, she left strict orders not to be disturbed. Oh, dear—"

"I'll make it six thousand dollars, Miss Worth, plus an extra thousand for yourself for the inconvenience we're imposing upon you. No, make that two thousand, but we must have an immediate decision, as I'm sure you'll understand."

"Yes, but—"

Nora Worth looked from Nigel to Moody and back again. "Could I . . . may I . . . have your autograph?"

"With pleasure, Miss Worth, and I shall also send to you a picture of myself, likewise autographed, for your quick thinking in this important matter. I think Empire can be relied upon to provide a block of tickets also to provide a free viewing for Miss Worth and all her friends and family, isn't that so, Wolfgang?"

"Certainly. Where is Miss Flowerdew at the present time, Miss Worth?"

"This way. You're absolutely sure you need to take her with you tonight?"

"Absolutely sure. We'll return her on Sunday morning at the very latest, I assure you, and in between takes on our soundstage we'll make sure the . . . uh . . . receptacle is kept cool with ice and electric fans. Miss Flowerdew will be returned to your care as fresh as when she left. Mrs. Yaddigan will also be given a mention in the closing credits of the picture, I want you to be sure and tell her that."

"She'll be thrilled, I know," said Miss Worth, sounding less than sure of her own words.

She led the men to a small room draped in black velvet, in the center of which stood a bier similarly draped. Reposing on top of this was a walnut casket, the upper half of its curved lid raised to display the fragile and hirsute corpse within. Moody and Nigel approached with hushed reverence and stared down at the tiny woman ensconced within the plush satin lining. Her carefully brushed facial hair gave her the appearance of a Pekingese asleep on its favorite cushion. "Perfect," said Moody. "We were not misinformed. Miss Flowerdew meets all specifications and qualifications for the job . . . the role assigned her. Now, as for removing her to the vehicle outside, the . . . um . . . casket of the deceased appears to be quite heavy."

"Oh, that isn't a problem at all," Miss Worth assured him. She raised the velvet drapery to reveal a sturdy metal platform on castors beneath. "Mrs. Yaddigan had this specially made to assist our usual funeral company with their work."

"Mrs. Yaddigan clearly is a woman of tremendous foresight. This makes things much easier. No need to bring in our assistants, I think, Nigel, we can take care of this all by ourselves."

"It would be an honor and a privilege," agreed Nigel. "Shall we begin?"

The casket lid was gently closed, then the velvet drapes were lifted clear of the floor and thrown over the polished lid to keep them clear of the castors. Nigel and Moody got behind the head of the casket carrier and began to push. After some initial resistance it began to move, the rubber wheels squeaking a little as they proceeded across the chapel and turned, with the assistance of Miss Worth, into the corridor and headed back toward the foyer. Moody trudged on, his soles slipping a little on the smooth parquet flooring. Under his breath, Nigel began singing, "Hi ho, hi ho, it's off to work we go," before Moody jabbed him with an elbow to make him stop.

Miss Worth held open the front doors as they maneuvered the casket carrier through and began easing it down the wheelchair ramp outside, holding its considerable weight back before it could begin to escape from them. The front wheels met the driveway's gravel, slowing progress, and when the rear wheels also sank into the loose stones, the carrier came to a halt. By then Lester and Marty were aware of developments, and left the hearse to assist in pushing the carrier across the intervening distance to the Cadillac's yawning rear doors. The casket was slid off the carrier and into the hearse in one smooth movement. Marty closed the doors. Moody and Nigel were breathing a little deeper than usual.

"Thank you so much for your assistance, Miss Worth. You've done an enormous service for Empire Productions."

"Yes, and the check . . . checks? For Mrs. Yaddigan and . . . me?"

"Company policy forbids the issuing of checks by anyone but the chief accountant," said Moody. "However, I am able to provide an IOU stating the sums concerned, signed by myself. Simply present this to the studio, and a check will be instantly forthcoming."

Miss Worth appeared dissatisfied with this, but she said nothing as Moody took from his jacket a sheet of paper bearing the Empire Productions letterhead. He wrote:

Received from Morning Glory Retirement Home one guest (deceased) on loan for a period not to exceed thirty-six hours. Monies owing: $6,000 for Mrs. . . .

"May I ask your employer's Christian name?"
"Hortense."

Hortense Yaddigan, proprietor, and $2,000 for her assistant, Nora Worth. Above sums to be issued on presentation of this document to Empire Productions, Financial Division. Wolfgang Hufnagel.

Moody dated the sheet and handed it to Miss Worth. She scanned it with some trepidation, but seemed to accept it as genuine.

"You'll be sure to bring Miss Flowerdew back Sunday morning," she said.

"You have my personal guarantee, or my name isn't Wolfgang Hufnagel."

"I do wish Mrs. Yaddigan had been here—"

"You conducted yourself according to the circumstances, Miss Worth. I'm sure Mrs. Yaddigan will approve. The sums involved are considerable, after all."

"Yes, you've been more than generous."

"And now, good-bye. Every minute is precious in the world of motion pictures. Nigel, do you have anything further to add?"

Nigel took the small and rather moist hand of Nora Worth and brought it to his lips. "Miss Worth, you are without doubt a woman among women. I look forward to our assignation . . . excuse me, our appointment together at the premiere of *They Came in Darkness.* Until then, I shall remember your face, your smile, your cooperation in this delicate matter. Au revoir, mademoiselle. Your dreams shall be my dreams."

Miss Worth appeared to be annoyed by such blatantly insincere wooing. Nigel seemed a little taken aback; Moody had the impression he had expected Miss Worth to swoon into his arms. Instead, she asked, "Where's my autograph?" in a slightly peeved voice.

Nigel patted his jacket pockets. "Dash it all, I seem to have come out minus quill and parchment."

Moody was about to offer another sheet of Empire stationery, but Nora Worth delved into the pocket of her cardigan and produced a business card, which she turned over and presented to Nigel. "This will do. I don't need a dedication."

"There's hardly room for one," said Nigel, sounding a little put out.

He scribbled his name and handed back the business card. "With my very best wishes," he said, smiling stiffly. His expression hardened as Miss Worth tilted the card toward the available moonlight to check what was written there. "It's very difficult to read," she said, squinting through her glasses.

Nigel responded, "Therefore difficult to forge, my dear."

"We really have to go," Moody reminded him.

"Good-bye, Miss Worth, and always remember—all the world's a stage."

Moody and Nigel crammed themselves into the front seat of the hearse, and Marty Montgomery started the engine. Nigel gave their victim a cheery wave as they departed. The Cadillac accelerated around the driveway's curve, paused at the exit from Morning Glory, then was launched onto the street with much squealing of tires and a noticeable bump from the rear. Moody, attempting to remove his gummed beard, lurched sideways against Nigel.

"That coffin there," Marty said, "it's one heavy bastard.

This baby, she's got an extra leaf in her springs to handle the stiff boxes, but that one there, that's heavy all right."

Lester said, "I thought you had 'em put in the extra leaf to handle all the nighttime canoodling that goes on back there."

"Comes in handy for that too," Marty acknowledged with a leer. "Okay, gents, where to now?"

"Alhambra. Miss Flowerdew will be staying at my place for the moment."

"She been gutted and stitched?" asked Marty.

"No, she only died this morning."

"They didn't scoop her guts yet? Hey, you better have a big refrigerator, Keith, know what I mean? That little lady back there, pretty soon she's gonna puff up and relieve herself inside that box so bad the lid'll pop. You don't got no better plan?"

"Uh . . . no. The object was simply to return Miss Flowerdew to her family."

"Okay, where they living? You let them handle a dead lady."

"That won't be . . . convenient, I'm afraid. The body has to be kept somewhere else until a decision can be made about what to do with it. They don't want a conventional funeral."

"You take it from me," Marty said, taking a corner at high speed, "there's only three things you can do with a stiff—bury it, burn it, or sink it. You better start figuring."

"Thanks for the advice."

"Don't mention it. You got the hundred on you personally?"

"Right here," said Moody, patting his pocket.

Lester said, "Good wages for a couple hours' work."

"Yeah," agreed Marty. "Listen, Keith, I don't do no spadework, and setting fire to the problem, that's risky inside the city limits, but if you decide to sink her, I know how."

"Uncle Reuben!" declared Lester. "He's got this boat, this

fishing boat down at Long Beach Marina. You slip him some dough, he's gonna play ball, I bet. He'd take you out to international waters anytime and slip that box over the side so nobody'd ever know, I mean, if you didn't want nobody knowing."

"I'll bear it in mind," said Moody.

"We might set it ablaze first," said Nigel. "The casket, I mean, and watch it burn down to the waterline. A Viking funeral! I must say I like that idea."

"You put that thing in the water," cautioned Marty, "and it's gonna go down like a stone, believe me. Besides, Uncle Reuben, he wouldn't wanna be fooling with no fires on his boat. Sailors and fishermen, they hate fires except on land, you know?"

The matter was left unresolved; the means of disposal would in any case be determined by Henry Gallagher. When they reached Moody's home in Alhambra, Myra's car was parked outside, and the living room lights were on. The hearse was backed into the driveway, its rear toward the porch for easier unloading of the cargo. Lester and Marty, assisted by Nigel and Moody, wrestled the casket out of the Cadillac and up the front steps to the door, which Myra held open. All four men were grunting with strain by the time Amanda Flowerdew's wooden bed for the ages was deposited on the living room table. Myra had wanted it placed on the floor, but Marty assured her it couldn't be picked up again from such a position. "You'll never get your fingers under it, see, plus you'll bust a gut lifting this thing from ground level. On the table is best. Not so far to lift it, and the ends poke over the edge for grabbing hold of, see what I mean?"

Myra saw, and the casket was put where Marty wanted it. Myra made sure the drapes were tightly closed; anyone peering through the front window from the street couldn't help but notice the table's unusual burden. Moody handed over one hundred dollars and was reminded again of the probable availability of Uncle Reuben's boat. Lester and Marty departed, and Myra poured drinks from a prepared pitcher of martinis.

"Of course, we're quite insane for doing this," she said, handing Nigel and Moody their drinks. Both drained their glasses before replying.

"I agree," said Nigel.

"More," said Moody, extending his glass.

"When are you going to tell Mr. Gallagher?"

"As soon as my whistle has been thoroughly wetted."

Downing his second drink, Moody went into the kitchen to make the call, leaving Nigel and Myra talking together. He waited, and the phone was picked up.

"Who's that?" was Henry Gallagher's unconventional response.

"Henry, it's Keith Moody. I have Amanda, Henry."

"You what?"

"I have her right here in my house. You remember the house you tailed me from to the Homeaway Hotel when Myra and I moved out? That place. She's here in the living room, large as life." Moody wanted to kick himself for that last phrase.

"Who's there? Myra?"

"No, Henry—Amanda. We have the body of Amanda Flowerdew in our living room. This is not a joke."

"The hell you say. How'd that happen?"

"I stole her for you, Henry, with the help of a good friend."

"Stole her? Outta that Morning Glory place?"

"Yes, sir."

"Got her there right now, you say?"

"Right here."

There was a lengthy silence, then Moody was asked, "What you gonna do with her, son?"

"That's up to you, Henry. You didn't want her to be exhibited in Florida, so I went and . . . took her for you. You have to decide what to do now."

"Hell's bells. This is a real thing you're telling me you went and done?"

"I wouldn't lie to you, Henry. She's here."

"Maybe I better get down there and see for myself."

"We'll be waiting."

Moody hung up and returned to the living room. The pitcher of martinis was already almost empty, and Nigel was giving his version of the night's events to Myra, who was laughing. She poured herself another drink and asked, "What are you two going to do when Mrs. Yaddigan attempts to collect from Empire?"

"Deny everything," said Nigel.

"And keep on denying it," said Moody.

"But you weren't disguised, Nigel, in fact you gave your name."

"That wasn't me, that was some outrageous impostor! How dare the bounder pass himself off as me! I'm infuriated by the cheek of the fellow!"

"Excellent performance," Moody commented. "I advise you to practice it often. By the time the police are involved, you'll be completely convincing."

"I say, old man old fruit old sport, didn't you find me convincing from the start? I must be losing my touch."

"Miss Worth wasn't convinced by your Latin lover routine either. I thought she was going to swat you when you kissed her hand."

"Miss Worth is that rare creature, the female impervious to my charms. She seemed pretty keen to have my autograph, though, did you notice?"

"Probably wants to sell it for fifty cents," said Myra.

"You two are hard on a chap," Nigel protested. "Any chance for more of this delicious stuff?" He thrust the empty pitcher away from himself. Myra picked it up and went to the kitchen. Nigel began rummaging in his breast pocket. "Actually," he said, "the estimable Miss Worth was in such a rush to have my jolly old autograph she gave me two bits of cardboard or whatever it is. I didn't want to embarrass her by pointing that out. Gentleman, you see, avoiding the awkward moment with a little sleight of hand. Here we are." He pulled a business card from his pocket, turned it over to read the printed side, then tossed it onto the small portion of table not occupied by the casket. "Can't win 'em all," he said, doing his best impression of philosophical resignation.

WHEN HENRY GALLAGHER arrived at 11:27, he had Kurt Flowerdew with him. They raised the half lid and peered into the casket at Amanda. "More than a little family resemblance there," Nigel whispered to Myra, and was given a kick in the shins.

"She looks like she's asleep," said Kurt, whispering also, as if not wanting to risk waking Amanda.

"She's dead, though," Henry assured him. "Now what do we do?"

"Dignity," Moody reminded him. "She has to be disposed of with dignity. And I'm told it needs to happen fairly soon, for obvious reasons."

"Dignity," mused Henry. "Hmmm."

Kurt was staring at Nigel. "I seen you before."

"Possibly," admitted Nigel. " Are you a cinemagoer?"

"Huh?"

"Do you ever attend the movies?"

"Oh, sure. Everybody does."

"Then that is undoubtedly where you saw me."

Kurt snorted. "How the hell could I do that? It's dark in there."

He turned away, unwilling to waste time with a fool. Nigel gave Myra a look of barely restrained amusement. She ignored this and said, "What kind of burial sites do you have on your farm, Mr. Gallagher?"

"I got plenty, all over the place, nice ones, some of them, under a nice tree maybe, only I can't bury her there."

"Why not?"

"Two reasons. Number one, the police, they'll come looking, and maybe see where there's been some digging and make me dig it up, and number two, I already buried my dog out behind the barn, and Amanda needs more than just what got done for the dog. She's a human, even if she didn't look like it, and I don't say that with disrespect or anything. She just deserves better than the dog got, is all I'm saying."

"I agree," said Moody. "Henry, were you ever in the Navy?"

"Nope. Neither was Amanda."

"Have you ever seen a movie where they had a burial at sea?"

"I saw *Mutiny on the Bounty*. Didn't they have a sea burial in that? Maybe it was another sailor movie."

"Would something like that be appropriate for Amanda, do you think?"

"Well, I don't know. She sailed on the sea a few times, going over there to Europe and them places. Maybe it'd be all right. She never did say if she liked to be on the ocean."

"I don't think we have a lot of choice in the matter," Moody urged. "I happen to know of someone with a boat. I'm told that the owner will help us give Amanda a sea burial. Would you consider that, Henry?"

"I reckon. It's gonna have to be a big boat. That coffin, it's real big and heavy."

"It's a fishing boat, quite big enough for the job."

"Kurt, what do you think?"

"Uncle Henry, I wanna go on the boat. I was never on a boat before! Let's do that with the boat."

"All right, then." Henry nodded his head several times in agreement with himself.

"Excuse me while I make a phone call," said Moody, heading for the kitchen.

He dialed Lester's number. An angry woman answered. "Well?"

"Uh . . . is Lester there, please?"

"It's late!"

"This is an emergency. Tell him it's Keith."

Moody heard a wrangling argument for several seconds, then Lester came on the line.

"Hello?"

"Lester, it's Keith. Is that offer of your uncle's boat still good?"

"You mean tonight?"

"Well . . . yes."

"Jeez, Keith, I dunno. I didn't talk to him yet."

"Lester, there's another hundred in it for you and Marty, and two hundred for your uncle, but it has to happen tonight. Can you have Marty come back here with the hearse?"

"No can do. Marty, he crashed the Caddy ten minutes after we left your place, ran it into some guy's car at a cross street. He was going too fast and didn't wanna stop for the yellow light, then this other car comes across and *Wham!* We bailed outta there fast and run off. We only just got home a little while ago. But the hearse, that's a wreck. Blakiston's is gonna figure someone took it for a joyride, I hope. Marty, he's real worried, so him and the Caddy, they're outta the picture."

"I understand. Call up your uncle anyway, would you, Lester? I'll figure out a way to get the goods down to the wharf. Call me back when you have an answer."

"Will do, Keith. Uh . . . the hundred, that's all mine? With Marty outta the picture?"

"Certainly, but it all has to happen quickly."

"I'm gonna call Reuben right now."

Moody returned to the living room. "Is everything all right?" Myra asked.

"Yes and no. I'm waiting to hear about the boat's availability, but we can't use the hearse again. Marty crashed it. That means Amanda will have to be removed from the casket and transported by car to the boat."

Looks were exchanged all around the room. "Well, I just don't know about that," said Henry. "She's all parceled up in there nice and peaceful. I don't know as I'd care to take her out again. That's a nice coffin, nice wood. I'd like to think that's what she'll be in when she goes under the water. Damn! If I had've known, I would've brung the truck, not my car. She'd fit in the back of that all right."

"May I make a suggestion?" said Nigel. "The question has come down to this—which car of those available will be used. It's as simple as that."

"Where are you from?" Kurt asked. "You don't talk like everyone else."

"North London, old man. Finsbury Park. Heard of it?"

"No. "

"Thought not."

"And I'm not old," said Kurt. "I'm twenty-two."

"Congratulations."

"There are five of us," said Myra, "six, including Amanda. We'll take Keith's car and mine so we can all fit."

"Might as well go ahead and get Amanda loaded up," said Moody.

"We haven't heard about the boat yet," Nigel said.

"Yes, but . . . I'm sure it'll be all right, and frankly, I'd rather be doing something than standing around waiting for the phone to ring."

As if on cue, the phone rang. Moody lifted the living room receiver.

"Yes?"

"It's me, Lester. It's okay with Reuben about the boat."

"I'm relieved to hear it."

"Only he wants five hundred, not two. He says it's very illegal, what you wanna do, so it's five, to cover the risk and all. That okay with you?"

"Uh . . . I suppose it'll have to be. Where do we meet?"

"Long Beach Marina, slip number forty-seven. The boat's called *Angela*."

"We'll be there as soon as we can."

"How about that big problem you got there?"

"Oh, we've decided to lighten the burden for purposes of transportation, if you see what I mean."

"No box, just the stiff, huh?"

"Exactly."

"See you there," said Lester, and hung up.

Myra drove with Nigel beside her and Amanda Flowerdew propped up in the backseat. Moody was treated to the unusual sight of his wife putting up the top on her convertible, a practical necessity, given Amanda's similarity to a werewolf. Stiffened by rigor mortis, the body leaned across the backseat like a small totem pole. Henry and Kurt rode with Moody in his Ford, and both cars stayed within sight of each other all the way to the Pacific. By then it was almost one o'clock. Lester Montgomery had stationed himself beneath a streetlight near the marina entrance, and Keith pulled up beside him.

"Park over there," Lester said, pointing.

Both cars were parked side by side. Their drivers and passengers got out, and a quick scan of the parking lot and street indicated no pedestrians or bystanders. Henry and Kurt lifted Amanda carefully from Myra's car and carried her between them across the street to the marina.

"We gotta get past the night watchman," said Lester. "It's okay, he knows me. I told him Reuben and me's taking out a bunch of folks that wanna go for a moonlight cruise. Just let me do the talking."

The night watchman's shack had a strong light beside it, illuminating the narrow entrance to the marina. As they approached, the watchman, a middle-aged man in a captain's hat, leaned through an open window, a cigarette dangling from his lip.

"This your party, Lester?" he asked.

"This is them, okay?"

"I guess. Who's that?"

"Who?"

"That one there being carried. Too much to drink already?"

"Ha, ha, yeah, that's right. She's out before we even started."

"That's a man, Lester. Got a beard. Wait a minute... that's a dress he's wearing. Lester, you care to explain this?"

"Well—" Lester smiled at the night watchman, but no further word came from his lips. Scenting potential disaster, Moody stepped forward.

"That's a dummy, not a human. It's a stage prop. Show the man, Henry."

Gallagher and Kurt edged closer to the light and presented Amanda, full face.

"Jesus H. Christ—that's the ugliest thing I ever saw! What the hell are you folks doing with a thing like that?"

Moody dredged his mind for a plausible answer, but none presented itself.

Nigel Lawson swept his arm across the entourage in a grand gesture. "Sir, we are picture people, therefore all certifiably insane. We have among us this fine night a dazzling creature, a bewitching curiosity, as you see, and although not a word has passed from her lovely face to our eagerly awaiting ears, nonetheless we are fascinated by her, and insist on our right to take her with us on our cruise over the waters. I ask you, sir, is there any law preventing this?"

The night watchman rubbed his jaw, then admitted there probably wasn't.

"Thank you," said Nigel. "Let us proceed."

They began moving away from the shack. "Hey, Lester," called the night watchman, "how come you know picture people?"

"Oh, just lucky, I guess," Lester called back.

The party continued along a hundred yards or more of wharf, the air heavy with the smell of salt water and diesel fuel and fish. Moody, Myra, and Nigel walked as close to the pallbearers as possible to shield the true nature of their burden from any sleepless person aboard the dozens of moored vessels they passed. But no one challenged them, and soon Lester announced they were beside his uncle's boat. A cigarette glowed in the darkened wheelhouse as they came aboard. Lester immediately cast off the bow and stern lines, and a diesel engine beneath the hatch coughed quietly into life. *Angela* began moving slowly away from the wharf.

Nigel began to sing. "Sailing, sailing, over the bounding main—"

Henry Gallagher turned to Moody after setting down the body of Amanda Flowerdew. "Who's that feller, Keith? He a friend of yours?"

"Yes, his name is Nigel."

"He oughtn't to be singing."

"That's just Nigel's way of coping with a tense situation, Henry. He helped me steal Amanda away. He's really very useful. We just have to overlook his social shortcomings."

Nigel overheard this and stopped singing. "Sorry," he said, beaming.

"This is a serious business here," Henry scolded him. "There's got to be some dignity."

"I agree absolutely. I do beg your pardon."

Henry appeared satisfied, but Kurt moved closer to Nigel, eyeing him with obvious suspicion and dislike.

"I know now where I saw you," he said, peering at Nigel through his bottle-end lenses.

"Oh, yes? And where was that?"

"You were on the stairs when I went up."

"Stairs?"

"Where that feller got killed."

"Killed? Ye gods and little fishes, I do hope not."

Kurt turned to Moody. "Where was that place you sent me, only you weren't there anymore?"

"You mean my old apartment on El Segundo? What about it?"

"That's where the feller was killed, that Dookey feller."

"Dulkis, Morton Dulkis."

"Him, yeah, and this guy was on the stairs, I seen him."

"I doubt that, Kurt. Why would Nigel be there?"

"How should I know? He was going down the stairs when I was going up."

"If you say so," said Nigel. "I wouldn't want to contradict you."

"You had a black hat on," insisted Kurt.

"Yes, that's right. I always wear my black hat when I go prowling around the scene of a murder. It's called keeping in character. Did you notice any blood on my coat, by the way? How about the cleaver grasped in my hand?"

"No," admitted Kurt, sounding less sure of himself now.

"Perhaps I should have worn my vampire's cape, and escaped by changing into a bat," suggested Nigel, winking at Moody. "It's terribly frustrating for the police that way."

Kurt snorted. "You couldn't do that."

"I certainly could, with the aid of a pulley and wire."

Kurt looked at Moody. "What's he mean?"

"Nigel's an actor, Kurt, and quite a well-known one at that. I think you saw him in the movies, not in real life. You're misremembering, probably."

"Oh."

"No hard feelings, old man," Nigel assured him.

"I'm not old."

"Of course not."

The boat plowed steadily toward open water, where the throttle was opened up a little more. Reuben Montgomery called from the wheelhouse, "Lester, get up here!"

While his nephew took the wheel, Reuben came down on deck, a short and stocky man with several days' growth of beard. He said to Moody, "You the one that's paying?" When Moody said he was, the captain of the *Angela* said, "Five hundred."

"I don't carry that kind of cash around with me, but I did bring my checkbook."

"Cash only. A check, there's a bank record of that. I don't like paying taxes on money that Uncle Sam don't need to know about."

"Could I possibly bring the money to you on Monday?"

"Sure, if you want me to turn around and you take the stiff away and bring it back Monday along with the cash."

"That isn't what was agreed. The arrangement was for tonight."

"The arrangement was for cash. You want me to turn around?"

Nigel stepped forward, taking out his wallet. "Five hundred, Skipper? I think we can accommodate you."

"Nigel, you don't have to," Moody protested.

"I most certainly do have to. We've had a lucky run so far tonight, and I don't want to see our spell of good luck broken for want of a few shekels. Here you are, Captain, all crisp and new." Nigel handed over a wad of bills.

"Lester, he gets a hundred," said Reuben.

"And a hundred he shall have," said Nigel, peeling off more bills. "So nice doing business with you, sir."

"Likewise."

The captain went back to the wheelhouse. "You're rich," said Kurt.

"Actually, I'm not," said Nigel, "I just happen to have collected some winnings from a chap I beat at cards. All in a worthy cause."

"I'll pay you back on Monday," Moody said.

"No hurry, old chap. Glad I could help."

"He isn't old," protested Kurt. "Why do you say that about everyone?"

"Just a figure of speech, not to be taken literally."

Kurt clearly was dissatisfied with this explanation, but he said nothing. He moved away from the rest as the boat continued heading south by west. Amanda Flowerdew lay on the deck, giving the appearance of deep asleep. The proceedings lacked all dignity, in Moody's opinion, but Henry Gallagher was not complaining, and Moody didn't want to hear him start, so he said nothing. The waters of San Pedro Bay were oily smooth, the swell barely noticeable. Moody was enjoying himself, he realized. The entire evening had been an adventure, starring himself and Nigel Lawson, who usually engaged in deeds of derring-do only on the screen.

"I'm very grateful for all this, Nigel. You really didn't have to."

"Not at all, Keith. I'm just glad I had the cash on me. Bit of luck, really."

"No, I mean everything, the whole . . . idiotic stunt."

"I wouldn't have missed it for worlds. I should be thanking you for letting me in on it."

Myra said, "You should both have your backsides kicked for putting yourself at risk. It could have come apart at any moment from the beginning."

"Yes," admitted Moody, "but it didn't."

"The gods are smiling on us tonight," said Nigel, lighting a cigarette.

Moody reminded his wife, "You said yourself we should do something to prevent Yaddigan from exhibiting Amanda."

"I know I did, but now I want it to be over. He makes me nervous."

She glanced in the direction of Kurt, who was studying the hypnotic motion of *Angela*'s bow wave. Henry was too far away, standing by Amanda, to overhear.

"You just have to know how to take Kurt," Moody said. "He really isn't the way he seems."

"He pointed a gun at you," Myra said, "and got you involved with the homicide squad. I don't think it's just a question of knowing how to take him."

Moody shrugged. "Kurt hasn't hurt anybody, it's just an impression he gives."

"I hope so," said Nigel, flicking ash into the water. "That accusation he made. Is the chap all right in the head?"

"Kurt's a little unsophisticated," Moody assured him, "that's all. He's probably already forgotten about it."

"I do hope so. Hate to see him coming at me on a dark and stormy night."

"He won't."

Reuben came back down from the wheelhouse. "How far out you folks wanna go? I'm not gassed up enough for a long trip."

Moody said, "Lester mentioned international waters. That sounds like the obvious place to do it. That way we can all say with a straight face that we didn't illegally dispose of a body in the United States."

"Okay by me. Be a half hour maybe."

"What do you have on board to use as a sinker?"

"I'll have Lester get something."

What Lester found, after searching for a while belowdecks, was a length of heavy pipe and some nondescript machine parts, plus rope. "Uncle Reuben had some work done on the engine last week, so this must be the old busted stuff that come out. It was just lying there."

"Where's the canvas?" asked Henry.

"What canvas?"

"To stitch her up in like a shroud. That's the way it's done.

Then you put her on a plank and say some words from the Bible and slide her off into the water."

"Got no canvas. This is a diesel boat, no sails. No plank either. That's only on pirate ships anyway."

Henry became agitated. "You're telling me that for five hundred—six hundred dollars you fellers can't even provide the decent necessaries for a sea burial? That what you're saying?"

"Well, yeah, only this got put together fast, mister. You can't blame me and Reuben. You have to take things the way they come sometimes."

Moody said to Henry, "I'm afraid he's right. Look on the brighter side, Henry. Amanda will go to her rest with two family members nearby, and she'll never have to suffer the indignity of being stared at by strangers."

The fact that Amanda Flowerdew had made a profitable living from doing exactly that was not something Moody deemed wise to mention. Henry shook his head; there were tears in his eyes. "This wasn't what I had in mind. There should be a box if there's no canvas. This way isn't right, not by me."

"What're we gonna do?" asked Kurt, adopting his uncle's look of disappointment.

"Do? We're gonna do the only thing we can do and put her over the side like she is, with a bunch of junk tied to her ankles, is what we're gonna do. That's for you and me to be taking care of, not anybody else, so get busy and tie that stuff on."

Kurt set to work binding the metal parts to the dainty ankles of Amanda. Moody went to the stern and smoked a cigarette, feeling vaguely guilty. Nigel and Myra joined him there, and conversation was kept to a minimum until the job was done.

The engine stopped. *Angela* slowed, wallowing slightly in the swell. Reuben came down onto the deck and said, "Okay, this is it. Let's go."

"You got a Bible on board?" Henry asked.

"No."

"It just don't seem right to put her over without a few words. Anyone know some words?"

Nigel said, "I believe I can help you there, Mr. Gallagher, if you and your nephew would just lift up Miss Flowerdew and hold her along the rail for a moment."

Henry and Kurt picked up Amanda and balanced her above the water, Kurt taking care of the heavy end. Nigel cleared his throat, then began:

> "Fear no more the heat o' the sun,
> Nor the furious winter's rages;
> Thou thy worldly task hast done,
> Home art gone, and ta'en thy wages:
> Golden lads and girls all must,
> As chimney-sweepers, come to dust."

Henry waited for more, then realized Nigel was finished. He nodded to Kurt, and together they pushed the body over. Amanda Flowerdew hit the water with a soft splash and was gone instantly. Concentric circles began moving away from the boat's hull and were subsumed by the swell before reaching very far. The stars were very bright and distant, the moon a stage prop dangling in the sky. It was done. Henry was crying. Moody felt less satisfied than he had thought he would. A cruel deception had been thwarted by guile and cunning; what was right had been accomplished; and yet satisfaction eluded him. It had been a caper, not a quest; a jolly jape, as Nigel might have put it, never a balancing of the universal order. The woman with the hairy face was plummeting through darkness to be anchored many fathoms down, there to rock and sway in the currents like a strange anemone until her flesh was consumed by fishes. It was a private place, this watery tomb Moody had brought her to, where nobody could stand and stare, but it was not enough, not anywhere near what Henry Gallagher had wanted.

The captain returned to the wheelhouse and restarted the engines. *Angela* turned and headed for shore. No one spoke on the way back to harbor.

Moody drove Nigel back to the Wilshire Hotel while Myra took Henry and Kurt back to Alhambra and Henry's car. As they drove, Nigel and Moody prepared a plan to counter any efforts that might be made to implicate them in the incident. Nigel insisted on being dropped off at the nearest corner, so there would be no witnesses at this late hour to their having been together.

Moody drove home. Henry and Kurt had long since driven away, to his relief; he simply didn't know what else to say beyond the few halting words he had spoken to Henry aboard the boat. The episode had ended with a whimper and the silent disbursement of the protagonists.

Moody felt tired. Myra was already in bed, asleep. Moody stood in the living room, looking at the casket, wondering what to do with it. The extra card that Nora Worth had accidentally given to Nigel was still where Nigel had tossed it, on the table beside the casket. Moody picked it up, motivated by nothing more than idle curiosity; what kind of card would a colorless individual such as Miss Worth carry in her pocket?

THE KUMQUAT CLUB
The Right Place for the Right People

On Saturday morning Moody and Myra returned to the Homeaway Hotel for their things. Passing through the lobby in both directions, they saw no trace of Knobby, much to Moody's relief. Their bill settled, they drove home again, to find a dark blue car parked at the curb outside the house. Two men with snap-brim hats were in the front seat. They got out of the car as Moody and Myra exited theirs.

"Police," whispered Myra. "They're onto us already!"

"Don't panic. They can't possibly have any proof. Wait, I think I've seen these two before somewhere."

"Mr. Moody, how are you today, sir?"

"I'm fine, thank you."

He recognized them now, the two FBI agents who had attended the stakeout in San Diego. From the anonymous suits and ties to the angle of their hats, they resembled mirror images of each other that spoke of self-assuredness and propriety. "Mrs. Moody," said one of them, dipping his head a little. "Fully recovered from the incident?"

"Oh, yes—thank you."

"Agent Buller, Agent Denton. Would it be possible for us to have a few words with you folks?"

"Of course," said Moody, wondering if body snatching was a federal offense. "Come right in."

Only as the agents passed through the door did Moody remember that the casket was lying in full view of the hallway. It was too late to uninvite the agents inside, and so he said, as they removed their hats, "Let's go into the kitchen, gentlemen. As you can see, the living room is occupied by a rather depressing object."

"Death in the family?" asked one of the agents; Moody thought it was Buller, but it might have been Denton. He would have to separate their identities fast, and be as polite and cooperative as possible without incriminating himself or Nigel. Now that their hats were in their hands, the agents no longer resembled twins; Buller had short black hair and Denton had short brown hair.

"Actually . . . my uncle Henry is expected to pass away soon. We're doing the practical thing and preparing for the inevitable."

"It's a little unusual to hold the coffin in your house, isn't it, Mr. Moody? Usually it's kept at the funeral home until needed."

"Quite true, but in this case we had to take immediate delivery. Just between you and me, it's . . . secondhand, and the funeral home director wanted it off the premises as soon as possible. I think those fellows are sometimes a little on the superstitious side."

"Secondhand? You mean it was used before? It looks like new."

"Well, when I say secondhand, I don't mean it was put into the ground, but it did have a previous occupant, whose family reneged on the contract and left their loved one at the funeral home, unpaid for, so to speak. When that mess was sorted out, the director wanted to dispose of the casket just as soon as possible. We got it for a bargain price, frankly, but they insisted we take it away with us, so there it sits, waiting for Uncle Henry to pass on. If we had a garage we'd keep it there, but we don't." As he spoke, Moody led the agents into the kitchen. "Please sit down. Myra, any chance of coffee for our guests?"

"My pleasure," said Myra. Ordinarily it was Moody who brewed the coffee, but husband and wife had fallen by unspoken consent into a pose of utter convention, the better to fool the FBI men into believing them incapable of breaking any law. Myra smiled sweetly. "Can I take your hats, gentlemen?"

"Thank you."

They sat at the kitchen table. Moody looked at them with what he hoped would pass examination as an expression of interest and slightly baffled concern.

"How may I help you?" he asked.

Buller said, "You've probably guessed why we're here, Mr. Moody."

Moody had thought so himself, until the agents appeared to swallow his nonsense about the casket.

"No."

"It's about the stamp," said Denton.

"The stamp?" said Moody, relief washing over him.

"There's more to the story than we first thought. Mr. Hoover has given us direct orders to inform you of the nature of the investigation."

"Investigation? I thought it was a straightforward case of kidnapping and attempted extortion."

"The San Diego incident was exactly that, Mr. Moody, but the story has wider implications," said Buller.

"Concerning the war effort," said Denton.

"The war effort," repeated Moody. "I don't think I understand. How could a stamp be involved with the war?"

"This is a very special stamp, sir, so special it came to the attention of Hitler himself. That information has only just reached us in Washington. Director Hoover wants an all-out effort to get to the bottom of it. This is serious business, Mr. Moody."

"I'm sure it is, but I still don't quite see—"

"The stamp," said Denton. "Describe it for us, please, to the best of your recollection."

"Well . . . I couldn't really say. It was a circle, wasn't it, Myra?" To the agents he said, "I just had a quick glance at it before we stuck it in a bank vault for safekeeping. Myra's actually more familiar with it."

"Two rings," said Myra. "One inside the other, very close together, with some little bumps inside the inner circle."

"Those bumps, Mrs. Moody, are mountains."

"Pardon me?"

"Mountains," said Buller. "The rings represent the outer and inner surfaces of a hollow earth, with landscape features such as mountains and seas on the inside. That's what the experts the Bureau consulted have told us."

"How remarkable."

"The thing is," said Denton, "the Finn who designed the stamp was some kind of eccentric character who believed the earth is hollow, with another world, you might say, all around the walls of the inner globe, just like our world, only fitted onto a concave, instead of a convex, surface. The Finnish government in 1901 went ahead and printed the stamps, or a small portion of what was intended, before they found out what it represented, and the stamps were recalled. Almost all of them were destroyed, but five were excluded, probably by some stamp fanatic who knew they'd probably be worth big money someday."

"This is fascinating," said Moody, "but you did mention Hitler."

"This is where the story gets a little strange. Hitler, as you know, is a madman. What you may not know is the extent to which madness has taken him over. We have reports from British Intelligence that suggest Hitler actually believes the world may be hollow. Some say he thinks we live on the outside, and the inside world is awaiting discovery. Other reports say he thinks the entire world is already on the inside, with the stars and moon and sun and so forth occupying a very dense space in the very center of this inner space. They'd be a fraction of the size we assume they are, of course."

"The man's a complete lunatic," Moody said. "What does Hitler think is on the outside of the planet, a giant parking lot?"

"We have no information on that, sir."

Moody looked at Myra. "This is beyond belief."

Buller said, "The fact is, Hitler is fascinated by anything to do with the inner world, and when he learned there were some rare stamps depicting the theory, he sent out orders to snap them up."

"He wants the complete set," said Denton. "He already has four. You have the fifth."

"But how on earth," said Myra, "or *in* it, did my uncle Barney manage to get hold of such an important stamp? He wasn't rich. All the other stamps in the album are worth about ninety dollars. How did it happen?"

"We've looked into that, ma'am, and it seems that a shipment of stamps was sent from Europe just before the war by a collectors' distribution company. It included the Finnish ring stamp by accident. The shipment was subdivided by a similar agency here, and apparently nobody noticed the ring stamp in among all the rest. The shipment was arranged into small lots and sold off by way of philatelic magazines. Your uncle was the lucky recipient. I'd have to say he didn't know what he had, or he never would have left it in his album all this time."

"It's a good thing old Adolf doesn't know we've got it," said Myra.

"There's the problem, Mrs. Moody. It seems he does."

"You're joking."

"No, ma'am. Word has come to us at the Bureau that Hitler's right-hand man, Goebbels, has dispatched a special team to locate and steal the stamp and take it back to Germany so the Führer's set will be complete. The team came in by submarine last month by way of Canada, a three-man team, two of whom were caught as they crossed the Canadian border into the States. The third man got away."

Moody asked, "How could he trace the stamp to us?"

"The same way we did—by utilizing their government's secret services and some plain old detective work. Mrs. Moody, have you been in contact with any of your family members in Yellowtail since you were up there recently?"

"No."

"No one has tried to get in touch with you?"

"Keith and I have been away from home for the past few days, so there might have been telephone calls that we don't know about. Why do you ask?"

"Because the house of your late uncle Barney was gone through with a fine-tooth comb just after you left. Obviously someone was searching for the stamp."

"Oh, my God—" said Moody, slapping his cheek.

"Sir?"

"That explains why Dulkis was killed. . . . The killer was

looking for the stamp! He must have looked us up in the phone book—and used a book that was out of date, so he went to El Segundo instead of Alhambra."

"That doesn't make sense," said Myra. "The old address was listed to you only, and whoever's after the stamp could only know about you through me, by way of marriage, so he would have been looking for a phone listing for the two of us, not just you."

"Oh," said Moody, disappointed, then he brightened. "But it could still have happened that way. He knew you were married to Keith Moody, so when he found a listing for me in the out-of-date book, he went ahead anyway, even though you weren't listed along with me. And the search that took place here a few days after that must definitely have been for the stamp, after he fugured out that I'd—we'd—moved."

"So it definitely wasn't Kurt looking for you," said Myra. "That's a relief."

Buller coughed. "May we know what murder it is that you're referring to, Mr. Moody?"

Moody said, "Myra, is that coffee anywhere near boiling yet? We're going to need a full pot."

By the time the pot of coffee was consumed, Buller and Denton were convinced Moody's theory of telephone listings, old and new, was probably correct. Almost from the moment the stamp album had come into Myra's possession, the nameless, faceless German agent had been attempting to track her down and retrieve it. Moody insisted that the incident in San Diego be gone over for any possible link to the Germans. Had Lemuel Spaulding, owner of the Los Angeles philatelic shop Stamp of Approval, and his partner in crime Paul Geery been working on behalf of the Nazis, or had they simply been independent operatives anxious to possess the stamp Spaulding was astute enough to recognize as a valuable rarity? Buller patiently explained that any connection with Nazis was unlikely, since Myra had of her own accord chosen Spaulding's stamp shop to make the first inquiries regarding her inheritance. Moody was annoyed with himself for not having reached the same conclusion. The FBI men stood up to leave.

"Mr. Moody, Mrs. Moody, it's possible your lives are in danger. We'd like to suggest that you relocate to a more secure place for a while, just until this is over."

"What exactly would be the point in killing us?" Myra asked. "The stamp is in a bank vault."

"A second attempt at kidnapping isn't impossible," Denton said. "We're dealing with Nazis. They're capable of anything."

Buller added, "The Bureau has several safe houses in the Los Angeles area. I advise you folks to take advantage of the safety they offer. Two or more agents would be close by at all times, in the unlikely event an attempt was made to kidnap you, or worse."

"Worse?" Moody inquired.

"It could be that they'd kill one of you to completely intimidate the other into handing over the stamp. I say again, they're capable of anything."

"I have an important job to complete," Moody said. "I can't stop now and go into hiding."

"Of course you could," said Myra. "The job consists of sitting in front of your typewriter all day. You could do that anywhere, and an FBI man could go with you when you deliver the pages to Empire and when you had to attend script conferences. I won't have you exposed to risk, Keith."

"I can't work in surroundings that don't suit me," Moody stated.

"It's up to you," Buller said. "The Bureau can't force you into protective custody."

"There's another possibility to take the heat off you," suggested Denton.

"And that is?"

"Sell the stamp. It's worth a lot of money. Offer it for private auction, maybe. Sealed bids, that's the way. It takes time, and it'd give us the chance to investigate anyone making an offer on it, to see if there's a connection with the Nazis. They'd probably be willing to buy the stamp rather than cause any more ruckus with criminal activity. The main thing from the Nazis' point of view is to get the stamp. They should've made you an offer on it in the first place and avoided killing Morton Dulkis."

"For all we know," said Moody, "that's exactly what they did. Don't forget that Dulkis owned a shotgun and had a very paranoid character, in my opinion, I mean, that's the impression I formed just from talking with him for a minute or so. It could be that this Nazi agent approached him, thinking he was me, and when Dulkis threatened him with the shotgun, the agent had no alternative but to kill him. It might have happened that way. Spies are trained to kill, aren't they?"

"You may be right, Mr. Moody. You still have a decision to make, however."

Moody turned to Myra. "You should definitely take the safe house offer."

"And why shouldn't you?"

"Because I need to get on with the script, and I couldn't do it surrounded by FBI agents." To Denton and Buller he added, "No offense, gentlemen, it's just that the creative juices require freedom to flow the way they need to. It simply wouldn't work."

"If that's your decision," said Buller.

"What about *my* decision?" Myra insisted.

Husband and wife argued back and forth for several minutes until they noticed Denton looking at his wristwatch. In the silence that followed, Buller suggested, "Mr. Moody, do you have a friend you could stay with? Someone who wouldn't interfere with the flow of your creative juices? I ask this because it isn't advisable for you to stay here anymore. They've been here once, and there's nothing to stop them doing it again, especially if they know you're here on your own, without protection of any kind. That's too big a risk for an intelligent man to take, I think you'd have to agree."

"I suppose I could always go back to the Homeaway," said Moody.

"But they called you there, you said."

"It was Geery who called me there, telling me to go and wait on the corner of Hollywood and Vine. Wait—there was another call, muffled with a handkerchief or something, that came to the Homeaway early Tuesday morning. . . . That first call was only one word—my name, then the caller hung up. Could that have been this German agent?"

"Anything's possible," said Buller. "I'd definitely rule out the Homeaway."

Myra said, "Are you absolutely determined to avoid a safe house?"

"Yes."

"Then go and stay with Nigel. There can't be too many Nazi agents at the Wilshire. Is that a good idea?" she asked Denton.

"The Wilshire Hotel? Probably as good a place to hide as any, if you're determined not to drop completely out of sight."

"Who's this Nigel?" asked Buller.

"Nigel Lawson, the actor," Moody explained.

"The movie star? That Englishman? You know him?"

Moody had the impression Buller was impressed, despite his unflappable Bureau demeanor. "Yes, I'm writing his next movie, *Traitor's Dawn*. Nigel and I are good friends. Been through a lot together, actually. You'll like this—the movie I'm writing is about Nazi spies."

"Is that right? How reliable is Lawson, in your opinion? What I mean is, if there's a dangerous situation, and there might well be, would he be able to handle himself okay, or would he fall to pieces?"

"Nigel Lawson would crack a joke as they tied the executioner's bandanna over his eyes," said Moody. "I'd have to let him in on the reason for my staying with him, of course."

"That's only fair," agreed Denton. "Why don't you give the man a call."

"He may not be there today," said Moody, reaching for the phone. "On weekends movie stars tend to play, to make up for the strains of the working week."

"I've heard those actors work pretty hard," said Buller. Moody wondered if he was being sarcastic. He dialed the Wilshire's number.

"He's probably still snoring," said Myra. "I believe he had a very late night last night, some kind of party on a yacht. Those Hollywood types," she said to the agents, "they're always up to something, pulling pranks of one kind or another, indulging their silly selves with behavior that's not so different from that of little boys." She was looking at Moody by then.

"Please be quiet," Moody scolded. "I can't hear the phone ringing."

Myra made a small "I don't care" sound with her mouth.

"Hello? Nigel Lawson, please. Tell him it's Keith Moody. . . . Well, wake him up."

NIGEL GREETED HIM at the door to suite fifteen with an exaggerated welcome, the kind of effusiveness reserved for long-lost brothers. "Keith! What a pleasure to see your smiling face again! It's been at least twelve hours since we saw each other! This calls for a celebration! I've ordered up a couple of bottles of champers, all on Margolis's bill, you know, and some savory treats from the kitchen. Hungry, old man?"

"I am a little. Could you take one of these suitcases?"

"Glad to, glad to. Come right in."

Moody wrestled his remaining two suitcases through the door. "I hope I'm not putting you out at all."

"Nothing of the kind! Pleased to have some masculine company about the place. Had to kick out a bevy of strumpets to make room, of course. Didn't want to place temptation in your way, not with you married to that lovely creature. It'll do me good to take a rest anyway. Been overdoing it a bit with the ladies of late. Must conserve one's strength once in a while, what?"

"I thought maybe you and Gloria were an item. I don't mean to pry."

"No secrets between us, old chap. Gloria and I, as a romantic team, you understand, are the exclusive creation of the Empire publicity department."

"You certainly had me fooled. I'm disappointed, in a way. None of my business, of course."

"Gloria detests the usual Hollywood private life hullabaloo, and I say, more power to her. Now then, this will be your room. Like it?"

Moody entered a bedroom of impressive size and style, complete with its own bathroom. He set his suitcases down, and Nigel set the one he was carrying beside them. "It's . . . what can I say, Nigel? It's magnificent."

"Isn't it? And all on the Empire dollar, that's the part I like best. Ready for the champers? I want to hear every last detail about your visit from Mr. Hoover's G-men. Were they tall and stern, the way they are in the flicks?"

"They were, actually."

Nigel led Moody to a table set with baskets of fruit and some exquisitely assembled sandwiches, so small and dainty they might have been made for fairies. Two bottles of champagne stood in silver ice buckets; two delicate glasses stood beside them. Nigel wrestled expertly with the first cork until it flew over their heads and landed with a discreet *bonk* against one of the many elegant mirrors adorning the walls. He poured generously and handed Moody a glass. Nigel lifted his drink and clinked it against Moody's.

"To artistry of whatever type, and the befuddlement of those who oppose it."

"Hear, hear!"

"Now then, tell me all, dear chap."

MOODY SPENT A weekend of riotous relaxation in the company of Nigel Lawson. They played golf badly and tennis tolerably well, and swam and sunbathed and talked of everything under the sun. Myra called on Saturday night to let Moody know she was installed in an FBI safe house, the location of which she couldn't reveal, even to him. "Good," he said. "Don't forget that there are two of you there. Do everything they say."

"Two of me? You mean one and a half of me. The other half of the baby's yours. We still haven't decided on a couple of likely names. How about Thomas and/or Thomasina?"

"How about Salmon and Salmonella?"

"Keith, you're so clever with words. How's life with Nigel?"

"Hectic, to say the least. I'm trying to determine where his off switch is."

"Hot and cold running women in every room?"

"Not at all. Are you surrounded by husky and attentive young agents?"

"Yes."

"Tell them no. You're married and pregnant."

"All right. I have to go now. Take care."

"I will."

"Promise."

"I promise."

On Sunday afternoon, as they lay beside a swimming pool, Nigel broached the subject of Edward Traven by asking Moody if he'd got any further along with the psychological background they had decided to inject into the screenplay. Moody fetched a carbon copy of the opening scenes, wherein young Traven witnesses his father's brutality toward his mother, and Nigel read it quickly.

"Yes, that's all right, but I really wish we could go ahead and put in the juicy stuff about Edward being responsible for his mama's death as well as that of the old man, the way we originally planned. The two of them dying in a boating accident is just a bit too pat, don't you think?"

"I agree, but if we go too far, Margolis is going to say nix to everything. There are always compromises in every script."

"I suppose you're right." He lit a cigarette. "This chap or chaps that are after your stamp, what kind of fellows would they be? A secret agent for the Nazis, what would he be like? Ruthless? Born killer? Fanatic?"

"I doubt it. Those are the qualifications for someone in the SS or Gestapo. No, I think the one over here's probably a bit more on the subtle side. There wouldn't be anything overtly nasty about him, nothing that would attract attention."

"Your ordinary man, at least on the outside."

"Yes, more than likely, in fact he's probably a bit on the gray and anonymous side, just so he can blend in anywhere he goes. That's what the best agents are capable of."

"A normal, rather boring-looking sort of chap, then."

"Yes."

"Let's call him Fumpf."

"Fumpf?"

Nigel flipped up his palm in a mock Nazi salute. "Secret Agent Fumpf reporting for duty, mein Führer!" His voice was high-pitched and slightly strangulated. "Vat iss my assignment for today? Ach, so I am to go to Amerika, to Hollyvood vere all der movie stars shine? Iss gut! Vat? I am to find der schtamp vid der circles? Zis is not vat I am trained for, mein Führer. . . . Yes, mein Führer. I am alzo to assassinate der traitor Marlene Dietrich und to get for you der autograph of Betty Grable, but I am not to be telling Frauline Eva Braun. You can rely on my dizcretion, mein Führer. Ach! Und you vill give to me der Iron Cross? I am so glad. Vid zis I vill decorate my schmall penis to make him larger, no?"

Moody laughed until he fell off his cane lounger.

MOODY'S WEEKEND OF entertainment and laughter came to an abrupt end on Monday afternoon. He was summoned to the office of Marvin Margolis, where he found Nigel already waiting, his expression that of a naughty schoolboy who has been sent to confront his crimes under the stern eye of the headmaster.

"Keith, Nigel, Empire Productions has been accused of a loathsome deed. Someone has accused us of stealing the body of a deceased individual. Not only stealing it, but failing to return it. The accusation is absurd, of course, particularly in light of the fact that you, Nigel, have been directly implicated. The Morning Glory Retirement Home accuses you, and some fictitious person called Wolfgang Hufnagel, of conspiring to defraud a Mrs. Yaddigan, owner of Morning Glory, of one dead retiree, this being a person by the name of Amanda Flowerdew."

"May I ask why I'm here, Mr. Margolis?"

"You, Keith, are suspected of being this Hufnagel fellow."

"I don't quite understand the connection."

"Hufnagel left an IOU for the deceased with Mrs. Yaddigan's assistant, and included her full name, Nora Worth, on the document. Miss Worth swears she at no time revealed her Christian name to Mr. Hufnagel, and so it was assumed the person masquerading in disguise was someone who had already visited the place. A search was made of the visitors' registry, and after coming across your name Miss Worth recollected your appearance and voice, and stated that you were Hufnagel, despite the fact that Hufnagel wore a beard, and you have no such facial hair. However, Keith, the person you and your wife visited at Morning Glory was the very same Amanda Flowerdew who was spirited away in a hearse belonging to Blakiston's Fine Funerals. The owners of this firm have been contacted by studio detectives, and indeed one of their hearses was stolen on Friday night, the night of the body theft, and later abandoned after being involved in a traffic accident. There is a highly complex mind behind this incident, which is totally baffling in its purpose. Why did the body thieves pretend to represent Empire Productions? Why would someone pass himself off as so famous and well known a personage as yourself, Nigel? These are deep mysteries. Can either of you shed light on the subject?"

"It's simply outrageous, Mr. Margolis," said Nigel, his voice conveying a perfect imitation of outrage. "Only an insane person would imagine that someone in my position, very well known to the public as you said, would attempt any such criminal act. The very notion is, as you so very rightly suggested, absurd. And, as you so brilliantly pointed out, the other impostor had a beard, so I fail to see why Keith is implicated in this disgusting farrago of lies."

"Those were my own feelings on the matter," said Margolis. "However, this Hufnagel fellow's beard was, according to Miss Worth, of a different color to his hair."

"A false beard!" Nigel scoffed. "How stupid these thieves and con men must be."

"Exactly, but Empire Productions now has to either pay the sum signed for on the IOU or face a lawsuit brought against us by Mrs. Yaddigan."

"May we know how much, Mr. Margolis?" Moody asked.

"Twenty thousand dollars" was the reply.

Moody controlled his face. As Hufnagel, he'd signed for a total of eight thousand.

"Someone clearly has it in for the studio, sir."

"Exactly, but with Nigel as our newest star, Empire cannot allow the faintest breath of scandal to besmirch his name, even if it was some criminal with a similar appearance. Miss Worth admits she isn't a fan of yours, Nigel, so it may be that she failed to notice the many differences in appearance between yourself and this cunning impostor. She might also have convinced herself it was you behind the false beard, Keith, simply to assure her employer she was duped by actual people such as yourself and Nigel. Miss Worth has been fired from her position at Morning Glory as a result of all this, naturally."

"That's a shame," said Nigel.

"A matter of no consequence," Margolis assured him. "Only a woman of limited mental ability would have fallen for so blatant a ploy. They said, these impostors, that they needed the body of Miss Flowerdew for use in a motion picture currently being produced by Empire. The stolen deceased was of an unusual type."

"Will you pay the twenty thousand, Mr. Margolis?" Nigel asked.

"It may prove to be the simplest and quietest way out of this situation we find ourselves in, gentlemen, don't you agree?"

"Yes, sir."

"Oh, absolutely. Can't have any scandal clogging up the works."

"Good. The monies will be deducted from your weekly salaries at a rate of one hundred dollars each per week, ten thousand apiece, until the full amount has been paid off."

The office was quiet for a long moment.

"Us?" said Nigel. "I thought we were the victims here?"

"The victim," said Marvin Margolis, "is Empire Productions."

"But—"

"Empire Productions," Margolis continued, "has never allowed itself to be victimized by con men, liars, or scoundrels of any description. That is not the Empire way. When a person or persons attempts to defraud the studio of its good name and hard-earned cash, then those individuals must pay the price. Balance must be restored, harmony encouraged to return, the unfortunate incident smoothed over. That is the Empire way, and Empire Productions makes no exceptions."

"But to take the cash from our salaries—" protested Nigel.

"There is an alternative," admitted Margolis, "and that is to take you both for identification by Miss Worth. Keith, you'll be obliged to wear a false beard."

"It hardly seems fair, Mr. Margolis."

"Come now, Keith. You'll hardly feel the pinch. The newspapers inform me you own a most valuable stamp."

"Ten thousand dollars is still a lot of money."

"Twenty thousand is twice as much."

"May we see the IOU?" Nigel asked.

"You doubt my ability to read figures on a page, Nigel?"

"No, of course not—"

"Ten thousand apiece, and the matter will be allowed to go away. Do you take my meaning to heart, gentlemen?"

Moody and Nigel said nothing. Moody wanted to vault across the desk and throttle Margolis, pausing only to allow Nigel his turn.

"I take your silence for consent. Good day to you both, gentlemen."

Moody and Nigel turned and began walking away.

"Nigel," said Margolis. Nigel stopped and about-faced. "The Wilshire Hotel, Nigel. A very expensive place. You've begun to search for a permanent home, I hope?"

"Of course. Just can't seem to find the right place."

"You have one week. The studio will be happy to arrange the financing of your new home, Nigel. Provided, of course, that you pick something in an acceptable neighborhood. I recommend West Hollywood, Bel Air, or Beverly Hills. Properties in these locations never lose their value. The studio wouldn't want to invest in something of lesser worth. Think about it, Nigel."

Margolis lowered his eyes to his desk in dismissal.

Moody and Nigel marched past Miss Harrison, who ignored them, and proceeded along the corridor to the outdoors and sunlight.

"My God, the colossal cheek of the bastard—!"

"He knows it was us. He may be an oaf in some respects, but he's no fool."

"All the same, old sport, ten bloody thousand each is a bit steep. And what a fucking liar the bugger is! How much did you sign for? Eight thousand, wasn't it? We're being taken for an expensive waltz down the garden path by that odious . . . bloody . . . thief! It's obvious what's going to happen to the extra twelve thousand, isn't it? It'll go straight into Margolis's pocket. Rich as he is, the bastard wants more, courtesy of you and me. I'd like to strangle the little monster outright! I'd be doing the world a favor—"

"It's my fault, Nigel. I'm the one who talked you into it."

"Never accept blame for a good deed, Keith. Those peculiar friends of yours needed assistance to overcome the plans of the wretched Mrs. Yaddigan—another one deserving of strangulation, I might add—so you need apologize for nothing. I'm going to get my own back, though. Margolis is going to pay dearly for what he just did to us."

"What can we possibly do? Let's face it, we're both owned by the studio. You need Empire's money for your acting, and I need it for my writing. He's got us right where he wants us, deep in his damned pocket."

"It's a matter of pride, old boy. Nobody owns Nigel Lawson, let me assure you of that. No, what the situation calls for is a good calm think. There's a plan somewhere in the ether that needs to be allowed into our skulls. Make no mistake, Margolis will pay, and I'm not just talking about his precious bloody dollars. Are you with me?"

"I suppose so, if we can think up something that'll do the trick without getting us into more hot water."

"Thinking caps on, old man. There's got to be a way."

They walked on.

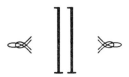

That evening Moody had just finished ordering a snack from the Wilshire's kitchen when a call came through. He handed the receiver to Nigel.

"For you."

"Hello?"

Nigel's face went pale as Moody watched. Clearly the small voice buzzing in his ear was conveying unwelcome news. The conversation that followed was largely one-sided; Nigel confined himself to a few terse phrases, then concluded by saying he would call back. As he hung up the phone, their food arrived. Moody let the delivery boy in and showed him where to set the trolley, then tipped him. When they were alone again he asked, "Bad news?"

"Yes. Go ahead and eat without me, Keith. I couldn't face food at the moment, if you don't mind."

"Is it something you'd care to talk about?"

"Not really, thanks. I have to do a bit of solitary pondering. Back in a while."

Nigel went to his room. While he ate his chicken sandwich,

Moody heard Nigel speaking on the extension phone, but the closed door prevented anything but the general tone of the conversation from reaching him. By the time Moody was finished, Nigel returned. His face indicated he was extremely upset. He went to the bar and began fiddling with various bottles, but didn't make himself a drink.

"Nigel, if there's anything I can do—"

"As a matter of fact, old boy, you can." Nigel sat and lit cigarettes for them both. "Here's the situation in a nutshell. What I'm going to tell you, I tell you because I trust you. We haven't known each other for very long, but speaking for myself, I recognize a friend, a true friend, when I meet one. As a friend, I'm about to tell you something, a secret that I wouldn't share with anyone else. I warn you, you may think less of me when I've done talking. Shall I begin?"

"Please do."

"The gentleman on the phone, would you say he had a foreign accent?"

"No, not really."

"His name is Guzman, a Mexican. He's a lawyer, representing one Tomas Moreno. The thing is, old man, I had what you might call a little fling with Moreno's daughter, Margarita. He's a gardener, looks after the lawns and flowers and so forth out at Margolis's grim little palace. When I got off the train from New York, I stayed a few days with the Margolises, very uncomfortable days, I might add. His wife's a decent sort of woman, but completely under the thumb, same for the kids. Hard to imagine MM as a husband and father, isn't it? I'm beginning to digress. . . . That's because this is so damned difficult to talk about. I'll get directly to the point, so you can see exactly what I'm faced with, and make your choice accordingly. There really is a choice involved here, Keith, I want to be quite sure you understand that. A choice between right and wrong."

"I'm still listening."

"Well, to make the proverbial long story short, I impressed the hell out of Mr. Moreno's daughter, who happened on that particular day to have come with her papa to his place of work. MM and the family Margolis were out somewhere, attending some social gathering or other, but I wasn't invited—just an actor after all, you see; good enough for the masses, not good enough for MM's personal friends, the bankers and so forth you get at his country club. . . . I'm doing it again, aren't I? Here's the crux of it. I took little Margarita upstairs to my palatial guest room and had my way with her. Didn't take much effort to persuade her, and it didn't take long to do the deed. There was some mess on the sheets afterward, virgin, you see, probably no more than sixteen, trying to be sophisticated, wanting to forget her father's a gardener, something like that. Anyway, I thought that was the end of it. This was only a little more than a month ago. A month—that's important."

"Why?"

"Monthlies?"

"Oh, you mean—she's pregnant?"

"That's the easy part. Know what the hard part is? She panicked when things didn't proceed as normal, and tried to abort herself. With a wire coat hanger, apparently."

"Oh, no—"

"Know what the hardest part of all is? She's dead."

"Christ, Nigel—"

"And if I don't compensate Mr. Moreno handsomely and ship his daughter back to the ancestral home in Mexico forthwith, he'll make a big stink, go to the newspapers, and make damn sure they print the story. No need to explain to you what that'd mean. Margolis couldn't possibly keep me on at Empire. The contract I signed had a morals clause, you see, and a pretty stringent one at that. Sex with anyone but the missus, if I had one, is pretty much ruled out. Bit of a prig, Margolis. So there goes *Traitor's Dawn* and *Below the Salt* and anything else you and I might have collaborated on. Back to dear old Blighty for yours truly, most likely."

Moody allowed the situation to penetrate his thoughts. While appalled at the tragic fate of Margarita Moreno, he was aware, painfully aware, that his first concern was for himself and Nigel and their professional standing. He was ashamed to feel that way, but could not deny the reality of what he thought and felt.

"How much does he want?"

"Twenty thousand dollars will buy his silence. And a fancy casket with all the trimmings. Silk lined, brass handles, polished wood."

"You mean you want—"

"Afraid so. Do you still have it at your place?"

"It's where we left it."

"He wants her taken back across the border tomorrow. He wants me to go along for the ride, probably to make me feel humiliated. Frankly, whatever he wants, I'll do it. I deserve it, Keith old man. I did something selfish and stupid and stopped thinking about it the minute it was over. And now this. What a fool . . . what a *bloody* fool I've been!"

"Mr. Moreno's behaving somewhat badly too, in my opinion. He's willing to settle for a price. If he was genuinely grief-stricken, he'd go directly to the newspapers and crucify you, or else do the Spanish thing and shoot you to satisfy the family's honor."

"Let's not criticize the father. The man has no money, and

Mexican gardeners don't just walk into a newspaper office and start making a fuss. No, it's probably the lawyer, Guzman, who's talked him into all this, for a percentage, of course. Anyway, that's the situation."

"The casket's yours, of course. I mean, you helped steal it, after all."

"Can we ask a favor of your farmer friend with the truck?"

"I'm sure Henry would be happy to help. I'd rather not spell out the details for him, though. Nephew Kurt's the kind who'd blab if he got wind of it."

"Absolutely. He's already accused me once of being a murderer."

"That meant nothing. Kurt's a tad simpleminded."

"But he was right, in a peculiar kind of way. Here I am, a murderer by implication. I killed her with my own stupid carelessness—"

"Stop it. What's happened has happened. Do you have the money?"

"Twenty thousand? Keith, you're joking. I've spent every penny Margolis has advanced me, and now he's going to be docking a hundred a week from my wages. I haven't got a bloody thing. I'll have to borrow it from somewhere, sign my future earnings away to some shady type who'd be interested. Los Angeles is full of characters who make deals like that, I'm told, gangster types."

"Nonsense. You're in enough trouble already without involving yourself in bad company. I'll get the money for you, Nigel."

"Gosh, Keith, you're a brick. I feel so utterly stupid, having to ask."

"Stop feeling that way and call Guzman back. Tell him you have a casket, one of the very best, available immediately."

"And the . . . other?"

"Tell him you have something valuable to sell, but the sale will take a little time to set up."

"But I don't have a damn thing to sell, except my bloody soul."

"The stamp, Nigel. I'll sell the stamp."

"What? You can't do that! Don't be ridiculous."

"I'm not being ridiculous. The FBI already hinted that sale of the stamp by private auction might bring the Nazi who wants it out of the woodwork. I'd have to get their okay for this, I suppose."

"Then it's best forgotten. The FBI can't know about any of it. That bugger Hoover has secret files on everyone who's anyone in Washington and Hollywood. I won't allow him to know how stupid I've been. Knowing it myself is one thing, but knowing that J. Edgar Hoover knows is quite another thing. Thanks anyway, Keith."

"Then we'll sell it without letting them know. I'm sure Myra wouldn't mind. There'd still be plenty left over for us. It's supposed to be worth eighty thousand."

Nigel crushed out his cigarette, then looked directly into Moody's eyes. "You're sure? It takes a lot to fool those federal fellows. You and Myra will need your wits about you."

"We've handled trouble before. The important thing is to get you out of this jam."

"I . . ." Nigel lowered his eyes. His lips, the lips dreamed about by millions of women everywhere, were compressed into a wretchedly thin line. "I simply don't know how to thank you. That poor little kid. . . . She really was just a kid, Keith . . . . I've done a terrible thing, a bloody *awful* thing . . . and the only way out of it is to use two of my very best friends, use their goodwill and trust and generosity. . . . I'm just a fucking *user*! I used *her* . . . that poor kid . . . Christ, what a fucking mess!"

Moody went to the bar and began making two Scotches on the rocks, Nigel's favorite drink. He could see Nigel in the bar mirror, slumped on the plush sofa, his head in his hands. Nigel's shoulders were shaking. Moody was shocked; he'd never seen a grown man cry, other than himself, when Bess was killed. But the two situations were not comparable. Nigel's grief was more than heartfelt; it was tinged with guilt, and the death in this instance was human, a young girl stripped of the remaining years of her life, cut short on her road to womanhood. He tried to place himself in Nigel's shoes and could not. The man's suffering was extreme, and it was his obvious shame that made Moody determined to help him. If Nigel had simply wanted a way out of his potential embarrassment, Moody would have helped, but this way, knowing that the actor was sincere, crushed by his own guilty conscience, asking for assistance as a last resort, made the helping easier. He and Myra would be better off without the stamp in any case. It was bad luck.

He took the drinks over to Nigel and sat beside him. "You could use this."

Nigel sipped at his Scotch. Moody saw tears on his cheeks, and when Nigel saw that Moody was looking at his face, he wiped the tears away. "Brings you up a bit short, something like this. No more Happy Jack. This changes everything. Am I a bastard, Keith? I know I'm not exactly the world's deepest thinker, but I know now I'm not going to be myself anymore, not after this. Someone else will live inside me. A better man, I hope. I don't have unrealistic expectations of myself, I mean I'm not about to become some kind of saint, but the old me has . . . gone away."

"Don't let him go too far. I'm rather fond of the old you."

"Thanks, Keith. Thanks for everything." He touched his glass to Moody's. "To coming through this and out the other side."

"Out the other side."

They drank, then Moody called Henry Gallagher. It was arranged that Henry and Kurt would drive into Los Angeles in the truck Tuesday morning and meet with Nigel and Moody at Moody's house in Alhambra. Henry asked no questions, for which Moody was grateful. He replaced the receiver. Nigel was preparing more drinks. The phone rang before Moody had taken three steps away from it.

"Hello?"

"Front desk, sir. I have two gentlemen here who wish to speak with you."

"Put them on."

"Moody?"

"Yes." He recognized the voice but couldn't immediately place it.

"Lieutenant Huttig, Moody."

"How did you know to call me here?"

"Empire, they gave us the number this afternoon. Got time for a little chat with Sergeant Labiosa and me, Moody, you and your movie star pal?"

"In regard to what, exactly?"

"Murder, exactly."

"Murder? Whose murder?"

"We're on our way up, Moody."

He set down the receiver. "Brace yourself," he said to Nigel. "Two homicide cops are coming up to talk with us?"

"What the hell for? I'm in no shape to be talking with the police."

"You'd better get in shape, Nigel. They'll be here in a minute."

"They'll be able to see that I'm upset. They'll smell it."

"You're an actor. Act confident. Be the usual breezy you."

Nigel tossed his drink down and handed the other to Moody. "Right you are."

"It'll be about Margarita, I expect," said Moody. "I didn't think self-inflicted injuries counted as murder, though. Mr. Moreno must have gone to the cops after all."

"He couldn't have. I was just speaking with Guzman."

"Who else do we know who's died recently of unnatural causes?"

"This doesn't make sense, old boy. Homicide?"

"Are you ready to talk with them? Think breezy."

"If you're referring to nervous farts, I can accommodate you."

"There, that sounds like the old Nigel."

"Fact is, I'm a bit on the petrified side."

"Have another drink, and prepare to deliver an Oscar-worthy performance."

Nigel twitched as several loud raps sounded on the door. Moody opened it. Huttig and Labiosa entered the suite, walking slowly, looking all around them.

"This is nice, Moody. How come you move from place to place every few days, huh? I mean, this is the best place yet, wouldn't you say, Vinnie?"

"I'd say this place is for faggots. Silk curtains, that means faggots."

"Welcome, gentlemen," said Nigel, smiling too widely. "How may we help you this evening?"

Huttig looked him up and down, lingering on Nigel's exotic smoking jacket. "So you're the movie star, or what?"

"Or what, some people might say, ha, ha—"

Nigel's laughter stopped. The detectives stared at him.

"Lieutenant," said Moody, "we'd like to know who died. Nigel and I have been wondering what you could possibly want to talk with us about."

"That can wait. So you went faggot or something, Moody, walked out on that nice little wife you got and moved in with this guy? Explain that to me, Moody. Make me believe you don't wear silk panties."

"I resent your tone, Lieutenant, and if it doesn't stop, I'll complain to the chief of police."

"You do that. We're waiting."

"You'll recall that my wife was kidnapped last week, for a certain valuable stamp?"

"We remember it," said Labiosa. "We remember stuff that happened last week. So what?"

"So Myra is currently in the protective custody of the Federal Bureau of Investigation. If you don't believe me, call the Los Angeles office of the FBI and ask for Agent Denton or Agent Buller."

"And you moved in here so the movie star could protect you, is that what you're saying to me, Moody?"

"I'm staying with Nigel because he kindly offered to let me. We happen to be working on a project together, so this was the most sensible arrangement."

"A movie project?" Huttig asked.

"Yes."

Labiosa said to Nigel, "People that make movies with Moody here get killed. He tell you about what happened to a bunch of people he was making a movie with a couple years back? You should ask."

"My curiosity lies in another direction," Nigel said. "Like, Mr. Moody, I'm waiting to hear who was killed. Are we suspects in something?"

"Maybe. You girls know someone by the name of Yaddigan?"

"I do," Moody said quickly. "Nigel doesn't, never having been out there."

"Out where?"

"Morning Glory Retirement Home."

"You were at that place, Moody?"

"I've just said so."

"No, you just said your friend Nigel was never there. That's a different thing to you saying you were there."

"Point taken. Now what?"

"So you know this Yaddigan dame, is what you mean to say?"

"I wouldn't say I know her, but I've met her. I don't want to get into a game of semantics with you, Lieutenant."

"We don't go for that either," said Labiosa. "The lieutenant and me, we're Americans, so we don't go for anything those Nazis like. They're antisemantic, so us, we're the other way around."

"Jews we like," said Huttig.

"Captain Meyer, he's a Jew. He's a good cop, Meyer."

"Lieutenant, has Mrs. Yaddigan killed someone?"

"First things first, Moody. You went out to this Morning Glory place for what reason?"

"To see someone there."

"By the name of?"

"Amanda Flowerdew."

"Check. Amanda Flowerdew. Now I want you to put your brain in reverse and think about what happened between you and us just a week or so back. Have something to do with that name, did it, that Flowerdew name?"

"Yes, but I thought I'd managed to convince you that Kurt

Flowerdew had nothing whatever to do with the killing of Morton Dulkis or the vandalism at my house. I've since learned all that was the work of Nazi agents."

Huttig and Labiosa looked at each other. "Nazi agents," said Huttig.

"Moody's got spies chasing after him," said Labiosa.

"I refer you again to Agents Denton and Buller. The Nazis want my wife's stamp."

"So those fellers that kidnapped her and then ended up dead, they were Nazis now?"

Moody took a deep breath and exhaled. "No, they weren't. They were common criminals who also wanted the stamp."

"So anyway, this stamp, how come everybody wants it?"

"Because there are only five in all the world, and Hitler has four of them."

"Hitler the antisemantic guy with the little mustache and the big voice?"

"The same."

"Moody, you wouldn't be shitting us, would you?"

"I mean every word. That's why the FBI has Myra in protective custody. Now, would you mind telling me who it is that Mrs. Yaddigan is supposed to have killed?"

"You got it wrong, Moody. She's the one that was murdered, just this afternoon."

"Why? What reason could anyone have for killing her? How?"

"By getting shot in the gut, that's how, right in her office there."

"And you think I'm implicated in the killing?"

"Maybe. We got told about you and your friend here while we're out there investigating. You steal a dead body last Friday night, Moody?"

"Certainly not. Whose body are you referring to?"

"Amanda Flowerdew, that's who."

"Really? That's most peculiar. Why would anyone do that?"

"Beats the hell outta me. An old dead lady, what good's something like that to anyone? But someone took her, Moody, so there's a reason behind it."

"I'm afraid I can't help you there, Lieutenant. I visited Miss Flowerdew last week, just to satisfy my curiosity, following the mistake about Kurt."

"Who told you where she's at? She's not in the book."

"Her nearest living relative, Henry Gallagher."

"Yeah? Where's he live?"

"Santa Clarita."

"Yeah, we know about him. He's in the records there at Morning Glory."

"And you asked me where he lives to see if I'd give an honest answer, I suppose."

"You suppose right, and you got a good grade for honesty, Moody. We also got told he didn't like Yaddigan, wanted her to not bury the old lady or something. Know anything about that, Moody?"

"No. Henry Gallagher didn't shoot Mrs. Yaddigan. He's just not the type."

"Yeah? You might be surprised what types commit murder. We see all kinds, don't we, Vinnie."

"All kinds. Even old farmer guys. What kinda dough does it take to stay in a ritzy joint like this?" he asked Nigel.

"I couldn't say. Empire Productions is footing the bill."

"They must like you a whole lot, Nigel."

"Officer, I'm an investment, nothing more. Investments must be nurtured to bring about a profit."

Labiosa snorted, then looked at Moody again.

"So you're saying you went and visited this old Amanda lady before she died, just because she's related to the guy you figured was trying to kill you on accounta he's a little cuckoo, and you never did go back and steal her outta there, and you definitely had nothing to do with the fact that someone went and killed the owner. That right?"

"Yes, and I'd like to know who told you Nigel and I did any such ridiculous thing as stealing a dead body."

Huttig said, "The suspect, that's who."

"The suspect? You have someone? It isn't Henry, is it?"

"According to you he's not the type, so relax."

"Then who?"

"Nora Worth."

"Miss Worth? That's even more absurd. She wouldn't hurt a fly."

"Nobody says she hurt a fly, Moody. She killed Yaddigan."

"I don't believe it. For what reason? What's her motive?"

"She had a good one. Yaddigan fired her this morning on accounta that body-stealing deal. Worth's the one that sold the stiff, only there wasn't any sale because nobody coughed up any cash. The lady loses her job, gets mad, and shoots her ex-boss."

"You have her in custody?"

"She flew the coop sometime this afternoon, after we had a little talk with her. It was a .22 Yaddigan got shot with, a ladies' type gun. A popgun like that, you could fire it a couple or three times, and no one that wasn't right there'd even hear it. Three shots, that's what Yaddigan took, right in the belly. It was a big belly, so I guess Worth wanted to make sure at least one of the slugs did some harm in there. It worked."

"I can't believe Miss Worth did that."

"Believe it or not, like Ripley says."

"So, Moody, this Henry Gallagher, does he know where Kurt Flowerdew lives? We just wanna be sure about all that stuff from last week."

"I asked him that myself. He . . . happened to be visiting Amanda at the same time, and he told me the last he heard about Kurt was years before, back in Wisconsin. You're not suggesting it was Kurt who shot Mrs. Yaddigan, I hope."

"We got a suspect that makes sense already," said Labiosa. "Forget Kurt. Maybe you think it was a Nazi that did it, huh, Moody? If Nora Worth's too much of a nice lady to kill her boss, maybe it was Hitler or somebody."

"Unlikely, I think, Sergeant."

Huttig and Labiosa began moving toward the door. "So long, Moody. We like you, you're interesting."

"Always with interesting people around him," Labiosa agreed.

"Don't forget the interesting events around him too," said Huttig, "like murders. So, Moody, you look out for any falling bodies."

"Thank you for stopping by," Moody said.

The door closed behind the detectives. Nigel said, "What kind of a professional attitude is that for police officers to have? Are they friends of yours, Keith?"

"We're acquaintances," offered Moody.

Nigel sat on the sofa again. "My mind feels as if it's coming apart. First there's Guzman, striking deals, then there's Yaddigan's murder. You don't suppose it was really that little mousy thing Worth who did it, do you?"

"I have no idea. Having put the notion into Huttig and Labiosa's heads that it was Kurt who killed Dulkis, and then finding out he didn't, I'm reluctant to go pointing the finger at anyone. Yaddigan was an unpleasant woman, and I'm sure I'm not the only one who thought so. Anyway, we have problems of our own at the moment."

"My problems, you mean, which I've foisted upon you."

"That's what friends are for, Nigel."

"Care to step out for a drink, old man? I feel a bit cooped up in here."

"You go ahead. I want to wait for a call from Myra. If we're going to dispose of the stamp, she needs to be aware of what's happening, and why."

"I say, you couldn't possibly fudge the issue a bit with Myra, could you, Keith? What I mean to say is, I'd hate to lose the respect of a decent woman like her—or do you think I'm being a bit on the mealymouthed side? No need to answer, old sport. I'm definitely being a coward. Tell her everything. It's her stamp, after all."

"I think that's best."

"Right you are, then. But I don't have to be here to listen to a description of my crimes against morality, so I'll just shuffle on down to the bar for a snort, in fact I think I'll get absolutely blotto. Join me later on if you feel like it."

When Nigel had gone, Moody paced about the suite, wondering about Nigel and the sixteen-year-old Margarita, wondering also about Nora Worth as the purported killer of Hortense Yaddigan. He wanted all of it to be over and done with; the stamp gone from their lives, Nigel restored to some semblance of normalcy, albeit with his moral senses strengthened as a result of the tragedy. Moody surprised himself by wondering if Nigel's shock and self-imposed reappraisal of his own character would in some way aid his performance as Edward Traven when shooting started. Would Nigel's recent travails give him additional depth on the screen? It was an unworthy thought, and Moody felt a mild guilt at having allowed it into his head. In any case, the definition of an actor was his ability to convey everything required by the role, whether or not the actor had ever experienced anything akin to whatever his screen character was going through. It was irrelevant, really. It's all fakery, thought Moody, and I write the words. He had another drink. He was mildly drunk when Myra called.

Two hours later Nigel returned, his face creased with a drunken smile. "More developments, old boy," he said. "I just met Guzman down in the bar. Bloody fellow invited himself over here to discuss matters face-to-face. Cheek of the chap. Desk clerk saw me go into the bar earlier and sent the bugger in there after me. Sat down beside me and started talking business. Oily hair. Didn't like the fellow at all. Um—did Myra call?"

"Yes, she did. I told her everything. She's going to go to the bank tomorrow and take the stamp out of our safety-deposit box in the vault."

"Bloody good show. Couple of damned good friends, you two are."

"We haven't worked out how to go about selling it yet. We'll need to be careful if we don't want the FBI pushing their noses into the sale before it's done."

"Believe I can help you there, friend Keith. Bloody old Guzman, he wants to see the stamp himself. Doesn't believe a stamp could possibly be worth twenty thousand. I told him it's worth eighty, and that's when he really started not believing me, the silly sod. Now he's anxious about getting the twenty thousand, and he wants to be involved in the sale, you see, down in Tijuana. Knows some people down there who'll help sort it out, he says. Do we trust a Mexican, old man? I don't trust him at all, personally."

"He's just doing what's right for his client. I suppose a sale in Tijuana would be just as straightforward as a sale in Los Angeles, in fact it might be a lot easier, with less red tape and so on. Everything's a bit more relaxed down there."

"So you're happy about this? I told Guzman to bugger off, actually."

"That wasn't wise, Nigel. You have to keep this man off your back if you want to avoid a scandal."

"He said he'd ring at midnight. What time is it?"

"Eleven thirty-four. Sit down, Nigel, before you fall down, and don't drink any more tonight. Tomorrow's going to be a long day."

Nigel staggered over to the sofa and allowed his lanky form to collapse onto it.

"I don't think I could handle this without your assistance, Keith, old man. Definitely a waker-upper, all of it. What a bloody old mess I've made of everything."

"We've been over this before. Keep your chin up."

"Bloody old chin, British chin, have to keep it up, put on a good show, what?"

"Nigel, stop it."

"All right, old fruit. For you I'd stop a train with my British chin, really I would."

"I don't think that'll be necessary. Sobriety from this point on will be, however."

Nigel saluted briskly, nearly poking his eye out with a fingertip. "Roger to that, squire, pip pip, tally-ho and all that. Not another drop, word of bloody honor." He paused. "Did Myra have anything to say about me? Criticism and so forth?"

"She said you need to grow up."

"Oh . . . Think I'll turn my back to the world for a bit and think about that, if you don't mind." Nigel faced the back of the sofa and buried his face in a cushion. His breathing changed almost immediately. Moody listened, worried that Nigel might be suffocating, then realized that his friend was asleep. Moody went to his room, returned with a bedcover, and placed it over Nigel, who by then had begun to snore.

Duty done, he sat and waited for the phone to ring. Now might be the best time to insert himself more directly into the legal proceedings, assert his right to parley with Guzman along with Nigel, since it was his wife's stamp that would get Nigel off the hook, after all. Myra's stamp and Moody's casket. The right objects in the right hands at the right time, and a problem was solved. There was something serendipitous about the entire affair that Moody didn't feel like questioning. He had never believed in the hand of fate interfering in human lives, but there was, in this instance, a certain element of predestination about the events he'd become involved in. Such mystical thinking offended Moody's usual mode of scientific/rational beliefs, and he pushed them away. The important thing to remember was, with the stamp and casket gone from their lives, there remained nothing to interest Nazi agents or cops inquiring into a stolen body, and as a side benefit, his friend Nigel would be allowed to slip unscathed through a tangled web of his own devising. Everything fitted together in just the right way. Moody wasn't going to question any of it for fear of bringing something worse down upon his own head.

When the phone rang, he jumped, having lost track of time. It rang again. Moody looked over at Nigel, who snored on, oblivious to the third ring. Moody stood and went to the phone. It would be better this way; Nigel was too drunk to bargain, and in any case Moody wanted to learn a little more about the lawyer who would be receiving the stamp.

"Yes?"

"Mr. Lawson, please."

Moody could detect no accent at all. It could be that Guzman was American-born.

"Mr. Lawson can't come to the phone at the moment. My name is Moody. Am I addressing Mr. Guzman?"

"You are, sir. Can I assume Mr. Lawson is drunk?"

"You can. Will you talk with me concerning matters of mutual interest?"

"That would be very much to my satisfaction, Mr. Moody. Mr. Lawson is subject to tantrums and somewhat insulting comments. To business, then. This stamp you have, it's a genuine rarity?"

"One of only five in the world, you have my word on that. My wife was kidnapped last week by certain parties interested in bargaining for the stamp."

"I recall the incident in the newspapers. Good. I accept your description. Now then, Mr. Moody, it will be necessary for Mr. Lawson to bring to a certain location the casket he has promised. The casket exists? You'll pardon my asking, Mr. Moody, if you could have attended the chat I had with Mr. Lawson a short while ago. His attitude toward me was belligerent, to say the least, and along with the stamp I began to doubt his truthfulness regarding the casket."

"I have the casket. It's a very fine example of its type."

"May I inquire how it is that you have such an article conveniently to hand?"

"I regret I cannot answer your question, Mr. Guzman. Rest assured, I have what Mr. Moreno requires for his daughter. May I offer my condolences?"

"They will certainly be conveyed to my client, and I thank you on his behalf. He, of course, does not wish to take any part in the—transaction ahead of us. Mr. Moreno has in fact already departed for Tijuana. I will be his sole representative in this matter at all times, until the terms of the agreement have been met. Is this acceptable to you, Mr. Moody?"

"It is."

"Mr. Lawson has told me the stamp is worth far in excess of twenty thousand dollars. Is this true?"

"Four times twenty, Mr. Guzman, and that is the opinion of Mr. Elliot Moxham, a national authority on such matters."

"I see. In that case, I'll arrange for a private auction in Tijuana. I have a number of contacts there who would assist me in ensuring the sale proceeds quickly and smoothly. At this point, Mr. Moody, I should make clear my own interest in this matter. For any sum above the twenty thousand agreed to by my client, I would expect to receive a ten percent commission from you."

Moody hesitated; he hadn't anticipated this.

"Mr. Moody?"

"Yes—I'm here. I have a counterproposal. For any sum in excess of eighty thousand, you may have a ten percent commission. Getting the price up to eighty thousand should present no difficulty. Anything beyond that is money I consider suitable for charging a commission against."

"Perhaps you don't quite understand the enormous trouble I must subject myself to, Mr. Moody, in setting up an unusual exchange such as this, but I prefer not to risk upsetting anyone so the transaction can proceed. Here is my new proposal. For money in excess of twenty thousand, a seven percent commission. I think, if you make inquiries, that sum is perfectly fair. Do you wish to think it over?"

"No, I accept."

"Very good. Do you have a pen or pencil and paper near to hand?"

"I do."

"Write down this address. Twenty-seven seventy-three Pacific Coast Highway. This is a group of abandoned warehouses, set far back from the road. Between the first two buildings there is an alleyway. Back your vehicle into the alley and wait. At no time are you to get out of your vehicle. Please be sure Mr. Lawson understands this. Are you able to meet me there at noon tomorrow with the casket?"

"Yes."

"A transfer of my client's deceased daughter will be made at that time. Further instructions will be given to you when that has taken place. I myself will leave for Tijuana tomorrow. You will hand the stamp to me when you arrive. Do you have any questions?"

"I don't believe so."

"I have a suggestion to make, Mr. Moody, if you don't mind. You should, in my opinion, accompany Mr. Lawson at all times until this unfortunate episode is behind us all. You have a maturity of outlook sadly lacking in your friend. Please don't take that as criticism of yourself. I mean simply to imply that all will go well if Mr. Lawson isn't left to accomplish this delicate matter alone."

"I agree. I'd insist on being there until the stamp is disposed of in any case."

"Of course. Until tomorrow, Mr. Moody."

Setting down the phone, Moody asked himself if he was doing the right thing, and could find no suitable answer. He hadn't left the suite all evening, and yet all around him the world had changed; Moody found himself at the very hub of strange and unsettling new developments. He hoped that his mission tomorrow would resolve all doubts in his own mind. All he wanted, really, was a quiet life.

At eight-thirty on Tuesday morning Myra met Moody at a restaurant for breakfast. Moody had half expected her to be accompanied by an FBI man with a bulge in his armpit, but she was alone. "They let me come and go," she explained, "and I always have the option of having one of their young men go with me for protection, but I told them I wanted a private breakfast with my husband, so they dropped me off just down the street a little way. I'm supposed to call them when I'm ready to go back to the safe house, and they'll pick me up wherever I happen to be, just like a yellow cab."

"They don't suspect anything?"

"Why should they? All I'm doing is meeting my hubby. I'm going to have an omelette, how about you?"

"Nothing for me."

"Darling, you must have something, or you'll fade away and die. You've got so much to do today."

"I don't need reminding."

"Oh, dear, did we get out on the wrong side of the bed this morning? Are you upset with me, or upset with Nigel?"

"Nigel, if anyone."

"You're going out on a limb for him, I must say. Don't take this the wrong way, Keith, but has he mentioned repaying the money at some future date?"

"The arrangement is that Nigel and I support each other, professionally speaking, for as long as his star continues to shine. In the long term, given the ability of Nigel to act and myself to write, the earnings will be considerable. There's no strict payback, if that's what you're asking, but consider what'll happen if I don't help get him out of this jam he's in. He loses everything at Empire, and no other studio will touch him. It isn't the underage sex so much as the attempted abortion and death. Nobody could get out from under that kind of cloud, not even Clark Gable. By helping Nigel, I help us. And there'll be plenty left over from the sale of the stamp, don't forget. All Moreno wants is twenty thousand. Nigel's lucky he didn't ask for forty."

"You make it all sound so cut-and-dried, so—businesslike. I can't stop thinking about that poor girl—"

"Let Nigel think about her. He's the one in need of some soul-searching, not you."

"My, you are in a mood today. Moody Moody, that's you."

"Myra, this has all been a bit of a strain—"

"No, don't apologize. I'll play my part and get the stamp out for you. God knows what Buller and Denton are going to say when they find out it's gone. They want to use the stamp to set a trap for the Nazi spy."

"Then we simply keep our mouths shut about it. So far as the Bureau is concerned, the stamp remains in the vault until the war's over, which presumably won't be long now. Have you seen this?"

Moody showed her the morning newspaper. Three-inch headlines announced:

EUROPE INVADED
NORMANDY BEACHES STORMED

"It's the beginning of the end for the Nazis. There's no possible way for them to resist an invasion of this magnitude. It says here that it's the largest assemblage of military manpower and matériel in history. We'll push the Germans back to the Rhine, then follow them across and wipe out everything clear to Berlin, you can depend on it."

"You sound like a paid propagandist, Keith."

"Aren't you sick to death of it, all this killing? Don't you want to see it end, once and for all, with the Nazis smashed to pieces?"

"Of course I do, but you and I aren't exactly playing our part in the grand scheme of things, are we? Here we are, letting our stamp go to put an end to a private scandal before it even begins, when we ought by rights to be letting the FBI use it for Nazi bait."

"If there's a Nazi in Los Angeles who knows how to read, he'll know the game's up over there. If he's smart, he'll go to ground until the armistice is signed."

"That could take another year or more. You're not a military expert, darling."

"I'm just saying that I have to think about the world you and I will live in when the war's over and done with. The stamp assures me of an ongoing professional and personal relationship with Nigel for—possibly decades to come. I can't turn my back on my obligation to him, and to us."

"And the dead girl and the FBI can go to hell, is that it?"

"I'm saying no such thing. If you don't want to get the stamp for me, I can't make you. It's your decision."

"Oh, and your feelings in the matter don't count at all, I suppose, in which case, why are you making so damn sure I'll fall in with you and Nigel and your rotten little plan?"

"If you genuinely think it's rotten, don't take that first step toward making it happen."

"This is emotional blackmail, Keith, I hope you're aware. I certainly am."

"I can't help how you choose to define it. I know it isn't . . . clean. The entire thing involves moral compromise. I'm just trying to do what's right for three people I happen to be very fond of—you, Nigel, and myself. Margarita Moreno is dead. The Nazi, if he's really out there, will have to be captured by some other means. Those are my thoughts on the matter."

"And very eloquently expressed, as usual. I just realized the waiter hasn't even come to ask for our order. Where's all the staff in this place?"

"Probably out in the kitchen, reading the headlines and thinking about the end of the war."

"The end of the war can wait," Myra said. "I want my damn breakfast." She waved her hand at a man carrying a notepad. "Waiter? I'm waiting—"

BY ELEVEN O'CLOCK Moody and Nigel, with the aid of Kurt and Henry, had succeeded in loading the casket onto the back of Henry's slat-sided farm truck and covered it with a tarpaulin. Kurt asked, "Where you taking this thing?" and was told by Moody that a certain person was in need of a coffin, having recently suffered a death in the family. "Anyone I know?" asked Kurt, who knew absolutely nobody in Los Angeles. Moody told him no. Kurt then offered to go along for the delivery, to assist in unloading the casket at the home of the grieving family. Moody had to convince him his help was not needed for that task. Kurt began to sulk. He expressed his unhappiness by glowering at Nigel until Henry told him to quit.

Moody offered them the use of his Ford to return to Santa Clarita, promising to bring the truck back to the farm late in the day. Henry agreed and drove off with his nephew, who was sulking all over again because Henry wouldn't let him drive the Ford.

"That fellow really doesn't like me, does he," said Nigel.

"Kurt's a puzzle," admitted Moody, consulting his watch. "We'd better be going."

They drove to the rendezvous at 2773 Pacific Coast Highway. As Guzman had told him he would, Moody found the address to cover several acres formerly occupied by the California Import Company, now apparently defunct; the sign was there, the employees and business were not. Moody backed into the alleyway between two high warehouses and turned off the motor. "Bit cloak-and-dagger, all this," said Nigel, who had chain-smoked from the moment they left Alhambra.

"I'm simply following instructions. The whole thing is peculiar, in my opinion."

"Peculiar?"

"Having us transport the girl back home, instead of leaving it up to a funeral service. I haven't the faintest idea what to tell them at the border."

"Guzman's probably arranged something. He's a cocky bastard, didn't you find?"

"He seemed polite and very capable."

"Then it must be me who's at fault. I just didn't like him. You might change your mind if you meet him face-to-face. Wonder if he'll show up along with the girl?"

"He may send a surrogate. Lawyers as a rule don't involve themselves directly with corpses."

"No, their hands must be kept clean and lily-white at all times."

"Guzman didn't create this mess, Nigel."

"Sorry."

They waited another ten minutes. The area appeared to be deserted, nothing more than wide expanses of concrete and asphalt and the blank, windowless walls of warehouses. Moody began to get hot despite being parked in the shade of the alley. Nigel lit yet another cigarette. "I don't think they're coming, old sock."

"Wait—there's a car coming toward us from the other end of the alley. It's coming in backward. It's a station wagon."

Nigel looked into his side mirror as Moody was doing. "How many inside, can you see?"

"No."

The vehicle approaching from behind was now so close Moody couldn't see it at all. He heard the engine stop, then a door slam. A man appeared at his window, a large man, non-Hispanic. "Mr. Moody?" His manner was bright and friendly, his well-scrubbed face smiling.

"Yes."

"And you must be Mr. Lawson," the smiling man said, looking past Moody.

"I am," said Nigel. "What can we do for you?"

"Absolutely nothing, for the moment. Just sit tight and let others do the work. What time do you have, Mr. Moody?"

Moody looked at his watch. "Twelve-ten."

"At exactly twelve-fifteen, start your engine and drive south. You know the way to the border at Tijuana, I suppose?"

"Yes."

The smiling man thrust several sheets of paper at Moody. "Show these to the border guards if they ask for them. They may not even bother. These are certificates of conveyance for a body and casket, in case you're wondering. There shouldn't be any problem getting through. If there is, give them fifty dollars, and the problem should evaporate. Once you're on the other side, follow these instruction for delivery."

He handed in another sheet with a diagram of streets and arrows, then asked, "You have the article for sale?"

"Yes."

"Let me see it, please."

Moody took a folded envelope from his pocket, extracted the stamp, and showed it to the smiling man, who scrutinized it for a long moment, then said, "Okay. Now remember, twelve-fifteen exactly." He then went to the rear of the truck. Moody watched him by way of the side mirror's restricted view until he disappeared. He felt the truck lurch a little as someone climbed onto the back. The truck had no central rearview mirror above the dashboard, since everything on the other side of the rear window was obscured by the solid wooden slats on the front and sides of the truck bed. There was no possibility of observing anything that went on behind them.

"Bloody fishy" was Nigel's muttered comment.

"Fishy or not, I'm doing it their way. I want this to go off without a hitch."

The truck lurched several times more. Moody could hear the canvas tarpaulin being slid off the casket, and thought he detected the sound of the lid being opened. There were more sounds, more lurchings, then nothing. Moody still could not see how many men had accomplished the transfer of Margarita Moreno's body from the station wagon to the truck.

"What time is it?" Nigel asked.

"Twelve-fourteen."

"I think they're all finished back there. Can't hear anything, and no more bumping around."

"We'll wait until twelve-fifteen. This may be some kind of a test."

"I don't like it, not one little bit of it. Have we even seen the girl? How can we be sure we're not being involved in some elaborate scheme to smuggle illicit goods into Mexico? Let's think about this for a moment, Keith. I'm not at all sure that's a body they loaded into the back—"

"Nigel, please listen to me. Smuggling in southern California is pretty much a one-way street, and the direction of the flow is south to north, not the other way around. We have legitimate papers of conveyance. The casket contains Miss Moreno. It could be that you don't want to accept that because of . . . your involvement with her, and what followed. You're not thinking logically at the moment, Nigel, so please leave the thinking to me, all right?"

"All right, old thing. Had to slip in a bit of writer's psychologizing, didn't you? Probably right, though. I'm panicking. God, I could use a drink. . . . What time is it now?"

Moody checked his watch, then reached for the ignition switch. The truck pulled out of the alley, and Moody turned left. Only when he was heading across the wide expanse of asphalt did he regret not having taken one last look into the side mirror to gain some clue to the number of men who had occupied the station wagon, but by then it was too late. He suspected that even if he turned around and cruised past the end of the alley, the station wagon would already be gone. There was no point now in wondering about any of it. Moody and Nigel had a simple task before them that would require most of the afternoon. They were deliverymen, nothing more. Forces larger than themselves had dictated their actions, and the appropriate choices had been made. There was a plan, and they would stick to it.

Soon the truck was heading south along the coast highway at its top speed of fifty miles per hour. Moody, his mind preoccupied with the Allied invasion of France, his less than amiable breakfast with his wife, and the morally skewed nature of his assistance for Nigel, was unaware that the tarpaulin had come loose and was flapping wildly in the wind, until it came completely off the back of the truck and flapped across the highway. He saw it then in the side mirror, as it drifted like a billowing sail over the roof of a car traveling in the opposite direction before settling along the highway shoulder. He trod on the brakes and slowed to a halt.

"What's up, old man? Second thoughts?"

"The tarp just came off. They must have done a lousy job of tying it."

Nigel and Moody both got out and hurried some hundred yards back to retrieve the heavy canvas, gathered it up, and returned to the truck. Nigel climbed up beside the casket, and Moody handed one end of the tarpaulin up to him for dragging aboard. When the entire thing was loaded, Moody joined Nigel to pull its stiffness over the casket again.

"Now's your chance to check and see," he said.

Nigel looked at him. "Check what?"

"Open it up and make sure it's really Margarita Moreno in there."

Nigel stared at the polished walnut, then shook his head. "I couldn't. I suppose I'm a coward, Keith, but I just can't bear to look. You can look if you want to."

"It wasn't me who suggested we were hauling contraband instead of a corpse."

"Appreciate it if you wouldn't use that word, old sport. Respect for the dead and all that."

"The deceased, then. You're sure you don't want to see her one last time?"

Nigel shook his head and began dragging his side of the tarpaulin across the casket. Moody followed suit, then they tied it down securely and resumed their journey south to Tijuana.

Moody attempted to fill the silence between them with talk of the invasion and its signaling of the end for the Third Reich, but Nigel was withdrawn and uncommunicative, so Moody let the subject languish, and soon all talk was subsumed by the sound of the motor and the warm breeze rushing through the partially opened windows. It was a beautiful day, and Moody, daydreaming at the wheel, was convinced that all his troubles soon would be behind him. Nigel would require some assistance in regaining his former lightheartedness, if indeed that was possible. Moody was reasonably confident that his friend would bounce back sooner or later from the shock of discovering he had inadvertently brought about the death of a young girl. Nigel's basic nature, his tendency to insist on having a good time despite everything, would reassert itself in due course. The man's natural ebullience would win out in the end. Moody would be there to hasten the process along and reap the reward when it finally was accomplished. He felt pleased with himself for having helped engineer the stealing of Amanda Flowerdew and, more important, the rescuing of Nigel Lawson from the dreadful pit of public humiliation and the end to a skyrocketing career. He was proud of himself, and when she was ready to overcome her doubts, Myra would also be proud of him. June 6, 1944, would prove to be a day of destiny in more than just the historical sense.

As they drove, Nigel sipped occasionally from a hip flask. He offered it to Moody, who shook his head. Nigel kept his head turned toward the Pacific for most of the journey. Moody supposed he was contemplating the nature of the events that had brought them to this time, this place, custodians of a girl Nigel feared to look upon in death. For Moody, the time for contemplation was long gone; the time for action, for resolution, was at hand. He felt he was dragging Nigel along in his wake as he set about fixing what was broken, reassembling Nigel's life for him the way an older brother might. It was undeniably a good feeling.

Nigel became agitated as they passed through San Diego, and drained his flask dry as they approached the traffic lanes slowly funneling vehicles across the border into Mexico. "You'd better do all the talking, old man. My English accent might set them wondering, you never know."

"Leave it to me. Here, put this on."

Moody passed him a battered hat that Henry had left on the dashboard.

"For my next impression," said Nigel, dropping it onto his head with a grimace, "Farmer Giles, for whom all answers lie in the soil."

"Almost there now."

"Steady as she goes, Cap'n. Spaniards off the port beam! Ahoy!"

"Shut up, for God's sake."

"Sorry."

The truck inched forward until it was level with the Mexican customs post. A smartly dressed customs officer with beautiful olive skin approached the driver's side. "Good afternoon," he said.

"Good afternoon," said Moody, smiling.

"Your purpose in entering Mexico, please."

"We're . . . delivering a recently deceased person," Moody explained.

"Deceased?"

"Dead," said Moody. "Umm . . . *morte*."

The officer appeared very interested. "You have him there?" he asked, indicating the back of the truck.

"Yes, only it's a she. I have the papers here." He handed them over.

The officer perused them briefly. "This woman is Mexican?"

"Yes. It's a girl, actually. Margarita Moreno."

"How did she die?"

"Well . . . she attempted to perform an abortion on herself."

"Abortion?"

"She . . . didn't want to have a baby, so she . . . tried to get rid of it."

"To kill it, the baby?"

"Yes, unfortunately, and ended up killing herself."

"Why to kill the baby?"

"I don't know. She was very young."

"You are the father?" The officer's expression was severe.

"No, we're just delivering the body of the young lady to her homeland, at the request of her father, Tomas Moreno. I think all the information is there in the papers—"

"This does not happen in Mexico," said the officer sternly. "Here all babies are welcome. This could happen only in America."

"Yes, I'm sure you're right."

"Wait."

The officer went into the post and was gone for several minutes. Nigel began nervously humming to himself. Moody could feel sweat pouring from his armpits. Were the papers correct? He'd barely glanced at them when they were given to him.

The officer returned, his face still dark. "You have no stamp for bringing into Mexico a dead person." He smacked the base of his right fist into the palm of his left hand, an action suggesting two things to Moody: stamping and punishment.

"We don't? I was told all the proper paperwork had been done. I only have what was given to me by the funeral home."

"Why to bring the dead in a dirty thing like this?" He glared at the truck.

"Uhh . . . the company hearses were all booked for funerals, apart from one that broke down and was unavailable."

"It is insulting to the dead."

"I agree; however, it was all we had. Mr. Moreno wanted his daughter returned to Mexico by this afternoon. He was most insistent about that."

"You do not have the stamp."

"I'm sorry. What can we do?"

"Go back."

"Sir . . . *señor*, if we did that, we would lose our jobs, and then our wives and children would starve."

"Take them to the man who did not give you the stamp. Show him your women and children starving."

"That will take time. In that time the girl we have with us will begin to smell very bad. Today is hot. Mr. Moreno will be angry if he opens the coffin and his daughter smells very bad. Mr. Moreno is a powerful man, I'm told, and a very bad-tempered man. He will want to know why we brought his daughter to him in a rotting condition that insults his family, and we will have to tell him about the man in Los Angeles who didn't give us the stamp, and the border officer who did his duty by making us turn around and go back all the way to Los Angeles for it."

The officer stared at Moody for fully half a minute. Behind the truck, an impatient tourist honked his horn, and several others followed suit.

"You may get the stamp here," said the officer. "With special permission. For dignity, for the poor girl who is dead."

"Aah, yes, for dignity."

"There is a cost for the stamp."

"How much?"

"Fifty dollars. Also fifty dollars for the use of this filthy thing to bring the dead home. It is not a proper car for the dead. You must have a certificate."

Moody took a hundred dollars from his wallet and handed it to the officer, who counted it carefully, then waved them through.

"Where's our precious bloody certificate and stamp, then?" asked Nigel, as the truck passed to the Mexican side of the border.

"Forget them, they don't exist. We paid a hundred wicked American dollars because the dignity of Margarita demands it. She wouldn't have died if she became pregnant in Mexico. Her father may have whipped her to within an inch of her life, and she would've been ruined forever as marriage material, completely disgraced in fact, but all babies are welcome in Mexico."

"Where to now?"

Moody dug the instructions from his pocket and handed them to Nigel. "You do the navigating."

"Right you are." Nigel's dark mood seemed to have lifted now that the border had been passed. "All right, it looks as though we have to keep going straight ahead for quite a bit, till we see a church on the left." He looked up through the windshield. "Don't these Mexicans know about staying off the road? Did you see that little bugger back there? Practically ran under the bloody wheels—"

"It's okay, Nigel. I'm driving slowly."

The truck passed along a street flanked by stores with

brightly colored awnings, their facades festooned with signs in English and Spanish. Even in daylight the neon danced and flickered. The air itself seemed different from that on the border's northern side, hotter somehow, laced with unusual odors that seemed to lodge in the back of the throat. Traffic crawled for block after block, and Nigel became agitated again. "Can't they do something about this? It's worse than Piccadilly Circus, worse than bloody Oxford Street."

"Nigel, please relax."

"Sorry. Nerves are shot to pieces."

"The border was the hard part, and that's behind us."

"It may have been the hard part for you, old boy, but I suspect the hard part for me lies ahead."

"What do you mean?"

"I mean, now that I'm here in Mexico, Moreno can do what he bloody well likes with me, can't he? I expect he'll get some beefy chaps to bash me about a bit, teach me a lesson, you see? Twenty thousand isn't going to be enough for that fellow, no indeed."

"You're guessing. Try to stay calm. There's the church. Was it left?"

"The left-hand pathway to outer darkness and damnation. Actually, we carry on past the turn until we get to a fountain, if I'm reading this correctly."

"Which way then?"

"We stop there, apparently."

Moody made the left turn, and five minutes later saw the fountain in the center of a crowded square. He drove around the fountain once, then parked in one of the streets leading into the square. Before he could turn the engine off, a small boy jumped onto the truck's running board and pointed ahead, telling Moody, "That way! Go!"

Moody hesitated. This was not the emissary he had expected, but neither was it the gang of roughnecks Nigel had been anticipating. "Go! You go!"

Moody engaged the gears, and the truck moved on, the boy still clinging to the door pillar, facing into the wind like an enthusiastic dog. He directed Moody through several intersections. The traffic eased, and it became clear they were heading toward the edge of town. The boy began to sing. Nigel, still drunk, began waving his hands in time with the tune. Moody concentrated on avoiding potholes and pedestrians and telephone poles that seemed to have been placed as close to the roadside as possible.

"There! Go there!" The boy pointed to what looked like a loading yard in front of a low warehouse of recent construction. Trucks were grinding in low gear across to the loading bays and backing up to receive wire crates of what appeared to be bottles of beer. "That way! Go there!" Moody steered to a less congested corner of the yard, where the boy told him, "Stop!" then jumped down from the running board and disappeared.

"This doesn't seem right somehow—" Nigel muttered.

"I thought we'd be going to a funeral home," Moody agreed.

A face appeared at his window. "Gentlemen, welcome." The face was Hispanic, the smile broad. "Stay where you are, please. Not to move, yes?"

"Yes," said Moody, having little choice other than to do as he was told.

The back of the truck dipped and groaned as several men leaped onto it. Moody heard the tarpaulin being removed. There was much scuffling and talking as the casket was slid backward off the truck bed. The back of the truck sprang up several inches as the load was removed. All Moody could see was an occasional figure surrounded by the dust raised by many feet. Then the same face returned, and a hand was thrust at Moody. "Give it to me, please."

"Give what to you?"

"The thing you have with you. Give it to me now."

"Just a minute. The 'thing' is for Mr. Guzman, to be handed over in person. Do you work for Mr. Guzman? He said nothing about giving it to anyone else—"

The hand held open for the stamp was withdrawn, then returned, closed around a pistol. The barrel was placed lightly against the orbit of Moody's left eye. He could smell gun oil on it. "Give it to me."

"Certainly. Please be careful with that gun—"

He took the envelope containing the stamp from his pocket. It was snatched from him by the gunman. "*Gracias,*" he said, stepping away. He made a motion with his hand, the one still holding the pistol, and the boy returned from nowhere to take up his position on the running board again.

"They've stolen it," Moody said to Nigel. "What the hell do we do now?"

The boy pointed to the loading yard's exit. "Go there!"

"I think it's all over, old chum," said Nigel. "These chaps were hired by Guzman. They've got what they came for. Now we're supposed to scarper."

"Scarper?"

"Go, and quickly, before their mood changes."

"But—the arrangement was for the stamp to be auctioned, with everything over Moreno's twenty thousand to go into my pocket, minus a percentage for Guzman—"

"He's changed the arrangement, it looks like. We've been double-crossed. Guzman wants it all."

"Well, he's not going to get it!"

Moody ignored the boy's protestations, opened the door, and got down from the truck cab. Now he could see a half dozen men bearing the casket away across the yard. He ran after them, recognizing the pink shirt of the gunman who had Myra's stamp.

"Stop!"

The pink-shirted man turned. He seemed surprised that Moody was so close to him. He lifted the gun, aiming at Moody's chest. "Go," he said. It was his utter calm in giving the order that convinced Moody the man meant what his gun implied; another step forward, and he would be shot. Moody stopped. "Go now," he was told, and this time the hammer was cocked to reinforce the message. Moody turned away and walked slowly back to the truck, defeated. The boy opened his door with exaggerated politeness and Moody climbed back into the driver's seat.

"No luck?" asked Nigel.

"None. We've been had, hook, line, and sinker. Fuck that Guzman! I'm not going to let him get away with it. When we get back home I'm going to the police. . . . The man's nothing but a damn crook!"

"Go, go, go!" said the boy, reaching through the window to punch the horn.

Moody turned the ignition, his face grim.

"I feel responsible," said Nigel. "It's me who got you into this mess."

"Eighty thousand . . . sixty thousand dollars, down the toilet. How *dare* he rob me like that!"

"He wouldn't have done it north of the border, that's definite. He lured us down here with this casket delivery nonsense just so he could have his way with us."

Moody steered across the yard to the road and headed back toward central Tijuana. The boy was singing again, this time unaccompanied by Nigel.

They were directed to the border customs post, at which time the boy simply dropped off the running board and joined the crowds along the street. The truck crawled forward until an American customs officer confronted Moody with a cheerful grin.

"Bringing anything back, sir?"

"Nothing."

"No fruit or foodstuffs?"

"Nothing at all."

"Go on through, sir."

Moody drove back into the United States.

I t was evening before the truck reached Santa Clarita. Henry Gallagher asked if everything had gone all right, and Moody said it had; there was no point in burdening the man with problems he could do nothing to alleviate. Moody and Nigel got into the Ford and began driving back to Los Angeles. Nigel insisted on stopping for liquor and began consuming his purchase immediately.

"Know you don't approve of this, old cock, but I've simply got to take the edge off things. It's all my fault, losing the stamp. You know it and I know it, and sooner or later Myra's going to know it, and there's not a damn thing I can do about any of it except have a drink and hope you and Myra can forgive me. Anything else I might say, or you might say, would be completely and utterly beside the point. It's a monumental balls-up, and yours truly made it happen, end of story, full stop."

"Then there's no use in drinking, is there."

"Beg to differ with you, Keith. Each to his own. Used to know a girl who ran and hid herself in a broom cupboard whenever she got upset. Stayed in there for hours sometimes, then she'd get over whatever it was, and come out as good as new. It takes all sorts. My sort takes a nip to cope with unkind fate, outrageous fortune, and all that. Bottoms up and hooray for our side."

"I'm going to have to admit what we did, you know that, don't you, Nigel?"

"Admit? Admit what? Sounds as if you feel guilty about something."

"I do. I feel guilty about deceiving the FBI. They wanted me to offer the stamp for private sale so they could screen the potential buyers, and I ignored them, sneaked the stamp out of the vault, and did . . . what we did. I even had to convince Myra to do what I wanted. I feel worse about that."

"But the point, dear chap, is that you did it for *me*, not just to bamboozle old Hoover's lads in trench coats. Your motives were pure, don't you see? That's the important thing, the thing to remember."

"At the moment I just feel that any kind of thinking along those lines is nothing more than self-justification of the lowest order."

"You're a decent sort of fellow, Keith, that's why you feel that way. Now I, on the other hand, accept my responsibility, but I'm afraid I can't do so with any kind of manly, chin-up-and-let's-hear-it-for-the-hero sort of feeling. I'm from somewhere else, you see, a lower order, to borrow your phrase, possibly the very lowest, in fact, so I don't look at things the way you do, old sport. Horse of a different color. No, I'd have to say warthog of a different color. More appropriate."

"Nigel, you're taking this too much to heart."

"Have to have a heart to take too much into it. No heart, no guts, no backbone. Not much of anything there at all, I have to say. I'm practically the invisible man! Barely here at all sometimes."

He drank deeply from his bottle. Glancing at him, Moody could see tears on his cheeks reflecting the soft dashboard lights. "Nigel? Are you all right?"

"Actually, no, but it's too late now. Nothing to be done, really."

"Stop it. This came on when I said I'd tell the FBI what I did. You're obviously worried about them finding out about Margarita. The FBI isn't interested in such things, Nigel. That's a police matter, if anything, and I'm not talking about her death, which was caused by her own actions; I'm talking about sex with a minor. That's your crime, if you insist on seeing it that way. The FBI wants to catch Nazis, not actors who think with their pricks."

"If you say so."

"I do, and I fully intend informing Denton and Buller. I'm going to need the Bureau's help in grabbing Guzman to get the stamp back. I'll have to tell them tonight. If I wait any longer than that, Guzman might hold a lightning-fast sale, and the damned thing'll disappear into some wealthy collector's album forever."

"That's what you intend doing as soon as we get to the Wilshire?"

"I should have done it the minute we came back across the border. It's taken me all this time to make up my mind. It's going to hurt, but I have to do it."

"Bravo, old man! You should write a script about yourself. Call it . . . *Back from the Brink*, or *The Cliff's Edge*. Says it all, don't you think? You went to the edge, but then came back. That's the name for your character: Cliff Edge. Very American, very sexy, very bloody heroic."

Moody forced a laugh from his throat. Nigel was behaving in a most peculiar manner that disturbed him. It was more than drunkenness. "Care to play the role, Nigel?"

"Oh, by all means. Dress up the invisible man with some lines and a story, and he can play anything at all—hero, villain, brave man, coward—there's really no end to the possibilities. That's the joy of being an actor, you see, the putting on and taking off of faces and costumes, the sliding into and out of roles, the *pretending* we do, just like spies, really. What must it be like to be a spy, a real spy? Not a dashing hero like Edward Traven, more of a type that no one would ever suspect of being what he is."

"You mean the anonymous type, like you imagined the German agent to be? What was it you called him?"

"Fumpf! Good old Fumpf. Yes, like him, toiling away in the shadows, doing his master's bidding by shortwave radio and secret drops and coded messages and whatnot. A very strange breed is the spy."

"There's a better title—*The Strange Breed.*"

"I offer it to you without mention of monetary compensation."

"Nigel, I'm the one who thought of it."

"Oh, did you? Of course you did. I must be getting a bit blotto."

"We'll be home in another half hour."

"The jolly old Wilshire? I suppose you could call it that. Home is where the heart is, someone or other once said. Don't think we'll find my heart at the Wilshire. Can't imagine where we'll find it, actually. Might not have one to be found. One more vital organ missing from the invisible man!"

Moody said nothing. He was too tired now to try and divert Nigel from his maudlin ramblings. He felt as if he'd been driving for a week. When they got back to the hotel, he'd tip Nigel into a hot bath and then into bed, and hope he woke up in the morning in a less self-pitying frame of mind. Moody had his own demons to confront. His call to the FBI would be a humiliating experience. They would ask and ask again why he had compromised the security of the nation by secretly attempting to sell the stamp, and he would have to mention Nigel at that point, despite his reluctance to implicate a friend. It was not anything he wished to do, but do it he must.

"I DEFINITELY NEED a drink" were Nigel's first words as they entered the suite.

"Don't you think you've had enough?"

"Certainly not. I'm still standing, aren't I?"

"It's your liver. Why don't you have a nice hot bath instead?"

"You sound like my nanny. Nice hot bath for little Nigel? No, thanks. Wouldn't work anyway. Need a bloody great steam hose to get me clean. Are you going to make that phone call now?"

"In a minute." Moody felt like having a drink himself before attempting that task.

"Make little Nigel a drink first, would you, old man? Last one I'll ever ask you to make for me. Promise."

"All right, if you also promise it's the last you'll have tonight."

"Cross my heart and hope to die. Oops . . . forgot I don't have a heart to cross. Oh, well . . . where's that drink?"

Moody went to the bar. "I'm going to have a Scotch. Same for you?"

"Think I'll try something a bit different, something American. How about making me a margarita, Keith?"

"A margarita? Is this some kind of ironic joke?"

"No joke, old man. There's a bottle of margarita mix right

there next to you. Interesting drink, the margarita. Study the label, why don't you. Might learn something about life."

"I know how to make a margarita."

"But that's no good, Keith. You need to study the label to learn more than you already know. That's the definition of learning, isn't it, to know something now that you didn't know a minute ago?"

Moody ignored him and poured a measure of the ready-made mix and lime juice into a glass, then looked around for tequila to add.

"Just read the fucking label, why don't you!"

Moody turned to face Nigel. The actor's expression was twisted with desperation and drink, his eyes filled with an anguish Moody had never seen there before, even when Nigel had bathed with considerable gusto in a sea of guilt.

"Nigel—?"

"Just read it!"

"If you insist."

"Read it aloud."

" 'Margarita mix . . . ' " read Moody, before Nigel stopped him.

"You didn't read the bit above the 'margarita mix' line."

" 'Guzman's . . . margarita mix,' " read Moody, and felt a queasy sensation beginning to assert itself among his intestines.

"Read the bottom line, the one in small print."

" 'Bottled by Moreno Brothers, Los Angeles—' "

"Beginning to catch my drift now, old boy? Picture forming in the old noggin, is it? Certain things becoming clearer?"

"You . . . made it all up?"

Moody felt himself becoming dizzy. He put a hand against the bar, then set the bottle down to support himself with both hands. He had the uncanny sensation that the city was being shifted several inches sideways by an earth tremor. Nigel had a ghastly grin etched onto his face.

"And there you have it, my friend. Brilliant bit of impromptu bullshitting, if I do say so myself."

"I don't understand."

"Oh, I think you do. Cast your mind back twenty-four hours. I get a phone call, I start looking worried, I have to go into my room and think for a bit, then I go across to the bar and dither about over there until you ask me what's wrong. One glance at a label, and I've got an answer for you. Margarita, Guzman, Moreno, a cast of three, right there on a bottle of drink mix. I spun you a yarn, old man, right off the top of my head."

"There was no girl called Margarita?"

"And no outraged papa called Tomas Moreno, and no lawyer called Guzman."

"Then—who was in the casket?"

"Care to guess?"

"No. Tell me."

"Fumpf."

"What?"

"Fumpf, Secret Agent Fumpf, was in the casket. He made it all right from Canada to Los Angeles, but things were getting a bit hot for him once the FBI got wind of his connection to the stamp. He wanted to get out, you see, out of America and into Mexico before they caught up with him. Into the jolly old casket with the blighter, and away we go. That was him who gave you that false undertaking documentation. Doesn't look particularly German, does he? Brilliant chap in his own way. That was him pretending to be Guzman on the phone, too. There was only him in the station wagon that pulled up behind us, nobody else. Stolen vehicle, I should imagine. He did a pretty good job of convincing you a body had been put into the casket by several men, didn't he? Of course, a body *was* put in, but it wasn't sweet, soiled Margarita, it was Fumpf. He couldn't fix the tarpaulin very well, though, not from inside his fancy traveling box, and that's why it blew off before we got very far. The German embassy in Mexico City did the rest, organized our welcoming committee in Tijuana and relieved you of the stamp. Two birds killed with one stone. Fumpf out, stamp collected. All it took was some phone calls and your own good nature, Keith. Would you believe me if I said I'm terribly sorry?"

"No. Who *are* you?"

"Me? Nigel Lawson, clever little lad from Finsbury Park, London, recipient of elocution lessons to put the upper-class plum in the mouth, then knockabout actor from one end of Blighty to another, till there came a very handy affair with a lady of a certain age who just so happened to be somebody big in theatrical circles. No more spear carrying for little Nigel, oh no, leading roles from then on, old fruit. 'Anyone for tennis? Surely you can't mean to imply, Inspector, that you suspect me of murder? My darling, if one could look at you without swooning with desire, one would. Really, one would. You're too, too divine, my darling. To be, or not to be, that is the question.' Then they put me in the flicks. Bags of money, lots of adoring types hanging on my every word. Had to let go of the lady I mentioned. Didn't want anyone thinking I couldn't get something younger, you know. A picture or two, some speechifying to the hoi polloi about surrendering all their pots and pans to make Spitfires, some radio addresses to the nation, uplifting stuff about the glory of old England, bit of Shakespeare, bit of Kipling, anything to keep me out of active service, didn't want to cop a bullet, did I? Then Hollywood beckoned—and here I am."

"You haven't told me anything—"

"Oh, right you are. You want to know why I'm doing my

bit for the Nazis, I suppose. Bit embarrassing, this part. Fact is, old man, I met a young chap on tour, my last theatrical engagement before leaping to the silver screen, awfully nice fellow, tremendously good-looking, and he . . . well, he asked me if I'd ever had it sucked by a chap, and I had to admit I hadn't, and he dared me to find out what it's like. I suppose I'd had a few drinks, so I said . . . all right, and you know, it's exactly the same as being serviced by a woman. Then he invited me to sample the tight delights of his back passage, you know, and what with being drunk and a little pleased with myself for having had the nerve to overcome convention thus far, I thought to myself, in for a penny, in for a pound, and we went at it. Not as enjoyable as the first, but then, it gives you something to compare women to, doesn't it. I do believe I've appreciated women better since that little episode than I did before. Trouble was, the chap set me up for blackmail, you see. Fellow in the closet with a keyhole camera, lots of interesting pictures. They got in touch with me later and showed me. Had to think of the career. Had to buy them off. They didn't want money, though, nothing so common as blackmail. They said they'd be in touch if they ever needed some helping out, delightfully vague about it all. I said right-o, look forward to hearing from you, ha, ha, and then I heard nothing for years. Ten days or so ago they got in touch. That's when I found out who the chaps with the cameras were. Had to make a decision on the spot."

"And you chose to help them."

"Afraid so. But look at what I did. Was it so awful? A nervous agent wants to get out of the country, and Hitler wants his bloody stamp. Did I betray any state secrets, any crucial war plans, steal the blueprints for a new kind of plane or torpedo? Not a bit of it. In the grand scheme of things, it doesn't amount to a thimbleful of warm pee. Career saved, which, as we've discussed, is a good thing for you too, Keith old man, and what's been lost? An agent who couldn't get the job done, and a stamp. Admittedly, you're down a few dollars on the deal, Keith, and I intend doing my utmost to reimburse you and Myra for your loss. It's the least I can do, but frankly speaking, you're liable to make back that much and more by sticking with me as my screenwriter of choice. Even a bugger like MM would let you keep writing my stuff for as long as it all made money. The eighty thousand that went bye-bye isn't so much when you consider what you'll be earning by the honest sweat of your intellectual brow. That's the sensible way to look at it."

"Nigel . . . Nigel, the man you gave a ride in the casket was a murderer. He killed Morton Dulkis, thinking he was me, thinking the stamp must be in my old apartment—"

"You said yourself, old boy, the Dulkis fellow was a bit deranged, owned a shotgun for heaven's sake. Who knows what went on between them? It might very well have been self-defense on the part of . . . let's continue calling him Fumpf, shall we? I haven't the slightest idea what his real name is. No, it's all a fog of this against that, and who's to say what it all means? Tale told by an idiot, full of sound and fury, signifying nothing."

"Nothing? All of this is . . . nothing to you?"

"Probably understating the case, it's true, but what's a chap to do? Don't think I'm happy about what's happened, gosh no, but in the end, it's water under the bridge, no real harm done. One day we'll all be dead, don't you see, and none of this will matter in the least. Out, out, brief candle! Best thing is to move on, burn your bridges, and look to tomorrow."

Moody stared at the plush carpet. He felt sick. He could barely comprehend the scope of Nigel's betrayal. His friend had lied to him and used him to smuggle a murderer out of the country. The loss of the stamp was secondary. He felt a yawning emptiness inside him in the place where he had once held a friendship. His thoughts were nine parts emotion, one part reason. Anger, shame, regret; they swirled through him in shifting gusts and eddies. To look at Nigel was more than he could bear.

"The thing to consider now, Keith, is whether to pick up the phone or not. Do we think of tomorrow and the good things to come, or do we look to yesterday and bring the house crashing down? MM isn't going to like hearing that his new star aided and abetted the Nazis, and he'll come down hard on you too, Keith, by association. Isn't that what happened the last time, with that Baxter Nolan chap? Out on your ear, that's where Margolis will put you. Think about it."

"I have thought about it."

"And you concluded?"

Moody went to the phone and picked it up.

Nigel said, "Wait one moment, old fruit. . . . You aren't seriously considering turning me in, are you? Consider the consequences."

"I have," said Moody, beginning to dial.

"There won't be anyone there, Keith. Business hours and all that—"

"The FBI gave me a twenty-four-hour emergency number."

"Really? Very considerate of them, I must say. Better not call them, though, not if you want to write another book and make love to your wife again."

Moody turned. Nigel had a small automatic in his hand.

"Just like in the movies, isn't it, Keith. Bit melodramatic, I must admit. 'Put down that phone or die.' You do know I'd shoot with the utmost reluctance, don't you, but I *would* shoot. Self-preservation, you see. Actors have oodles of it, keeps them going when the audiences boo and the critics jeer. I won't lie down and let you ruin my life, Keith. Part of me is tempted to, of course, the decent part, but that's not very big at all, not when considered against the entire man, possibly just a small toe's worth. The rest of me wants to carry on as if none of this ever happened, and I remind you again, old man, that if you adopt the same wise philosophy, there's no saying how successful we couldn't make each other. Please don't make me pull the trigger—"

Moody set the phone down.

"Tell me what you want to do, Nigel."

"Do? Absolutely nothing. Keep my mouth shut, the same as you. We never did go to Mexico. You took a day off yesterday to discuss the Traven role with me in depth, that's what we'll tell Margolis if he asks. It never happened, Keith, none of it. Please, let's be sensible."

"And if I don't see things your way, you'll shoot me."

"Have to, old boy. The self-preservation instinct, as I said."

"And how will you explain my dead body?"

"Hide it. Smuggle you out in a laundry cart, something like that."

"You wouldn't care to chop me up into more easily managed parcels?"

"Don't be grotesque. What kind of man do you think I am?"

"I don't know. I thought I knew, but I was wrong. You had me fooled completely. I have to give you this, Nigel; you're a brilliant actor. That bit of extemporizing with the bottle label to concoct an entire scenario on the spur of the moment—amazing! The way you expressed doubt over the presence of Margarita in the casket; the suggestion that maybe we were being conned into smuggling something illicit across the border—stupendous! And that bit of inspired nonsense when the tarpaulin blew off and I told you this was your chance to reassure yourself there really was a dead girl inside, and you went all cowardly and declined, and *then*, the masterstroke—you invited me to take a look on your behalf. What colossal balls you have."

"Thanks, old man. I did pretty well in a tight spot, didn't I."

"I doubt that Edward Traven could have done better. But I'm afraid it puts me in the same position as Bruno von Eschen."

"Come again?"

"Count von Eschen, the husband of Maria, Countess von Eschen, who'll be played by the lovely and talented Gloria Gresham."

"Not following, old man."

"Bruno discovers that his wife has fallen for the spy Edward Traven, and he's faced with a dilemma. He loves his wife, and if he reveals her perfidy to the high command, she'll be shot along with Traven, but if he doesn't say anything, his wife leaves Germany by a secret route along with Traven and a host of Nazi secrets, and Bruno does actually love his country almost as much as he loves his wife. There's the dilemma."

"Having read the book, we both know he stays mum, and Traven and Maria make it back to England with their bag of codebreaking booty. Bruno did the right thing."

"Yes, but he did the right thing because it hurt the Nazis. If I keep mum about you, Nigel, I'll be doing the wrong thing, because it'll *help* the Nazis. I don't know that I could live with myself."

"Fix us a couple of drinks, would you, Keith? Have to keep my gun hand free, you know."

Moody went to the bar and began pouring Scotches.

"Are you saying," Nigel continued, "that the love of the count for his wife is the equivalent of the friendship between you and me?"

"Kind of. It's an interesting parallel, don't you think?"

"Fact is, I'm having a bit of trouble thinking at all just now. You're telling me that even though we're friends, you have to turn me in."

"Yes."

"Then I have to shoot you."

"Go ahead, get it over and done with. I'm definitely making that call when we finish our drinks. Want me to leave yours here on the bar?"

"Do that, old fruit, and step away. No sudden moves, please."

Both men sipped at their Scotches. Moody could tell that Nigel was genuinely at odds with himself. The man could act like a spy but never do what a true spy does when in a tight corner—cover his tracks with blood.

"Of course," said Moody, "there is another way out of this."

"Really? Surprise me with it."

"I hold off on the phone call and give you a head start."

"Head start for where? Germany? Wouldn't want to go there at all. Place is being bombed to pieces. The war's going to end soon, now that our side's landed on European soil to take it back from the Hun."

"*Our* side, Nigel? What a confused actor we are."

"No need to be snide about it. I did explain the bind they put me in."

"It wasn't bad enough to make you do what you've done."

"Depends on your point of view, I'd say, and from where I was standing, the situation looked disastrous."

"You might like to make a run for Mexico."

"Too hot. Don't like spicy food."

"Canada?"

"Too cold, too far away, too boring."

"Japan?"

"Don't be funny."

The telephone rang. Nigel waved Moody away from it and came closer to pick it up with his free hand. "Hello?"

He listened for several minutes, his face revealing nothing, then hung up, a sickly grin revealing his teeth.

"As a writer, Keith, you'll appreciate this. Fumpf is dead."

"Dead?"

"The bloody casket was an airtight model. Poor old Fumpf started poisoning his air the minute the lid was lowered. They do say a body doesn't react to slow toxification. Every breath he took, every exhalation, made him a little bit drowsier than the one before. He fell asleep, then became unconscious, apparently, not knowing anything. . . . He was dead from asphyxiation before we even got to the border. Ironic, what?"

"Extremely."

"Want some more? The stamp's a fake."

"No, it isn't. An expert philatelist, Elliot Moxham, studied it personally and verified its authenticity."

"That's right, and then what did you do with it? You put it in a bank vault, so nobody would have another go at pinching it, correct? That's when the substitution took place, if I'm any judge."

"There was no substitution. Myra had the only passkey to our safety-deposit box."

"Imagine you're an FBI man, Keith. You go to the bank manager and tell him what it is he's got in his vault, a tiny little piece of gummed paper that's actually a vital part of the war effort against Germany. You tell the manager you want to make absolutely sure the stamp remains in the right hands. You remind him of all the publicity surrounding Myra's kidnapping. You suggest he cooperate in the late-night substitution of a fake stamp prepared by those cunning chaps in the FBI for the real thing, then you walk away with the genuine article, leaving the fake behind for Myra to collect. Beginning to make sense, old man? The stamp you handed over was worthless. They're very angry with me down in Mexico City. Dead agent, fake stamp. They don't like me anymore, Keith."

"You're making it up, every word."

"No, I'm not. Clever I may be, but not this clever. Catch."

He threw the pistol to Moody, who caught it in midair.

"No need for bloodshed now, is there? Would I attempt such a risky bluff as this and hand over my gun, if I wasn't telling the truth?"

"Probably," said Moody, pocketing the automatic, "given your past performance."

"Gosh, what a compliment. I'm as earnest as any man ever was, and you think I'm acting, because I've been this convincing before. I can't think of a greater compliment. You're really unsure if I'm telling the truth?"

"Yes."

"Wizard! I can't begin to tell you how chuffed that makes me feel!"

"No charge," said Moody.

"Doesn't help us out much, though, does it."

"Not really."

"Isn't it obvious that turning me in now is an utter waste of time? No Nazi agent escaped, no precious stamp was stolen. . . . *I haven't done anything wrong!*"

"You're lying to me again, Nigel. It's another brilliant performance from the master, nothing I could base my own reactions on."

"But hang it all, man, I'm bloody sweating like a pig, can't you see? Could an actor sweat on demand, even a great actor? Stop being such an idiot!"

Nigel collapsed onto the sofa. "I think I must be going mad," he whispered.

Moody put his hands together for some light applause. Nigel responded with a smile even sicklier than before. "Hoist on one's own petard," he said, "or should that be hoisted? What's a bloody petard, anyway? Can I have my little gun back, please?"

"That wouldn't be wise."

"The damn thing isn't even loaded. See for yourself, if you don't believe me."

Moody took the automatic from his pocket and ejected the magazine. Empty. He pulled back the slide to check the chamber. Also empty.

"I never did buy any bullets for it," admitted Nigel. "I got the thing in a pawnshop for fifteen dollars. It probably wouldn't even work if you put bullets in it."

Moody tossed it onto the sofa. Nigel picked it up distractedly and slipped it into his pocket again. Now Moody began to believe him. The casket lid's craftsmanship had ensured a tight fit. "Fumpf" could indeed have suffocated. And the stamp? Would the FBI have allowed Myra to leave their safe house without assigning a surveillance team to follow her? And would that team have allowed her to visit the bank and then hand over to Moody the stamp the Bureau set so much store by? Unlikely, he now saw. The Bureau had switched stamps, as Nigel insisted. Moody had thought himself so clever at outwitting them, and he had himself been outwitted. Now he was angry, with the FBI and with himself. He was lost in a maze of mirrors, turning and turning, seeing himself and Nigel and everyone else concerned with the stamp whirling in an ever-increasing gyre of reality and reflection, reality, reflection . . . until everything became a whirlpool that funneled down into darkness, where one thing was indistinguishable from another. He felt sick all over again.

And one question remained to bother him: Could he now, in the light of the most recent revelations, allow Nigel to be his friend again? He was sorely tempted to let the incident slide away from recollection like a dream, but a part of him resisted. Nigel had done what Nigel had done; had betrayed him, lied to him, knowingly put up a false front to deceive him. How could such two-faced behavior be forgiven? The man himself, the actor, lay on the sofa, staring at the ceiling, his Scotch ignored. Moody actually felt sorry for him. The phone call from Mexico City was real; the plot had come undone. Was any real harm accomplished? Had the United States lost anything? Had the Germans gained a single thing they wanted? The real stamp was doubtless at FBI headquarters by now. Moody would have to humiliate himself by asking for its return. The prospect did not appeal. They would ask him why he'd used his wife to take the stamp from safe custody for a private sale that allowed no FBI access to the potential buyers. He would have to lie, to avoid implicating Nigel. Thinking that, and becoming aware that he had thought it, Moody realized he wanted to protect the actor. Was Nigel anything but a rather pathetic pawn in a game of incalculable size and scope, a dupe, shanghaied into doing what he did by way of a threat every public figure would think about twice before ignoring? Moody had deceived the FBI for friendship; Nigel had betrayed his friend and the Allied cause for the sake of his career and good name. The two motives were not comparable, but Moody nonetheless wanted to forget everything Nigel had done, simply push it all over the edge of a cliff and watch it dwindle to nothingness far below.

"All right," he said.

Nigel rose onto one elbow and looked at him.

"Sorry?"

"I won't tell."

"You won't?"

"No. There's no point."

"Keith . . . you mean it?"

"Against my better judgment, perhaps."

"Dear old chum Keith!" Nigel leaped up from the sofa, suddenly invigorated. "What an absolute brick you are! I know I've behaved shamefully, done things I shouldn't have, used you in the most awful fashion, taken advantage of your decency. . . . Let's get out of here and have a real drink downstairs in the bar! I feel like celebrating!"

"There's absolutely nothing to celebrate."

"Nonsense, old man, there's bags of things. Friendship, for one, albeit a tiny bit tarnished on my side—and the confounding of the enemy by an unexpected twist of fate, two of them, actually . . . and . . . we'll think of some more downstairs!"

Moody threw up his hands. "If that's what you want," he said, not knowing what else to do.

"It's what we both need, old boy. Hang on a sec while I change my clothes. I've gone and sweated right through what I've got on."

Moody finished his drink while Nigel dashed into his bedroom, to emerge minutes later looking every inch a movie star. The man's transformation from defeated wretch to celebrity triumphant was, Moody acknowledged, worth the price of admission.

igel took Moody's arm and steered him out of the apartment. He jabbered excitedly throughout their descent in the elevator, reminding Moody of the creative bonanza awaiting them after the undoubted success of *Traitor's Dawn* and thanking him several times over for his generosity of spirit, his tremendous grasp of both sides of the issue.

Moody was a little annoyed by the time they found a booth and were seated with their first round of whiskies. Residents and their guests came and went throughout the length of the bar, talking excitedly, wearing their finest, pleased to be who and where they were. To Moody they resembled creatures from another planet. By the third round, Moody's sense of removal from reality was complete. He allowed Nigel to prattle on enthusiastically, nodding in agreement with the little conviction he could muster, quickly becoming disassociated from everything around him. It had all been too much, the lies and deceit, the believing and not believing, the spinning mirror-world of pretense. He was dizzy and tired and becoming drunk, and he simply didn't care anymore. The morning would reveal any truth associated with events of the past twenty-four hours, if any remained to be made.

"I always said these movie people work hard, Vinnie, and here's the proof."

"Yeah, they've been working real hard on those drinks, I bet."

Moody looked up. Huttig and Labiosa stood over the table.

"Detectives!" said Nigel, his speech a trifle blurred. "Welcome, and pray be seated! Join our party of two in celebration!"

"Celebration of what?" asked Huttig.

"Why, celebration of life itself, Captain."

"Lieutenant."

The detectives sat down at the outer ends of the U-shaped bench seat. Moody noticed that this seating arrangement effectively trapped himself and Nigel. Had the investigation of Mrs. Yaddigan's death come full circle back to them?

"May we offer you chaps a drink?" Nigel offered.

"We're on duty, Lawson," said Labiosa. "Don't be corrupting us."

"Oh, certainly not. Furthest thing from my mind."

"If you're on duty," said Moody, "that means you came in looking for us."

"Check," said Labiosa, smiling. "You could be a detective yourself, Moody, with that logical brain you got."

"Thank you. I assume you have more questions for us concerning the Yaddigan murder."

"Nope," said Huttig. "Answers."

"Pardon me?"

"Answers, Moody, we got answers for you and your pal the body thief."

"I think I resent that," said Nigel.

"Don't act so angry," said Labiosa. "On you it don't look

convincing. I could act angry better myself. They should pay me what they pay you for acting that way."

Nigel smiled and said nothing. Moody said, "What answers, Lieutenant?"

"We got the one that did it, that's what."

"Miss Worth?"

"Not her, she's not the one. The old guy."

"Excuse me, what old guy?"

"Out there at that Morning Glory joint. The old guy in the wheelchair."

"Mr. Hardiman?"

"The cowboy cripple. He's the one. Couldn't keep his mouth shut, wanted to brag about what he did to some of his cronies out there till the whole place knew what happened, and finally someone called us."

"Good God," said Moody, "I never would have suspected it was him. He didn't like Mrs. Yaddigan, of course, but then, she wasn't a terribly likable woman. How did he get hold of a gun?"

"The gun was Yaddigan's. He told us someone knew where she kept it in her office drawer and told Hardiman, and yesterday morning he went in there and grabbed it when she's outta the office, and he waits there for her and plugs her when she came back."

"Does this mean he'll be charged with first-degree murder, or will he be able to plead diminished responsibility?"

"He won't be pleading nothing," Labiosa said.

"I don't understand."

"He's dead," explained Huttig. "He still had the gun when we got him cornered in the laundry room this afternoon. He used it on himself. Didn't want to give up and come quietly."

"Saves the taxpayers the cost of a trial," added Labiosa. "We thought you'd like that angle."

"I . . . don't know what to say," said Moody, truthfully.

"Know what his last words were, Moody, before he put a bullet in his head? He said, 'No more stinking custard,' then he pulled the trigger."

"He did make it known that he was less than pleased with Morning Glory's cuisine, the desserts, anyway."

"So if you know where Worth's hiding out, Moody, you can tell her she's got nothing to worry about anymore, not being a suspect in the case now that we got Hardiman."

"How would I know where Miss Worth is hiding?"

Huttig shook out a cigarette and lit it. "Come on, Moody. You and Nigel here and Nora Worth did that body steal between you, it's obvious. Not that we care or anything, we're Homicide dicks, not Larceny, so why don't you come clean, just so's we can sleep nights without wondering what good's an old lady's body? You wanna tell us maybe?"

"There hadda be money in it somehow," said Labiosa. "We're just curious, honest."

"Gentlemen," Nigel said, his manner offended yet dignified, "Mr. Moody and myself had absolutely nothing to do with this alleged body stealing, and we resent your insinuation that we did. If you don't cease and desist immediately with your unfounded accusations, we'll have no other recourse than to consult our attorneys in the matter."

"My attorney," Moody added, "is Mr. Guzman, a brilliant man."

Nigel began to laugh.

"Never heard of him," said Huttig.

"You will," Moody assured him.

"You girls better not try anything dumb like that again," Labiosa warned. "Any more bodies get stolen around town, we'll know where to come looking."

"Of course you will, Lieutenant," said Nigel.

"Sergeant, smart-ass."

"Quite."

The detectives stood. They hadn't bothered removing their hats before entering the bar. Huttig pulled his a little lower onto his forehead.

"We'll be in touch, Moody."

"You could always send me a postcard instead."

Huttig and Labiosa turned together and left.

"Sergeant Smart-ass," joked Nigel. "The name suits him. Let's order champagne."

"Nigel, do you have any idea what the Kumquat Club is?"

"The what?" Nigel beckoned to a waitress.

"The Kumquat Club. One of the journalists interviewing Gloria and you and Myra and myself dropped a card in my office the other day. The Kumquat Club, it said. No address or phone number."

"Never heard of it, old man." A waitress hovered over them. "Champagne, my dear, and I refer to the good stuff."

"Yes, Mr. Lawson."

The waitress hurried away as Nigel admired her rear. Moody was mystified by Nigel's ability to shrug off his anguish and resume playing his former self as if nothing had occurred to shake him to his core. The man who had held a gun on him now was buying champagne for them to share, and was genuinely happy to do so. Moody shook his head to clear it.

"The reason I ask is, that card Nora Worth handed you accidentally, when you gave your autograph, was another one from the Kumquat Club. It bothered me at the time, the coincidence, but events put it out of my mind until Huttig mentioned Miss Worth. What connection could she possibly have to reporters?"

"No idea at all. Don't get all perplexed over nothing, Keith. We have some serious drinking to attend to, and I want your undivided attention on the task before us."

"Is a kumquat a fruit or a vegetable?"

"Haven't the foggiest."

A sudden thought came into Moody's head. "Damn," he said.

"It can't be that important," said Nigel.

"No, it's . . . something else." He looked at Nigel.

"What is it, old man?"

"The accusation Kurt made, that he saw you coming down the staircase as he went up to my old apartment, is it true?"

"True?"

"Were you there, Nigel?"

"You're taking that ridiculous story seriously?"

"Having learned what I've learned tonight, how ridiculous can it be?"

Nigel's eyes skittered away from Moody's. Moody felt his heart sink.

"Just because a chap is at the scene, so to speak, doesn't mean he had anything to do with the rotten thing that happened."

"So you *were* there."

"Didn't even set foot inside the place, just accompanied our friend Fumpf. He's the one who went in and demanded the stamp. I had absolutely nothing to do with what happened, I want you to believe me, Keith. Bloody old Fumpf must've panicked or something. He said the chap inside showed resistance and reached for a shotgun, of all things, so Fumpf had to put a stop to that, naturally. He went a bit too far with the strangulation, he said, so instead of simply rendering the chap unconscious, he sort of . . . killed him. Regrettable, I admit. Horrendous balls-up all around."

"Did he tell you he finished him off with a straight razor across the throat?"

"Actually, he was a bit reserved about the whole thing when we talked about it later. I didn't go inside with him, not wanting to take part in any rough stuff, you understand, so I waited outside. When things started getting nasty I got a bit panicky over what I could hear through the door and just . . . left. That's when your friend Kurt came up, and we passed on the stairs. I kept my face turned away from him, but he must've got a good look at me anyway. I say, this doesn't queer things between us, does it, old fruit? I happen to be a victim of circumstances in this particular instance, you can see that, can't you? I don't know why they wanted me to go along with him, just a bit of deliberate involvement to make yours truly know who's issuing the orders, I suppose. He could've done the job alone, but they told me to go with him. There, now you know everything."

"Morton Dulkis is dead."

"As I say, a regrettable error."

"You were there."

"Not in the actual room, dear boy. Waiting outside, you see—"

"Yes, I see."

"Are wheels spinning inside your head, Keith? Are you wondering what to do now? Life's full of compromises, you know."

"Yes, I know."

The champagne arrived. Nigel told the waitress to bill it to his room. This time, as she walked away, he didn't watch her. Nigel was watching Moody closely.

"Tell you what, Keith, let's take this bottle of champers and go for a drive. I can see you've been shocked all over again. This isn't the place to be debating the rights and wrongs of the situation. A long drive in the cool of the evening, that's what we need to sort things out, all right?"

"All right."

They left the bar and went to Moody's car. "Drive east, old man. Do you know, I've never seen the desert? I'd like to have a look at it by moonlight. Want me to drive? You look a bit shagged out. Understandable, of course."

"I'm fine."

Driving south into Orange County, then east toward Riverside County and the desert, Moody's senses were dulled to the point of numbness. Nigel, on the other hand, became more animated as the drive progressed, sucking at the champagne bottle, putting his head out through the open window as the city was left behind to let out a scream that seemed to Moody's ears one part excitation to three parts desperation. Nigel clearly was not yet back on an even keel; nor, Moody reminded himself, was he.

The car passed through darkness, its headlights a weak cone of light playing across the road ahead. "Let's go to Corona," suggested Nigel.

"Why?"

"No reason, old man, I just like the name. It isn't far, is it?"

"Another thirty minutes."

"Good show." He took a deep swig from the bottle. "Sure you don't want any?"

"I've got a headache."

"Best thing for headaches is champers, I always say. My own head's splitting, and I just don't care anymore. Bottoms up!"

Nigel drained the last of the drink and flung the bottle into the desert scrub alongside the road, then turned to Moody and said, "You can't do it, can you, Keith old man."

"Can't do what?"

"Forgive me. Forget what happened. You can't do it. I can tell what you're thinking, you know, always had a knack for that kind of thing. It's all been too much, hasn't it. A shock to the jolly old system. It's there in your face. You despise me, and you despise yourself a little bit too, for not despising me sooner than this. I really do wish you'd forgotten what Kurt had to say about seeing me. If not for that, we'd be fine, I'm sure of it, but knowing I was hovering around in the vicinity when that Dulkis chap was murdered has set you back on your heels, hasn't it, Keith. Can't say I blame you. Of course, this means we can't go on as a creative team, doesn't it. There'd always be a certain awkwardness between us. The magic has gone. I feel its loss too, I want you to know. Anyway, it's all over now. You fully intend reporting me to the authorities, don't you. It makes you sick to think about losing *Traitor's Dawn*, but you can always go back to writing novels."

"Why am I losing *Traitor's Dawn*?"

"Because, old man, I'm going to do a moonlight flit. They told me to over the phone, you see. We're going to the airport in Corona. There's a plane waiting for me."

"What plane?"

"The one that'll take me to Mexico. You see, Keith, when they told me what a shambles our little expedition today turned out to be, they said I had to get rid of you, as the only witness. Naturally I didn't want to do any such thing, you being a good chum of mine, but they were adamant, old sport. I have to give up everything in Hollywood and go south, but before I do, I'm supposed to bump you off, isn't that a tricky situation?"

"How are you going to do it?"

"Shoot you, obviously. I'm not the kind to go strangling people. The very idea makes me want to vomit."

Nigel took the small automatic from his pocket.

Moody said, "Too bad you didn't get around to buying any bullets for it."

"As a matter of fact, that was a little white lie. I did buy bullets, and I loaded it up before we went down to the bar."

"I don't believe you."

Nigel put his arm out the window and fired a shot into the air. Moody swerved slightly at the sound of the pistol's sharp crack. Nigel went on, "I was going to shoot you in the suite, but when you said you weren't going to tell on me to the FBI I changed my mind, but I loaded the gun anyway, because as you may have noticed, things have a way of changing from night to day at the drop of a hat. I was going to ignore both orders, the one to kill you and the one to fly away to Mexico, and hope they didn't try to get me, but of course that option's no longer open. Once you learned I was a party to Dulkis's murder, the die was cast; you simply couldn't ignore it any longer. I'm not saying I wouldn't do the same thing in your place, but it pretty much washes me up in Hollywood, doesn't it. Pity, really. I honestly think I had a chance to make something of myself there. It's all over now. But I won't shoot you, Keith. I can't. I've grown too fond of you over these last few days. You were going to stay mum for me, and I appreciate that, but it's all in the past now. I'm getting on that plane, and when I face them down in Mexico City, I'm going to hope they don't mind that I only obeyed one out of the two orders. There's really no point in them getting angry with me. What purpose would killing you serve? None at all, in my opinion, so I won't do it."

"Thank you."

"No need for that, old man. I'm a washout, completely

buggered myself. All my fault, really, the choices I made, the company I kept, present company excepted, of course. This will be my first plane ride. I'm rather excited about it."

"Don't take that plane, Nigel. Stay here and face the music. I'll do everything I can to make things easier for you."

"Too late. Opportunity gone. Paradise lost. Drive on, Keith. My mind is made up. Good thing for you, though, my going away. Nobody can connect you with anything. Good for Margolis and Empire too. No scandal if I vanish, just a mystery, provided you don't talk. If I can't go down in history as a great actor, the very least I can look forward to is making my mark with a mysterious, unsolved disappearance. Not a terribly satisfactory kind of fate, but better than nothing, I suppose. I could never live in a prison cell, Keith. I'd rather die."

"They may kill you in Mexico."

"What on earth for? It wasn't my fault the FBI switched stamps, and it wasn't my fault Fumpf was asphyxiated. It's all just bad luck. No, I'll be better off down there. At least I'll be free. Bit of an ignominious ending, but a chap can learn how to adapt to unexpected circumstances. A change of plan, that's all it is. Enough said. Let's have some music to cheer us up, shall we?"

Nigel turned on the radio, and Moody drove on, his doubts and misgivings swamped by the lush sounds of Glen Miller.

Much too soon, the lights of Corona appeared in the distance. Nigel said, "Would you like me to drive on alone? That way you're covered if anyone puts two and two together. You could always say I held you at gunpoint to make you drive out this way, then forced you out of the car in the middle of a desert road, so you couldn't try to warn anyone at the airport. I'll leave the car somewhere obvious, with the keys under the driver's seat.

You won't have to walk far to get it, and you won't have to walk
back to Los Angeles."

"No."

"No? Rather a good plan, I thought."

"I'm taking you to the plane, like it or not."

"If you insist."

The airport was north of the town. Moody followed the
signs and pulled into a parking lot in front of a low building
flanked by several small metal hangars. He turned off the engine.
Nigel looked at his wristwatch. "Plenty of time yet. The chap's
going to come in at the west end of the runway with his engine
off, glide in so no one even knows he's here until he turns the
engine on again for takeoff. I'm supposed to wait for him out of
sight, away from the lights. Good thing it's a clear night. Might
as well say our cheery-byes now."

"No, I'll go with you till you get picked up."

"What for, old man? Parting is such sweet sorrow."

"I don't know what for, but I'm seeing this through till the
end."

"Just as you like."

They left the car and walked back along the airport road for
several hundred yards, then climbed a wire fence onto airport
property and began walking toward the west end of the runway.
Neither man spoke until they reached the rendezvous. Nigel
checked his watch again. "Should hear the chap pretty soon now,
or rather, not hear him. Hope he doesn't miss the runway and
bowl us over. Be an ironic end to things, wouldn't it."

"Yes."

"Poor old Keith. Betrayed by his pal. I do apologize."

"It isn't necessary."

"No, suppose not. What's been done's been done. Nothing
to do now but hope nothing worse happens to us, you here, me

in Mexico. Imagine MM's face when I go missing. The bugger'll probably have a heart attack. Shouldn't say that, should I, after everything that's happened. I really do hope that none of this gets smeared on you, Keith. That's the one thing that bothers me."

"You have enough to worry about."

"True. Wonder if I could sort of . . . pop up again after the war, when everything's calmed down a bit? I mean to say, if a chap can't be an actor, what's he going to do for a living? This is all I know, the only thing I've ever been any good at. Hate to give it up, just like that, forever. Think I might be able to sneak back into the good graces of the powers that be after the peace is signed? Not right away, of course, but after a year or two, perhaps. Think that might happen?"

"I don't know, Nigel. I don't know anything anymore."

"Nor I, old chum. Pair of woebegone buggers, we are."

A whispering sound came to Moody's ears, the sound of wind passing over wires and canvas, and suddenly a dark shape passed swiftly overhead, coming from the west. The biplane's wheels touched onto the earthen runway, raising faint clouds of dust; then it continued rolling, its upper wing and fuselage gleaming faintly.

"Bang on time. Well, this is it, old sport. Sorry about all this."

"Good-bye, Nigel."

"We . . . we *were* friends, weren't we?"

"Definitely."

"That makes it easier, somehow. Or harder . . . I don't know which." Nigel put out his hand. "So long, old man. I'll send you a postcard."

"Please do."

They shook hands. Nigel seemed reluctant to let go. The

plane had stopped, and now sat waiting a short distance away. Nigel released Moody's hand and began running toward it, his long legs pumping. Moody watched him talk briefly with the pilot, then stand by the propeller, arms lifted to take hold of one blade. He heard the pilot call "Contact!" and saw Nigel swing the prop. The engine came to life with a spluttering roar. Nigel climbed up onto the lower wing and lowered himself inside the rear cockpit. The plane swiveled around and began charging toward Moody, still standing at the end of the runway. He hurried out of its path as the plane picked up speed. The wheels were barely off the ground as it sped past him and began to climb. Moody saw Nigel waving, but he could not bring himself to wave back. The plane was by now too far away in any case. Moody asked himself, as the plane vanished into darkness, the throbbing of its engine quickly dying away, why it was that he didn't wave. A part of him had wanted to; another part had not. As he had said to Nigel, he didn't know anything anymore.

The desert air was thick with the smell of sagebrush, he now noticed. He supposed his attention had been elsewhere while Nigel was still with him. With Nigel gone, Moody was aware of other things. He felt terribly sad. What was it about the actor that made his absence cause this feeling? He had lied to Moody, had tricked him into running a fool's errand, thinking he was helping a friend out of a tight spot, and now, by his leaving, had put Moody's career as a screenwriter back where it had been just a short time before—deep within the realm of the impossible. A friendship betrayed, a job almost certainly lost, and yet Moody already missed the company of the man responsible. Was he so very stupid that he couldn't distinguish where honor lay? Moody had chosen—finally, in the Wilshire's bar—to do the honorable thing and report his friend's misdeeds to the FBI, but it had not been easy making that choice, and then the choice had been taken from him before he could act, removed by Nigel's ability to know Moody's mind. And even then he had performed one more task for the actor, by driving him to Corona. He hadn't seriously believed Nigel might shoot him if he chose not to cooperate, once the loaded gun was produced. He had wanted to help the man get away. Was he nothing more than a willing dupe for spending these last few hours assisting Nigel Lawson? In a sense, the actor's loss was greater; he would forever be branded a traitor for his willingness to assist the Germans in their pursuit of Myra's stamp. That is, if Moody told anyone.

It occurred to him then that he alone held the key to Nigel's future, or at least, the future of his public memory. No one else was aware that Nigel was a spy. Should Moody tell what he knew? That he would confide in Myra was a foregone conclusion, but need anyone else know? The murder of Morton Dulkis would be explained, even though the true identity of the killer "Fumpf" would never be revealed. What point was served by implicating Nigel, now that he had gone? Moody knew he was a poor custodian for the legend that might grow around the missing star; sooner or later something approaching the facts about Nigel Lawson would find their way into a book written by Moody, and tongues would wag. The easiest thing would be to confess everything to Agents Buller and Denton, just to set the record straight. But the FBI had stolen his stamp, if Nigel's theory was correct. Why should Moody help government thieves?

He began walking back toward the airport fence, mulling over the possibilities open to him, and decided, before jumping over the fence and onto the side of the road leading to the parking lot, that he would give the FBI a chance to exonerate themselves. He would ask them to return the stamp, and if they complied (they might, after all, have switched it for a fake solely to protect it), he would tell them everything he knew. If they did not, and by doing so proved themselves unreliable and dishonest, to say the least, then he would tell them nothing. Let them wonder about whatever he might one day write about a missing actor who spied for the Nazis; he was a writer of fiction and could always claim to have made it all up. Nothing could be proved against Nigel, because Nigel was gone, and nothing could be proved against Moody, because Moody himself was the only witness. It was an insubstantial reward for his labors and his losses, but it was all he had.

oody went back to work on Wednesday as if nothing had occurred and booked out of the Wilshire that evening, asking the management if they had by any chance seen their famous guest recently. That question set a ball rolling. The ball rolled to Empire Productions and the office of Marvin Margolis, where Moody was summoned on Thursday. MM was in an interrogative frame of mind.

"Keith, Nigel Lawson has disappeared. What can you tell me? I'm told you were sharing his suite at the Wilshire until Tuesday."

"Yes, I was, Mr. Margolis, and Tuesday evening is the last time I saw Nigel. We went for a drive together, and he asked me to drop him off along Mulholland Drive. He said he had a lot of thinking to do, and he wanted to walk alone for a while. He didn't say what he wanted to think about."

"Why were you sharing his suite at the Wilshire, and why have you since moved out?"

"That's classified information, Mr. Margolis. I can't reveal the reasons."

"What? Tell me what you know immediately."

"I can only refer you to Agents Denton and Buller of the Federal Bureau of Investigation. The matter concerns the war effort."

"The war effort?" Margolis stared at Moody for a moment. "Where are you now living?"

"In my house, with my wife. Myra left the protective custody of the FBI yesterday."

"Protective custody? I need to know more. This may relate in some way to Nigel's disappearance."

"It concerns the stamp my wife was kidnapped for. Certain other parties were also in search of it. Denton and Buller can explain, if they wish."

"I see. It may interest you to know, Keith, that I have a personal relationship with J. Edgar Hoover. If any of this information is incorrect, J. Edgar will inform me."

"Then I suggest you telephone Mr. Hoover immediately. If Nigel has fallen afoul of enemy agents, the Bureau should be aware of it."

"Enemy agents?"

"I'm sure Mr. Hoover will tell you everything, sir."

"That will be all."

On Thursday evening Myra and Moody were visited at their home by Agent Denton and Agent Buller. The first questions asked were in relation to Myra's leaving of the safe house to return home. Myra said she didn't feel afraid of further kidnappings. When asked why, she had no answer other than her "instincts." The agents appeared dissatisfied with this.

"The stamp is still wanted by the Nazis, Mrs. Moody, yet you say you don't fear them?"

"Not anymore, no."

"Mr. Moody, can you explain why you moved out of the Wilshire and came back home?"

"I missed my wife, and Nigel Lawson can be a bit hard to take after a while."

"You're aware that Mr. Lawson has disappeared."

"Yes. I took advantage of that to pack my bags and come home. It would've been awkward explaining to Nigel why I didn't want to share his suite anymore."

Buller hesitated, then said, "But you're not telling us why you don't fear further interest from the Germans."

"The stamp is a fake," said Moody. "They're not interested."

"Excuse me?"

"We took the stamp from the vault last Tuesday. It was a clever forgery, I could tell that at a glance, even though I'm no expert. Someone substituted the fake for the real stamp while it was supposedly protected inside the vault."

"This is a remarkable charge, Mr. Moody," said Denton.

"Yes, isn't it. Either the Germans broke into the vault and made the switch without leaving a tace, or the bank manager did it, or someone else did it with the cooperation of the manager."

"Someone else?"

"The FBI," said Moody. "Purely in the interests of safeguarding the stamp, of course."

"You're accusing the Bureau of taking the stamp without consulting you first?" asked Buller. His professionally neutral expression was hardening.

"For the national interest," said Moody. "It's bait, isn't it, for the Nazi agent you mentioned?"

"Mr. Moody, you should have informed us that you intended removing the stamp from the vault."

"And you should have informed us that you substituted a fake. We'd like the real stamp back."

"Where's the supposedly fake stamp you took from the vault?"

"We have it hidden in a safe place, as evidence of theft," bluffed Moody.

Denton said, "You may be charged with interfering with a federal case, Mr. Moody. Are you aware of what you've done?"

"Yes, quite aware. That's why I have the fake stamp in a safe place. I'll keep it there until the real stamp is returned to us."

"As far as the Bureau is concerned, you have your stamp. You took it from your own safe-deposit box, under your own volition, and any implication of impropriety by the Bureau made by you will be treated as a hostile act."

Myra said, "Can we stop this nonsense? Give me back my stamp."

"Mrs. Moody, we don't have your stamp. *You* have your stamp."

"A clever fake. I want my own stamp back. It's worth a lot of money."

"Bring the 'fake' to the Bureau, and we'll investigate," said Buller. "You folks are acting like shakedown artists."

"We simply want our stamp back."

"The Bureau takes a dim view of attempted blackmail, Mrs. Moody."

"No one's attempting to blackmail anyone. I just want my stamp back."

Denton said, "Show us the fake, then we'll talk."

The agents looked at each other, then stood up to leave. "The next move is up to you," Buller told the Moodys. "Agent Denton and myself will look forward to it."

They walked toward the front door, and while passing by

the entrance to the living room, Denton asked, "Where's the coffin, Mr. Moody?"

"Oh, Uncle Albert died, finally."

"I thought you said his name was Henry."

Henry Albert, yes. He went peacefully."

Myra opened the door, and the agents passed through. Buller turned to Moody and said again, "Your move," before leaving. Myra shut the door.

"They're not going to give it back, are they," she said.

"No, and we can't prove they substituted a fake, not without producing it."

"They stole something worth eighty thousand dollars."

"We can't prove it, and they know that. It's a stalemate."

"Bastards!"

"Indeed. It isn't Buller and Denton's doing, though. An order to fake the stamp had to have come from higher up. They did say the case had been brought to the attention of J. Edgar Hoover himself, because of the Hitler connection."

"J. Edgar Hoover stole my stamp."

"Probably. All we need to do in order to get it back is admit I smuggled a Nazi agent across the border into Mexico, with the help of my good friend Nigel Lawson, who worked for the Germans."

"We're not going to see that stamp ever again, are we."

"I doubt it."

"Double bastards."

WORD OF NIGEL'S disappearance soon became front-page news. The story flourished for a week, then began to fade, and was revived when a housewife in Escondido found a body in the dense growth at the bottom of her overgrown backyard.

The body was badly decomposed, but police called to the scene found documentation suggesting it was none other than the missing movie star. After an autopsy it was revealed that almost every bone in his body was broken. Nigel held in his hand, even at the moment of death, a lap or safety belt of some kind, with a buckle that functioned perfectly; however, it was obvious the ends of the belt had been sliced almost clean through. It was eventually concluded that Nigel Lawson had gone for a ride in an open-cockpit plane and had fallen out when the plane turned upside down, subjecting the tampered-with belt to more strain than it could accommodate. Why any of this should have happened was never explained.

Moody was not surprised at being summoned again to the office of Marvin Margolis.

"Keith, this tragedy is a severe blow to Empire Productions; however, we'll proceed with *Traitor's Dawn* using another actor, probably Wallace Ewing."

"Wallace is an American, Mr. Margolis. Edward Traven's an Englishman, and I don't think Wally's ever been known to do a convincing English accent."

"Edward Traven will become an American agent with the Office of Strategic Services. It's clear that the presence of American forces in Europe is what turned the tide against the Nazis. We've played our part over there, in the field of espionage as much as in the military sense. Traven should be an American. The role has more meaning that way, don't you agree? Mr. Hoover has suggested to several heads of the studios that we have failed to beat the patriotic drum as loudly as we should have in this particular area. There will be no more movies about heroic Englishmen produced at Empire until the war's end, and possibly not even then. It's our turn at center stage as spies and secret agents and so forth. Very little rewriting will be required to accommodate Wallace. Now then, do you wish to continue with the screenplay, Keith?"

"Yes, sir, I do."

"Word has come to me concerning the late Nigel Lawson that you might be interested in hearing. This comes from the office of J. Edgar Hoover himself, so its truthfulness is beyond dispute. Inquiries were made in London, and it has been learned that Nigel was a troubled individual since boyhood. I would never have suspected that myself, but that's a measure of the man's brilliance as an actor, to be capable of deceiving a man such as myself. Nigel was a difficult boy, willful, hard to control, according to his aunt, who raised him. You see, Nigel was responsible for killing his parents. Apparently he caused his home to explode by tampering with the gas stove. He was unaware that his mother was upstairs sleeping at the time. He reportedly wished to bring about the death of his father, someone he hated, according to the report that has come to me. Guilt is a terrible burden for anyone, and I must presume Nigel carried just such a weight upon his shoulders. Who knows, it could be that he became an actor to escape from himself and his burden of guilt and shame. I thought you should share this special knowledge, Keith. I'm told you and Nigel got to be great friends during the short time he was with us."

"Thank you, Mr. Margolis. It clears up some lingering questions in my mind."

"Good."

"Is Mr. Hoover a stamp collector?"

"Why do you ask that question, Keith?"

"Idle curiosity, sir."

"Mr. Hoover does have a small collection, yes."

"More than just one stamp?"

"I fail to follow your train of thought."

"It doesn't matter. That train is better derailed."

"Keith, are you quite all right . . . in your mind?"

"Never better. A mind without illusions sees things more clearly."

Margolis stared at him for a moment before going on. "Regarding your next assignment, I have an entirely new concept for you to tackle."

"Next assignment? I haven't really begun work on *Traitor's Dawn* yet."

"That project will be handed to another of our writers."

"But—you just asked me if I wanted to continue with the screenplay."

"I asked out of politeness. Your wishes play no part in decisions made on my side of the desk, Keith. It's my feeling that without Nigel in the lead role, your work would be distorted, lacking perception, also unfocused."

"I can assure you, Mr. Margolis, that the screenplay will be the best possible, Nigel or Wallace notwithstanding."

"I appreciate your commitment to the project, Keith, but the correct decision has already been made. As I was saying, Empire wishes to try something new, and I've decided that a man with your talents is the one to bring the new concept to fruition. This will be a personally rewarding task for you, Keith. You have, I'm told, lost a valuable friend recently."

"Nigel was more than just a friend."

"I refer not to Nigel, but your dog."

"My dog?"

"Your dog was killed, isn't that so?"

"Yes, but—"

"And you and your wife are currently childless, am I correct?"

"Myra's expecting—"

"But not yet delivered of her precious baby, so this will give you the opportunity, Keith, to sample the delights of fatherhood at first hand, a valuable experience for any man intending to raise a family."

"I'm not sure I understand."

Margolis pressed a button on his office intercom. "Miss Harrison, send in our new stars, if you'd be so kind. Mr. Moody wishes to become acquainted."

"Yes, Mr. Margolis."

The bronze door opened. A small girl came through. In her hand was a leash; at the end of the leash was a collie dog. The girl was eight or nine years old, with a mass of curling red hair.

"Keith, meet Missie."

Moody swallowed hard and managed to nod his head. "Hello, Missie."

"Missie is the dog. The young lady is called Bunty, Bunty Wells. Say hello to Bunty, Keith."

"Hello, Bunty—"

The girl suddenly broke into tears and said, "She peed on my shoes! Look what she did! I hate her!"

Bunty Wells extended a shapely little ankle and foot. Her shoe buckle was wet.

"Now then, Bunty," said Margolis, with a grimace attempting to become a paternal smile, "we don't want to upset Missie by complaining about her natural functions, do we. Collies are sensitive creatures, and Missie is a purebred, so we must learn to accommodate her, mustn't we, dear. Yes, we must do that."

"I dowanna!" insisted Bunty, stamping her wet shoe.

"But you will," said Margolis, now leering like a gargoyle. "Won't she, Keith."

If she knows what's good for her, thought Moody.

. . .

THAT EVENING, AFTER Moody had revealed the full
extent of his humiliation to Myra, she took his hand in hers and
patted it. "There, there, darling. Who cares if the movie was
taken away from you? There'll be other movies."

"Yes, and the first one's called *For Love of Missie*."

"You could always quit."

"And feed you with what? Soon there'll be three of us."

"Baby mustn't have an angry, bitter daddy."

"Daddy will restrain all signs of his inner torment when
Baby arrives."

"Goody. Mommy likes Daddy better when he smiles."

"Daddy will continue smiling. Daddy will concoct baby-
poo dialogue with many a Woof and Arf. Daddy will be nomi-
nated for a new category of Oscar—Best Emetic."

"Daddy's being grumpy and sarcastic. Daddy mustn't."

"Daddy wants Mommy to disrobe and soothe his addled
brain with her erotic techniques."

"Mommy will, for Daddy."

"Daddy's appreciative of Mommy's willingness, also impatient, in a smiling kind of way, naturally."

The telephone rang. Myra went to pick it up.

"Hello? Oh, hello, Morris. Keith, it's Morris, your agent."

"Of course it is. I don't know any other Morrises."

He took the phone. "Hello, Morris? Good to hear from
you." He could hear loud music in the background.

"Sorry to be calling so late, Keith, but I've had a hectic day.
Just wanted to let you know I finally got around to reading *A
Desert Island of the Mind*, and I think it's great! Very interesting
characters, diabolically cunning plot, and highly original concept to boot. You must have pulled this bunny out of your ma-

gician's hat. I'm going to start sending it out to a select few publishers for a first look. I predict an early buy for this one, Keith."

"Morris, *Below the Salt* was a flop, so I can't see anyone clamoring to be the publisher of the followup book."

"Don't be so hard on yourself. The reviews were excellent. Some authors take tim to catch on with the general public. Have faith."

"I do, also hope and charity."

"Have to ring off now, Keith. I'm at a party absolutely swarming with people who count. I might even sell your book tonight."

"Circulate, Morris, circulate."

He hung up. "Morris likes the new book."

"Of course he does. He knows brilliance when he reads it."

"He won't get much for it, though, I can't kid myself about that. I'm stuck with Bunty and Missie, for the sake of the mortgage and groceries."

"Should I begin my erotic techniques now?"

"In a minute." Moody lit a cigarette. "Morris reminded me of something with his talk about people who count. It's been at the back of my mind for weeks now, and I can't even find it listed in the telephone book."

"Find what?"

"The Kumquat Club. A reporter left one of that place's cards in my office when he was interviewing us, and Nora Worth had one too, but what the hell is it? Why don't they advertise more widely than those little cards? 'The Right Place for the Right People.' Presumably those would be people who count."

"Is that what's worrying you? Mommy has the answer."

"She does?"

"The Kumquat Club is a discreet downtown establishment

that caters to the sexually disenfranchised, to give them a place of their own to hobnob with like-minded ladies."

"Pardon?"

"It's a dyke joint."

"A dyke joint? Daddy wants to know how Mommy came by ths interesting snippet of information."

"First, Daddy has to ask himself if the card he found really came from a reporter."

"Of course it did. There were swarms of them in my office at the time."

"And who else?"

"You and me."

"And who else?"

"Nigel, and Gloria Gresham."

"Which of those last two is female?"

"Gloria, obviously, but are you telling me she's a lesbian? Nora Worth, yes, I can believe that, but Gloria—?"

"How like a man to assume that all lezzies are big truck driver types or little mice with glasses. There are glamorous dykes too, mister."

"You're just guessing."

"Listen, do you recall having lunch in the commissary with Nigel and Gloria after the interview?"

"Yes."

"During that lunch, Gloria and I went to chat with some of the women I used to know in the research department. One of them was Ariane Roberts, a lady known to swoon over other ladies. There was recognition in their eyes, darling, I saw it, and I also saw Gloria slip a card to Ariane. Just think, Gloria might bump into Nora Worth at the Kumquat Club and fall in love with her, or Ariane might. Wouldn't that be nice?"

"I suppose so. My God, Empire's most dazzling sex symbol, and she's—Margolis had better not find out."

"Kumquat Clubbers are notoriously cautious, darling. Gloria's safe so long as she keeps her head down. I could make a naughty joke about that, but I won't."

"Apply your lascivious thoughts instead to your husband."

"Since he's in the doghouse, all right."

EPILOGUE

Years later, following the phenomenal success of the Missie series—*Here Comes Missie, Letter for Missie, Missie in Danger*—Moody drove his Cadillac to the highest point in the Hollywood hills so he could look down upon the glittering city below and ask himself if the disappearance and inexplicable death of Nigel Lawson was not the very cause of his success. *Traitor's Dawn* had been made, starring Wallace Ewing as Traven, with a screenplay by someone other than Moody, and had been a resounding flop. Moody had taken secret satisfaction from that, and he often wondered if his efforts, and Nigel's, might not have made all the difference. There could never be an answer to his wonderings, but the box-office hits he was responsible for (MM would say Bunty Wells and Missie were the parties deserving of credit) had certainly changed his life. Myra and the children were healthy and happy, and the Moodys' worldly comforts were the result of his screenplays. At the rare parties Moody attended, he never introduced himself as the author of the Missie films, but as a novelist. If someone happened to know about his screen successes, he cringed. It was the price he had to pay, he supposed.

Looking out over Hollywood beneath a canopy of winking stars, he watched the roving searchlights of a movie premiere stabbing at the sky and felt nothing but loss; his hopes of fame as a screenwriter were gone, and his books, although well received, continued to sell in low numbers. The eventual filming of *Below the Salt* brought nothing but more disappointment, more money. One of the sideliners; that was Moody's honest description of himself. The headliners were another breed. Nigel would eventually have been one of them and drawn Moody along behind, like a leaf caught up in the roiling wake of a racing car. But it was not to be; Fate had ordained otherwise, and left Moody twisting and turning briefly before settling back to his point of departure, the side of the road.

It was a familiar place, and not uncomfortable. Moody asked himself if such pedestrian environs were not worthy of exploration. The ordinary man, going about his ordinary business, far removed from the world of adventure and glamour; was there subject material in such stuff? There could be if he made it so. His reputation might yet be made by embracing his failure, examining it. The postwar world was one where the ordinary was celebrated, a return to normalcy the dream. He already had the title: *An Ordinary Man*. It could be done. It *would* be done.

He drove home slowly, thinking. ___